# Just in time for June...
# Janet Dailey's <u>The Hostage Bride</u>

It's been said that Janet Dailey "wrote the book" on romance. And Silhouette Books is thrilled to announce that Janet Dailey, America's best-loved romance author, will now be writing for Silhouette Romances, starting with *The Hostage Bride* in June.

You may have enjoyed one of Janet's recent novels: *Touch the Wind, The Rogue* or *Ride the Thunder.* All three made *The New York Times* best-seller list—and together sold well over three million copies! Her latest book, *Night Way*, is currently on the best-seller list, and is another million-seller.

More than eighty million people have already fallen in love with Janet Dailey. Her books have been translated into seventeen languages and are now sold in *ninety* different countries around the world.

We're sure that you too, will fall in love with Janet Dailey's romance novels. Be sure to watch for *The Hostage Bride* this June.

Dear Reader:

Silhouette Romances is an exciting new publishing venture. We will be presenting the very finest writers of contemporary romantic fiction as well as outstanding new talent in this field. It is our hope that our stories, our heroes and our heroines will give you, the reader, all you want from romantic fiction.

Also, *you* play an important part in our future plans for Silhouette Romances. We welcome any suggestions or comments on our books and I invite you to write to us at the address below.

So, enjoy this book and all the wonderful romances from Silhouette. They're for *you!*

Karen Solem
Editor-in-Chief
Silhouette Books
P. O. Box 769
New York, N.Y. 10019

# LAURA HARDY
# Burning Memories

*Silhouette Romance*

Published by Silhouette Books New York

**America's Publisher of Contemporary Romance**

SILHOUETTE BOOKS, a Simon & Schuster Division of
GULF & WESTERN CORPORATION
1230 Avenue of the Americas, New York, N.Y. 10020

Distributed by Pocket Books

ISBN: 0-671-57076-5

First Silhouette printing May, 1981

10 9 8 7 6 5 4 3 2 1

America's Publisher of Contemporary Romance

Printed in the U.S.A.

# Burning Memories

# Chapter One

London was asleep, but the fuzzy glow of the orange streetlights lit the sky for miles. From a distance, thought Nicola, they looked like the campfires of some enormous army. Martin hadn't spoken for some time. They were both tired. They should have left the party earlier, but they had been enjoying themselves and somehow the time had flashed by.

The spring night was clear and chilly, the stars bright pinpoints of light. As they reached the top of Highgate Hill, London lay stretched below them, a cluttered huddle of roofs, spires, tower blocks, with a sickle moon climbing the sky behind them. Nicola stared sleepily at the city, snuggling into her warm, thick wool jacket.

"It was a good party."

Martin started, glancing sideways at her. "Wasn't

it?" Broad and fair, he had a comforting solidity about him and he never said much. Nicola did not mind that. She didn't talk much either. Martin was frowning, though, which was unusual. His calm good temper was one of the qualities which had drawn her to him.

"Have you got something on your mind?" she asked him. He had been very cheerful all evening. Whatever was bothering him had only come up during the drive.

"You," he said, smiling.

"Me?" She laughed. "That's nice. Why, especially?"

He took one hand off the wheel and touched her knee caressingly. Nicola stiffened. She knew Martin sensed that involuntary withdrawal but she couldn't help it. Her cheeks glowed with anxious color.

Martin did not wait for her to say anything. He took his hand away, grimacing. "You see?" he asked. "That's what is on my mind."

"Oh," Nicola said, fighting down a desire to shift away in her seat.

"We're neither of us children," Martin pointed out. "We've been seeing each other for months now but we never seem to get any further than a good-night kiss."

"I can't; not yet," she stammered, her fingers twisting in her lap.

"Look, I respect your point of view," Martin came back quickly, his face coaxing. "I do understand how you feel, Nicola, but can't you understand how *I* feel? You can't say I've tried to rush you. I've been patience itself."

She sighed. "Yes, you have. I'm sorry. I can't . . ." She broke off and Martin looked at her sharply, the streetlights giving him a clear view of the tension in her trembling mouth and worried eyes.

It was not the first time they had had this discussion. With some men, of course, they would have started to argue on the subject after a first date. Martin had been less impatient. He had realized, perhaps, from the start that it would do him no good to try to rush her into bed, but, in any case, Martin was not the type of man who rushed anything, especially in personal relations. He was cautious, methodical, his own valuation of himself too high for him to want to grab at an instant pleasure. Martin took himself seriously.

The car drew up outside her home and he turned toward her, his eyes half apologetic. "Don't look so upset," he said, smiling wryly. "I shouldn't have brought it up tonight. We're both tired. But your attitude is old-fashioned, Nicky. People aren't going to condemn you, you know, even if they found out. Hasn't anybody told you? This is the age of sexual freedom. You do your own thing." He used the phrase with a rueful grimace and Nicola laughed.

"Maybe my own thing is to wait and see."

He put a hand to her cheek, his fingers caressing. "You are exceptional, do you know that? I meant what I said. I admire your integrity. It may mean I have to wait too, but you're well worth waiting for."

Her doubtful little smile made him laugh. He bent forward to kiss her with lingering tenderness, his fingers still stroking her cheek. "Am I still invited to lunch tomorrow?"

"Of course," she said, getting out of the car. "I was planning on roast chicken."

"Great," he said. "I'll bring a bottle of white wine. See you at twelve?"

"Twelve," she agreed and stood watching his red taillights streak away into the darkness before she let herself into her flat. It was on the ground floor of a large Victorian house. Nicola had been living there for over two years. She had spent time and energy on making it a comfortable, pleasant home. Standing in the living room she looked around her, shivering slightly. It wasn't just the cold dead of night which sent that tremor down her spine. She felt, as she always felt when she came back here, abruptly alone, as though suddenly aware of a pressing silence, an emptiness. Martin's company, hours spent with friends in lively talk, could chase away that loneliness for a while, but the moment she walked back into the flat it all fell back on her like an icy wave.

With a sigh she walked into the bathroom, inspecting her face as she removed the traces of makeup. Her skin was very pale, the translucent pallor emphasized by the frame of black hair curving around her face. Her eyes had the golden warmth of some amber liquid, their dark pupils lending depth to them, but that warmth disguised the obstinacy which lay behind her gentle smile.

She always had a rapid shower before she went to bed. Stepping under the warm water she closed her eyes, feeling the relaxing spray jet down her back. Why had Martin brought up the subject of sex? It had been the last thing on her mind. She wanted to go to bed tonight only to sleep. She did not want to carry any worries into the bedroom with her.

A white toweling robe hung by the shower. Yawning, Nicola wrapped it around herself and switched off the bathroom light. The shower had done its work, leaving her warm, relaxed and increasingly sleepy. She walked into the bedroom, put a hand to the light switch and then shrugged. The darkness was inviting and so was her bed. She wouldn't bother to put on the light and look for a nightdress.

Walking across the room in the dark she took off her robe and dropped it on the end of the bed. Turning back the thick, comfy quilt she slid underneath it, her body turning onto its side, searching for warmth.

A split second later she was wide awake. Her body had touched another body.

With lightning speed her nerve ends flashed their message to her brain. There was a man in her bed.

She screamed. At the same instant she leaped out of the bed, grabbing her robe and huddling into it with shaking hands as she ran. Her cries of panic were involuntary but her mind was working as she screamed. The phone was in the living room. Could she get there before the man caught up with her? He was moving, she heard the bedsprings creak. Would anyone hear her? And would they come if they did? People in a big city tend to ignore strange noises in the night. They don't want to get involved. They might ring the police but by the time a patrol car got here it might be too late.

"What the hell are you doing?"

The voice stopped her in her tracks. The bedside lamp came on and she turned, her face incredulous.

The man in the bed was staring at her, his bare brown shoulders gleaming smoothly, rippling with muscle as he ran one hand through jet black hair, brushing it back from his face. A sardonic smile twisted his mouth as Nicola stiffened, speechless and slowly flushing.

"What are *you* doing here? How did you get in?" She did not recognize her own voice. It sounded dry and rusty, as though she hadn't used it for a long time.

"I used a key," he drawled.

"A key!" She repeated the word helplessly, trying to think, her mind in total disorder. She did not like the way he was looking her over, his blue eyes oddly bright and mocking. Fumbling with her belt she tied the robe more tightly under those bright, watchful eyes.

"Forgotten I had one?" His mouth twisted again, wry humor in his face. "So had I, to be frank. Lucky I remembered it."

"What are you doing here?" she asked again, recovering from her first shock. "I thought you were in Africa."

"I flew back today."

Something in the way he said that made her look at him sharply, her gaze flicking over him in search of some visible sign of injury. That was usually what brought him back to London. Had he been caught in crossfire again?

He registered that hurried inspection and laughed shortly. "No, I'm not hurt."

Nicola reacted with a flare of angry color. For a moment she had experienced the old familiar fear, the anxiety, the pain, and she was angry now. "Get dressed and get out of my flat," she ordered tartly.

"Don't be ridiculous—at this hour?"

"The hour has nothing to do with it. This is my flat and you have no right in it."

"As I recall, I paid for it," he pointed out drily. "That gives me some rights, I think."

Nicola's teeth came together with a grinding hiss. "Get dressed and go!"

She felt at a distinct disadvantage standing there, her slender body so inadequately dressed in that thin white toweling robe, her legs bare to the thigh, her damp hair ruffled after the shower she had had before she came to bed. She would have liked to pretend she was unaware of the constant lazy inspection of those blue eyes, but she couldn't quite convince herself.

He gave her a shrugging grin. "I'm not going anywhere."

"You are," Nicola insisted, meeting his gaze with determination. He regarded her, his eyes narrowed now, then he slid over and switched off the light. In the sudden darkness he said, "To hell with you. I'm going back to sleep."

Nicola's temper boiled over. She marched across the room and switched the light back on, looking with rage at the tumbled black hair against the pillow. "Who do you think you are? What do you think you're doing? Walking into my flat . . ."

"Our flat," he interrupted.

"My flat; mine," Nicola seethed.

13

She was so angry that she missed the wicked look
in his blue eyes. "Our flat; ours," he said and Nicola
began to tremble with fury.

"I'm not going to argue with you."

"Oh, good," he said and she caught the bland
note and gave him another angry glare.

"This flat is mine. We agreed."

"I don't recall agreeing."

"Your solicitor did!"

"Did he, indeed? He didn't have my consent to
that."

"Whether he did or did not, that's not the point."

"I'd say it was very much the point," he murmured, eyeing her with amusement.

"I'm not getting into one of your endless debates
about definitions," shrieked Nicola. He would never
concede a point. He had nearly driven her out of her
mind with his infuriating circular habits of arguing.

"Why are you shouting?" He sounded so calm and
reasonable and he was nothing of the kind. Nicola
looked at him with dislike.

"Get dressed, give me back the key to my flat and
get out of here."

"Can we discuss this in the morning?" He yawned
again, sitting up, the quilt dropping off and giving
her a clear view of his bare wide shoulders and his
deep chest, the tanned skin roughened by wiry dark
hair which curled up from the flat planes of his
stomach.

Hurriedly averting her eyes, Nicola said, "No, we
can't discuss it in the morning. I want you out of here
tonight."

"Nicky, I'm dead on my feet," he said plaintively.

"I'm tired too," Nicola retorted. "But if you think I am allowing you to sleep in my bed, you're wrong. In fact, I'm not even talking to you while you're in there, so you can get out of it now. We'll discuss this in the living room."

She should have realized she had made a mistake in making that statement. He gave a mock sigh, his wicked blue eyes fixed on her. "Oh, well, if you insist . . ."

Her pulses leaped with alarm as he pulled back the quilt, his bare legs sliding out. Turning, she fled into the other room while he laughed behind her. Over her shoulder she told him, "Get some clothes on before you come in here."

"My word, you're a shrew," he drawled.

Nicola switched on the light and went over to turn on the electric log fire, shivering. It was a crisp, cold night. Her robe was too thin and she was tired. This was the wrong end of the day for having a row. Nicola hated having rows; they made her feel ill. She had had too many of them in the past. She had thought all that was over. How dare he waltz in here and take up a comfortable spot in her bed?

She heard a movement and tensed. "Are you dressed?"

"Yes," he said tersely, adding, "although why you should start being coy about seeing me without my clothes on, heaven alone knows."

Nicola turned round slowly, not quite trusting him. He was wearing a short quilted black satin robe. She had bought it for him two years ago. He

15

had hardly worn it, and it looked brand new. She skimmed a glance over him reluctantly. She had never quite got used to the vital impact of his appearance. He was a tall, lean man, with a physical magnetism which kept you staring at him, especially when he moved; his body in motion had a powerful grace, the muscled elegance of some predatory creature. That impression of lethal force was echoed in his face, his features strong and sardonic, his blue eyes electric, their intelligence masked by mocking humor which was visible in the lines of his mouth too, the hardness sometimes curving into aware sensuality when he smiled.

It was a long time since Nicola had been able to look at him. A pulse began beating in her throat as she looked hurriedly away.

"Is this going to be a long session?" he asked drily. "Because if it is, I could do with some whiskey. It's bloody cold in here."

"It isn't going to be a long session." Nicola meant it to be short and far from sweet.

He put his head to one side, surveying her with wry comprehension. "I wish I could believe that, but you have that obstinate look again."

"It would save us both time and trouble if you would just get some clothes on and go."

"No doubt," he agreed. "But it *is* the middle of the night and I'm exhausted. What do you expect me to do? Camp out in the middle of Trafalgar Square?"

"I don't care what you do. You're not staying here."

He pushed his hands down into the pockets of the

robe, his wide shoulders grimly set. "I can see I'm going to need that whiskey."

"There isn't any," Nicola retorted.

"No whiskey? I must say, your hospitality has taken a downward turn since we last met," he said, walking over to the cabinet in which she kept drinks.

"Do make yourself at home, won't you?" she told the back of his black head with frustrated fury, watching him as he took out a bottle of red wine which she had been saving for some evening when Martin came to dinner.

"Is this all you've got?"

"Yes," she flung at him. "Sorry."

"How about coffee?"

"Look, I want to know what you are doing in my flat!"

Ignoring that, he padded off into the kitchen, his bare feet silent on the cream-colored carpet. Nicola looked around the room, biting her lower lip. Maddening, she thought. He is every bit as maddening as he ever was—what am I going to do?

She followed him out to the kitchen and found him hunting through the contents of the refrigerator. "Cream?" he asked over his shoulder and she said through tight lips, "No."

"You know I like cream in my coffee," he complained.

She counted to ten. If she hadn't, she would have screamed. "Since I was not expecting you, you can't be surprised if I haven't got any cream."

He found a jar of powdered cream substitute. "This any good?"

"I like it," Nicola said. "If I didn't, I wouldn't have it."

"That's what I like about you," he said. "Logical." The mocking little smile got absolutely no response.

"Stop trying to put off our discussion."

"Was I?" He made the coffee, stirred in the powder, and bent to sniff at the result with apparent enjoyment. "Ah, coffee, the smell of real instant coffee. The stuff I've been drinking smelled of ground acorns."

"Steve!"

He swung around, the electric blue flash of his eyes making her throat close in alarm. "So, you *do* remember my name."

Her flush mounted and her stare became even angrier. "I don't think that's funny."

"I wasn't being funny," he told her, and let his eyes wander down over her from her damp hair to her bare feet. "That's just how I used to imagine you." He paused. "Well, almost," he added wickedly. "Minus the robe."

Her face made him laugh under his breath. "Stop looking as though I'd broken in here with intentions on your virtue—all I want is a few hours sleep."

"Why didn't you go to a hotel?"

His face altered, the amusement vanishing and a strange grayness creeping up over his skin. "I was tired," he said tersely. "I wanted to sleep. I haven't slept for three nights."

"You can sleep in a hotel."

His mouth twisted. "I can't." For a moment he stared at the coffee. She saw the fixed brooding

18

tension in his whole body. "I had to come here," he added.

Nicola watched him, frowning. Something was seriously wrong, she suddenly realized. There was some indefinable difference in him. He looked fit enough—the long body had the same poised vitality, the potential menace of a cobra in it. Under his smooth bronzed skin, however, he was taut, strung-up, on edge. She could believe him when he said he hadn't slept for three nights. His blue eyes had a deepset, burning exhaustion in them. His mouth had a drawn look. A tiny muscle jumped at the corner of his eye, indicating some nervous tension.

"What's wrong?"

Her quiet voice disturbed his brooding. He looked around, thrusting one sinewy hand through his thick hair. "I've had a bad week," he said lightly. "One of the worst weeks of my life." Picking up one of the mugs of coffee, he handed it to her and she automatically accepted it, her trembling hands clasping it tightly, the warmth of the hot liquid seeping into her palms.

Walking past her with the other mug he sat down next to the log fire, holding one hand toward it. "I'd forgotten how cold London can be at this time of year."

"We're having a slow spring," she agreed, sitting down on a chair opposite.

He sipped his coffee, his heavy lids half closed. "How's the new job?"

"I like it." She had been working in the features department of the paper for six months, since just after Steve had left that last time. She was used to the job by now. It was a much slower way of life and reassuringly calm. She wouldn't go back to the way things had been before.

She hadn't been taking much notice of the news since her change of job. After several years in the newsroom she had been glad to forget the daily adrenalin rush of the news. It filtered through, of course, via the television, and her occasional glance at a newspaper, and she knew there was a civil war going on in the African state where Steve had been working. That was what had taken him out there, after all. Steve only turned up in trouble spots. War and the rumor of war brought him zooming in like a carrion crow.

She looked at him, torn between cynical anger and a reluctant anxiety. What was wrong? She knew that shuttered face. Steve never talked about his job. He wrote his stories and what you got from the curt paragraphs was all Steve ever betrayed.

His reputation had been based on the cool, rational reporting of what he saw. Steve was not the sort of reporter who used adjectives to excess. He was objective; he just told the facts. He was famous for his terse, crisp style and the unblinking eye which saw so clearly.

"The paper knows you're back?"

"Of course. They were expecting me today."

"I'm glad somebody was," Nicola said, brushing back a few loose strands of black hair from her cheek.

"I thought I'd surprise you," he drawled, looking amused.

"Oh, you did that, all right."

He laughed, the blue eyes sparkling. "Scared you stiff, did I?"

"What do you think?" She was furious, remembering her terror as she had leaped out of the bed and run for the door. "I had no suspicion it was you. I haven't seen anyone from the newsroom for weeks."

His lip curled sardonically. "No regrets?"

There was far more to that question than a simple inquiry about her views on changing her job, but she pretended not to understand that. "None," she said coolly. "I don't miss the newsroom. Life is much easier in features."

"Dead boring, you mean." He swallowed some of his coffee, his bare throat rippling. His tan was so deep it seemed to be imprinted on his skin, increasing the dangerous brilliance of those blue eyes. He had always had a tan of one sort or another; he took the sun easily.

"Can we cut the polite conversation? We still haven't got anywhere on the subject of what gave you the idea you could walk into my flat—and my bed—without so much as a polite request."

"You weren't here to ask. The flat was empty."

"Why didn't you ring me at work?"

"I only flew in at nine o'clock tonight." He threw her a sarcastic grin. "If I had asked, what would you have said?"

"No way," she admitted, meeting his eyes.

"That's what I thought." He finished his coffee. "If the discussion is over . . . ?" He rose, the movement displacing his satin dressing gown and giving her a brief, disturbing glimpse of his hair-roughened thigh.

Looking away hurriedly, she said sharply, "It isn't. You don't seem to get my point. You had no business coming here. You don't live here anymore. I do. So get dressed, get out and give me back my key."

He put down his mug with a crash which made her jump. "Look," he snarled, "I'm going back to bed. Any further argument can be postponed until the morning. I'm going to sleep and I don't want to have any early calls, either. I'll wake up in my own good time."

As he walked away she went after him, trembling with anger. Nicola had always thought of herself as good-tempered. It had taken Steve Howard to teach her that she could be so angry that her head could feel like it might blow off. She grabbed at his arm, her fingers digging into the quilted satin, and he halted to look down at her.

"Haven't you forgotten something?" she demanded. Was he going to ignore the fact that they were getting divorced?

He eyed her, his mouth crooked, a weary quizzical mockery in the lift of his brows. "Yes," he said slowly, then his hands were fixed on her slender shoulders and before she could evade him he jerked her against him.

"You dare," she burst out.

His mouth had already fastened onto her lips as the words left them. Parted, trembling, her mouth had no hope of escaping his abrupt, sensual possession.

She grasped his arms to push him away but there was an ache somewhere deep inside her, a burning sweetness pouring through her veins, and while she hesitated, Steve kissed her deeply, one hand sliding down her back, pressing her toward him so that she felt the tense masculinity of his body from breast to thigh.

Shuddering, she broke free, a shaking hand at her lips. "That's enough!"

"It will have to be, for tonight," he said huskily, giving her a slight grin. "I'm too tired even for you. I'm so tired I can hardly keep my eyes open."

He had gone before she had a chance to stop him. The bedroom light went out; she heard the bedsprings creak as he turned over heavily, giving a smothered yawn.

This is insanity, Nicola thought. I can't let him do this to me. He has no business walking into my life again. He is selfish, thoughtless, ruthless. Her hands clenched at her sides, she stood there trembling with anger, staring at the open door.

Marching over to it she stared into the room. The light from the room behind her fell in a pale shaft across the carpet, showing her the dark head buried in the pillows.

Nicola slammed the door viciously.

"Bitch," he murmured in a sleepy voice which held a muffled amusement.

"You're leaving tomorrow morning, the minute you're out of that bed," she yelled back.

He didn't answer. All she heard was the slowing sound of his breathing, a rustle as he shifted under the quilt.

She curled up beside the log fire, staring at the artificial flames with unblinking anxiety. It had been a disaster from the first day, their marriage. If she hadn't been so crazy about him, she would have realized what madness it was to consider marriage with a man who never stayed in one place for long, needed to duel with death as though it gave some desired consummation, was deaf to all pleas for him to change his way of life.

They had been temperamentally unsuited. Nicola was gentle, quiet, domesticated, a girl who never took risks and was terrified of violence. Steve Howard should never have entered her orbit. Working in the newsroom, though, she had met him with the casual collision of fate, an accidental encounter which, if they had known anything about each other at the time, would have had no consequence. All they had known, however, was what they saw. Nicola had been dazed by his electrifying sexuality. Those blue eyes had flashed over her and she had been head over heels in love at first glance.

She was never sure what Steve had seen but he had seemed as instantly fixed by her. Perhaps it was because they were such opposites, both physically and mentally. Nicola was slight and delicate, the warmth of those brown eyes matching her gentle smile, and Steve was not the first male member of the staff to have noticed the seductive nature of her femininity. Nicola was as strongly female as Steve

Howard was strongly male. The polarity of their natures pulled them together from that first meeting.

After their marriage, Nicola had secretly expected that Steve would settle down, give up his roving existence on the foreign reporting staff and take a desk job in London. The paper had offered him several. He was highly thought of—he could have walked into a good job whenever he chose to do so. He refused. Nicola had to learn to live with fear as her daily companion. While Steve was abroad, she struggled to come to terms with his way of life, but her nerves cracked under the strain.

He was so rarely at home and while he was away she waited with terror to hear that he had been injured, or even killed. Her temperament just could not take that permanent, nervous life on a tightrope. Steve's idea of marriage did not match hers. She wanted her husband with her, not on the other side of the world. Steve's electric sexuality and the reactions of other women to it increased their difficulties. Nicola couldn't help wondering what he was up to when he was away for months.

While he was reporting a war in the Middle East he was caught in crossfire and flew home, slightly injured. Nicola gave him an ultimatum. He had to choose, she said. Her—or his job. Steve laughed at her at first, refusing to take her seriously, trying to tease her out of it. Nicola's gentle obstinacy came to the fore. She would not budge. She refused to argue but she kept repeating that ultimatum. "Me—or your job."

When Steve had recovered, he flew back to the

war zone. Nicola at once began divorce proceedings. She got one letter from Steve after that—a terse, sarcastic note which made her so furious that she tore it up and did not reply.

At first she had huddled in their flat, grim with misery. She did not hear from Steve again. Their marriage was over, she told herself. It should never have begun. She began to get angry. She wasn't going to let Steve ruin her life. She forced herself to start going out. At first she went with other girls in the office—theaters, cinemas, parties. At one of those parties she had met Martin. His quiet, dependable kindness had been like a fire on a cold day. Nicola had drifted into seeing him, a little guiltily at first, keeping him very much at a distance.

The quality which had drawn Steve to her was the same quality which attracted Martin. Most men found Nicola's warm gentleness attractive. Nicola had warned him that she was in the process of being divorced. She hadn't been ready to feel emotion again. She was lonely, uncertain, in need of comfort. Martin rushed to offer what he saw she needed. Steve had left scars on her; Martin set about healing them.

He was a patient man. Inch by inch, day by day, he had somehow infiltrated her life. Nicola could not remember actually saying she would marry him after her divorce. The idea had been planted in her mind insidiously. She had become very fond of Martin but she knew she did not feel for him the fierce attraction she had felt toward Steve. That overwhelming passion, though, had led to disaster, and Nicola instinctively turned away from the idea of passion now. Martin's love was so much easier to live with and so much less dangerous. He made her feel loved, cherished, wanted. He made her feel safe.

She did not feel safe tonight. She felt like someone who has gone up to a tiger's cage in the happy expectation of seeing him behind bars only to find the door open and the tiger padding toward her.

# Chapter Two

At around three o'clock she got a spare quilt from the airing cupboard in the bathroom and made herself up a bed on the couch. It was four o'clock before she finally fell asleep. She woke up when the newspaper came through the front door, the clack of the letterbox making her wake with a start. Her eyes were dry and ached from lack of sleep. She was stiff, her limbs cramped. The couch was, she had been told when she bought it, designed for conversion to a bed at a touch. A dwarf might have been comfortable on it, Nicola decided, as she got up, stretching. She felt as if she had been on the rack all night.

Going into the small hallway, she brought in the milk and found the newspaper on the mat. She went slowly into the kitchen and got down the percolator. By the time the coffee was hitting the top of the glass dome she had made some fresh orange juice and toast. She sat down at the table and sipped the juice, her weary eyes fixed on the front page of the paper. Her eyes widened and darkened as they read the lead story.

Lowering the paper she looked toward the door. So that was what had put the drawn, haggard look into his face.

A civil war had been raging in the African state from which he had been reporting. It had been a minor affair until now. Steve had become a shocked witness to the acceleration of the struggle. He had seen the wholesale massacre of the rebellious inhabitants of one small township.

How had he got out alive? Nicola wondered, wincing. She pushed the paper away. She could not read any more of it. The details were so painful that even to read them made her feel as if she had been present.

Getting up, she threw her uneaten toast into the bin. Suddenly she wasn't hungry.

Why did he keep on with the job? Hadn't he had enough of seeing death at close quarters yet? One day his luck would run out and he would end up like the men, women and children he had seen mowed down in that African township—shoveled into a hastily dug grave and forgotten about.

She stood looking down at the newspaper, her lips trembling, tears burning behind her eyes.

She snatched it up, crumpled it into a ball and threw it across the room, swearing hoarsely under her breath.

"Temper, temper." The mocking voice made her swing around, tense and feverish, her brown eyes still hot with unshed tears.

Steve ran his glance over her face, his dark brows meeting above his arrogant eyes. "I see you've been catching up with the news." He said that coolly, but his scrutiny was intent.

"You made the front page, don't worry," Nicola muttered with bitter irony.

A harshness invaded his face. "So I should damned well think."

She sagged back against her chair, her body trembling on a low deep sigh. "Yes, it sounds pretty bad."

"You have a genius for understatement." He walked forward, his lean body, clothed only in the black robe, moving with that casual animal grace, and picked up the coffeepot. "This still hot?"

"Yes."

She watched him pour himself a cup, add the top of the milk and sip, his eyes half closed, a tired absorption in his face.

"Was it worse than you made it sound in the story?" she asked, her voice low.

"It was as close to hell as I've ever been."

She drew a painful breath, then her pain became anger and she said icily, "I'm sure you can't wait to get back there."

He shot her a dry smile. "I've been told on good authority that if I try to go back, I'll be shot on sight." That seemed to amuse him. He began to laugh, his blue eyes fierce. "They seemed regretful that they had to let me on the plane at all."

"Why did they?" Nicola was trying to control the helpless shaking of her body, and her voice was only just under the high edge of hysteria.

"I went out with the British Consul. They decided not to risk a scandal."

Nicola was afraid she was going to cry. She had to get away from him before the tears started. She swung around and her chair crashed to the floor. She left it there, and almost ran to the door.

"Going somewhere? What about my breakfast?" Steve inquired in a calm tone.

"Get it yourself. There's plenty of bread and eggs. I'm going to have a shower and get dressed and then I want you out of my flat." She did not wait to see how that was received. The tears were already spilling out from under her lids, trickling down her cheeks. She slammed the door behind her and got to the bathroom before her legs gave out beneath her. Leaning on the door, sobbing and trembling, she felt she hated him.

When the first bitter storm had passed she had a shower, taking her time, the warm water spraying over her skin and easing some of the terrible tension.

She was going to have to get Steve out of the flat before Martin arrived. Martin knew about Steve, of course, although they had never met. All the same, it was not going to be easy to explain his presence in her flat, especially if he was still half-naked. Martin was a good-tempered, level-headed man, but even his calm approach to life might be somewhat strained by the sight of her ex-husband wandering around her flat in nothing but a short robe.

Nicola had only briefly discussed Steve with him.

She had told him as much as she felt he ought to know. Martin had never evinced any real curiosity about her marriage. He had listened without doing anything more than look grave.

"That was no marriage at all, was it?" he had asked her. "He didn't deserve you."

"How true," Nicola had agreed ironically. "I wish he could hear you."

"I wouldn't mind a chance to tell him a few home truths," Martin had agreed. "Men like that have no business getting married at all. He's the type to have a woman in every port. I wouldn't mind betting he doesn't lead a celibate life while he's abroad all those months."

Nicola had ground her teeth. That thought had occurred to her, too. She had sometimes questioned Steve about other women, in the first months. He had been evasive about them.

"No confessions, darling," he had said. "I don't believe in them. After all, what good does it do to rake up the past?"

"So there is a past?" Nicola had demanded, burning with jealousy.

He had turned those electric blue eyes on her, grinning. "Why have your eyes gone green?"

"I've told you everything about my ex-boyfriends," she had said. "Why can't you tell me?"

Rueful amusement had shown in his face. "My past stretches back a lot further than yours, darling. I'm ten years older, remember, and I've traveled further, in every sense of the word."

"I can imagine," she had said tartly.

He had begun to laugh, his black lashes curling

back from his wicked eyes. "Now I'm beginning to feel married," he mocked. "Is this what I'm to expect? You're worse than the secret police. Nicola, there's nothing so dead as an old love affair. Sweep it all under the carpet, all the ash of yesterday. We don't need it." Then he had begun to kiss her, his hard mouth demanding, and, yielding to him, Nicola had let her jealousy slip away.

She pushed away those memories now, too, concentrating her thoughts on Martin. He was always punctual. He would arrive, as he had promised, at midday. So that gave her two hours to get Steve dressed and out of the flat, and before he went she was going to get that key out of him. She wouldn't have him walking in and out of her flat while he was in London.

Dripping, she groped for the towel. It was put into her hands. Her eyes flew open on a reflex action, her wet lashes fluttering back, the brown eyes all pupil in shock.

Steve's blue eyes flashed down over her naked curves and Nicola felt her breasts ache with the inflow of blood under his stare, her body stiffening and fiercely awake. Her breath caught painfully. She wound herself into the towel, hands trembling. "How dare you walk in here? Get out."

"You've lost some weight," he said coolly.

She had lost nearly a stone during the months of their marriage. She had never put it on again. She had always been a very slim girl, but that weight loss had made her waist tiny, her hips even more slender, increased the fragile delicacy of her small face.

"It suits you," Steve decided. "I like girls to be a bit skinny."

She lifted her chin, her eyes defiant, the towel tucked firmly around her breasts and covering her wet body to the knee. Stalking past him she went out, her wet feet leaving footprints on the carpet. This time she not only shut but locked the bedroom door before she dried herself and got dressed.

When she emerged in skin tight blue jeans and a white silk shirt, Steve was listening to the radio in the kitchen. He had had a shower, too, she saw. His hair was curling in damp clusters on his head.

Nicola had decided to try the calm, polite approach. "Now, will you please get dressed and leave?" She stood watching him, her hands on her hips, her freshly brushed hair immaculate.

He switched off the news, glancing at her. "I'm not going anywhere. I'm only home for a week's leave and an in-depth conference with my replacement, then I'm going off to the Middle East. While I'm in London I planned to stay here."

Her head almost exploded. "Are you crazy? Or just plain awkward? You can't stay here."

"Why not?" He surveyed her with a little smile.

She took a long fierce breath. "Steve, we are in the process of being divorced. If anyone found out you were living with me, there could be unfortunate repercussions. You can't stay here. You don't live here anymore."

He yawned, stretching his arms above his head, the movement dislodging his loosely tied belt and giving her an unwanted glimpse of the damp black hair on his chest.

"I'm still tired. I'm going back to bed."

"You dare," she burst out. "Listen to me . . ."

"Later, sweetheart. Right now, I am going to sleep for another twelve hours."

As he walked out, she followed, protesting to deaf ears, ready to throw things if she had to, her fury spending itself without getting any response from him. He dropped his robe without warning, and her nervous eyes flickered over him, from the muscled shoulders and deep chest burned dark brown by the African sun, to the lean hips and hair-roughened thighs. Averting her eyes she swallowed, her skin heated. She knew he was watching her, although he didn't say a word.

He climbed into the bed and stretched, his arms crooking over his head as he yawned. Nicola looked back at him, her hot face irritable.

"Why can't you go to a hotel?"

"Why should I? This is my home."

"Not anymore," she said, on a deep, angry breath. "You're making it very difficult for me." She paused, then said defiantly, "I'm expecting someone here today."

Steve lay still, watching her through suddenly sharp blue eyes, a chill menace in the way his stare fixed her. "Expecting who?"

Nicola was trembling slightly, her nerves prickling with tension. "That's my business. But I don't want you here when he arrives."

"He?" Steve asked very softly, his black brows a heavy line across his forehead.

"Yes," she muttered, lifting her rounded chin to face down the threat in that stare.

"Give him a name." He said that in a terse voice.

"Martin," she said huskily. "Martin Eastwood."

Steve was silent for a moment, then he said coolly, "Well, I'm sorry to louse up your date, of course. I can see it might be inconvenient to have the bed otherwise occupied . . ."

"Oh," Nicola interrupted fiercely, her lips parted on a cry of fury. "How dare you suggest . . ."

He ignored the interruption, his face sardonic. "But my need is greater than his, I'm afraid. You'll just have to make do with the couch."

She was insulted, her body tense. "Martin and I don't . . . haven't . . ." She broke off that stammered denial under his ironic stare, her face scarlet.

"No?" He lifted his brows quizzically. "Poor Martin; what a patient fellow he must be."

"He is," Nicola threw back. "He's prepared to wait until our divorce is through and then . . ."

"He'll make an honest woman of you? Great. Fill me in with all the romantic details later, will you? Right now all I need is sleep, not the secrets of your love life."

He slid down the bed, his eyes closing, and Nicola looked at the bronzed profile, which was all she could see now that he lay on his side, facing away from her. "Look, Steve," she began irritably, and he suddenly sat up, fixing those haggard, glittering eyes on her, the tan not hiding the exhaustion which held his bones in a vise-like tension.

"Damn you to hell," he roared. "Can't you see, you stupid little bitch, that I'm out on my feet? I crawled here because I needed a safe hole to go to—don't you understand? My head's jammed with pictures I don't want to remember, would give the earth to forget. I don't want to talk about the divorce, the flat, your bloody boyfriend. I want to sleep for days on end and forget everything. So get out of here and let me sleep."

Falling back against the pillows, he dragged the quilt over his head, and after a moment of consternation Nicola turned, trembling, to walk out of the room, closing the door very quietly behind her.

She went into the kitchen like an automaton and stood at the window, staring at the sky without seeing it. Steve's rage burned behind her eyelids. What terrible memories had he brought back with him from Africa? It was rare for him to get so involved in what he reported. He had learned, during his years in his profession, to tell the story as he had seen it happen without letting his own emotions get in the way.

She would get no clue from the story in the paper. The subbing staff would have watered down what he had written, carefully softening it for public consumption. Steve, like all the other reporters, constantly complained about that. The paper would never print all of the truth, they said, only a carefully selected part of it.

She closed her eyes, shivering. Why did he have to come here? His long silence had seemed an admission that their marriage was over. She thought he had accepted the idea of divorce. Finding him in her bed last night, all she had felt was anger, but now his outburst had given birth to other feelings. He had made her feel guilty, disturbed, anxious.

It was so unlike Steve to break out like that. He

was a tough, experienced newsman with a cool head and nerves of steel. That, at least, was the impression she, in common with everyone else on the paper, had got of him.

As she surfaced from her thoughts, her eye focused on the low, livid bank of cloud which had spread over the quiet city. A tentative sun was trying to struggle through the gray layers, but the sky was as dull as Nicola's mood. The street was empty. The houses had that deserted look which Sunday usually brings. Most people would be staying in bed, reading the papers, their eyes skimming casually over the horrific news as they drank their Sunday morning tea and hoped the children would not start clamoring for food too soon.

Food, she thought, remembering Martin with a start. He was coming here for lunch and she could not have him here with Steve in the flat.

She went through into the living room and dialed Martin's number. The phone rang for some time. Frowning, she wondered if he was too deeply asleep to hear it, or if he had gone out. After a while she replaced the receiver. She would try again later.

It was difficult for her to concentrate on anything but the man sleeping in her bed. Martin seemed to fade, dissolving like a ghost into the recesses of her mind.

How had she been expecting Steve to react when she told him she was dating another man? Well, whatever she had expected, it had not been what she got. She had not imagined he would make cold jokes about it. Biting her lower lip, she trembled with rage and pain. Did he really believe she would sleep with another man so lightly? Was that the sort of woman he thought she was? The memory of his cynical shrug stabbed her, made her wince.

If that was what he thought, he knew nothing about her, but then, what *did* he know about her? What did she know about him? Their time together had always been so short. Their marriage had been spent largely apart. Had Steve been unfaithful to her? She wouldn't be surprised to find out he had. At the back of her mind she had always suspected it. That had been the most painful of her problems, that suspicion. She had never told Steve that, of course. She hadn't wanted him to know about the bitter fantasies with which she had lived while he was away from her. How could she help suspecting that a man of his sexual vitality was likely to be unfaithful?

Jealousy wasn't one of Steve's hang-ups. If he had really loved her, he would have reacted very differently just now when she told him about Martin. But then, if he had really loved her, he wouldn't have gone shooting off all the time. He would have stayed with her, got a London job, taken her with him if he felt he had to go abroad.

She dragged herself out of her grim thoughts to get the lunch ready. It helped to have something to do. When she had got the chicken into the oven and prepared the vegetables, she rang Martin again, but got no answer. Making herself a cup of coffee she sat down, her brows creased. Where was Martin? Was he on his way here?

A muffled cry made her start, her coffee cup

jerking in her hand. She put it down, listening. The sound came again, louder. Nicola got up and slowly moved toward the bedroom. As she opened the door Steve gave a hoarse yell which made all the hair rise on the back of her neck. He was having a nightmare, his body convulsed under the quilt, his lids flickering rapidly.

She went over to the bed. Steve twisted restlessly, muttering. "For heaven's sake . . ." That came out in a raw agony which Nicola found unbearable.

She could not listen to him. His mumbled words were building up too painful a picture. Sinking onto the bed she caught hold of his shoulders, bending toward him.

"Steve. Steve, wake up." Her voice was shaking and she was very pale.

He jerked convulsively at the touch of her hands, his own hands flying up to clamp over her wrists, their grip like a vise. She was pulled forward, sprawling over the bed. The next moment she was on her back with Steve holding her down, his powerful fingers around her throat. Choking, trembling, Nicola looked up at him in desperation. As she gasped out his name again his lids lifted and she saw the dangerous blue eyes staring down at her.

The locked bones of his face unclenched. His fingers relaxed around her throat although they did not fall away.

"Nicky," he said in a blank voice.

Still trembling, she whispered, "You were having a nightmare."

His mouth twisted. "Yes," he admitted.

"Have you had many of them?" She could guess

the answer to that but she wanted to keep him talking, give him time to recover his balance.

"Yes," he said in a terse voice. There was perspiration on his forehead, beads of it along his upper lip.

A lock of thick black hair had fallen over his temples. Nicola absently put up a hand to brush it back, her fingers lingering on the vital strands, remembering the feel of them, the way the hair had clung to her skin when she ran her fingers through it as Steve kissed her.

"Bad nightmares?" she asked gently.

"Bad enough." He closed his eyes again, shuddering. "Don't ask me, Nicky."

She could not remember Steve ever betraying weakness before. She saw that tiny muscle flickering beside his hard mouth and instinctively put a finger on it to stop it.

He turned his head with a blind, seeking look and his mouth brushed her finger, slid into her palm, the faint tremble of his lips making her heart wince with pain.

"Oh, Nicky, I needed you," he muttered against her skin, the warmth of his breath sinking into her pores, making her blood sing in her ears. "I thought it was my turn any minute. It was so bloody hot. The sun made the place feel like an oven and all around me there was nothing but death. I've never been so angry or so scared in my life. I kept thinking . . ." He broke off, his teeth coming together.

"Thinking what?" she asked, her hand against his cheek, the fleshless angularity of skin and bone alive under her touch.

"When you think you're going to die any second, you can get quite hooked on the idea of being alive," Steve said with grim humor.

She could believe that. She watched him anxiously. Under his tan his skin looked gray.

Had she imagined it, or had he said just now that he had needed her? He had never said anything like that to her before. She had not imagined Steve could ever need anyone. He didn't give the impression of feeling the need for other people which is a part of the human condition. People in general cannot exist alone. They need each other, however briefly, however reluctantly. We are all interdependent. Our lives are knit together in a loose weave and the fabric of one life is never strong enough on its own. Nicola's eyes moved over Steve's face, tracing the strong bone structure which proclaimed his fierce individuality; the arrogant nose, deep-socketed blue eyes, the assertive, self-confident jawline. No, she thought. Steve Howard didn't need anyone but himself.

He watched her and as their eyes met she realized she had been absently smoothing his cheek in the instinctive gesture of comfort one might offer to a child.

Nervously, she pulled her hand away, and Steve smiled at her. "Don't stop, I like it," he said huskily.

"You had better get back to sleep," she said in a low voice. "And no more nightmares."

"Give me something more enjoyable to dream about, then," he murmured in a mocking voice, his hands sliding over her collarbone and fingering the rounded bones of her shoulder sensually, yet the implicit power of those long, sinewy fingers warned that Nicola would not be easily able to unlock their hold on her if she struggled.

"Don't," she muttered, twisting to avoid him but unable to escape those controlling hands.

"What sort of lover is he? The guy you're dating? Sexy, is he? Good looking?" The questions came out drily, a thread of derision running below them, and Nicola hated the way he was talking. He sounded indifferent, amused. He did not sound jealous.

"Martin is a stockbroker," she said and Steve broke into jeering laughter, his blue eyes wicked.

"You're having me on."

Her face irritated, Nicola shook her head and his smile broadened, the lines around his mouth deep in his brown skin. "A stockbroker?" he repeated. "You must have been desperate."

Indignantly she threw back a denial. "Martin is a very charming man."

"Rich, too, I suppose," mocked Steve.

That stung. "I'm not interested in his money."

"What are you interested in? What has he got— apart from this charm?"

"He's attractive. We get on well."

"What do you talk about? The way the market is going? The cost of money? Which company is going bust and who is taking over who?"

Nicola did not like the way he was looking at her or how he was talking to her. His eyes spat blue fire, their mockery cold.

"I'm not discussing Martin with you!"

"I hope you haven't discussed me with him," Steve said, his icy smile going.

"No," she said, her eyes shifting, because of course she had once or twice talked about Steve, although it had been very brief and very cautious.

"Because I would not like that," Steve said through his teeth. "I wouldn't like it at all, Nicola, if I thought you had been discussing me with another man."

"I haven't," she said.

"He does know you're married, though," Steve murmured, watching her closely.

"Of course."

"Then you must have talked about me," he said shrewdly, leaping to the obvious conclusion.

Nicola was annoyed. "Only when I had to—I prefer not to think about you, let alone talk about you."

He did not like that, his brows meeting. "Don't annoy me, Nicola. Take some well-meant advice for once in your life and try not to make me angry. I'm pretty hyper at the moment—if I lose my temper, I could get very nasty."

"Nastier than usual, you mean?" Even as she asked him that she inwardly regretted coming back with that crack. It was a mistake; she saw that as the dark color crept under his tan.

His hands closed around her face, biting into her. "Much nastier," he said thickly just before his head swooped down.

She was angry enough herself to meet his mouth with a furious attempt at escape, her slender body writhing under the pressure of his, bitterly aware of the naked thigh clamped over her own, the wide shoulder pinning her to the bed. She pushed at his chest without managing to shift him. As her palms slid over his warm skin her pulse began to thunder. Her closed lips parted; her open eyes shut. Her fingers dug into Steve's bare shoulders, clinging, holding on with desperate intensity. It was so long since she had been in his arms. Time seemed to rush her away at top speed, back to the first days of their marriage. She stopped thinking and was all feeling. Her hands moved around to the back of his head and clasped it, feeling the vital hair clinging to her palms.

Steve lifted his head to look down at her. Exhausted, limp, Nicola lay with closed eyes, shuddering. She could not meet his stare. She knew what she must look like, her lips burning and parted from those kisses, her skin flushed, her body weak with the desire he had woken in her.

"That's how I remembered you," Steve said huskily.

Slowly her lashes fluttered back. The dazed brown eyes looked up at him, her pupils dilated with passion.

The doorbell rang briskly.

Steve muttered something terse under his breath. Nicola jumped, her nerves wincing at the unexpected noise.

"That," Steve drawled, "is the stockbroker, I presume."

She pulled herself back from the hectic memory of their lovemaking. Defiantly, she said, "I suppose so."

Steve's mouth was crooked with icy humor. "You'd better let him in, then, hadn't you? He sounds like an impatient fellow." The doorbell had rung again, even more briskly. Martin would wonder why she hadn't opened the door.

Sliding off the bed, she stumbled, her legs weak. Steve laughed and she gave him a cold glance.

"What's the matter, darling?" he mocked, satisfaction in the curve of his mouth. "Something bothering you?"

"Nothing is bothering me," Nicola denied. She walked rather less steadily than she would have liked to the door. "While Martin is here I'd be grateful if you would stay out of sight, though," she said as she left, closing the door firmly behind her.

She did not hear any answer but somehow she felt very uneasy as she made her unsteady way to the front door.

# Chapter Three

Martin was smiling as she opened the door. "I thought you must have forgotten I was coming and gone out," he told her, moving forward to kiss her lightly.

"Sorry," she said, lying instinctively. "I was in the bathroom." Her body leaned away from him, as she spoke, in an involuntary movement of evasion which she picked up even as it happened.

He was flushed, his firm, smoothly shaven skin freshly colored after walking in the cold spring air. Taking off his overcoat he handed it to her, showing her the bottle of wine he carried.

"How does that grab you? It's a very good vintage."

"Lovely," she smiled, hanging his coat up. "I'm afraid lunch is going to be a little late."

Martin looked at her with amusement, his eyes

dancing. "I get it—you overslept, didn't you? You look pretty hectic. Have you been rushing around trying to make up for lost time?"

Nicola put a trembling hand to her hot face. She looked hectic, did she? Well, she wasn't surprised to be told so, but she was furious with herself.

"Something like that," she said, in as cool a tone as she could manage. "Would you like to open the wine now? I haven't got anything else to drink, I'm afraid, except some red wine."

"How long will lunch be?"

She glanced at her watch. "Another hour, Martin. I'm sorry."

"Then why don't we have some coffee?" He was always so calm and easygoing. She looked at him with warm appreciation. Martin was a man you could depend on, a man who wouldn't rush off to dangerous places on the other side of the world and leave you aching with misery, not knowing if he was alive or dead.

"I'll make it now," she promised, moving into the kitchen with Martin behind her.

"It looks as if it might rain," he said as she plugged in the percolator. "I'm beginning to wonder if we're going to have a spring at all this year."

"It has been rather cold," she agreed absently, half of her attention given to any hint of sound from the bedroom. Would Steve stay in there? Should she take this opportunity to explain to Martin that they were not alone in the flat? It might be better for her to tell him now rather than wait on tenterhooks to see if Steve betrayed his presence.

She knew she ought to do that but Nicola disliked

confrontations, arguments, angry voices. She wasn't sure how Martin would react and she half hoped that Steve would not make it necessary for her to tell Martin anything.

"You should get quite a good price for this place when you sell," Martin told her, looking around the kitchen.

Nicola nodded. She would have liked to ask him to keep his voice down but she could only do that if she told him why she wanted to be quiet.

"How much did you pay for it?" he asked as she got down the coffee cups.

She looked around, frowning. "Twenty thousand but prices have shot up since, of course."

Martin looked immaculate. He always did, his clothes conservative but carefully chosen to match his image. He had explained to her that his clients liked to be sure their money was in good hands. They liked their stockbroker to be safe, trustworthy, reliable. Martin was all those things. He was everything Nicola felt a husband should be. He was the opposite of Steve.

"You haven't got a date fixed for the divorce hearing yet?" he asked.

Her hand shook as she switched off the percolator and Martin looked at her in surprise. "You're very edgy this morning."

"Sorry," she said, trying to smile. "The divorce won't be heard for ages. There's a long waiting list, my solicitor tells me. I'll have to wait until my name gets to the top." She hesitated. Now was the moment to tell him that Steve was back in London. Moistening her lips, she tried to get the words out, but she was not certain of her voice. She needed time to think, work out how to bring him into the conversation. She had never been able to talk to Martin about Steve. She was half afraid of what she might betray if she said anything.

Swinging away, she began to pour the coffee, watching the black stream of liquid as it filled the cups.

"Darling, could you press my pants before I get dressed?" Steve's casual voice made her jump ten feet into the air. Scalding coffee sprayed over her hand. She put the pot down with a crash, gasping and trembling.

Martin stood up in a reflex action, his face torn between concern for her and surprise at Steve's sudden arrival, his head swinging from one to the other and his frown growing as he absorbed the fact that Steve was wearing nothing but a short robe which he had only tied loosely.

Steve was beside her before Martin had moved, taking hold of her hand and thrusting it under the cold tap. After a moment he turned off the water and inspected her reddened skin, his expression concerned. "How does it feel now?"

She pulled her hand away and put it behind her back like a child, her lower lip sulky. Her eye moved nervously to Martin. He was staring at them. "This is my husband," Nicola mumbled, very flushed.

Steve ran his blue eyes over Martin in a casual assessment before giving him a crooked smile. "We had better introduce ourselves, as Nicola has fallen down on the job. I'm Steve Howard." He did not offer his hand although Martin, always polite and conscious of the social niceties, had moved forward with his own hand held out.

Martin let his hand fall, embarrassment written all over him. "Martin Eastwood," he responded.

"I imagined you must be," Steve drawled. "Of course, it is possible she has half a dozen ardent suitors but somehow I don't see Nicky in the role of femme fatale."

Nicola looked at him irritably. "Thank you," she muttered.

He crooked a mocking eyebrow. "Oh, would you rather I saw you as one? Sorry. I'll try, if you like." His blue eyes drifted down over her in her jeans and discreet shirt. "You don't quite look the part, though. Something in clinging black would be more appropriate."

"Oh, shut up," Nicola said, her face scarlet.

Steve looked at Martin, who was staring, his mouth open. "So you want to marry my wife," Steve said pleasantly.

Martin had grown very red. This scene was not going the way Martin felt it should—the way, no doubt, he had imagined his first meeting with Nicola's ex-husband would be.

He had a vague grasp of the fact that Steve was getting at him. "I didn't know you were here," he said, stammering slightly.

Steve looked under his lashes at Nicola, the oblique mockery deepening in his eyes. "Oh, Nicky, you didn't tell him," he said sweetly, pretended reproach in his tone.

Martin had made up his mind about Steve. He did not like him. Keeping his eyes on Nicola he said with

51

all the calm he could muster, "What's he doing here, Nicola?"

"We *are* still married," Steve pointed out before she could answer. "The deed to this flat is in my name."

Deciding to ignore that, Martin kept his eyes on Nicola's disturbed face. "You should have warned me," he said.

"I'm sorry." She knew she should have warned him. She wished she hadn't been such a coward. "I was going to," she explained rather limply.

Steve picked up the coffee cup nearest to him and sipped some of the black coffee. "Just what I need," he told Martin, who looked at him as if he hoped the coffee would choke him.

Moving toward Nicola, Martin lowered his voice to a confidential, chiding murmur. "He shouldn't be here, Nicola. Surely you realize that? It could prejudice your divorce."

"I've told him that," she said. "He doesn't take any notice."

"Oh, doesn't he?" Martin bristled, swinging around to face Steve, who went on drinking coffee, his blue eyes very bright. "Now, look here," Martin began aggressively.

"No, you look," Steve said, putting down the cup. "Of the two of us, I have more right in this flat than you do, so mind your own business."

"Nicola wants you to leave," Martin informed him. "Don't you, darling?"

"I've told him I do."

"You see?" Martin said, turning back to Steve. "You heard what she said."

"I heard," Steve agreed indifferently.

"Then you had better go," Martin pointed out. "You can't insist on staying if Nicola wants you to leave."

"Why not?"

Martin was staggered. "Why not?" he repeated. "Well, obviously . . ."

"Obviously what?" Steve was enjoying himself, leaning against the draining board, his long body relaxed and at ease, his eyes watching Martin like a cat with a mouse.

"Nicola has told you . . ."

"I never listen to anything a woman says," Steve drawled with enjoyment. "If you do, you're a fool. They never mean half of what they say. You should have worked that out for yourself by now. You have to read between the lines with them. It's a bit like doing the crossword in the papers—half guesswork, half an informed suspicion."

Martin had the look of a man about to explode. He squared himself, his elegantly clad body tense. "If you won't go, I'll have to throw you out," he told Steve.

Nicola closed her eyes.

Steve laughed. The sound of his laughter told her that that was precisely what Steve had been angling for—the offer of violence. It could only have one outcome. Martin was slim and active but he hadn't a chance against Steve's powerful, muscled strength.

"You and whose army?" Steve asked him softly, not shifting from his casual stance.

Martin went at him with a furious gasp. Steve moved too fast for Nicola to see what happened but

53

the next second Martin was flat on his back, a hand to his nose, making muffled gasps of pain.

Nicola ran to kneel beside him, full of contrition and distress. "You're a brute," she yelled over her shoulder at Steve as she tried to see what damage he had done to Martin's nose.

Steve strolled away, stepping over Martin's feet with composure on his way to the door. "Don't forget I want my pants pressed," he told her as he vanished.

"My nose," Martin grunted, still clasping it.

"Oh, dear," Nicola groaned, looking at him in flushed, anxious disturbance. "I am sorry, Martin."

Martin gingerly removed his hand. His nose seemed perfectly normal, except that it was rather red. "He's got a fist like a steamhammer," he said sulkily. "Anyway, he took me by surprise. He jumped at me before I was ready."

Nicola was suddenly irritated with them both. Martin looked like a little boy who had lost a fight.

"I'll be ready for him next time," he said and Nicola got up, stiff with impatience.

"Don't be ridiculous. What good would that do?"

"It will do me a lot of good," Martin said. "I owe him a good punch in the nose, remember."

Steve had left his trousers over a chair. Nicola picked them up absent-mindedly. They were very crumpled. What had happened to his other luggage? she wondered. Did he have to leave it behind to get away? It wouldn't be the first time he had lost a whole wardrobe. Once before he had had to abandon all his belongings to escape with a whole skin.

Martin slowly got to his feet, staring at her as she

let down the ironing board from the cupboard which held it. "What are you doing?"

"Pressing his pants," Nicola said, getting out the iron and plugging it in.

"You're not going to do that for him, are you?" He sounded so furious she looked around at him.

"He can't wear these as they are. He must have slept in them for days."

"Too bad," Martin muttered. He switched off the iron, his expression black with temper. "Let him get someone else to do it. You aren't his slave."

Nicola looked at the creased trousers. "No," she said. "I'm not, am I?" He was right. She hadn't been thinking properly.

"Who does he think he is?" Martin said rhetorically.

"Good question." She had often asked herself that in the past.

"He's an arrogant devil," Martin said, his lips tight.

"I couldn't agree with you more."

"I had no idea. You said he was difficult but I didn't realize how much so."

"He's a brute." She looked at Martin, her face warm. "Your poor nose." She leaned toward him, kissing it gently. "How does it feel now?"

Martin slid his arms around her slender waist and kissed her lips. "It's getting better all the time."

The door opened and Steve lounged there in a shirt, his long legs very brown. Nicola instinctively jumped away from Martin and got a hard unsmiling look from the blue eyes.

"Where are my pants?"

"She isn't pressing them," Martin told him, but he said it with a wary eye on Steve, poised to move back if Steve moved an inch.

"If she hasn't pressed them in five minutes, I'll have yours," Steve informed him silkily. He smiled as he said it, the reasonable smile of the tiger regarding the tethered goat which it would claim any minute, then he walked out again, letting the door slam.

Martin said something Nicola ignored. She plugged the iron back in and began pressing the trousers.

"I'll break his neck if he comes near me again," Martin told her but he didn't try to stop her.

"He's got a horrible temper," Nicola said as she watched the steam hissing up.

"He looks as if he has," agreed Martin, straightening his tie with one hand. "What is he doing in London?"

She nodded toward the paper. "That's his story— the lead. He was thrown out by the government there. They said they would shoot him if he went back."

"I'll buy him a plane ticket," Martin muttered, picking up the paper and beginning to read. His face changed. Nicola finished pressing the trousers while he made his way through the story.

She heard him swallow. "I didn't realize," he said under his breath.

Nicola met his eyes. "You hadn't heard about it?"

"Oh, they had the story in my paper but not in this detail."

She nodded. "I think Steve was the only reporter

in the area." He would be, she thought. Typical of him to be on the spot when something like that happened.

"It must have been murder," Martin said, and she began to laugh hysterically.

Looking at her in impatient bewilderment, he asked, "What's so funny about that?"

Her laughter died, as if it had been switched off "Nothing," she said wearily. "Not a thing."

Martin did not understand her, she could see. He was looking as if he thought she needed her head examined. "You're upset," he told her gently. "No wonder you looked distraught when you opened the door. Why on earth didn't you tell me he was here?"

"I didn't want any trouble," she said, and that was funny too. She couldn't help laughing but her laughter had that edge of hysteria which bordered on tears.

Martin looked at her grimly. "Well, you got it anyway," he said, and she nodded.

"I did, didn't I? There's always trouble when Steve Howard is around. All over the world people say, 'Oh, no!' when they see him flying into the country. They know that where he goes, trouble follows."

Her trembling voice cut off as Steve came back into the room. He had shaved now, his tanned face smooth and still slightly damp.

He didn't say a word, just took his trousers and slid into them, ignoring Martin and Nicola.

Martin looked at him with embarrassed concern. "I've just read your story," he said, clearing his throat. "Terrible."

Steve pretended not to understand him. "Is it? Well, the subs will take a hatchet to my best work, you know."

Martin struggled to be polite. "I meant that the news was terrible," he expanded. "A shocking story—it must have been a nightmare for you."

Steve shot Nicola a hard, querying look, as though asking her something. She met his stare with surprised bewilderment, then, as he said brusquely, "Yes, it was," she realized that he had wondered if she had told Martin about his nightmare. Steve hated to reveal anything of himself, particularly anything anyone might read as a weakness.

"When will that lunch be ready?" he asked, turning to her, and Nicola exclaimed, "The chicken!" She flew to the oven to inspect it. An appetizing aroma wafted out into the room and Steve sighed deeply.

"I'm starving. I could eat that all by myself."

The phone rang in the living room and Steve glanced around. "That will be for me, I expect. I left this number." He went out and Martin watched as Nicola tested the vegetables.

"Nicola," he said slowly, his tone thoughtful.

She looked up. "Yes?"

Martin was looking at her very oddly. "You haven't . . ." He broke off, his face rather confused, coloring. "How long has he been here?"

"He was here when I got back last night," she told him, not getting the point.

"He's been here all night?" His tone made it clear then; she felt herself going pink.

"Yes, and before you ask me, he slept in the bed but I slept on the couch." She could not help the slight acidity with which she said that. Martin was looking at her accusingly and Nicola did not like it. He had no right to look at her like that.

He relaxed. "Oh."

"Yes, oh," she snapped, and Martin tried to placate her, giving her a coaxing smile.

"You don't still fancy him then?" That was a very heavy attempt at humor and she wasn't responding to it.

Her face cold, she said, "No, I don't fancy him."

Steve loomed up in the doorway, catching the words, and giving her a hard stare, his brows meeting above his eyes. He did not speak to her, however; he addressed Martin with brisk courtesy, a threat still lurking in the clear blue of his eyes.

"I'm expecting some people from the office any minute, but there isn't any whiskey in the place. Would you do me a small favor? There's an off-license on the corner. I'd be grateful if you would go down there and get me a bottle of whiskey. I'd go myself but I ought to stay here in case they arrive."

Martin looked to Nicola for guidance, and she shrugged. Apparently deciding that as Steve seemed to be ignoring the incident he might as well, too, he picked up his coat, departing like a lamb. Steve glanced at Nicola who was straining the carrots, her attention fixed on what she was doing.

"I can see why you picked him," he drawled.

Nicola pretended not to hear that. She was not going to talk about Martin to him. She was still angry with Steve for the way he had behaved earlier. He had had no business taunting Martin into a fight which Steve knew very well he would win with one hand tied behind his back. Martin led a very sedentary life. He was fit enough for the life-style he enjoyed but Steve was a much tougher proposition. He had to be, his job demanded it. He had learned to look after himself in a rough school. He had the alert instincts of a jungle animal.

"What turns you on?" Steve demanded, watching her closely. "His smooth manner or his looks?"

"Martin is nothing like you," Nicola said coldly. "That's what turns me on."

"I thought it might be something like that." She had hoped to prick his thick skin but she could see that she had only amused him instead. He was grinning and looking as if he liked that idea.

"At least this time I shall be getting a husband when I marry, not just a flying lover," Nicola muttered, turning away from him.

She wasn't looking at him as she spoke and she hadn't heard him move. When his voice came just behind her it made her jump, her eyes opening wide, startled and alarmed.

"For the next week I'm not flying anywhere," he said, his voice deep and husky, then his mouth burrowed into the back of her neck and her pulse went crazy, her breath hurting as she tried to drag air into her lungs.

"Don't do that," she whispered breathlessly.

His arms had gone around her waist, his hands moving just below the uplift of her breast.

60

"I've been waiting for this for months," he said, his kiss sliding to her ear.

She pushed at his hands, wriggling in the cage of his embrace, trapped between him and the sink. "What do you think I am? You must despise me if you think you can just fly in and out of my life like a homing pigeon. If you wanted me, you wouldn't have stayed away so long. The only thing that matters to you is your job."

His hands shifted upward and she felt those long fingers closing over her breasts and her pulse accelerated once more. This warm possession sent waves of excitement pulsing through her.

"Nicky," he whispered, his lips moving softly against her neck again.

She knew what he was doing. The temptation of those experienced hands, the teasing mouth, did not need any explanation. Nicola shut her weakening mind to what he was offering. She reminded herself of the empty nights, the lonely days, he had given her in the past.

"Will you leave me alone?" She broke away, turning to face him and he watched her intently, staring into her angry eyes with a frown.

"We're still married, Nicky," he reminded.

"We've never been married!" It had not been marriage as she understood the word.

"Don't talk nonsense," he said impatiently, shifting his stance in an uneasy movement. He had always avoided discussions of this sort. He had not wanted her to bring it all out into the open. He wanted to keep things light between them. That left him free to fly away whenever he chose without feeling that he left any problems behind him. Steve ran from involvement. He felt trapped when she tried to make him admit that their life-style was no longer going to work. Marriage was a trap; that was how he saw it. So he had tried to be married and yet free, but Nicola was not prepared to share him with his job.

"We went through a legal ceremony," she threw back. "But as far as real marriage was concerned, you never even considered it. You put a ring on my finger, took me to bed and then went back to what you really enjoy—your job."

"You're being ridiculous," he argued, his face darkening as he listened. "You can't expect me to take that seriously."

"I don't," she agreed scathingly. "You've never taken me seriously."

"You're wrong." He moved nearer, a harsh light in his eyes. "I take you very seriously."

"No," she denied. "To you I'm just a woman you like going to bed with."

"If that was true, I'd never have married you at all," he said furiously. "Do you think you were the first girl I'd ever wanted to take to bed?"

Jealously, she muttered, "I'm sure I wasn't."

"I didn't marry any of the others."

"Maybe they had more sense than I did. Maybe they wouldn't have you."

"Maybe I didn't ask any of them," he told her, his eyes growing cold.

"I wish you hadn't asked me!"

The coldness deepened, hardening all the lines of his face. "Thank you."

"If I'd realized you didn't intend to take our marriage seriously, I would have turned you down. I want a normal marriage with a husband who comes home to me every night." Her voice had begun to shake, she was afraid she was going to cry. She tried to steady herself, biting on her inner lip. "I want a house, children . . ." Her voice broke. She couldn't finish; it hurt too much.

He moved restlessly, watching her as she brushed the back of her hand over her eyes. When he moved closer and tried to put an arm around her, though, she pushed him away, giving him a bitter look.

"I don't want you touching me!"

He fell back, taking a deep breath. "Why are you in such a rush? There will be plenty of time for children. But if you want one that badly we could have one right away."

"While you go back to Africa, leaving me to have it on my own? No, thank you. I want a baby, but not like that. I'm not planning on a one-parent family."

"Neither am I," he retorted. "I'm intending to give up foreign reporting one day. I'll get a desk job in London."

Nicola's breath stilled. She looked at him sharply, searching his face. "When?"

He grimaced. "Sometime."

Her body sagged. He was talking at random, making vague promises. He didn't mean them. Steve liked the way his life was arranged. He had the best of both worlds—an exciting job which gave him plenty of travel, glamor, the danger he loved—and a wife waiting in London for him whenever he chose to come back to her.

"If they don't send you home in a coffin first," she said with biting rage.

Steve gave a sudden grin, reckless amusement in his eyes. "They'll have their work cut out."

He thought he was indestructible, did he? Nicola wished she could believe he was—she looked at the all-too-human vulnerability of his amused face and hated him. One bullet could stop that laughter forever. His lean body was a beautifully streamlined machine, the taut brown skin smooth over those strong bones, the mind behind the blue eyes quick and clever. Unlike machines, though, Steve was flesh and blood.

"Well, I'm not waiting around to find out," she told him with bitterness. "You go on risking your life for as long as you like, but count me out. I've had enough." She could not face any more of the interminable waiting, worrying, the nights without sleep and the days when her nerves jumped every time the phone rang.

Steve pushed his hands down into his pockets, watching her with an unreadable expression. "And when you've divorced me, you plan to marry your stockbroker?"

"I haven't made up my mind what I'm going to do." Martin was always talking as though she had said she would marry him when the divorce was through, but she had never committed herself. Martin took too much for granted. Men always did, she thought, her face impatient. They seemed to think it was up to them to make decisions and all a woman had to do was fall in line obediently.

"How long has it been going on?" Steve demanded.

She didn't like the way he phrased that, or the narrowed glare of his eyes. "I met Martin a few months ago," she said coldly.

He laughed, a vicious mimicry of amusement, his mouth twisting and his blue eyes scathing. "The minute my back was turned . . ."

She interrupted that sentence with a gasp of fury. "I'd already started the divorce proceedings, and if you turn your back, you can't be surprised if I walk away. Did you think I enjoyed living like a widow? How much time did you actually spend with me after we were married? It's surprising I remembered what you looked like. If I hadn't had a few photos, I would have thought you were a mirage."

"So you scouted around for someone else, did you?"

Flushing, she snapped, "No, I met Martin purely by accident."

"Oh, of course," he sneered.

"It was! I was at a party when we met. I was on my own and so was he . . ."

"What a touching story," Steve interrupted. "I've heard it before, though. Adultery always starts like that."

"I told you," she broke out breathlessly. "We haven't . . ."

"You told me," he agreed, watching her with a harsh frown. "But how do I know you told me the truth?"

"I don't happen to believe in . . ." she began, and he laughed unpleasantly.

"How high-minded. Doesn't a lot depend on your definition of the word adultery? Where do you draw the line, Nicola?" He moved closer and looked down at her, his face hard. "Does he kiss you?"

She looked away, her eyelids fluttering.

Steve caught her face between his hands. "How does he kiss you?" he asked thickly. "Like this, Nicola?" His mouth moved sensually against her lips, parting them, probing between them. She felt his fingers unbuttoning her shirt and moving under it, the cool tips of them gently sliding over the flat plane of her midriff until he was cupping one breast. "Does he do that, my darling?" Steve whispered against her trembling mouth.

There was a tremulous feeling deep inside her and her pulses beat fiercely. She couldn't answer, her mouth too dry to speak.

Steve's hand moved around to her back. She felt him unclip her bra and she tried to break away. His hand closed on her waist, holding her. "Oh, no," he said. "Not yet, my darling. We haven't finished our little experiment. You haven't told me enough yet."

She felt his fingers brushing gently over the warm white flesh he had exposed and her eyes closed helplessly. She was breathing fast, her lips parted on a stifled moan.

"Has he had your clothes off yet?" The terse question broke into her weak surrender and she shuddered.

"No, no, no." There was mounting pain in her voice.

Steve cupped her breast, bending to touch his lips to the hard pink nipple. "I hope he hasn't," he muttered, his breath warm on her body. "Like most women you have a positive genius for telling lies with your eyes wide open and a look of indignant innocence on your face."

"I'm not lying, but if I wanted to sleep with Martin, I would," she said bitterly.

"I'd kill you if you did," Steve said, with raw rage threaded through his voice. He straightened and brought his mouth down on hers with demanding fire, the force of the kiss driving her head back, her throat stretched and aching. She felt his hand caress her neck, push into her hair and wind among the black strands. He pulled her head back even further and the kiss became violent, cruel, a punishing possession which sapped all her will to fight him.

The jangle of the doorbell snapped them both out of their passionate trance. Steve lifted his head, breathing sharply, a dark red color in his face and leaping desire in his eyes. Nicola swayed, moistening her bruised lips with her tongue. The pressure of Steve's mouth had driven them back upon her teeth, and she felt the tiny soreness, grimacing.

The bell rang again. "That will be Martin with the whiskey," Nicola whispered in an unsteady voice.

"You'd better let him in then, hadn't you?" Steve released her and ran his derisive eye over her open shirt, the firm pale breasts he had been caressing. "You had better tidy yourself up before you do, though. We wouldn't want your boyfriend to know I'd been sharing your favors."

Her hand flew out in an involuntary gesture. The

slap of it as it connected with his face surprised them both. Steve stared as she jumped back, her eyes enormous. Putting one hand to his cheek he grimaced. "You'll pay for that later," he promised silkily.

She turned away, trembling even more, and hurriedly did up her bra and then her shirt before she went to open the door.

# Chapter Four

Martin thrust the bottle of whiskey into her hands. He was looking rather annoyed and at once broke out, "I've been thinking. I can't stay to lunch now, can I? If he refuses to leave, we must go. Why don't we have lunch elsewhere? We'll eat out at a restaurant."

She was tempted to agree out of sheer defiance, but the heated trolley in the kitchen was full of food she had spent the morning getting ready, and if they did go out, she knew Steve would never bother to eat any of that food. That was one thing she had learned about him during their strange, sporadic marriage. Steve was very vague about meals. He might make himself a sandwich but she knew he wouldn't dream of serving the meal she had prepared.

"I can't," she told Martin. "I'll have to stay." After all, this was her home. Why should she let Steve drive her out of it? She did not quite trust him, anyway. She wanted to keep an eye on him while he was in the flat. Seeing Martin's frown, she added, "He *is* expecting people. I'm not going out and leaving them all here. Who knows what sort of orgy they might have?" She could imagine coming home to find the flat full of noisy newspapermen, the air full of cigarette smoke and the smell of whiskey. She knew those parties. Once they got talking about their job they forgot everything else.

Martin had begun to look very sulky. That calm manner of his did not tend to the sort of savage temper Steve could fly into, but it did produce the occasional fit of the sulks. "It puts me in a very false position," he said. "You aren't changing your mind, are you?"

"What about?" She was thinking about the lunch which was going to be ruined if someone did not eat it soon and she did not get his drift.

"The divorce," he said, and Nicola gave him an angry look, going rather pink.

"No, I'm not." She paused, and decided that that was not definite or vehement enough, so she said, "Certainly not!" She hoped that left no room for doubt.

"You're very complacent about letting him stay here," Martin said with more shrewdness than she liked.

"Nothing of the kind," she retorted. "I've told him to go over and over again. He takes no notice."

It was like talking to a brick wall to try to get Steve to take any notice if he chose not to do so.

"You could make him go," Martin informed her and she looked at him scathingly.

"Oh, yes? What do I do? Pick him up and throw him out? You try it." Her tone made Martin turn very red and she was apologetic as she met his eyes. He was hurt. Although she had not actually said so, she had implied that Martin couldn't stand up to Steve. The sting in that implication was, of course, that after what had happened between the two men earlier, Martin was angrily aware that he couldn't.

"He's a nasty piece of work," Martin said, almost as though he was blaming her for that, as though she had deliberately produced Steve out of a hat. "I can't see what you saw in him."

"Neither can I," she lied, her eyes shifting away and her mouth wry. She sighed, shrugging her shoulders. "I'm sorry to spoil your day for you, Martin, but I suppose you're right. You had better go."

He lingered, chewing on his lower lip. "I'm worried about leaving you here alone with him."

"I'll be okay," she said reassuringly.

Martin did not quite meet her eyes. "I don't like it," he said, and she knew perfectly well what was in his mind. Martin was far too conventional to come out with it but he was worrying about the idea of her being alone in the flat with her husband in case Steve talked her into bed.

"I can manage him," she said, with less truth than optimism.

"Can you?" Martin clearly did not believe her. "Sure you don't want me to stick around?"

"No," she said. "Steve's my problem."

Martin gave her a look then opened the door, his face blank. "If you want me, you know where I live," he said, stalking out. Martin was not the sort of person to make a noisy protest. He was too conscious of his dignity. It came over, though, that he was angry with her. What also came over was that Martin was less deeply wounded than he was annoyed. The hurt was to his self-respect rather than his heart.

There had always been some sort of unreality about her relationship with Martin. They had been too nice to each other, too careful, too polite. She had told herself that that was because Martin was a nice, polite man, but it had been more than that.

Martin had never been in love with her. Love would have been more urgent, more demanding. Martin liked her, he found her attractive. He felt she would suit his life-style. He had had a number of sound reasons for asking her to marry him, but love had not been one of them. It was just that Martin was conventional enough to believe love must be the only reason for marrying anyone, so he had pretended feelings he didn't really have.

Holding the bottle of whiskey, she walked slowly back into the kitchen. Steve was leaning against the sink, his arms folded, and a harsh frown on his face.

The blue eyes fixed her. "Well, where is he?"

"Gone," Nicola said, putting down the whiskey.

Steve began to grin and she resented that. Today she was ready to resent a lot of things.

"You can take that grin off your face," she yelled, turning on him like a wildcat.

"Don't shout at me," Steve said, the grin vanishing.

"I'll shout all I want to," Nicola informed him. "Who do you think you are?"

"I think I'm your husband."

"Not for long," she said with bitter satisfaction.

A hard, cold expression came into his face. "Then I'd better make the most of the time that's left, hadn't I?"

"You're not touching me," she said, a thread of panic in her voice as he moved toward her.

"You sound scared, Nicola," he taunted, smiling tightly. "Why is that? What are you scared of? That you might enjoy it, by any chance?"

She had backed involuntarily away from him, trembling, but now she stood her ground, her chin lifted and her eyes burning with anger.

"I'm not scared at all," she lied.

He laughed, so close to her now that their bodies almost touched, looking down at her with mockery and cold appraisal. "Liar," he whispered in a low, intimate voice. He lifted a hand and touched the side of her neck. "What's that?" The little pulse beneath his finger beat faster. "A dead giveaway," he told her, his mouth twisting.

"Get your hand off me," she said shakily.

His fingers caressed her throat, wakening more pulses, and that made her angrier than ever. He had one easy way to get under her skin and he knew it. If he had any principles, he wouldn't be doing this. Hadn't he hurt her enough?

73

"You're a selfish, self-satisfied brute," she said with such passion that his hand dropped away from her.

She took advantage of his disbelief at her tone. Meeting his stare, she said, "How dare you criticize me for dating Martin? How dare you walk in here and expect to be welcomed with open arms after all this time? What do you think marriage is? This has never been your home. You've treated it like a hotel. I won't describe how you've treated me, but you're never doing it again."

"What do *you* think marriage is?" he retorted with a contemptuous stare. "Or don't you remember the words 'for better for worse?' I seem to recall you saying them."

"I wasn't expecting the worst so soon," Nicola muttered. "I had no idea that you married me with every intention of walking out on me almost at once."

He shifted irritably. "I didn't walk out. I was sent on a story. It's my job. You knew what my job was when we got married."

"I didn't know it was going to mean we never saw each other."

"I couldn't take you with me, it wasn't safe," he said, frowning. "It was too risky, Nicky."

"If it was risky, you could have given me the option. You didn't, did you? You didn't discuss it with me. You just flew off and left me."

"I missed you," he murmured, looking at her through his lashes, a coaxing little smile appearing on his face.

She was not going to let him wheedle her. She

turned away, her face cold. "The lunch is ready," she said, her tone ending the conversation.

"Blast the lunch," he roared, slamming out.

Nicola went on with serving the meal, her eyes grim. When it was ready, she called him and after a pause he came, his strong face expressionless now. During the interval, she got the feeling, he had been reviewing their argument. As they ate he kept shooting her quick, assessing looks, but he said nothing.

Only when they had finished their meal did he say, "I sometimes suspect you want a home more than you want a husband. You have a very fixed idea of what marriage should be."

Nicola didn't answer. She had been an only child, brought up in a very quiet, contented home life, and she couldn't deny that she had wanted to reproduce that happy atmosphere with Steve. Her parents had both died before she met Steve. For some years she had lived alone in London's lonely wasteland and perhaps she had expected marriage to give her back the warm background she had grown up in. She had no family and few friends. She only knew she needed to belong.

"I just want my husband with me all the time, not hundreds of miles away," she muttered.

"You make points like someone hammering in nails," he muttered.

"I hope you're getting them, then."

"You'll get something, in a minute," he threatened, and she gave him a defiant stare.

"You're so civilized. Faced with any argument, you react by making threats."

"That wasn't a threat, it was a promise," he said, his eyes dark with temper, getting up in a violent movement to move around to her.

The doorbell rang as she leaped up, sending her chair crashing to the floor. Steve swore under his breath. "Teddy," he said, spinning to stride away. Nicola picked up her chair with shaking hands. She heard the editor of the paper talking at the front door, heard Steve answering him in a calm and level tone which revealed nothing of the temper she had seen a moment ago.

Steve walked back into the room with Teddy at his heels, beaming over the rims of his spectacles. "Nicola, nice to see you."

"Hello, Mr. Wiseman," she said politely, giving him a pretense of a smile.

He was a large, untidy man whose clothes always looked as though he slept in them. Nobody ran around after Teddy Wiseman to make sure his suit was pressed. He shambled as he walked, his body rolling from side to side, but when things got heated up around the office, nobody could move faster. Teddy only really lived when a deadline was coming closer and his particular brand of urgent energy was required. Then he straightened up, his whole manner changing. That adrenaline was a necessary part of his job and it was probably all that kept Teddy from lapsing into a total stupor.

"Seen the story this man of yours brought back? Good stuff, isn't it? He's a miracle man. I like to have a scoop now and then—keeps us on our toes, eh, Steve?"

"Sure," Steve said, collecting the whiskey and glasses.

Nicola got an odd idea. She felt Steve was trying to steer Teddy away. He had a furtive, evasive look.

"He's told you, has he?" Teddy asked, and she felt Steve's uneasiness increase.

"Later," he said, grabbing Teddy's arm to pull him into the living room.

Teddy did not go. He gave Nicola a cheerful grin. "Try to talk him into it."

"Into what?" she asked, and he threw Steve a quick look.

"You haven't told her?"

"Not yet," Steve said curtly. "I haven't made up my own mind yet. Until I do, I'm not discussing it."

"Discussing what?" Nicola asked, and both men ignored her. They talked across her as though she was a child. She could have screamed.

"Shouldn't Nicola have a say in it?" Teddy asked him.

"No," Steve said, leaving no room for argument.

"In what?" Nicola asked. Maybe if she said it often enough, one of them might see fit to enlighten her as to what they were talking about.

"Nothing," Steve said. "Teddy, come into the living room and have some whiskey while Nicola does the washing up."

That puts me in my place, she thought. I do the domestic chores while they drink the whiskey. Who says women are emancipated? They may have made a law about it but it isn't worth the paper it's written on until it's women who drink the whiskey while men do the chores. She looked at Steve, trying to imagine him in an apron, but failed. It just wasn't his scene. It wasn't just women who had been conditioned to see themselves in certain roles. Men had, too. Steve had a vital individuality which sprang from his certainty about his role in life. He didn't have to think about it. He was sexually confident and it blazed out of those blue eyes.

Teddy detached his arm from Steve's guiding hand. "With all due respect, I think Nicola ought to be involved in your thinking," he said with a quick smile at her which she read all too easily. Teddy wasn't speaking as a representative of the male sex now. He was speaking as someone with an axe to grind. He was enrolling Nicola on his team. He wanted her to bring her influence to bear on Steve in whatever he wanted Steve to do.

"Well, I don't," Steve muttered, but he was too late.

"I've offered Steve the job of Deputy Foreign News Editor," Teddy told her.

Nicola stiffened, her eyes flying to Steve. He grimaced, impatience in every inch of him.

"I haven't decided yet," he said, frowning.

"Now," Teddy said, happily sure that she was going to help him persuade Steve, "what do you say to that, Nicola?"

She looked away from Steve, her face icy. "That it's up to Steve," she said. "It's his job."

For a moment there was total silence. Steve stared at her in what appeared to be stupefied disbelief. Teddy's face dropped like a stone.

"Oh," he said, ludicrously discomfited.

Nicola turned and walked back to the sink to get on with the washing up and after a moment she heard the two men depart, closing the door behind them. She scrubbed viciously at a saucepan, her teeth clenched together.

Nothing had altered. Faced with the threatened divorce, Steve was still not prepared to give up his way of life. What point would there be in trying to change his mind? She had pleaded, begged, argued and cried in the past. Not anymore. She was going to follow his example and just go ahead with her own plans, ignoring their effect on him.

The doorbell rang again, and from the living room Steve yelled, "Get that, would you, Nicky?"

"Get it yourself," she yelled back, banging saucepans down as she dried them.

There was a stunned silence, then she heard him going to the front door. Nicola rarely had visitors. Her social life had never been ultra active. She was too shy. At parties she tended to sit in a corner and watch; she didn't have much to say to strangers. It always seemed such hard work hunting for small talk. She had, in fact, had more visitors at the flat this morning than she normally got during a week. Steve had a lot of friends, and whenever he had been in London they had descended in a horde. Nicola hadn't got to know any of them very well. She was too silent. She had found her role confined to going around refilling glasses, offering sandwiches, smiling shyly.

For the first time in her life she was facing herself and the way she lived and not liking either very much. From the very beginning, she realized, she had unconsciously been presenting Steve with an image of her which had affected the way he responded to her. His behavior had been conditioned by her own.

She heard him talking, heard men's deep cheerful voices, the sound of footsteps. "Joanne," Steve said in a very different voice, the voice he reserved for the opposite sex, and someone laughed. The door was shut but through it Nicola fancied she got waves of perfume. She glared at it. Joanne Hollis, she thought darkly. What's she doing here?

Joanne was one of the reporters. She got all the stories with a feminine angle. She also got a lot of the men. Joanne was a vibrant redhead with a taste for variety and come-hither green eyes. Nicola had rarely spoken to her but she had seen her swaying through the building in very tight skirts and so much perfume that after she had vanished it hung around in the air stifling everyone.

Nicola flung the saucepans into their cupboard. The clatter brought an odd little silence from the other room. Then the voices resumed rather more loudly.

Steve appeared, closing the kitchen door behind him, eyeing Nicola with wary uncertainty. "I'll need some more glasses."

Nicola began to clean the sink, ignoring him.

"Why don't you come in and join us?" he suggested, hovering behind her.

"When they go, you go with them," she told him. She had no intention of walking in there in her jeans. She knew Joanne Hollis. Joanne advertised her sex appeal in neon lights and Nicola was not competing

80

with her. Not yet, anyway, she thought. She had a lot of thinking to do first.

"I'm not arguing with you," Steve said, collecting some glasses and slamming out of the room.

Nicola finished tidying the kitchen then she quietly slipped off to her bedroom. She heard the voices rising and falling in the living room. Secure behind her bolted door, she stripped and hunted for something else to wear. A lot of things were going to change around here, she thought. And they might as well start changing now.

She had never seriously thought about herself before. Life rarely gives one time to stop and look at oneself from the outside. Day succeeds day in such battering rapidity. From childhood upward, the image inside one's head is formed like the growth of a pearl, so gradually that it isn't noticed.

Nicola thought about herself now, eyeing herself in the mirror with distaste. We are all partial, fragmentary, shifting, but that's not the image we have of ourselves. The self we project is a mixture of self-appraisal and the expectations of those we meet. People are constantly in motion, changing shape and form as you grasp them, yet we all tend to see ourselves as static.

Nicola had responded to Steve without knowing what she was doing, giving him back the image he desired. He had reacted to her in response to how she reacted to him. She saw that now. She had made no demands on him. She had yielded helplessly, allowing him to dictate the course of their relationship. If you're weak, you invite others to push you around.

Not anymore, she thought. She didn't know yet what she was or how she was going to shape her future, but she did know that it was going to be she who shaped it, not Steve or Martin or anyone else.

I've been pushed around long enough, she thought. From the mirror her own face stared back, the amber eyes fringed now with thick black false eyelashes, her mouth warm and glowing moistly, her delicately applied makeup lending color to her translucent skin. That's more like it, Nicola told the reflection.

She only had one dress which would make Steve sit up. She had bought it on impulse and left it hanging in her wardrobe because when she wore it, she got the sort of looks which made her feel uneasy. Some women like to be stared at like that. Nicola didn't. She usually wore clothes which made her safely invisible, using them as camouflage. But not today—today Nicola was going to make sure Steve knew she was there.

When she walked into the room, the voices stopped dead. The men half rose, looking at her with surprised interest.

Steve had been talking, a glass of whiskey between both hands, but he looked up, eyes widening. Nicola sauntered across the room under his sharp gaze, hoping she looked cool and casual.

"Hello," the men all murmured, and she smiled around the semi-circle, her glance avoiding Steve but lingering on Joanne Hollis.

"Hello, Joanne." Her smile had a fake sweetness.

"Hi," Joanne said, giving back the smile the way she had got it. Joanne was a man's woman. She had no time for other members of her sex and she had no friends at the newspaper, particularly among the secretarial staff, whom she treated with offhand contempt.

"What can I get you to drink?" Joe Fraser asked as she sat down beside him on the couch. He was one of the London-based reporters and was an old friend of Steve's. He knew Nicola quite well.

"Whatever you're drinking," she said, because there wasn't anything else, and when he handed her a small whiskey she sipped it, stifling a grimace of distaste.

"I'd like to shift over to foreign," Joanne said, leaning back and crossing her silkclad legs while Steve's blue eyes observed the graceful little movement with enjoyment.

Nicola sipped some more whiskey. If she didn't drink the stuff, she might toss it at Joanne.

"Tired of home news?" Steve was asking.

Joanne shrugged elegantly. She was wearing a white sweater cut so low it left nothing to the imagination and the shrug drew Steve's eyes from her legs upward. Joanne had a figure which curved in all the right places. She knew what to wear to draw attention to it, too.

"No way," Teddy said, his face sphinxlike.

Joanne gave him a coaxing little smile. "I'm sure I'd do well on the foreign team."

"Women who go in for foreign reporting have to be tough," Teddy said indulgently.

"I am tough," Joanne said, swallowing some whiskey in a casual fashion.

The men all laughed. Nicola didn't. She wasn't

viewing Joanne through the same rose-tinted spectacles they all wore. Joanne *was* tough. She might have
a sexy figure, a pretty face and a flirtatious manner,
but she couldn't hide from another woman the
hardness in her green eyes, the acquisitive line of her
mouth.

"Have you ever looked at the sort of women who
work on foreign?" Teddy asked. "They can kick
down doors."

"I don't need to kick them down," Joanne said
demurely, and they all laughed.

"We're not talking about bedroom doors," one of
the other men teased her.

Joanne looked at him through her lashes. "Charming," she purred.

"Teddy's right," Steve said. "The job doesn't suit
women. Too much risk involved."

"Oh, I wasn't talking about turning war corre-
spondent," she explained. "There are plenty of
other jobs on foreign."

"Talking about jobs on foreign," Joe said, glancing across at Steve, "are you taking the deputy's
job? David Wakeman leaves in a month's time,
doesn't he?"

Teddy assumed a sweet smile. "Steve's thinking
about it."

Steve looked at Nicola, who looked at her whiskey. She wasn't making much headway with it. A sip
or two left far too much in the glass.

Joanne leaned over and put her hand on Steve's
knee. "Oh, do take it," she pleaded girlishly.

Nicola looked at the other woman sideways, her
teeth grating. Steve was smiling and looking into

Joanne's eyes. He didn't appear to object to the intimate way she was touching him, nor did he seem surprised by it. Steve had known Joanne for years. How well had he known her, though? Nicola wondered. He had never been communicative on the subject of his past relationships. Steve had a poker face when he chose to. He was wearing it now, under that smile. Nicola couldn't guess what was going on inside his black head.

"I'd need some persuading," Steve said, his lashes flicking toward Nicola, who ignored him.

"I'm very persuasive," Joanne told him, throwing all her sex appeal into the smoldering gaze of her eyes. "You're a natural for the job. You've been working out in the field for years and you wouldn't make any mistakes about the men you sent out to get a story."

"Or the women," Joe Fraser muttered under his breath. "She's flattering you, Steve. Watch out."

"I'm watching," Steve said with amusement. He looked as if he was enjoying Joanne's attentions.

Joe looked at Nicola thoughtfully. "I'm sure you want him to take the job."

"I don't care what he does," Nicola said, drinking some more of the whiskey and shuddering as the heat of it hit the back of her throat. Why do they drink this stuff? It tastes vile, she thought.

Steve was staring at her from across the room and their eyes met. "He's a free agent, he can do as he likes," she added.

There was a little silence. Joanne laughed softly under her breath. "I hope you're listening to this, Steve; I am," she said.

"Oh, so am I," Steve said through his teeth, with a recriminatory look flung toward Nicola which promised punishment when his friends had finally gone.

"I wish my wife took such an understanding attitude to my job," Peter Lewis said, brushing back his untidy hair. "She drives me nuts complaining about the hours I have to work. You must have a word with her, Nicola, teach her the secret of the perfect marriage."

Teddy Wiseman intervened hurriedly, "You shouldn't miss your chance of a London job, Steve. You can't stay out in the field forever. You have to give up that life one day, and the longer you leave it the harder you'll find it."

"I wasn't planning on coming home just yet," Steve said. "It gets into your blood. Life will seem pretty tame once I've come back to London for good."

Nicola looked into her whiskey. That says a lot for our marriage, doesn't it? she thought to herself. Tame and far from being an irresistible lure.

Joanne gave Steve one of her smoldering smiles. "You ought to be planning on an executive career. In your position, I would. You know you can't just walk into an editorship—you have to work your way up, but you'll never get there until you start."

Peter Lewis was watching them, his mouth wry. "Women these days are always trying to muscle in on the decision-making," he muttered. "My mother would have got slapped if she had tried to tell my father what to do."

"That sounds like a really happy marriage," Nicola said with a bite. "Just like mine."

There was a silence. Steve looked dangerously at her. Teddy got up, looking at his watch, and said he had to go. The others remembered urgent appointments too, and Steve walked with them to the door.

Joanne gave Nicola a malicious little smile. "That was rather silly of you," she drawled.

"Was it?" Nicola asked coldly.

"There will be repercussions," Joanne said with silky malice. "Mark my words."

"Oh, I will," muttered Nicola, wondering whether to get herself some more whiskey but deciding she just couldn't stand the taste of any more of it.

"Steve's not the sort of guy to take that sort of display in front of his friends." Joanne was looking at her curiously, one hand running through her red hair. Even while they were alone she was never able to forget herself. She posed self-consciously, taking up a catlike attitude of sleek elegance. "I've known him a lot longer than you have."

"Well, that's nice for you," said Nicola, baring her teeth in a smile as false as Joanne's concern.

Joanne gave her another long, considering stare. "You know, I had you down all wrong. I thought you were the domesticated species."

"Oh, did you?" That was what Steve thought too, presumably. He, in common with the rest of his sex, put women into these tidy little categories. It made them easier to cope with and easier to forget.

"No need to bristle at me," Joanne said, looking amused again. "We're on the same side, remember."

I am not on your side, lady, Nicola thought. I'd rather not win than fight alongside you.

"You have to cheat a little," Joanne said. "Kid them along. It doesn't hurt to lie a few times, does it? Let them think they're natural winners if it makes them happy. You should never try a head-on clash. It always ends up with you getting the worst of it."

Nicola looked at her dumbly. Joanne was actually trying to be nice, she saw. Her conspiratorial smile made that clear. It must be fair warning and all that.

"It's called diplomacy," Joanne said. "Try it sometime." She turned her head as Steve came through the door. "I'd better rush," she said, flicking a hand across his cheek in a tantalizing little gesture which Nicola disliked intensely. "See you, darling."

The front door slammed. Steve stood staring at Nicola with furious blue eyes.

# Chapter Five

"I ought to slap you," he said, his brown skin drawn tightly over the angular strength of his cheekbones. If she had ever needed to be told that Steve could be dangerous, the way he was staring at her now was an unmistakable reminder.

Nicola was feeling very brave, though. The whiskey was circulating, leaving a comfortable glow inside her, and she looked back at him with her chin lifted belligerently. "Just try it."

"I will, in a minute," he muttered, frowning harshly. "That dress." He gave it a slow appraisal which made her prickle with resentful awareness, his narrowed eyes lingering on the way the bodice clung to her. "It's too tight," he said. "And what do you mean by arguing with me in front of my friends?"

"I didn't argue. I didn't say a word to you."

"Not to me directly," he agreed. "They knew you were sniping at me though—all that stuff about being a free agent."

"That's what you want, though, isn't it? To be free?" She looked coldly at him. "Well, you are. As free as air."

He did not like that. "Don't you ever snarl at my friends again," he said, evading the earlier subject.

"I didn't snarl. I just made myself clear."

"Oh, very clear," he agreed, his face grim. "They've all gone away with the distinct impression that this isn't so much a marriage as a prize fight."

"Well, they're right about one thing. This isn't a marriage. You've never treated me as anything but a woman you sometimes come back to."

His blue eyes took on a glittering threat, his mouth twisting in a bitter smile. "Well, I'm back now," he mocked in a low voice, then crossed the space between them like a streak of lightning.

She looked up, startled, her mouth suddenly dry, the insolent brightness of his gaze sending a shock wave through her body, making her legs go weak underneath her.

"Hello, woman," he taunted in a husky whisper. Her heart distinctly turned over. Nicola had always believed that that was a piece of romantic fantasy. Hearts didn't turn over. Now she discovered that hers did, the strange somersault leaving her quite breathless.

She tried to pull herself together. "Don't you come near me," she hissed aggressively. "We're having a new set of rules around here."

"We certainly are," he agreed, but she didn't get

the impression he was talking about the same set of rules. He was running his eyes over her in that too-tight, sexy dress and taking his time about it. Nicola did not like that look. It made her feel threatened, and, she suspected, that was exactly how he meant her to feel.

"And they're going to be my rules," she said.

"Are you drunk?" he asked, and she lifted an indignant face.

"I only had one glass of whiskey."

"You never could take anything stronger than milk," he taunted, grinning. "Or you wouldn't try to take me on, sweetheart."

"Oh, wouldn't I?"

His arm had somehow insinuated itself around her waist. She looked down at his hand as it calmly appeared beneath the upward swell of her breast.

"Take that away," she demanded. "I don't want it there."

"You're right," he agreed, removing it, then spoiled the effect of this apparent obedience by placing it on her breast, his long fingers splaying to stroke upward.

"Oh," Nicola said with a little gasp.

"It's reprisal time," Steve said silkily, bending to kiss the beating pulse in her throat. His lips were warm and smooth, their sensitive caress sending shivers of pleasure down her spine. She swayed, her eyes closing, and felt his hand shift. The tight bodice of her dress opened and his fingers slipped inside.

"No, no," Nicola said without opening her eyes. She tried to summon up her earlier rage but it seemed to have evaporated. She couldn't remember now what it had all been about. She couldn't remember anything. Her mind submerged beneath waves of pleasure.

The dress had dropped off her shoulders. Without noticing it, she had somehow got her arms around his neck. Under her searching fingers, his thick hair curled and clung. When his mouth closed over hers, she gave a muffled moan of excitement, her lips parting, and Steve drew her closer with one hand while the other softly moved up and down her naked back, following the marked line of her spine.

This wasn't what I meant to happen, Nicola told herself. Then added, more honestly, was it? Under the mounting sexual excitement, her mind was struggling to fight back. There's a principle at stake here, she thought. But what was it?

. How could she think with clouds of desire weakening her brain? How could she even hear when her blood was singing in her ears and shutting out every sound but itself? How could she make Steve see her as an equal, a rational human being with a mind of her own, when all he had to do was touch her and she became a puppet, responsive to every movement of his fingers?

Her dress had gone altogether now. She was held against him, his heart beating rapidly, fiercely, against her and his caressing hands growing more urgent as they ran from her breast to her silky thigh.

That's the principle at stake, Nicola remembered suddenly. Here I am again trapped in the same old equation and losing my way as I try to struggle out of it.

Steve saw it as a simple matter. He saw her as the

female to his male, the victim to his victor, and he believed he could always get his equation to add up. All her loud protests could be disregarded so long as Steve knew that he could silence them so easily.

He lifted his head, his eyes half shut, breathing harshly. "I need you, Nicky," he muttered, and her body shook in unwanted, unwilling response.

She wanted him to feel like that. She wanted him to say that. But not until he meant it the way she meant it. Not until Steve understood what needing and wanting meant. At the moment he was still ready to make love to her and walk away afterward, back to the more enthralling world of his job. He had a very limited understanding of love.

"I don't need you," she said, her voice husky and uneven.

The words dropped into silence. Steve's lids lifted. The blue eyes focused on her sharply.

"Liar," he said, trying to smile but visibly taken aback. She had caught him off guard for once. He had been very high and now he had come down with a thud.

"You're sexy, I grant you," she said in a cool voice.

He smiled angrily.

"But then so are lots of men." She smiled back with bland sweetness. "And some of them are rather more reliable."

"Are we back to what's-his-name?" Steve's brows jerked together and an impatient look came into his face. "Don't bring him up again. You know he doesn't turn you on. I could see that. He couldn't turn on a gas fire."

"Martin has nothing to do with this. I'm talking about you. I don't want a husband who comes and goes but usually goes and stays away for months. I want a husband who's around all the time. I want a real marriage, not an intermittent love affair."

Steve's eyes moved restlessly over her, dwelling on the warm white cleft between her breasts under the thin silk slip. "We'll talk about this later, shall we?" He bent and placed his mouth on the smooth exposed flesh. Nicola's breath caught.

"We'll talk about it now," she managed to say hoarsely.

"Darling," he coaxed, sliding his lips over her skin. "There's a more important matter on my mind."

"I know what's on your mind." It was on hers, too, but this time she was not giving in to the tempting persuasion of his kisses. She had to force herself to ignore what he was doing. "I want to talk about the job Teddy Wiseman offered you."

"I'm thinking about it." He gently drew one of the straps of her slip off her shoulder.

Nicola pushed it back up again. "It's just the sort of offer you should accept. You'd get a big raise and you'd be moving up the career ladder several rungs, wouldn't you?"

"Mm," he agreed noncommittally, his finger hooking under her strap to pull it down again.

"Why are you even hesitating?" She slapped his hand. "And stop that."

"I'm not ready to become a vegetable yet," he said, getting irritated, his face faintly red. "Once I leave reporting I'll be stuck at a desk for the rest of my life. You don't go backward in this business. If I take that job, that's it. I'm out of foreign reporting for good."

"You said you planned to leave it one day," she reminded him.

"Not yet," he said in restless impatience. "I'm not interested in sitting at a desk, giving orders, watching other men send in the news. I want to be out there where it's all happening, not standing on the sidelines. It's a different ball game with different rules, Nicky. I need the adrenaline you get from being under fire. If I'd been the sort to sit safely at home, would you have wanted to marry me, anyway?"

"Your job didn't come into my thinking," she said, which was all too painfully true, because she hadn't been doing much thinking. She had been feeling and her mind hadn't been involved at all.

"Do you think you're playing fair?" he asked. "You knew what sort of man I was when you married me. I haven't changed."

"Don't you think perhaps you should have done?" She looked into his eyes and saw them flicker. "You want to have your cake and eat it too, Steve. You want me *and* your old way of life. You want me to make all the adjustments but you don't intend to make any. You said just now that you hadn't changed and that's what's wrong, don't you see? Because one thing *has* changed, Steve. You weren't married, but now you are, and you have to come to terms with that or we might just as well forget about marriage altogether."

"I'm not caving in under ultimatums," he said with sudden savagery. "Married or not, you're not issuing the orders around here."

"It isn't a question of orders. It's more a question of attitude of mind. So long as you continue to think of me as some sort of doll you can pick up and put down at will, I don't want to know about you."

His teeth snapped together. "Right," he said, "So we know where we both stand."

"Yes," Nicola said. "And I'd be grateful if you would get yourself a room at a hotel."

"Right," he said again, in an impeded voice.

"My solicitor tells me that under the new divorce laws I have the right to possession of the marital home."

"Oh, great," Steve said. "You have all the rights and I have none, I gather."

"You must take that up with your solicitor." Nicola could see that he was going to get nasty any minute.

"I ought to take it up with you right now," Steve muttered, giving her a harsh look. "But I'm not going to lose my temper with you. You'd like that, wouldn't you? That's what you've been angling for ever since I got back. Then you'd come into court with some vicious lies about cruelty and ill treatment."

"I don't need lies," Nicola said. "I just have to count up the number of days I've seen you since we were married. That should be enough to convince a court that our marriage never even got off the ground."

"Count away," Steve said. "I didn't know you could count."

"I can do that sum on my fingers," Nicola flung back.

"You can go to hell," he said, striding toward the door. She heard the front door crash open, crash shut. She was trembling, her legs weak under her. She sank down on the couch and sat there blankly for a long time.

She ought to be feeling triumphant. Instead she just felt cold. She had stood fast in defense of her precious principle, but somehow that wasn't much comfort. Principles do not make exciting bedfellows. Nicola wound her arms around herself, biting her lip to stop the tears. If he had been there, he would have had a walk-over at that moment. She told herself she was glad he had gone. It was hard to be convincing, though, when all she could remember was the feel of his hand sliding down her body, the sound of his heart beating next to her own.

What if he goes back to Africa and ends up with a bullet in him? she asked herself, the tears spilling. How will I feel then?

She had taken an enormous risk, gambling that Steve loved her enough to face up to the problem. What if he put his job first? He had before. He very well might again. What then?

Would she be left with nothing but brief, burning memories? It was a bitter prospect, and telling herself that she had been fighting for their future was not going to make it easier.

Nicola had never expected to find herself fighting

so hard for anything. She was not combative by nature; she didn't enjoy quarreling with Steve. It would have been so much easier to let her female instincts rule her and fall into his arms, but she knew that if she had, Steve would have been reinforced in his belief that what he wanted was all that mattered. He would have flown off again when he had a new assignment and Nicola would have been back in the old trap, prey to the old fears and misery.

When she walked into the features department next morning, she was met by a peculiar silence which told her that the excited chatter she had heard as she opened the door had been about her and Steve. Now everyone became very busy, their heads bent over their desks. Nicola pretended she hadn't noticed anything unusual in the atmosphere.

She was not the sort of girl to broadcast her affairs to everyone she met. It was general knowledge, of course, that her marriage to Steve was in trouble; she had not been able to hide that. Her transfer to features had aroused too much curiosity. Most people politely avoided the subject but there was always someone with the tact of an elephant and the curiosity of a jackdaw who seemed oblivious of the fact that his personal questions were unwelcome. Nicola had fenced whenever someone asked a direct question, and her quiet manner had usually managed to silence the questioner.

But that didn't stop the sidelong looks, the unspoken questions, that morning. She worked intently, trying not to notice them.

At lunchtime she did not go down to the canteen.

She went out into a wintry Fleet Street and had a quick salad at a local café. The wind was biting but the sun was trying to fight its way through the clouds blowing across the sky. When she had finished her lunch, Nicola walked down toward St. Paul's to do some hurried shopping. Through the wedge of tower blocks she gazed unseeingly at that stately dome, the sight of it too familiar to penetrate her thoughts.

She was so absorbed that she walked straight into someone, beginning to stammer an apology before she recognized the girl.

"Oh, hello, Jane," she broke off, smiling.

"Wake up," Jane teased, her hazel eyes friendly. She worked in the features department, too, and although they did not know each other very well, they liked each other. Jane was in her early twenties, a shrewd sensible brunette who spent all her spare time ice-skating with her boyfriend.

"I was sleepwalking," Nicola admitted wryly, glancing from Jane to the girl with her. She did not get a very friendly reception there. Mandy Graham had a critical eye. She always spoke her mind, she was fond of explaining, which meant in practice that she was devastatingly rude whenever she felt like it and felt quite justified about it.

"That could be dangerous," Jane said lightly. "Did you eat in the canteen? It could be food poisoning."

Nicola laughed and Jane said, "I'm going back to bringing my own sandwiches. That stew we had today was definitely suspect."

Nicola got the feeling she was talking to stop Mandy coming out with something. Mandy had her eyes fixed unwinkingly on her and she had the expression of someone who was waiting for a chance to speak. Jane began to say something else but Mandy was tired of waiting.

Overriding Jane's voice, she said, "We saw Steve coming out of the lift. Is it true they've offered him the job of Deputy Foreign Editor? Is he going to take it?"

Jane's eyes were ruefully apologetic as Nicola met them. They exchanged glances, then Nicola said calmly, "I don't know. If you ask him, I'm sure he'll tell you."

That was as far as she was prepared to go along the road of giving Mandy back her own coin. Nicola did not like scenes.

Mandy was not amused nor did she even seem to be offended. She had a way of staring at you stolidly, her brown eyes round and bovine, as though trying to force an answer out of you. "Don't you know?" she persisted.

Nicola shook her head, then glanced at her watch. "I must rush. I want to buy some tights." She lifted a hand in a vague wave and hurried away.

Jane caught up with her a few yards further on, falling into step with a sidelong look. "Sorry about her."

"It isn't your fault." Nicola often wondered why Jane put up with Mandy, but office friendships were often more a matter of convenience than personal liking.

"She isn't exactly tactful," Jane said, something hesitant in her manner.

"Not exactly," agreed Nicola. She had a feeling

Jane had more than that to say and was casting around her mind for a way of saying it.

"When something is burning a hole in her head, she just has to let it out," Jane said wryly. She paused. "You ought to know—sooner or later she's going to come out with something else."

"Give it to me," Nicola said lightly, smiling.

"The thing is," Jane muttered, "Steve wasn't alone."

Nicola stopped smiling but her lips curved in a dry, rigid grimace.

"Mandy is going to spill it out to you sometime," Jane said. "She nearly did just now. I thought you'd rather get it from me."

Nicola waited. She wanted to scream at Jane to get it out, not drive her crazy wondering.

"He was with Joanne Hollis," Jane mumbled, rather pink. "Sorry," she added under her breath.

Nicola had five seconds to pull a smile back over her face. She managed it, but it cost her blood. "Oh, that," she said with sparkling vivacity. "I know all about that." She laughed, a silvery little noise which she hoped sounded convincing. "You know Joanne."

Jane stared at her, then looked away. "Who doesn't?"

Nicola stopped to look into a shop window and saw Jane's faintly troubled face beside her own reflection. "I expect they were lunching together," Nicola said. "Joanne wants to move over to foreign and she's hoping to twist Steve's arm."

"Of course," Jane said with false enthusiasm. "That explains it. She's ambitious, isn't she?"

"Very," Nicola muttered.

"Very attractive, of course," Jane said.

"Very," Nicola said again, smiling like mad.

"A bit of a piranha," Jane hesitantly suggested.

"She's all teeth," Nicola said on a bitter rush, then could have kicked herself for betraying so much.

Jane gave a stifled giggle. "I was beginning to wonder if I ought to order your martyr's crown," she said, her eyes dancing.

"Not just yet," Nicola sighed. "Thanks for telling me before anyone else had the chance to take me by surprise with it."

Not that there was much in the news to surprise, she thought, as Jane left her to finish her shopping, but someone less scrupulous than Jane could have got her to betray far more and Nicola would have died if she had let her feelings be seen in public. She would be ready now if someone tried to use the news like some sort of hand grenade.

It was Mandy who did, of course. She sauntered past Nicola that afternoon and halted with a sweetly synthetic smile to say, "Oh, I forgot." Here it comes, thought Nicola, looking happily alert. "Guess who was with Steve," Mandy finished, watching her like a hawk.

"You tell me," Nicola invited.

"Joanne Hollis." Mandy waited with breathless eagerness, staring at her.

"She must be desperate," Nicola said. The phone rang and she answered it, detaching her eyes from Mandy casually. After a moment, Mandy walked away, looking almost shocked.

Across the office Jane signaled "I told you so" and Nicola made a wry little face.

Joe Fraser wandered in an hour later to talk to the features editor. He had a photographer with him who hung around trying to chat up the girls while Joe was closeted with their boss. Mandy liked the brand of repartee which passed for wit with him. She threw it back cheerfully and they laughed a good deal. The other girls were pleased to have an excuse for breaking off work.

The department was housed in an open-plan office full of desks, typewriters, phones and noise. It was used as a through passage from the newsroom to the great bank of steel filing cabinets which held clippings from the back issues of the paper. When Nicola had first started work there, she had found it impossible to ignore the constant comings and goings, but after a while she didn't notice when someone walked through the room. The slap slap of the swinging doors went right over her head. She sometimes felt like a blinkered horse. Head down, she worked, not aware of what was going on around her.

When someone leaned on her desk she looked up, ready to smile. "Oh, hi, Joe."

"How are you?" he asked soberly, as though he hadn't seen her for weeks.

"Fine," she said. She knew he was remembering her little outburst at the party Steve had had in the flat, and she gave him a wry, apologetic smile.

"Raymond says I can borrow you," Joe told her. "I'm doing a feature for him on the circus and he wants it by next week. There's far too much research involved for one person. He says you can go through the files for me. Is that okay with you?"

"I'd enjoy it," she said. It was polite of him to ask since Nicola had no real choice, of course. That was what she was here for—to do what she was told. Joe was always scrupulously courteous, though. "When will you want me to start?"

"Tomorrow," Joe said. "Phil and I are just off to take some shots of a couple of circuses playing around London. Maybe you and I could have a quick session tomorrow at nine? I'll draw up a few guidelines of what I want and let you have a list of names to look up."

"Fine," Nicola said.

The photographer, Phil Smith, came wandering over to give her his insolent smile and a quick inspection which set her teeth on edge. If there was one thing that annoyed her, it was getting that sort of look from men she scarcely knew. She looked back at him with frozen distaste.

"Hello, ice maiden," he said, with another of his smiles.

"Come on," Joe told him grimly.

"You've had your turn," Phil Smith said. "Now I get to chat her up." He winked at Nicola who looked away. "Talk about frost in May," he said. "What's he got that I haven't got?"

"Charm," Nicola said.

Joe chuckled as he dragged the photographer away. Nicola went back to her work, frowning. Over-familiar though Phil Smith always was, he would have drawn the line at that sort of come-on if he hadn't known about the newest blow-up in her marriage. Phil Smith did not try to flirt with married women. He either had some sort of principles or else he did not like trouble.

It was pelting rain as Nicola left the newspaper building that afternoon to make her way home across London. She hesitated under the concrete canopy which overhung the entrance, watching the splash of raindrops into a puddle in the gutter.

A taxi swerved through the busy Fleet Street traffic. Nicola was about to rush across the pavement to hail it when she saw Steve bolt out of the printer's entrance, his hand held up. The taxi pulled in beside him and he opened the door, glancing around. For a second Nicola thought he had seen her and was waiting for her, but even as she was about to join him she saw Joanne Hollis totter across to him on stiltlike heels, her red head bobbing under an umbrella.

Steve took her arm in a chivalrous gesture to slide her into the cab, then he shut the umbrella and got in beside her. The taxi chugged away, engine throbbing as it waited for a break in the line of cars. Nicola stared fixedly at the two heads she could see in the rear window. Steve was leaning toward Joanne, his bronzed profile clearly visible. Joanne put up a hand to brush back a rain-soaked lock of black hair from his forehead, then she ran her fingertips lightly down his jaw.

Nicola was swamped by a wave of jealous hatred which left her feeling sick.

She was not surpirsed, of course. She had known as she watched Joanne with Steve at the flat that the other woman fancied him and Steve had not exactly been slapping her down. The shrouded secrets of Steve's past love life could contain any number of other women, but Nicola knew nothing about them. The faceless procession she had always imagined had been a hidden threat to her peace of mind and she could not decide whether it was harder or easier to be able to put a face to what she had long suspected.

Steve's sexuality was too vital for her to imagine he had led a blameless life before he met her, but that had not mattered too much beside the realization that his affairs had never meant much to him. Looked at in a certain light that might seem reassuring. Steve had married her because he loved her, she had tried to tell herself. He had never loved any of the others.

Nicola had never been able to convince herself. The attitude of contempt and indifference which underlay Steve's casual treatment of women had been a dark thread in their relationship, too. It was the reason why he had married her and then rushed back to his job. Steve despised the opposite sex. He had always been able to get any woman he wanted. Nicola had tumbled at his feet the minute he looked in her direction. He expected it.

But not anymore, Steve, she thought. I'd rather lose you than spend the rest of my life as the wallpaper hanging in the ignored background of your life.

# Chapter Six

Great newspapers always carry a vast filing system from which reporters can dig out background facts to enrich the mixture of their stories. Nicola was used to quarrying in the Morgue, as it was known. All the back copies of the paper were stored there, along with everything known about anyone whose name had appeared in the paper in the past.

The huge room was always crowded with people rushing from one cabinet to the other in search of information. The staff had a calm, phlegmatic patience. You couldn't hurry them. They picked their way through the files carefully and could reel off the correct catalogue numbers on almost any subject. They had a row of shelves behind their desks which held reference books to back up what the files contained. The more esoteric a subject the more they enjoyed the challenge of finding out about it.

Nicola spent most of the following day in there, making elaborate notes in shorthand in a large notebook. She found it fascinating to read the history of the modern circus. Joe was spending the day looking for still photographs to go with his feature. Wryly, he had said that that would be the hardest part of the whole job. He already knew he could only have two pictures with his article and he was going to have to choose from a rich array of fantastic shots.

The cabinets were arranged in narrow alleys along which you had to squeeze if you wanted to pass someone else who was consulting one of the steel drawers. Nicola stood, flicking over files, with people occasionally apologizing behind her as they passed and forced her to move.

"Fancy meeting you here," a voice suddenly murmured intimately in her ear and she looked around in startled surprise.

"Oh," she murmured, her lips parting, color sweeping up her face. Today he looked quite different, far more rested, the strain and weariness she had seen in his face when he first got back quite gone. Steve was tough. He recovered quickly.

"What are you up to?" he asked, glancing at her notebook and then at the files she was consulting.

"Researching." Her eyes quickly flicked over him while he was not aware of it. He was wearing a new suit, she noticed. It was more formal than the clothes he usually bought. Steve wore jeans more often than suits, his taste casual.

Was he going somewhere special? The suit looked very good on him, the dark jacket open to show a close-fitting waistcoat which emphasized his slim waist and his crisp white shirt showing up that smooth, tanned skin.

"Researching what?" he asked, looking at her before she could look away.

Her color deepening, she muttered, "Joe's doing a feature on the circus."

"There's an apt subject," Steve said. "Joe should know all about clowns." He grinned, though. She knew he liked Joe.

Nicola detached her eyes from their survey of his lean-hipped figure. "Have you been to see Margaret yet?"

Steve had a casual attitude to family relationships. His sister, Margaret, saw little of him. Steve rarely visited her and even more rarely wrote. She had said, last time Nicola saw her, that it was only the occasional postcard that told her Steve was alive.

"Not yet." Impatience showed in the way his mouth tightened. "All I would get is a string of questions. Maggie never could mind her own business."

"She's very fond of you."

He made a face. "She's very fond of trying to boss me around, you mean."

"If you're only intending to stay in England for a few days, you ought to make the effort to drive over to Suffolk."

His dark lashes drooped suddenly across his brown cheek. "Don't nag," he said, watching her through them. "What's it to you? I thought you had washed your hands of me."

"I'm fond of Margaret."

His eyes mocked her. He knew Margaret made her feel hunted, too. "Come with me, then," he said, grinning.

I walked right into that, Nicola told herself. She shook her head firmly. "No, thank you. She's your sister, not mine."

"I thought you said you liked Margaret," he said innocently.

She didn't answer, her eyes sarcastic. He knew why she did not want to accompany him, and it had nothing to do with liking or disliking his sister.

Margaret was a lively woman in her late thirties with dark hair and blue eyes like her brother's, a slim active figure and enough energy for six women. She lived in a small village in Suffolk near the edge of some rough marshland. Margaret ran that village. She had three children and a busy doctor for a husband yet she found time to preserve her own fruit and jams, make her own bread, do all her own housework and still dictate the social life of every other woman in the village. Any social function organized there was capably masterminded by Margaret. Any local society only functioned under her eagle eye. She made Nicola feel weak and inadequate.

Steve had never hidden his view that Margaret was only to be taken in small doses. When he was young, his sister had organized his life, too, and he had been relieved to escape from her sharp-eyed dictatorship.

"I'm not going down there alone," he said, wistfully, now.

"Take Joanne Hollis," Nicola snapped, her color rising.

His eyes narrowed and a satisfied little smile curved his lips. "What a good idea," he said softly.

Nicola looked back at the files, her fingers tightening on the steel edge of the drawer. Why don't I keep my mouth shut? she asked herself.

"Very fetching creature, Joanne," he drawled, watching her with acute observation.

"I've seen her doing the fetching," Nicola said. "She's like a good gundog. She doesn't ruffle a feather on their backs."

"Meow," Steve mocked. "Now what gives me the idea you don't like her?"

"I don't give her a thought," Nicola lied.

"No?" He looked smug as her eyes flicked at him and away. She would have loved to wipe that satisfaction off his face.

"No," she said, slamming the drawer and almost catching her hand in it in her haste.

Steve saw her jerk of alarm and asked, "Hurt yourself?" He took her wrist before she could back off and viewed her hand for signs of injury. Her small pale fingers looked very colorless against the brown strength of his and Steve turned her hand palm upward, touching the center of her palm with one long finger.

"Tiny little hands," he said huskily. "You should be more careful. That skin of yours shows every mark."

Her breathing quickened. He lifted her hand to

his mouth, brushing his lips gently on the palm. Someone came hurrying around the end of the cabinets and Steve released her, faint color in his face.

Nicola walked away, her eyes down, trying to halt the queer trembling in the pit of her stomach. She went over to the desk to consult the clerk and a few moments later she saw Steve leaving.

At five o'clock Joe came into the features department and Nicola paused in her typing. "Hi," he said in his flat voice. A stocky, quiet man in his thirties, Joe was already slightly balding, his hair receding at great speed from the high dome of his forehead. Peering at the page in her typewriter, he asked, "How's it going?"

"I got all the checking done," she told him. "I'm just typing up my notes for you now."

"Oh, great. Can you let me have it tonight before you go?"

She looked at the clock and at once Joe added, "If it isn't any trouble." He was much easier to work with than some of the reporters. They had more sense of urgency and more sense of their own importance. Nicola had worked for Steve, and she knew he was the worst offender where that sort of attitude was concerned. Steve knew he was the hub and purpose of the universe. The world, in his opinion, revolved around him and he expected any work you did for him to be ready when he wanted it. Steve had no notion of other people's convenience or any sense of time. That was what made him such a good reporter. It didn't make him easy to work for.

"I'll try," Nicola promised and got one of Joe's calm, friendly smiles.

"Thanks." He did not waste words. "Bring it through to me when you're ready," he said. "I'll be at my desk."

At six she still hadn't quite finished but the other girls had gone, sheathing their typewriters and drifting out, talking. The great room had an empty feel under the blaze of the strip lighting. People still came and went through the swinging doors, their feet tapping along past her, but Nicola did not look up, her eye fixed on the notes she was transcribing.

It was almost seven when she finally finished the last line. She sat back, eyes closed, very tired. Her back was aching and her eyes were weary from staring at the squiggly shorthand.

"You look terrible."

She opened her eyes and gave Joe a wry smile. "Thanks, that's very comforting."

He was eyeing her with compunction. "If I'd realized it was going to take you so long, I wouldn't have asked you to finish it tonight. It could have waited until morning."

"Now he tells me," she said, grinning.

"I'm sorry," Joe apologized.

"It was no trouble," she said. She collected up the pages and clipped them together, handing them over with another smile. "There you are—would you like to check them now?"

"That can wait," he said. "You shoot off home, Nicola. Thank you very much for all the work."

He walked out of the room with her and on the stone-floored landing, as they both waited for the lift

113

down to the ground floor, they talked politely about the notes. "I enjoyed reading it all," Nicola assured him. "I was fascinated. I love the circus. I always used to enjoy going although I didn't care much for the animal acts, particularly the big cats. I think that's rather cruel. I can't believe it can be done with kindness, that sort of training. It's too unnatural."

Joe nodded soberly. "I think people only enjoy those acts because they half hope to see the trainer getting his head bitten off."

The lift stopped and they were met with cries of "No room, no room" from the crush of people inside it. Joe grimaced, moving back, and the doors closed again. There was always a long wait for lifts at this hour of the evening. The paper was reaching the peak period of activity before the deadline arrived.

"It might be quicker to use the stairs," Joe told her.

Nicola grinned. "I'm too tired. But you can if you're in a hurry, Joe. Don't let me keep you."

"I'm not in a hurry," he said, eyeing her with unhidden concern. "You do look tired. Your skin is always pale but tonight you look gray."

"That's what I like to hear," Nicola said lightly. "All this flattery will go to my head."

They heard the click of footsteps behind them. Nicola half turned and saw Joanne Hollis walking out of the newsroom with Steve at her heels. Joanne was talking in her light, quick voice and giving Steve one of her eyelash-fluttering smiles.

"It came over on the telex," she said. "An hour ago—another one of those quakes."

"Not my scene," Steve said, his blue eyes narrowed as he halted next to Nicola. "Well, well," he drawled. "If it isn't my wife."

Joanne laughed. Nicola ground her teeth, averting her eyes. The lift stopped, the doors slid open and Nicola walked into it with the others following her. She would rather die than allow herself to show a thing.

Joanne turned to view herself in the mirror on the wall of the lift, running a satisfied hand over her flaming hair, adjusting the tight belt of her green dress. "Going out for a supper break, Joe?" she asked as she turned around again.

He gave her a nod. "You?" He wasn't looking at Steve but Nicola was, her angry eyes watching him from behind lowered lashes. Steve was looking at Joanne with a lazy smile, but as if he felt Nicola's stare, he flickered a glance at her, taunting mockery in his blue eyes.

"We're having dinner at Ramiro's," Joanne purred, putting a hand on Steve's arm, her polished nails gleaming against the dark material of his jacket.

Nicola's hands clenched at her sides, the nails digging into her soft palms. She lifted her head, staring at the lift doors as it descended. She could feel them all looking at her. Joanne was smiling like a cat that has stolen the cream. She was competitive, feline, a woman whose nature it is to covet other women's property. Nicola fought not to show the bitter jealousy which was consuming her, biting into her inner lip to keep her mouth steady.

Calmly, Joe said, "Nicky and I are eating out, too, but I can't afford Ramiro's on my salary. All I can manage is the local Indian place—Chicken Madras for me, I like a nice curry." He grinned at Steve slightly. "I don't get my dinners on expenses, like some."

The lift stopped and Nicola walked out blindly. "Hang on, wait for me, Nicky," Joe said, hurrying after her, leaving Steve and Joanne to follow at a slower pace. Nicky waited, trembling, and together they walked out into the dark night. Fleet Street was a different place at this hour, all the traffic slowing to a trickle, the pavements empty except for a few printers here and there, talking and smoking.

Joe caught her elbow and steered her across the road. "I hope you didn't mind," he said.

"No," Nicola muttered, giving him a shaky little smile. "Thanks, Joe."

He flushed. The night wind lifted the thinning locks of his hair and blew them forward over the bald patch. "Joanne can be a bit much," he said.

"Just the tiniest bit," Nicola said tartly.

He laughed. "I suppose you wouldn't agree to eating a curry with me? It isn't bad at Mohal's. He does all the cooking himself and it's always edible."

"I've eaten there," she said. "I like their curry and I'd love to have a Chicken Madras with you, Joe."

"That's fine," he said, walking down the tiny side road which ended in the Thames embankment. Below them lay the dark waters of the river, their oily surface glinting with reflected yellow light. The sky behind the Thames was jagged with tower blocks, windows lit in some cases, in others pitch dark now that the office staff had gone.

"I like London at night," Nicola murmured.

"I like it any time," Joe told her, his face wry. "I was brought up in a small town in Cheshire. Come six o'clock and the place shut down for the night. I much prefer London."

They had reached the Indian restaurant whose oriental lamps glowed in the night like strange fruit. Joe shepherded her to a table and they ordered. They were the only customers. At lunchtime though, the place was always crowded. Office workers liked the lunchtime menu which was a set price meal with coffee thrown in, the price temptingly reasonable. "I've only eaten here at lunchtime," Nicola said. "It seems different at night." The heavy red curtains were drawn and the room had a hushed intimacy quite unlike the busy rush earlier in the day.

Joe had little to say and it was hard work making conversation with him. She was grateful to him for the way he had charged in to rescue her, but that did not help her to keep up a flow of small talk.

He relaxed more while they were eating, as though having the food on the table made it easier for him to be natural with her. Offering her a *paratha,* he said, "It must have been tough for you, with Steve away so much."

"Yes," she said, refusing the *paratha* with a smile. There was far too much food. "Why do they bring so much?" she asked Joe. "They must think we've got huge appetites."

He nodded, but he was determined to discuss Steve. "He isn't an easy guy," he said. "The way he's always lived demands a very self-sufficient sort of mind."

117

Nicola looked at the curry. She wished he would stop talking about Steve. It was ruining her appetite. "Self-sufficient describes him perfectly," she said.

"But nobody is," Joe said. "Not entirely self-sufficient."

She pushed her curry around the plate with a fork. It was very well cooked but she just did not want it. "Steve comes pretty close," she sighed.

"He took that business in Africa hard," Joe muttered. "I've never seen him so shaken by anything. He only just got out of there alive, did he tell you? One of the government troops hid him. Steve knew him, you see. They'd been out drinking together."

How typical, thought Nicola. They had a few drinks together and that made them pals. Men make me sick.

"I don't want to talk about it," she said. Her stomach was heaving. If Steve wanted to walk along a cliff edge, she couldn't stop him but she did not want to hear about it.

"He doesn't show what he's feeling most of the time," Joe said. "But seeing all those killings . . ."

"Don't," Nicola bit out. Reading about it had been bad enough. She did not want to talk about it.

"He's human," Joe insisted. "I know how he feels. He's angry, sick, horrified. And he's feeling guilty, too."

"Guilty about what?" She stared at him, bewildered.

"Being alive," Joe said flatly. "You know what he said to me? 'Why me?' he said. 'Why did I get out alive?' "

Nicola's lip trembled. "Maybe next time he won't," she said with savage pain, and Joe fell silent for a long time, as though recognizing he had said enough. It was some time before he spoke again.

"Joanne is a troublemaker," he said. "It isn't wise to give her the room to make trouble."

"She can only make as much trouble as Steve allows," Nicola said resentfully.

"Nature abhors a vacuum," Joe told her. "Didn't you learn that at school?"

"What if the vacuum existed anyway?" She did not look up to meet his eyes.

There was a little silence. The waiter brought the bill and Joe paid it before guiding her out of the restaurant. He insisted on putting her into a taxi and the subject of Steve did not come up again.

It was hard to go back to her silent flat, knowing that Steve was in the same city, but with another woman, and her imagination was working overtime as she sat listening to the ticking of the clock and the beat of the rain against the window.

It was not the first time, though, that she had sat here wondering jealously what he was doing, and at least her angry emotion was not increased by the fear that he was in deadly danger, risking his life for the sheer thrill of it. That had been unbearable.

When she got to the office next morning, Jane came over to groan about delays on the underground. "It took me an hour to get here today. In theory it's supposed to take twenty-five minutes. Staff shortages, they said. Living in London is becoming a nightmare."

"I came by bus," Nicola said. "That took ages,

too. I'm beginning to think it would be quicker to walk."

"You and me both," Jane grimaced.

Mandy walked toward them, and with a blank face Nicola hurriedly moved away. She wasn't letting herself in for any more of Mandy's prying comments about Steve.

The grapevine would already be busy with rumors about him and Joanne. She knew how people around here talked, but she wasn't listening to any of it. Her imagination could work hard enough without any help from the grapevine.

It wasn't easy to stop people talking to her, though. They took such devious routes to bring the subject up. All day she kept getting oblique comments and all day she kept changing to some other topic. Of course, they all wanted to know how she felt about Steve seeing Joanne. Nicola refused to give anything away.

She went home dead on time that evening. As soon as she let herself into the flat she knew Steve was there. She could hear him whistling under his breath in the kitchen.

A tide of rage swelled up inside her. She flung open the door and he looked drily at her furious face.

"I thought I told you . . ."

"I came to collect some things," he broke in before she had finished. "I went in such a hurry that I left behind a pile of papers I shall need."

"You should have asked me for them, not just walked in here." He was wearing jeans again, with a thick white fisherman's jersey, and he looked tougher than ever. Just the sight of him made her feel nervous.

He folded his arms, surveying her closely. "Did Joe stand you a good dinner?"

She met his stare with an assumed smile. "Yes, thank you. I enjoyed the evening very much. Joe's a nice man."

He gave her a jeering little smile. "Of course he is—just up your street. Joe's out of the same box as the stockbroker guy, isn't he? Another tame, security-minded type who will never be any problem to you. That's what you want to turn me into, isn't it? A nine-to-five commuter who trots home to you to get his head patted and his dinner put in front of him. You don't want a man—you want a dog."

"That's not true," she said angrily. "You're twisting things around again. You refuse to face facts."

"It's you who's doing that. *I'm* a fact. Myself, the way I am—that's a fact. I'm not the nine-to-five type."

"You mean you're not husband material! Well, okay, shove off then," she said with burning bitterness. "Who asked you to come here to shout at me? I'm giving you a divorce. You'll be free. Clear off and be yourself somewhere else."

"Maybe I will," he said, his temper rising too. "There are other women in the world and I don't get complaints from them."

"Joanne Hollis," she interpreted, her amber eyes hardening.

"Joanne," he mocked, his mouth twisting. "She's

a realist. She doesn't expect me to be anything but what I am."

"I'm sure she doesn't. She's just your type, if we're going to start classifying people. Joanne Hollis plays the field too."

His icy glare made her smile in angry sarcasm. He threw back, "I do not play the field, blast you."

"And you never have, of course," she said, hating him.

He shifted, shrugging his wide shoulders. "If you're talking about before I met you, well, maybe a little. Don't we all before we settle for someone?"

"You didn't settle for me. You just married me. There was no settling involved. Joanne is welcome to you. She should suit you nicely—I get the feeling she likes it without strings, too."

"She always has," he grated, cynical amusement in his blue eyes suddenly.

They looked at each other in taut silence. "I always suspected you had known her very well in the past," Nicola said.

His eyes flickered. He didn't answer but she knew him too well; he didn't need to. "Yes," she said. She was right; he and Joanne had known each other intimately some time. Joanne had hinted as much to her.

"Well, at least she knows what she's getting," Nicola muttered. "I had to find out the hard way."

"She isn't getting anything," he said with growing impatience.

"Not yet? Don't keep her waiting too long." Nicola was using a tone of voice she had never used in her life before, but then, she had never been so angry before, either. It was acting on her like acid. Her voice sounded raw and sharp. I sound hateful and vicious, she thought incredulously, but she couldn't stop herself.

"Nicky," he said hoarsely, staring at her. "Don't talk like that."

"Maybe I should take a leaf out of her book. Obviously I don't know what I've been missing. All this freedom is going to the wrong people. Why shouldn't I take advantage of it too?"

"Don't be ridiculous," he muttered, his frown black.

"You ought to approve," she said. "You can't expect to be set free without leaving me free, too. I'll have to start finding out what fun it is to have no ties."

He crossed the room in two strides and shook her violently, rage in his face. "I'm not listening to any more of it."

"You don't have to listen. There's the door. Go through it and don't come back." She was past being alarmed by his height or the dominating power of his blue eyes. She looked back at his angry face, defiant. "And give me back my key, too. I don't want you using this flat whenever you feel like it. I have no intention of coming back one evening to find you and Joanne in my bedroom."

His hands bit into her shoulders. "You little . . ."

She struggled, shoving at him to escape, but her slight build gave her no chance against his strength and Steve shook her again, her head swinging from side to side, the strands of dark hair whipping across her face.

"Let me go," she raged.

He stopped shaking her, staring down at her in grim silence. "No," he said thickly.

Suddenly Nicola was frightened. Her heart gave a convulsive leap. She stared up at him, unable to drag her eyes away from the dark intention she could see in his eyes. Swallowing, she said in a shaking little voice, "Don't."

"I'm going to," he said in that deep, hoarse voice, and her fear grew like a fire fed with petrol.

Under her fear a weak, smoldering excitement began to grow, too. "I should have done this the night I got back," Steve said, then he picked her up like a child, heaving her over his shoulder.

"Put me down," she gasped, banging on his broad shoulders with her fists, kicking her legs vainly, her head dizzy as he began to walk toward the bedroom. "You dare!" she screamed. "Steve, I'll never forgive you. You can't. I don't want to . . ."

"I don't care two cents what you want."

He kicked open the bedroom door, the wood crashing as the door hit the wall behind it. The next second Nicola was flung down on the bed, her helpless body off balance as she looked up at him, her eyes wide and nervous.

He flung his sweater to the floor, his bare brown chest gleaming in the light streaming in from the living room. As he began to take off his jeans Nicola tried to struggle off the bed on the other side. He grabbed her roughly and forced her back, his deep, hurried breathing sounding very loud in the room.

"You're my wife," Steve roared at her. "It's time you got that through your head."

"It isn't me who needs to realize that," Nicola told him in a bitter voice. "You say I'm your wife—you don't claim to be my husband."

"Don't let's start that again," he grated.

"It works both ways. You want me as your wife but you have no intention of behaving like a husband."

"The devil I haven't," he muttered. "I'm going to behave like one right now."

His lean body forced her back against the pillows, his mouth hungrily closing over hers, a fierce compulsive demand in the movement of it as it parted her lips. Nicola fought against her own weak need to yield to him. When she struggled, his hands and mouth grew almost brutal, refusing to allow her to escape. Under his passion his anger still raged, the savage insistence with which he made her give way to him a betrayal of it.

Her struggles weakened and as they did so her own desire flared up to meet his. Moaning, she relaxed under him, her hands grasping his black hair. Feeling that surrender, his hands began to stroke down her body and she felt her bones turning to wax inside her overheated flesh. She had been wanting to touch him for days. Ever since she saw him in her bed her body had been aching for this, and with trembling hands she touched his throat, his shoulders, the muscled chest, her skin burning at the feel of his flesh against it.

Her dress slid down and his exploring hands began to peel off her slip, his head buried between her breasts, blazing a path down her body which brought a weak moan from her. They had always been passionate lovers, but there had never been this stark necessity between them before. Steve lifted his head as he heard the cry she gave and his face held a confused mixture of triumph, hunger, desire. He was breathing as fast as she was, his skin burning hot.

"Darling," he whispered. "I need to make love to you. You need it, too, don't you?"

The weak, feminine side of her nature cried out in yielding agreement. Nicola's brain struggled to drown that cry. During her months alone while Steve was in Africa other elements had been working in her like leaven, changing her whole attitude. If I give in now, I give in forever, she recognized. It wasn't love. It was war. Steve meant to win that war. He might not even know what he was doing; he acted instinctively. Faced with her rebellion against his wishes he was falling back on the male imperative.

They had each retreated to entrenched positions— sniping at each other from opposite sides of the no-man's land between them. They were in a hand-to-hand, body-to-body struggle now, and in that conflict Nicola had little hope of winning. Steve had all the advantages. The driving, urgent power of his body could always defeat her. How could he lose with her instincts fighting on his side? The woman in her craved surrender, primitive instincts from a buried racial memory confident that that was the female way to win.

It had always worked for women in the past. When they softly submitted to the possessing male, they engulfed him with their warm bodies, possess-

ing him in the act of possession, retaining him when
he withdrew, always the victors on the abandoned
field of battle which the man imagined he had
conquered. Women had weapons too subtle and too
secret to defeat. Waxing and waning like the moon,
they drew men like the tides, men helpless in their
own strength, blind to their captivity.

Nicola was fighting a different war, though. Steve
was a nomad, always wandering away from her, and
she could not fight that with a gentle surrender. It
had not held him in the past. She had no hope it
would hold him now.

He was kissing her fiercely, her head framed in his
hands, but his urgency was growing. He moved away
to strip off the rest of his clothes. Nicola slid off the
bed, taking the quilt with her. She folded herself into
it and Steve turned, lifting his head in surprise.

He was smiling, though. The hard planes of his
naked body had a taut excitement as he moved
toward her, laughing under his breath. "Give up,
darling. You know you're going to."

"I can't stop you," she admitted stiffly. "But if you
do—I'll never forgive you."

"Don't be stupid, Nicky," he said, still amused.

'I mean it. Steve! I mean it!" The last words were
yelled, their sound clear and bitter.

He stopped dead in his tracks, a hand's breadth
away. The blue eyes focused on her searchingly; his
frown deepened.

"You wanted it just now; don't lie," he said undeniably.

"All right, I did," she admitted, deciding that
there was no point in lying to him. "And I want it

127

now," she went on, throwing that out huskily. She saw his frown vanish and his smile come back. The blue eyes held amused mockery.

"Darling," he said, about to touch her again.

"But I *won't*," she said fiercely, through her teeth. "Do you hear me, Steve? I *won't*."

His frown returned, darker than ever. "I should think half the street could hear you," he muttered. "Don't shout like that."

"It seems I have to shout to make you listen," she said. "I don't enjoy shouting. It makes my head ache."

"It makes mine ache, too" he said harshly, staring at her. "You've given me a permanent headache since I arrived back."

"Try using your head then," Nicola advised. "It's simple enough. I want a marriage based on respect, if you like."

"So do I," he retorted.

She shook her head. "No, Steve. You demand my respect but you don't give me any. If you can't bear living in London, take me with you. I don't mind where I live so long as I'm with you but I'm sick of living alone and I'm sick of this pretense of a marriage. Make up your mind about it. If you want me as your wife, you have got to change the way we've been living. Until you're ready to do that, you're not sleeping with me."

His eyes were metallic blue slits under the black line of his brows. She met them without any visible sign of alarm, her soft mouth hardening in determination. Nicola was fighting for her life, her back was to the wall, and she had no intention of backing down. Steve saw it. He swore savagely under his breath, the word too muffled to be audible, then he whirled in a movement jerky with temper, and snatched up his clothes. She watched, huddled in the quilt like a defiant squaw, while he dragged them on in rough haste.

When he was dressed he turned on her, his eyes shooting at her like bullets. "I was all wrong about you, wasn't I?" At last he was getting the message. "You're not the woman I took you for."

Nicola was glad he had noticed, her eyes told him.

"I thought you were so gentle," he accused in response to that look. There is a time and place for gentleness but the battlefield is not it, she thought.

"I thought you were just the woman I'd been looking for all my life." She could believe that. Steve wanted a woman who would never make any demands on him, who would yield and accept without question. She gave him a sarcastic little smile which brought a flare of red into his face.

"You're about as gentle as a bulldozer," he said viciously. "I don't admire women who lay down the law." Of course he didn't. If anyone was going to lay down laws, it was going to be he. That was how he saw the role of the male.

"I'm not running my life to please you," Steve grated. He ran his life to please himself and he expected his wife to fall in with it, no matter what it cost her. The world was masculine territory, run by men, organized by them, their birthright from the moment they opened their eyes. The female role was to accept, submit, do as she was told.

Nicola had tacitly understood that. It would never

have entered her head to challenge her sexual role if Steve had not placed the strain of fear and anguish on their marriage. He might not realize it but she was fighting for him as much as for herself. She wasn't humbly sitting at home while he risked his life for the kick he got out of it.

"Why don't you say something?" he demanded, glaring at her.

"I've said all I had to say."

"You obstinate little fool!" Steve roared, then he turned and stalked to the door. "Maybe Joanne will be more welcoming," he threatened as he opened it, and she knew he was waiting for her to call him back, his body poised in the doorway.

"Don't forget, I want the key to my flat," she said, unmoved.

The slam of the door almost deafened her. She trembled in the folds of the quilt. The strain of their fighting was eating at her nerves. Tears spilled from her eyes. Now that he had gone she stumbled to the bed and lay there, weeping for a long time.

# Chapter Seven

During the rest of that week Nicola was in a state of numbed suspension. She hardly knew what she was doing at work. She got through each day without anything that happened remaining in her head. People spoke to her and she answered them, but when they went away she could not have told anyone what they had said.

"Are you okay?" Jane asked, and Nicola looked at her blankly, a polite smile on her mouth.

"Sure."

"Sure?" Jane did not look convinced. "You're sleepwalking again, aren't you?" she teased with so much sympathy in her hazel eyes that Nicola wanted to cry, but she smiled again somehow.

"Am I? Sorry."

Jane had the hesitant look which meant she felt

she ought to say something but wasn't quite sure how to phrase it or whether it would be wiser not to say it at all.

"Steve's been having some long sessions with Teddy Wiseman, hasn't he?"

"Has he?" Nicola shrugged. "Debriefing sessions, I expect. He's probably giving his successor a rundown on the situation over there, the civil war."

Jane looked at her sharply. "Oh, is that what's going on?"

"I expect so."

"Steve isn't going to take the Deputy Editor job, then?"

"You, too?" Nicola asked with a dry glance and Jane went rather pink, making a little face.

"Sorry, I was prying, wasn't I?"

"The tiniest bit," Nicola agreed, her face breaking into a smile at the other girl's self-accusing tone.

"I ought to know better, but everyone keeps speculating about it. Rumor is rife."

Rumor ran around the newspaper offices at lightning speed. It reminded Nicola of the dome of St. Paul's—whisper something at one side and it is heard right around the other side a second later, and not always accurately. What people did not know, they guessed or invented.

"They *are* all dying to know what Steve will do," Jane said.

"They'll have to wait and see, won't they?" Nicola had no intention of admitting to Jane that she was waiting, too. Jane no doubt imagined that Steve had discussed it with her. Nicola had gambled and now she was waiting for the spin of the wheel which would tell her whether she had won or lost. Her need to know was much greater than that of the other staff members. Her whole future depended on it.

Joanne wandered past Nicola's desk that afternoon and paused to give her that sweetly feline smile. "Hi," she said, skating an assessing look over Nicola's face. "How are you?"

"Fine, how are you?" Nicola wondered what had brought Joanne in here and did not believe it was chance. Joanne was here with a purpose.

Joanne leaned on her desk, the curve of her body lazy. "I just heard a new rumor," she murmured.

"Oh?" Nicola watched her, a line between her brows.

"A little bird told me you and Steve were getting a divorce. Is that so?"

Nicola stiffened. "Ask him," she said, her whole body tense with anger.

Joanne's moist red mouth curled in a mocking smile. "I don't need to, do I? If it wasn't true, you'd have denied it."

Nicola began to type violently. "I'm busy," she said. "Do you mind?"

Joanne laughed and clicked away on her high heels, her body swaying with exaggerated sex appeal. Nicola threw a look after her. She wished it had been a knife.

Steve strode through the room an hour later. He did not stop nor did he look in her direction, slamming through into the Morgue without seeming to be aware of her presence. Mandy drifted over afterward to say, "Is it true that Joanne Hollis is going out to do a tour of the Middle East?"

Nicola looked up. "Where did you hear that?"

"Someone was talking about it in the canteen— Joanne has been angling for a job on foreign for months. It seems she finally got what she wanted."

Nicola pretended indifference and Mandy reluctantly went away. As she worked, Nicola wondered if it was true. It would remove Joanne from dangerous contact with Steve. When Joe came by and stopped to chat about his article, she waited for a chance to ask him about it.

It was hard to pretend an interest she did not genuinely feel. All her attention was centered on Steve, her mind drivingly obsessed with the need to know what he was doing.

Joe broke off to peer at her, frowning. "I'm boring you."

"No," she said quickly, smiling. "I'm fascinated by the circus."

"But you're on edge about Steve," he said shrewdly, and she laughed, her face wry.

"Sorry, does it show that much?"

"Neither of you shows much," Joe said. "In your different ways you're both pretty secretive, aren't you?"

"Are we?" Nicola hadn't thought she was but what does one ever know of oneself? From inside a life it's impossible to guess how it looks from the outside. Everyone's viewpoint is fixed at an angle dictated by a very subjective attitude. We only see life from our own pair of eyes. Maybe it would be easier, she thought, if we could occasionally switch heads and see how it looks from another angle, but life isn't arranged like that.

"You aren't exactly a chatterbox," Joe teased.

"No," she agreed. She found it so hard to make conversation. "I'm sorry."

"You're shy," Joe said. "And I wish you wouldn't keep apologizing for yourself." There was a touch of irritation in the way he said that and she flushed.

"Do I? Sorry." Then she laughed.

"You see? There you go again. You say that word far too often. Why should you apologize for being yourself? I like your quiet company." He was slightly flushed, his eye sliding away from her.

Nicola flushed too. It hadn't occurred to her before but now she hoped Joe was not taking too much interest in her. She liked him, but only as a friend.

"Some people are hard to talk to," Joe said. "Joanne Hollis, for instance—she makes me feel stupid. She talks too easily. Every man she meets gets some sort of come-on and you know she doesn't mean a word of it. It's all show. She makes me want to run a mile away from her."

Nicola waited until he had stopped talking before asking him, "I'd heard she was going out to the Middle East soon?"

She was surprised when Joe shot her a strange look, his forehead creasing in a frown. "I wouldn't know," he said, but his eyes moved away far too quickly. He looked at his watch. "Good heavens, look at the time, I must rush." He was gone like a rabbit disappearing down a rabbithole and Nicola stared after him in anxious speculation.

Over the next two days she saw Steve only at a distance. Martin rang her one evening but she refused his invitation to have dinner that night. "You aren't changing your mind about the divorce?" he asked her, and she sighed, and said she had not altered her plans. She didn't tell him that her plans depended entirely upon Steve's decision.

"Martin, I like you, but I'm not in love with you, you know," she said uncertainly. "I don't think you're in love with me, either, if you're honest with yourself."

"We hadn't got that far," he said in an offended voice. "Had we? I'd hardly been allowed to kiss you."

He rang off sulkily and Nicola sighed. Martin was a complication in an already complicated situation. She could have done without his intervention to-night. Although she knew he did not love her, she felt guilty about dating him in the first place. She had known in the back of her mind that she didn't really fancy him at all. He had been an antidote to Steve, that was all, his calm quiet manner soothing to her when she was deeply unhappy.

She had lunch with Joe the next day. It hadn't been planned; they just happened to arrive in the canteen at the same time and queued up together, talking about a freak hailstorm which had smashed some windows on the other side of London.

Nicola wasn't unaware of the whisper of comment following them as they sat down at a spare table. Her cheeks rather pink, she avoided Joe's eyes, wishing they had not bumped into each other at the door.

"Enjoying yourselves?" They both looked up as Joanne purred at them. She was alone, but Nicola did not need three guesses to know that Joanne would make sure Steve heard about his wife lunching with his best friend. Joanne had the glint in her eyes of someone suddenly given a birthday present. She did not wait for an answer, swaying away with a broad smile.

Joe looked at Nicola wryly. "Sorry, dumb of me not to realize it would cause talk."

"I don't care," Nicola muttered untruthfully. She felt the eyes staring from all sides and she couldn't wait to get this week finished. It had been the longest week of her life, she thought.

On Saturday morning she did housework and then went shopping. The shops were packed. Her baskets were heavy enough to contain stones, and her back was aching when she got back to the flat. She was dying for a cup of tea. When she opened the kitchen door, she did not see Steve for a moment, then she stopped dead, staring at him. He was sitting casually at the kitchen table with a cup in his hand.

"I've made some coffee," he said, as if there was nothing more natural in the world than that he should be there waiting for her when she got back with the shopping.

She put her baskets on the table with a sigh of relief before she looked angrily at him. "Will you stop wandering in and out of my flat?"

"I'm going over to see Maggie." He ignored her question without a sign of concern.

"Good." She began to unpack her shopping and heard him move. He poured her a cup of coffee and pushed it across the table.

"What are you doing here?" she asked, and he looked at her through his lashes, a coaxing look in those blue eyes.

"Come with me."

"No."

"Maggie would like to see you. I've talked to her on the phone and she asked me to bring you."

"Oh, did she?" Nicola could imagine. Margaret was always ready to give advice and manage people. It was her life's work, telling other people how to run their lives.

"She's fond of you."

"I'm fond of her," Nicola said, unmoved. "But I am not driving over there with you. I'll visit her some other time, on my own, when you've gone."

The coaxing look went as if it had been switched off. "You obstinate little . . ." He broke off the harsh growl, taking a deep breath.

"I wondered how long the sweet act would last," Nicola said. She never trusted him when he was being reasonable and coaxing. It was always an act. This was the real man, this scowling brute who looked as if he wanted to slap her.

She laid out salad items on the table. Steve glanced at them. "That your lunch?"

"Yes." She added some cheese to the clutter of food. "If you wouldn't mind going, I'd like to eat it, too."

"We could have lunch on the way," he said. "At that little hotel off the road through Essex. Remember? We ate there several times. They have that huge garden and a pond with ducks."

She got down the salad bowl. She remembered all too well. They had walked around the pond one wintry day and fed the ducks ham sandwiches which they had brought but had not eaten. Nicola had a clear picture of the bare willow trees beside the water, the weedy expanse of the pond, the yellow beaks of the ducks as they dived tail-up for the bread.

"They do a fantastic homemade steak pie," Steve said. "And all the vegetables are home-grown, too. I used to think about that place while I was in Africa."

"How charming," Nicola muttered. "I'm glad you were homesick for something." Not her, she gathered. Steve had pined in the steamy African sunshine for homemade steak pie and ducks on a winter pond but he had not yearned for her.

He moved restlessly. "You were part of it," he said huskily. "Part of everything I remembered. When you're on the other side of the world, you have to carry England in your head—green fields and rain and gray London streets." He sounded nostalgic, wry.

"I'm flattered," Nicola said. "It makes a woman feel so appreciated to be added to a list that includes ducks, rain and steak pie." But her smile was slightly shaky and she had to steady her voice. She might not have been a burning memory in his head but she had been there. He hadn't forgotten her altogether. She had suspected he had.

Steve had an impatient cast to his face. He didn't like talking about his feelings. Steve didn't dwell on his softer moments. She sometimes got the impression he would rather not have softer moments at all. His job demanded nerves of steel and a tough independence which was only weakened by emotion.

He stood beside her, watching her, and she could almost hear the little wheels going around in his head. He was trying to work out some way of persuading her to come with him to see Margaret. Nicola looked at the salad. It was a bright spring morning but it was still quite cold and she suddenly did not feel much like eating salad. Steak pie sounded much more tempting.

"The twins and Andrea will be at home," Steve wheedled softly. He knew she enjoyed seeing his sister's children. They were a lively trio, bursting with their mother's vitality, easy to talk to because their extroverted natures made them ready to meet you halfway.

Nicola hated herself. She knew she was weakening. She wanted to go. She wanted to be with him. Looking away, she struggled to force her emotions into line.

The temptation was insidious. It would undermine her, making her strength leach away every time their eyes met. She only really felt strong when she wasn't with him. The masculinity he exuded had a disastrous effect on her.

On the other hand, she told herself hurriedly, going down to see his sister could be a good idea. Steve would find himself wrapped in a warm, happy, family atmosphere which might prove to him that a marriage involved a lot more than the occasional bout of lovemaking in between months of work.

Nicola knew she was just looking for a good reason for doing what she wanted to do. We always have to rationalize our reasons for doing as we like. We snatch at any excuse, however thin, she admitted ruefully to herself.

"Well . . ." she said slowly, and Steve took hold of her elbow, smiling at her.

"Come on," he said, because he knew he had won.

She didn't need to be told he was pleased with himself. His blue eyes made that clear.

Although she let him steer her out of the flat and into the car he had hired, she resented that look. He needn't look so smug. If he thought that driving down to visit his sister was some great triumph, he could think again.

They drove north out of London, along the choked roads, between the rows of little terraced houses back to back, the skyline bristling with television aerials, tiled roofs, chimney pots. This was the shabby hem of London's spreading skirt, a dull sameness about the houses, the shops, the people.

"This is what I go abroad to get away from," Steve confessed, grimacing at it all. "Suburban life in all its deadly boredom."

"You don't have to go abroad to get away from it," she pointed out. "You could live anywhere within reach of London. We could live in the same village as Margaret."

"Heaven forbid," he groaned. "What a prospect."

"That isn't a very kind thing to say about your sister."

"Maggie would drive me to drink inside a month," Steve told her with grim vehemence.

Nicola laughed and he shot her a sideways smile. "And you know it," he added. "She would have you organized in no time. How would you like that?"

Nicola wouldn't, but she didn't bother to admit as much. Steve turned his blue stare back to the road, his mouth crooked.

"And stop trying to get a ring through my nose," he said.

Nicola stiffened, her cheeks reddening. She ignored the little dig but it had hurt.

"Heard from what's-his-name?" Steve asked, after a few moments of silence.

"Martin," she said tersely. "You know very well his name is Martin, so stop calling him what's-his-name."

Steve scowled. "Why should I remember his bloody name? I wish I could forget him."

"Forget away."

"How can I? While I was on the other side of the world you were dating other men."

"Man," Nicola said. "Martin was in the singular."

"So you say."

"It's true," she said angrily. "If it wasn't, I'd tell you. Why should I lie? It's my business how many men I dated, but as it happens, there was only one."

"Well, bully for you," he said with icy dislike.

"Why is it always me who makes confessions? What did you get up to while you were away?" She turned to give him a furious, jealous glare and saw his face relax into amusement.

"Oh, this and that," he said with deliberate, needling mockery.

"Particularly that," she muttered, knowing that satisfied grin. He was pleased to have got that reaction out of her. She shouldn't have betrayed any interest whatever.

"And anyway," she added, remembering, "seeing that we are getting divorced it was my business if I dated someone. I'm not going to apologize to you for it."

"Blast!" he said, putting on a burst of speed which made the tires screech as he took a corner, the hedges on either side of the road masking the view.

They had left the suburban sprawl of London behind them now. They were out in rural Essex, the fields bare and empty, the blue spring sky having that frosty sparkle which gives the light a deceptive brilliance in the cold spring weather. The flat fields of Essex were largely pasture in this corner of the county. Black and white cows grazed under elms and trod heavily over the muddy grass. There were few other cars on these narrow country lanes but Nicola did not enjoy driving fast along them.

"I hope we're not going to argue all the way to Maggie's," Steve muttered.

"Only if you insist," she retorted.

He slowed down, taking a side road, and she asked, "Where are you going now?"

"The hotel, remember? It's somewhere along here."

They found it a few moments later and parked beside a few other vehicles. They had no trouble getting a table. Although the food was good, the hotel was off the beaten track and people did not find it easily.

Steak pie was not on the menu today, but they had a delicious navarin of lamb, a rich stew made with a mixture of spring vegetables, and Steve was content with that.

The hotel dining room was old-fashioned, with heavy plush curtains, paneled walls and a faded dark red carpet. The cutlery was massive silver, worn with use, and the waitress looked as if she had been left over from the Edwardian Age. There was a cathedral hush about the whole place but the excellence of the food more than made up for that.

After they had eaten, Steve insisted on going to look at the duck pond, taking a roll from the table so that he could feed the ducks.

The willows were breaking into tiny bright green knots of leaves. They were alive with birds who flew in and out of the drooping branches. As Steve crumbled his roll and scattered it, the brown ducks fought and squawked, flapping aggressively at each other.

Nicola looked up at the spring sky, shivering in her fur-collared winter coat.

"Cold?" Steve asked.

"A little." It wasn't that, but she was not going to admit it. She felt a peculiar, piercing sadness. That was what had made her shiver.

Steve was laughing as he watched the ducks, his black hair blown across his forehead by the wind. She had one of those unforgettable moments of clarity when a memory is caught like a sharp snapshot in the mind. She knew she would never forget watching Steve today, with the pond and the ducks and the new leaves on the willows behind him.

Her sadness was that of someone recognizing the transitory nature of happiness, the inevitable end of every living organism. Steve was here now, he was alive and amused, but even as she looked at him the moment had ended.

"We'd better get on," he said, turning to her, and she forced a smile and nodded.

He took her arm as she stumbled slightly. "Hey, one glass of wine can't have made you drunk," he said teasingly.

"The path is slippery," she said. "When do you think we'll arrive at Maggie's?"

"I told her any time after lunch."

Margaret would have made elaborate preparations for one of her high teas, then, thought Nicola. Margaret liked to do things properly. The children would have been scrubbed until they shone. The house would be polished from roof to cellar. Margaret's husband, Derek, would be forced into a suit despite his sullen protests. On Saturday afternoons Derek was, given a little luck, free. The patients were given over to the care of another doctor to give Derek some time off. All the doctors in the area organized a rota, which meant they each worked one weekend in four. Derek spent his Saturday afternoons either on the golf course or in his garden, and he hated wearing suits in his spare time.

"Did I show you what I brought her?" Steve asked as they got into the car. He turned and produced a parcel from the back seat.

"Don't unwrap it," Nicola protested. "What is it?"

"An African drum made of deer hide," he said.

Nicola shuddered. "Oh."

Surprised, he asked, "Don't you think she'll like it?"

"She may, I wouldn't," Nicola said. "Every time I looked at it I would think of the poor deer."

Steve grimaced. "I'd forgotten how sentimental you are about animals."

"I'm not sentimental. I just couldn't bear to wear mink coats or have a handbag made out of crocodile."

His blue eyes were amused. "Soft-hearted little idiot," he said.

They drove toward the Suffolk coast through flat green fields punctuated by villages whose narrow streets had been built before the arrival of the motor car. Each one slowed them up as they crawled in a line of traffic through the center of the village. This area of England had once been famous for its wool, and the wealth from the sheep had left a visible legacy in ornate, timbered Elizabethan houses, town halls with high gables and crooked roofs, and great medieval churches left stranded in the fields after the villages around them had died, their spires piercing the blue sky and their high vaulted ceilings echoing with silence.

Margaret lived on the edge of the marshland, the sea within earshot of her house, the trees all bending the way of the wind, their branches crooked and protesting as they creaked.

The children met them at the crossroads, waving their arms and leaping up and down as they spotted the car. Steve slowed and they all climbed into the back.

"Hello, Uncle Steve, Auntie Nicky, what have you brought us?" They had found the packages on the back seat at once and the twins were pinching them inquisitively, exchanging suggestions as to the possible contents.

They were identical boys of seven, thin and small with dark black hair and bright blue eyes and that mixture of toughness and shy tenderness which makes small boys so touching. They hid the tenderness, shoving each other, scrambling to be noticed.

"Sit still," their elder sister commanded, and Peter and Luke made horrible faces behind her back. Andrea was ten, a slim neat girl with the same blue eyes, the same dark hair.

"I'll tell Mummy you asked," she told them. "You know what she told you."

"Those who ask, don't get," Peter repeated. "But this parcel has got Peter on it, so it must be for me." He gave Nicola a crooked little smile and she grinned at him. "How like you the boys are," she told Steve. The twins did not suffer from any inhibitions about presenting their demands, either.

They drove between deep-banked hedges, the air full of the salt scent of the sea, and saw Margaret's house framed between ancient elm trees, the red-tiled roof spotted with yellow lichen. The sea air encouraged the growth, Margaret had once told Nicola.

Margaret appeared through the front door, calm and unruffled in a beige blouse and pearls, a pleated brown skirt, her slim waist drawn in by a leather belt. She looked as casual as though Steve dropped in every day. Kissing him, she said, "Aren't you brown? One look at you and anyone would know you hadn't been in England lately. Did you have a good drive down? How are you, Nicky, you poor girl?"

Steve scowled. "Why is she a poor girl?"

"Married to you," Margaret told him, turning on the twins and asking sharply what they thought they were doing as they began to examine the parcels they had disinterred from the back of the car.

"They can have them," Steve said, taking the parcel containing the drum. "They're labeled."

He needn't have pointed that out. The boys were already tearing them open and giving cries of joy over the intricately carved animals they found inside.

Andrea opened her package to find a set of carved ivory beads which she seemed delighted with and wore at once, kissing Steve as she thanked him.

"Nobody is to play this," Margaret informed the twins with a steely glance as she carried the drum, with which she had been delighted, into the house.

Steve looked down at Nicola. "You see? She liked it."

Nicola was watching the twins fighting as they shoved each other into the house. Steve followed her eyes.

"Brats, aren't they?" he said, and looked at her in

148

amazement as she gave him a furious glare. "What have I said now?"

"Oh, shut up," she said, walking into the house. She was not going to tell him that she had been thinking how much she envied Margaret the two boys who looked so much like Steve.

# Chapter Eight

"Are you serious about this divorce or not?" Margaret asked later as they worked together in the kitchen to prepare the tea. Steve, Derek and the boys had strolled off to take a look at the distant sea from a nearby hill. Andrea had decided to take the opportunity to practice her piano piece. The instrument wasn't exactly in tune; the notes had a dull, flat sound but Andrea made up for that with the great vigor of her performance.

"Yes, I am," Nicola said, skimming plates across the table deftly, but her voice had enough defiance in it to attract Margaret's shrewd little smile.

"Yes?" she questioned, smiling wryly. "You're here with him, though, aren't you? Steve has a maddening habit of getting his own way. He had it in his pram. I'm not sure how he does it. Sheer bloody-minded obstinacy, perhaps."

"He made me come," Nicola said.

"Oh, charming," Margaret grinned.

"Oh, I wanted to see you all," corrected Nicola, laughing. "But I didn't mean to come down with Steve. I'm trying to get it through his head that I'm not living like this anymore. Either he takes me with him or he stays in England, but I'm not putting up with months of separation again."

"What did he say to that?"

"Nothing very pleasant."

"I can imagine," Margaret said. "He's a brute. I remember I warned you about that before you got married." There was always a slight edge to Margaret's voice when she talked about Steve. She was very fond of her brother, but Steve said Margaret had never forgiven him for being born at all. She was a few years his senior, and had enjoyed being an only child. Steve's arrival had put her nose out of joint and she had been resenting him ever since. Their relationship had been a continual struggle for power from the day he was born.

"You stick to your guns," she told Nicola.

Nicola meant to, but she changed the subject. She might find Steve maddening but she wasn't going to let his sister run him down. She had a sneaking suspicion that Margaret was quite enjoying the idea that Steve was not getting things all his own way for once.

The children charged into the kitchen, followed by their father and Steve, and Margaret ordered them all off to wash their hands. They trooped off obediently while Nicola poured the boiling water into the teapot.

The meal was a typical high tea: sandwiches, sliced cold meat, boiled eggs, pickles, several different kinds of cake and a great bowl of fruit salad.

"Did you see any pygmies in Africa?" Peter asked Steve, who grinned at him as he answered. The children were fascinated, staring at their uncle as he talked.

The food disappeared and Margaret presided over them all with regal grace, enjoying having visitors, pleased with Steve's compliments about her food. "No more cake," she told Peter.

"But, Mummy," he groaned, and Nicola watched, moved. There was something magical about sitting here while the windows darkened with the fall of night and the moths flapped at the glass, drawn by the flowering of light inside the room. On the windowsill stood a green glass jar of wild flowers: primroses, violets, early daffodils, the flowers squashed in among tapering sprays of catkins, a mixture of pollen and fresh scent drifting from them.

"We ought to get back," Steve told her.

"Not yet," his sister argued, but Steve insisted that they should leave. It was a two hour drive back to London, he pointed out, and it was nearly seven now.

Everyone crowded out to kiss them good-bye at the car. As they drove away a barn owl flew across the lane, white face peering, the huge span of wings silent on the dark air. Nicola watched it, sighing. She did not feel much like driving back to London or being alone in her silent little flat. She waved to the half-glimpsed faces clustered at the gate and saw the pale hands waving back.

They made good time. It was just before nine when Steve drew up outside the flat. Nicola looked at him with mute hostility.

"Good night."

He frowned, correctly interpreting the chilly note in her voice. "What's wrong now? I thought you enjoyed yourself. You seemed happy."

"I was," she said, and didn't he realize that that was what was wrong? She had been too happy, sitting in that room while the children chattered and ate slices of rich fruitcake, talking of swimming lessons and a motherless lamb at the farm next door, displaying a missing front tooth or giggling over something that had happened at school.

"Then what's up?" he asked.

You're an insensitive, selfish brute, Nicola thought, staying stubbornly silent. That is what is up.

"I thought it was a very good day," he said, tapping his fingers on the steering wheel.

"Oh, did you?" She couldn't help the sarcastic snap of that. It had been more than good—it had been a day lit with poignant beauty for her. The crowded house full of the scent of home cooking, the wild flowers in the jar, the laughter and talk—she had felt it all around her, the distant promise of the sort of life she wanted for them, and that magic had gone now.

"I don't understand you," Steve said, his eyes sliding sideways to study her like some strange specimen under a microscope.

"I know you don't," Nicola told him. "You never have."

"Why can't you tell me what's wrong? Why do you sit there with that blank expression? Do you think I can't see your eyes accusing me? What of, for heaven's sake? What have I done today? I thought you would enjoy visiting Maggie and those awful brats of hers."

Nicola got out of the car and slammed the door, walking very quickly across the pavement. He caught up to her on the doorstep.

"Don't walk out on me when I'm talking," he barked like some army sergeant.

She had her key in her hand and he took it and opened the front door of the flat. Nicola snatched it back. "Good night," she said, starting to shut the door.

He kicked it open again and hurtled past her while she could only fall back, trembling, as she caught sight of his face. Turning, he shoved the door shut and looked down at her, eyes blazing.

"Right—let's have it. What's wrong now?"

"I'm not having another of your violent rows," she told him, stiff as a poker.

He moved so close to her that they were touching. Barely moving his lips he said very softly, "If you don't tell me what is wrong with you, I shall get very violent indeed."

Her eyes fell. "Don't threaten me."

"Don't force me to," he said, caging her in his arms so suddenly that she looked up in alarm.

His blue eyes were smiling now. "You smell of country air," he told her. "Your hair's full of it. Much more attractive than all the scented shampoos in the world."

Her pulses hammered in reaction. "Go away," she said, though. She knew that look in his eyes.

"Throw me out," he invited, grinning.

Helpless, furious, she looked up at him. "You're a brute, do you know that?"

"You keep telling me," he agreed, his lips grazing across her cold pink nose. "Your skin smells of the country too," he said, his mouth making its leisurely way down her cheek. His hands were pressing along her back, holding her tightly.

"Oh, don't," she wailed, far too conscious of the temptation he was presenting.

"Nicky," he muttered, his voice going husky.

She had her hands against his chest. His heart was thudding harshly under her palms.

"Darling, don't send me away again," he whispered, and she listened half to what he said and half to the beating of his heart, the two sounds mingling in her brain.

"I've got to have you," he said. She didn't answer but her whole body shrieked consent although she hoped he could not see it.

He buried his face at the side of her neck, the warmth of his breath on her skin. She thought of the two boys as she had seen them last, their skinny bodies wearing jerseys and short trousers, their wide grins identical as they waved good-bye.

If she told him I want sons like that, I want a home filled with that warmth and happiness, what would he say? Maybe one day, he would promise, because under the urgent pressure of desire he would promise anything. But then he would fly off again and leave her, because Steve's idea of a happy life was not the same as hers and he was not ready to exchange his roaming freedom for the cage of four walls and a wife and children.

"You're driving me mad," he muttered.

What did he think he was doing to her?

"Say something," he ordered, lifting his head to look at her, the blue eyes demanding. "Why do you never say anything?"

"I've said all I have to say," Nicola said. "I'm sick of saying the same thing over and over again."

The telephone rang shrilly. Steve's hands dropped away and Nicola walked to pick the phone up. "Yes?"

"Nicola?" She knew that cautious voice.

"Hello, Martin," she said warmly, and felt Steve stiffen behind her.

"I rang earlier but you were out," Martin said with an undertone of reproach.

"Yes," she said unrevealingly.

"I was going to ask you to have dinner." Martin paused. "Is your husband still around?"

"He isn't staying in the flat," Nicola evaded, and heard Martin give a little sigh of satisfaction.

"Tomorrow, then—will you have dinner tomorrow?"

"I'd love to," Nicola said. "What time tomorrow?"

Steve appeared beside her, his brows together and his blue eyes harsh. He shook his head at her and she ignored him, her expression calm.

"I'll pick you up at seven," Martin said and she told him she would be ready.

As she put the phone down Steve broke out, "I want to see you tomorrow."

"Well, you can't."

"But I'm leaving on Monday," he said, and her heart winced in pain and anger.

Going pale, she repeated, "Leaving? For where?"

"A quick tour of the Middle East," he said.

All she could think was, I've lost. He's going. The words went around and around in her head while she stared at him, her amber eyes wide and fixed, a deep, burning pain behind them.

Steve's brows contracted. "Did you hear what I said?"

"Oh, I heard." Her voice was raw. "What do you want me to say? If you're expecting me to break into floods of tears, too bad. As far as I'm concerned, you can go where you like, when you like. It doesn't matter to me."

His skin ran with angry color. "I see."

"Now, I'm tired. Would you mind going?" She turned away, pretending to give a wide yawn, her hand at her mouth. "Good night. Thank you for the visit to Margaret."

"I'm not going anywhere," he said, catching her elbows and swiveling her around to face him.

"Let go!"

"Oh, no," he said in a deep grim voice. "Not tonight, Nicola; I'm not going anywhere tonight."

Fear concentrated at the back of her throat. She couldn't swallow. Her mouth was dry. She looked up at the darkened face, his bones clenched, the line of his mouth hard and bitter.

"I won't," she muttered.

"We'll see about that." The bitter line twisted in a derisive smile. It was not a smile anyone could enjoy watching. Nicola shivered as she saw it.

There was something pressing at the back of her mind, some vague memory bothering her. The Middle East? she thought. Where did I—and then she remembered, looking at Steve with pain.

"Is Joanne going with you?" The question shot out jealously and she saw his eyes alter, the hardness going and a sudden smile coming into them.

"Yes," he admitted, his mouth mocking.

Nicola winced. She couldn't help it. "I might have known," she said bitterly. "So she got what she was angling for after all, did she?" Joanne had got her foreign posting and Steve all in one. Nicola could imagine how triumphant she must be feeling tonight.

He grinned, watching her. "She worked hard for it—I'd say she deserved to get the job."

"Not to mention you," Nicola snarled. "She worked hard for you, too, didn't she?"

"Careful, sweetheart, you're beginning to sound jealous," he drawled, a gleam in the blue eyes.

"That gives you a kick, does it?" she threw back, her eyes hating him. "You're enjoying this."

His hands shifted to her back, the warmth of them penetrating her shirt and making her nerve ends tingle with awareness. "For tonight let's forget Joanne," he murmured. "Let's forget everything and everyone but us, Nicky."

"Forget? You forget it!" she blazed, pushing him away. "You don't honestly think I'm going to let you touch me when you've just admitted that you're planning to fly off with *her* on Monday, do you?"

"And what about you and what's-his-name?" he asked her coldly, his frown coming back. "You expect me to stand back and watch you dating another man, apparently."

"If you expect me to hang around this flat for months on end without any social life, you're wrong."

"Social life is a new name for it," he grated in a barbed voice. "I know a shorter one."

Her face burned. "For the last time, I have never been to bed with Martin." She looked at him with open hostility. "I can't promise to say the same next time I see you."

The blue eyes iced over. "Don't threaten me, Nicky. I don't like threats."

"Neither do I," she said, nervous under the stare of those cold blue eyes. "I ignore threats."

He moved so suddenly that she was taken by surprise. Swinging her up into his arms he looked down into her paling face. "This is one threat you're not going to ignore," he told her through his teeth.

She opened her mouth to give a yell of fear and anger but he silenced her, his lips clamping over hers and stifling her cry before it could escape. Struggling, she felt him striding across the room. He tossed her on the bed like a doll, the heavy weight of his body pinning her down before she could escape.

Nicola fought in frantic panic, helpless under him, her mouth unable to evade the scorching possession of his kiss. His hands moved slowly over her while she wriggled. She felt her clothes being pulled away and redoubled her efforts to push him off, her face hot, her breathing impeded. She felt she was suffocating and fixed her hands in his thick hair to drag his head away, without success.

"I won't," she groaned against his fierce mouth, but her long fight was weakening her, the writhing of her body lessening. Steve felt her weakening and lifted his head at last. Nicola dragged in air, shuddering, glaring at him.

"You're hurting me," she accused.

"Don't fight me, then," he bit out. "Because you aren't going to stop me tonight, Nicky. You've kept me at arm's length long enough. I should have done this the night I got back but I was too bloody tired. I must have been insane the other day, to go when you told me to get out. I should have taken you then."

"I don't want you," she breathed harshly and he laughed with bitter lack of amusement.

"You're lying and you know it. We both know it."

"No," she said, and then he touched her breast with one long cool finger and her husky, involuntary moan made him laugh again.

"No?"

Nicola closed her eyes, hating herself for that instinctive response. Her lips trembled and the fight drained out of her. What was the point? she thought. He was going. She might never see him again. Did it matter that her suspicions were true? She had always believed that while he was away from her for months at a time he had other women. It might hurt unbearably to know that it was someone like Joanne Hollis but being able to imagine the worst was only one step further down the path to hell. She had been on that path for a long time.

Steve touched his lips to the small hollow at the base of her throat, caressing the fast-beating pulse. "You're mine, that's all that matters." His voice was rough with triumph but the hands touching her were trembling, their seductive movements leaving a track of fire along her body, her skin burning with pleasure everywhere he stroked it.

The sensual trap yawned for her. Nicola tried to make her mind work, tried to escape the coaxing hands, the heated brush of his lips, struggling to remember all her reasons for denying him, but reason fled before the igniting passion Steve had roused in her.

Her arms went around him. She kissed him back, clinging, moving restlessly as desire took over her entire being. Only later, as she moaned with satisfaction, did her drowning mind come up with one sane excuse for giving in to him. Only when she was in his arms did she ever feel alive at all. Wasn't that excuse enough?

She fell asleep in his arms, her head nestled into the hard strength of his shoulder, a hand flung across his muscled chest, aware of the beating of his heart within his ribcage. Steve was already asleep, his long body relaxed against her, the heat of their lovemaking giving way to a tired peace. He had touched his mouth to her hair a moment before he fell asleep, whispering, "I needed that, Nicky. You don't know how I needed you."

He might even mean it. Nicky couldn't guess if he was lying or not, but at this moment she didn't care.

She only knew he was lying close to her, heavy and relaxed, his body warmth reminding her that he was alive, that a moment before they had been one creature briefly.

She woke up during the night to find Steve mumbling and thrashing around beside her, his body twisting on the bed. Was he still having nightmares about what he had seen? She leaned over him, touching his cheek, saying his name gently.

His eyes lifted, gleaming in the darkness, but for a few seconds he did not understand, then he gave a little groan. "Sorry, did I wake you up? Bad dreams again, I'm afraid."

"Would you like me to get you something to drink? Hot milk? Cocoa?"

He smiled wryly. "Just come back here and let me hold you," he whispered, his long arm reaching up to pluck her back into his arms. She settled against him, his cheek against her back, and they fell back to sleep after a short time.

She was alone in the bed when she woke up and stretched, her slim body warm and catlike with sleepy contentment. The curtains were still drawn and sunlight filtered into the room, dancing along the walls like golden water. She curved her arms above her head, a little smile on her lips.

Was Steve making tea? She listened, yawning, but couldn't hear a sound. Maybe he was having a shower, she thought. Slipping out of the bed she put on her dressing gown and went into the kitchen. There was no sign of him. She put on the kettle and as she turned to get the cups out she saw the little note on the table.

It was brief. "Had to rush. Will ring you. Steve."

Nicola's smile vanished. The contented warmth drained out of her, leaving her whole body ice-cold. Gone? Where had he gone? After last night, how could he just walk out on her again, without a word, just a curt little note with no feeling in it? She sank down at the table, her legs trembling under her.

Last night she had weakly abandoned her fight to hold him, allowing Steve to coax her into abject surrender, her pride going down before his with scarcely a struggle.

Now she sat and hated both him and herself. Steve had won. He had achieved the submission he had been determined to wrest from her and she was left with only emptiness. How could I be so weak? she asked herself, her hands clenched.

The phone rang and she leaped up, shaking. Running to answer it, she said nervously, "Hello?"

It wasn't Steve. It was Teddy Wiseman, sounding half asleep, his yawn obscuring his first word. "Sorry," he apologized. "Steve there?"

"No," Nicola said.

"Oh." Teddy sounded embarrassed. "I've been trying to get him at his hotel. They say he wasn't there last night."

"No, he was here," Nicola admitted flatly. "He left some time ago. I don't know where he's gone now."

"Must be on his way to meet Joanne," Teddy said. "Okay, Nicola. Thanks. Sorry to disturb you at this hour on a Sunday."

The phone clicked and he was gone. Nicola looked at the receiver blankly before she replaced it. Steve was with Joanne. Hadn't she suspected it? He had left Nicola in bed and walked out to go to another woman. She slowly walked back into the kitchen and made the tea. If Teddy knew he was meeting Joanne, it must be business, she thought. That made her feel better. A little better—not much. Joanne Hollis was capable of using any weapon at her disposal, even business. Nicola didn't really care why Steve had left her bed to meet Joanne. The fact was that he had, and that his note had given her no glimpse of any warmth or love. It had been a scribbled message, written hastily from the look of the writing. Steve had already forgotten their passion of the night before. His only true passion was his work. That was what separated them, not Joanne Hollis.

Nicola might be his wife, but his job was his mistress, and there was no real doubt as to which he truly loved.

She had a shower and got dressed. The hours passed far too slowly. She waited for the phone to ring but it didn't. By the time Martin arrived, Nicola was in a state of cold misery. She was inclined to tell him she had changed her mind, but why should she sit around the flat waiting for a man who never came and a phone that never rang?

Martin had booked a table at a very expensive restaurant. As they ate, he talked to her about the way he saw the situation. Martin did not rush into such discussions. He laid out his conversation like a railway track. You could see each sentence coming before it arrived.

"I think you owe it to me to be perfectly frank,"

he told her. "You've told me you intend to go through with this divorce, but do you mean it?"

He did not wait for her to answer that. It was, in any case, a rhetorical question. Martin was laying out the facts for her. Only when he had finished would he expect an answer. He had a neat and tidy mind and Nicola looked at him in despair, wondering why she had ever started going out with him.

"I have never believed in romantic love," he said with a faint smile. "Marriages aren't made in heaven. I think you and I could be quite happy together. We get on very well, wouldn't you agree? We're the same sort of people. That's very important in my opinion."

Nicola looked surreptitiously at her watch. Martin talked on and she let the smooth flow of words wash over her head.

He patted her hand, making her start, coming back to him. "So you see, the most essential point is to be very frank with each other."

"Yes," Nicola said. She took a deep breath, "Then, frankly, Martin, we aren't suited at all."

"Oh," he said, looking taken aback.

"You're a very nice man and I like you very much but that isn't enough for marriage and I think we should accept that we aren't suited and just forget about each other."

"I see," he said gravely. "Does this mean you are going back to your husband, after all?"

"No," she said, her smile wavering painfully. "It just means that I should never have started seeing you in the first place and I'm sorry I've wasted so many months of your time. It was my mistake. I am sorry, Martin."

"I think you're wise to stick to your decision to divorce your husband," he told her, a slightly sulky look on his fair-skinned face. "He is a rather nasty type, I'm afraid."

"Yes, he is," Nicola said bitterly. She looked at her watch again, almost relieved to see the inevitable progression of time. "It's getting late," she said. "I'm sorry, Martin, I must go."

They parted as politely as they had met, shaking hands in what she felt to be a rather hilarious fashion. Martin made a little speech about his hopes for her future. "I wish you the best of luck," he told her and she thanked him before she ducked into her flat with a grim sense of relief.

She had known, hadn't she? She had known all along that she felt nothing whatever for Martin. He was a very nice man but he was very dull and she couldn't imagine why she had ever dated him. Martin had felt no more for her than she felt for him. She wondered what he would say if she had told him that she wished for him to experience an encounter with deathless passion? He would smile politely and look amused, no doubt. It would explode like a bomb in his head if he ever fell in love. He didn't believe in the state. Serve him right if he goes crazy over the next girl he sets eyes on, Nicola thought.

There was no sign of Steve. She lay in bed listening for the sound of the phone but it did not ring. It was well into the early hours of the morning before Nicola finally fell asleep and her dreams were troubled. She kept waking up, her eyes hot with misery and lack of sleep.

When the postman came, she flew to the door to see if there was a letter from Steve, but all she received that morning were two bills in brown envelopes. While she got ready for work she kept hoping the phone would ring, but it didn't. She left at the usual time, telling herself that Steve might be at the office when she got there. Her nerves were on edge as she walked into the long, brilliantly lighted room.

There was no sign of Steve as the morning wore on and she finally decided to sink her pride and ring the editorial staff to find out what time his plane left. She sat there thinking up some plausible excuse. It would sear her if everyone knew that Steve had not told her when his plane went, but she could pretend she had forgotten the exact time.

It wasn't necessary. Even as she had made up her mind, Joe came past and smiled at her. She caught up with him as he was making his way into the Morgue.

"When does Steve leave?" She had abandoned all pretense. Joe wouldn't look at her with surprise and curiosity. He wouldn't smile behind his hand.

Joe didn't smile. He hesitated, frowning. "He left last night," he said at last and Nicola took a long, unsteady, bitter breath before she said, "Oh, I see," and walked away feeling like death.

# Chapter Nine

It was three weeks later that she discovered she was expecting a baby. Her first reaction was one of stunned disbelief. She had been so bitterly unhappy over Steve's sudden departure that it hadn't even occurred to her that she might have become pregnant. Once she had realized it, though, a fierce happiness filled her for a day or two. She wanted Steve's baby. She had wanted it for a long time. For months she had looked into prams and felt envious. Knowing that new life was growing inside her gave her a strange, tremulous pleasure.

Only later did she realize the irony of it. It was one of fate's little jokes. But Nicola was not laughing. She was facing the practical problems the baby would bring and she was feeling disturbed.

She had to talk to someone, but she refused to make a confidante of anyone in the office. That weekend she caught the train to Suffolk to see Margaret.

The house was sunny and full of the scent of bluebells. The children had picked them in a nearby wood, cramming the pale green stalks together into a vase, the deep blue of the flowers trembling as a spring wind blew through the open window.

Margaret had been baking bread. The golden brown loaves stood on a baking tray on the table in the kitchen. Margaret made coffee while Nicola looked out at the children. They were playing in the garden, their shouted words floating back to the house. Derek was out on his rounds through the local villages. A black spaniel slept under the table, his nose on his paws. Nicola sighed.

"What's wrong?" Margaret asked, pushing a cup of coffee across the table. "Have a doughnut?" They were hot, their surfaces coated with sugar. Nicola looked at them, shuddering.

"No, thank you. I'm not hungry."

"You look pale," Margaret decided, eyeing her. "I'm glad to see you, but why are you here? Something's up, I suppose? Steve? He hasn't had an accident again, has he?"

"No," Nicola said, pausing. "I have."

Margaret stared. "You've had an accident?" Her eyes ran over Nicola in surprise. "What sort of accident? What are you talking about?"

"I'm going to have a baby." Nicola had been rehearsing it all the way down in the train but she felt self-conscious and silly as she said it, all the same.

Margaret gave a whoop of amazement and pleasure. "No! You're not? That's . . ." She broke off, meeting Nicola's strained amber eyes. "That's complicated things," she finished more soberly.

"Hasn't it though?" Nicola tried to laugh but didn't quite make it.

"What are you going to do?" Margaret was frowning now, the excited look no longer in her face.

"I don't know," Nicola confessed.

"Are you still going on with the divorce? You can't, Nicky. You can't divorce him when you're expecting his baby."

"Can't I?" Nicola nursed her coffee cup in both hands, watching the way the bluebells swayed on the windowsill, their heavy perfume drifting to her nostrils.

"Oh, Nicky," Margaret said, her tone torn between reproach and sympathy.

"What will happen if I tell him? He'll be cock-a-hoop. He'll think he's won. I'll have to stay at home to look after the baby and Steve will carry on just the way he always has, flying around the world, living like a bachelor except when he's in London when he'll expect me to offer him home comforts until he's ready to clear off again."

Margaret listened to the hurried, impassioned words, frowning. She sorted out the only thing that made sense to her. "Don't you want to have the baby?"

Nicola looked at her with pain. "Of course I do. I want it badly. But that doesn't alter anything, does it?"

With maddening common sense, Margaret shrugged. "I'd say it did. The baby is a fact. You're going to need Steve's help whether you divorce him or not. You can't manage to bring up a baby on your own; don't be silly."

Nicola hadn't told her about Joanne. She wasn't going to, either. Margaret would be deeply shocked. She had old-fashioned ideas about marriage, ideas Nicola shared, and although Margaret might call Steve a callous brute, she was fond of her brother. Nicola wasn't about to destroy Margaret's respect for Steve.

"I'll manage somehow," she said stubbornly.

Margaret spent the rest of the time trying to persuade her to change her mind about the divorce. "I'm sure that when Steve knows, he'll stay in England," she said.

Nicola knew it would make no difference. Steve wasn't going to let a little thing like a baby stop him from leading the sort of life he enjoyed, and Nicola wasn't going to try to use the baby as a weapon against him. If Steve wasn't prepared to stay with her for her own sake, she wasn't going to blackmail him. Her pride wouldn't let her.

She spent the whole weekend in Suffolk. On Sunday she and the twins walked through the fields with fitful sunshine illuminating the stormy horizon. When they got back, Derek had mowed the lawn and the garden had that pungent odor of newly cut grass. Derek had gone to sleep in a deck chair and the twins tiptoed up to drop grass cuttings onto his face. Nicola went in to help their mother, laughing.

She did not want to go back to London. Her flat was so empty, as empty as her life, and although she was laughing, her eyes were weary. Margaret looked at her with sudden anxiety.

"You will look after yourself, won't you Nicky? I don't like the idea of you alone in London now."

Nicola hurriedly dragged a smile across her face. "I'll be fine," she lied with vehemence.

Steve was already sending back stories from the Middle East, but Nicola did not read them. Whenever her eye was caught by his byline she skipped past hurriedly, frowning. She could only manage not to think about him if she avoided him deliberately.

It was quite easy while she was at work. She could keep busy, her mind occupied by other things. But when she got home to the empty flat, the dead weight of that silence fell on her and her heart ached with misery.

People carefully did not mention either Steve or Joanne, but Nicola couldn't help noticing the gaps in their conversations. If there were reporters talking in the canteen and Steve's name came up, there would be a hurried change of subject if any of them noticed Nicola at a nearby table.

Everyone knew, of course. How could they help knowing? Steve and Joanne were out there together and, knowing Joanne, there could be little doubt as to what was going on between them.

Nicola heard next to nothing from Steve. That didn't surprise her. He hated writing letters; he always had. She got a few postcards with snappy little messages on them. She tore them up.

One afternoon as she left the building a car drew up beside her and she looked around to recognize Joe, grinning from ear to ear. "Like a lift home?"

Nicola was tired. She felt tired quite often these

172

days. Her doctor had given her some iron tablets and scolded her because he thought she wasn't eating enough. She had lost more weight when she should have begun to put some on, he said.

Joe watched her settle herself in the passenger seat, doing up her seat belt. "It's very kind of you," she told him, smiling. She hadn't seen much of him lately. He had been up in Scotland working on a big trial which had just ended.

"I've got a space in the car park at last," Joe said cheerfully. "I've only been waiting for three years." Space was very limited in the underground car park beneath the office block and a parking pass was highly coveted.

She congratulated him. "How did you pull that off?"

"I think it's a mistake," Joe said, laughing. "But I'm not arguing. It means I can bring my car into town and I'm sick of public transport."

Summer had come to the city. The girls wore light summery dresses and the floods of tourists had begun to swarm through the streets. It had been hot all day and Nicola pushed her hair back from her perspiring forehead.

"This weather is tiring," she said.

"You get paler every time I see you," Joe murmured, looking at her sideways. He frowned. "Are you okay, Nicola?"

She felt as if she was being dragged away, her body weak and slack, her head strangely buzzing. Forcing a little smile she told him she felt fine.

He wasn't convinced, watching her from time to

time as he drove, and she struggled to make polite conversation. I am not going to faint, she told herself firmly.

Joe pulled up outside her flat and she thanked him before she got out of the car, stumbling a little as the bronze gong of the sun beat down on her head. Joe got out and caught up with her, putting an arm around her.

"Are you ill?"

She lifted her aching head wearily. "No, of course not, it's this heat." The heat, the noise of the city, the long hours spent in the overcrowded office—they had all contributed to her lack of energy.

Joe took her key and opened the flat door. Nicola walked inside rather unsteadily, leaned on the wall with one hand, her head bent to recover her balance. The hallway was going around like a washing machine. She felt dizzy, sick.

Leaving the door open Joe hurried to put an arm around her again. "You *are* ill," he said anxiously, his hand over her dark head.

Nicola felt him turn her. She swayed forward and let her head droop onto his chest. Her legs seemed to be sliding out from under her. She clung to Joe to keep herself upright.

Sudden panic poured through her. Am I going to lose my baby? The very idea of that made her realize how much she wanted it, how badly she would feel if she lost it now. Whatever the problems, she wanted to have Steve's baby. It would kill her if she lost it.

"I'll get a doctor," Joe told her, stroking her hair.

He guided her through the flat and made her lie down on her bed. The room was still going around.

She kept her eyes shut, shivering. She could hear Joe talking on the phone, then he came into the room and looked at her. "Just lie still," he whispered with touching anxiety. "The doctor will be here soon."

Nicola wanted to sit up and assure him that she was fine, just a bit tired; she muttered incoherently, her voice just barely audible, and Joe bent over her to push her back against the pillow. "You stay where you are," he said. "You're as white as a ghost."

"The heat," Nicola whispered.

"Yes," said Joe, unconvinced.

It was easier to keep her eyes shut. The room stayed still and she didn't have to be afraid she was going to be sick. Joe had gone away, she thought. She couldn't hear him breathing and that meant she could relax. She just lay there, waves of tiredness breaking over her head.

"Now, then, what's all this?" The new voice broke in on her and she forced her eyes open to see her own doctor bending over her.

"Hello," he said cheerfully. "How do you feel now?"

Nicola's mouth felt numb and cold. "The baby," she asked. "Am I going to lose the baby?"

"Why should you think that?" He was a kind man, in his late fifties, very sensible and calm. He asked her questions and she answered them, but she kept sliding away into that dull silence which waited for her every time she shut her eyes.

"A few days in bed for you," the doctor told her.

She looked at him again, blinking as she tried to focus her eyes on him. "Is the baby all right?"

"Everything seems to be fine," he assured her.

"But you've been a very silly girl, haven't you? Not been eating, have you? Your face is gaunt, all bones. What did I tell you? You can't skip meals or the baby will suffer. I want you to stay in bed and eat three sensible meals a day, plenty of milk and fresh vegetables and protein. I'll give you a diet sheet, but for the moment just get some rest."

Nicola was already far away before he had finished talking. She didn't hear him leave. The silence beat around her and she gave in to it with relief.

It was dark in the room when she opened her eyes again. She cautiously sat up. Her head wasn't going around anymore but she felt sick. It was a different sickness now. She was sick with hunger.

She slowly slid out of the bed and began to get undressed. She had slept in her clothes and they were horribly creased. When she had put on a nightie and dressing gown, she walked unsteadily to the door. It opened as she got to it, and with a gasp of amazement she looked at Joe.

"Hey, what are you doing out of bed?" he asked.

"What are you doing here?" she asked in her turn. She had imagined he had gone. She thought he had left with the doctor, if not before.

"Someone had to stay with you." Joe looked sheepish. "I couldn't leave you alone in that state."

"Oh, you are kind," Nicola said, giving him a quavering little smile. "Thank you, Joe, but there's no need to stay now. I'm fine again."

"It's no problem," he said. "Can I get you anything? A drink? Something to eat?"

She tried to persuade him to go but Joe was being

obstinate, and in the end she had to accept that he was staying.

She made her way to the bathroom, pausing several times as she felt giddy, but when she had washed and brushed her hair she felt much better. She got back into bed ten minutes later and Joe brought her some scrambled eggs and toast. He sat on the end of the bed to watch her eat, as though suspecting she wouldn't eat at all if she wasn't under surveillance.

She managed to eat it all, smiling at him as he took the tray. "That was very nice. Thank you."

"You look a little better, less like a ghost. You really had me scared, you know." He smiled at her as she lay down against the pillows. "There wasn't a scrap of color in your face." She could tell from his solicitous manner that the doctor had told him about the baby. Joe was walking about on tiptoes, almost like an expectant father. He fussed over her covers, tucking her in again, and Nicola smiled up at him.

"You are a darling, Joe."

A harsh voice sounded from the doorway as she finished speaking. "What's going on here?"

Joe straightened and spun around, his face flushing a dark red. Nicola sat up, the covers falling back from her bare shoulders, her pallor only increasing as she looked across the room and saw Steve. His face was pale, too, the lines of it harsh, his blue eyes glittering in molten anger.

"Well?" he demanded when neither of them spoke. His stare flicked to Joe, his lip curling back from his teeth. "What are you doing in my wife's bedroom?" He looked at his wristwatch. "It's two o'clock in the bloody morning—what's going on?"

"Don't shout at Joe," Nicola said coldly. How could he have the nerve to behave like a jealous husband after all he had done? He was a hypocrite. She looked at him with scathing distaste and Steve stared back at her, the flare of a barbaric fury in his blue eyes.

"Shout at him?" he repeated. "I'll break his neck."

Joe looked nervous and shuffled back a little. "I know what it must look like, Steve," he began in a worried voice, and Steve's eyes spat bitter hostility at him.

"But it isn't like that," Joe added hurriedly. He was a mild man with no taste for violence and he could see in Steve's eyes that any minute violence was what was going to happen. Steve was standing in rigid menace, his long body taut with a desire to break things, principally Joe's neck.

"Don't tell him anything, Joe," Nicola interrupted coolly. "It isn't any of his business."

"The devil it isn't," Steve shouted hoarsely, his stabbing blue eyes turning toward her.

"Don't you come into my flat shouting and swearing at this hour of the night," Nicola said. "Joe is here at my invitation. You aren't."

That seemed to leave him speechless. He breathed audibly, his jaw clenched, looking at her as though he did not know her. After a moment he ground out, "How could you, Nicky? How could you let anyone else touch you?"

"Why shouldn't I? You have no right to criticize me. If you can, I can, so go back to Joanne Hollis and don't come anywhere near me again. I hate the very sight of you."

Joe had listened to their exchange with an embarrassed, worried face. Even his ears looked red. Now he moved toward Steve, saying nervously, "Don't take any notice of her, she isn't herself. I'll explain."

"I don't need any explanations," Steve said murderously, his sinewy hands clenching. "Save your breath. You're going to need it when I choke you to death."

"She's having a baby," Joe croaked, stepping back quickly, fear in his eyes.

For a few seconds Steve looked at him, his blue eyes narrowing, then he abruptly moved across the room to the bed. Nicola shrank back in it, looking up at him with icy defiance.

"Is that true?"

She didn't answer. She had nothing to say to him. Joe moved away to a safe distance, and after a moment said, "It is true, Steve. She fainted earlier and I got her doctor. He told me."

"It's mine," Steve said, only the faintest question in his voice, as though he knew already.

Nicola looked away, her mouth mutinous.

"She hasn't been eating," Joe said. "The doctor is worried about it. She's losing weight all the time."

"Get out, Joe," Steve said, without moving his eyes from her.

"But," Joe began and Steve repeated the curt order.

"Get out—and get out now."

"Don't talk to him like that," Nicola said. "Joe, don't go. He can't give orders in my home."

"Unless you want his head twisted off his neck, I'd advise you to be quiet," Steve said softly.

Joe hesitated, looking at her. "If you want me to stay . . ."

Steve swung, tense and dangerous, and Nicola said hurriedly, "You'd better go, Joe. Thank you for being so kind. I'm very grateful."

Joe nodded, looking back at her with anxious eyes, then he went out, closing the door.

Steve bent toward her, talking through tightly closed lips, his voice very low and rough. "You stupid little fool."

"I must be a fool to have married you."

"I ought to wring your neck," he said, then he sat down on the bed and stared at her, his eye traveling from her ruffled hair down her pale shoulders, the half-revealed breasts in the candy pink nightie, the pallor of her hands as she grabbed at the covers to haul them up against herself.

"You look terrible," Steve muttered. "What have you been doing to yourself?"

"What have *I* been doing to myself?" She gasped that in sheer incredulity.

"You're too thin and you look ill."

"And none of that would be your fault, would it?" she asked with bitter sarcasm.

His blue eyes closed and he gave a thick deep sigh. "I'm sorry," he muttered.

It made her even angrier to hear him say that. "I

don't want you anywhere near me," she told him with hatred.

"After I've flown halfway across the world to get to you?" Steve murmured wryly, opening his eyes and looking at her with a faint, coaxing smile.

"What are you doing in London again so soon? Tired of Joanne, Steve? Or did she ditch you and go off with someone else?" Her voice was full of barbed cynicism and he frowned.

"I hate to hear you talking like that. There was never anything between me and Joanne."

She laughed disbelievingly.

"There wasn't," he insisted. "Oh, Joanne was stalking me, all right, but her motive wasn't what you thought. She wanted to use me to get herself a job on foreign. She knew that if I moved back to London, there would be a vacancy. She wanted to persuade me to take the Deputy's job and leave a place that she could fill."

Nicola had already worked out a lot of that, but she knew Joanne fancied him. She had seen Joanne doing it, all too obviously, giving him come-hither smiles and flirtatious little glances.

"But you wanted her," she said thickly, biting her inner lip.

"I've never wanted Joanne," he muttered. "She's not my type at all." He looked at her through lowered black lashes, his face taut. *"You're* my type, except when you're shouting. I like my ladies to be soft and warm and feminine, not tough go-getting creatures like Joanne Hollis."

Nicola stared at him, wondering how much of that

to believe. "You've been with her for weeks," she accused.

"Taking her on a quick tour of her new district," Steve told her.

"What?" Nicola sat up, her eyes fixed on him.

"Joanne was taking over the job, not me," he said. "I was just there to give her some training, teach her some of the tricks of the job. I've left her nicely settled in a flat in Cairo."

"You aren't going back there?" Joanne was a matter of supreme indifference to Nicola now.

He shook his head, his blue eyes taking on a glint. "I've got a new base."

Her face froze. "Oh?" Not Africa again, she thought dully. Where was he flying off to now?

"Aren't you interested?" He leaned back, his hands propping him up and his lean body languidly at ease as he watched her. "Don't you want to know about my new job?"

Her heart leaped into her mouth. "You're taking the London job?" Hope made her voice shake but it went as he shook his head, smiling. She felt her skin quiver with icy nerves. "Where, then?" What did it matter, though? He wasn't going to be here with her. She was going to have her baby alone while Steve diced with death in some distant part of the world.

"Washington," he said.

Nicola was too stunned to speak, her eyes fixed on him almost pleadingly. "Washington?"

"The plum job," he said, grinning. "I've been angling for it for years but Don Sutcliffe was a fixture out there. He didn't want to come home and he was too good for the paper to move him if he wanted to stay. But his wife's parents are in their seventies and Linda has been nagging Don to bring her home so that she can visit them more often. Don finally caved in and asked for a transfer back to London."

Nicola could scarcely breathe.

Steve looked at her with sardonic amusement. "Women are a pain in the neck," he said, smiling. "They always get their own way."

"Do they?" Nicola's voice was very small and husky.

He leaned forward to run his fingers down the pale curve of her cheek. "Always," he said. "Do you think you'll enjoy living in Washington?"

"Yes," she said, before he could change his mind. "When do we go? I can be ready tomorrow."

He grinned, his mouth crooked. "No rush. Don doesn't come home until next month. That gives us time to sell this place or put it on the market anyway, and pack up the things you want to take over to the States."

Nicola was weak with relief and happiness, but under that glow of joy she still felt angry with him. "Why didn't you tell me this was in the wind? Why did you go off without a word last time? How could you do that to me?"

Steve looked at her for a moment without saying anything, then he sighed. "I hadn't made up my mind. I had a lot of thinking to do. You were right when you said I hadn't wanted to change my life-style after we were married. I liked the way I lived and I didn't want to alter anything. You made me see I couldn't go on doing things the way I'd always done them."

"Why couldn't you tell me what you were thinking?"

"I needed to think away from you." He looked at her with a frown. "Nicky, I've been a selfish brute. You were right. When I got caught in that massacre and thought I wasn't coming out of it alive, I realized how much more you meant to me than I'd ever admitted to myself. I realized how much I needed you, how much I loved you."

Her heart began to thud with violent happiness. She put a hand out toward him and he moved closer, encircling her with his arm, pushing her head down onto his shoulder, his hand stroking her hair.

"You're everything I've ever wanted in a woman," he whispered, brushing his lips across the stray strands of ruffled hair. "The minute I saw you I knew you were the woman for me. The trouble was, I didn't want to give up my job. I tried to have you and my job as well, and it didn't work, did it?"

"No, it didn't," she said huskily, but her voice was light because she had won, after all. She had suffered in the process but the final victory was hers and she could forgive him anything.

"I know I kept arguing with you last time I was here, but underneath I was thinking, and beginning to realize that I had to accept that I had to settle down. I was angry with you, I suppose. I love you like mad, my darling, but I wanted to have my cake and eat it too, as you rightly said. Even while I was quarreling with you I was admitting to myself that it was all up with me. I knew I'd have to find a way for us to be together."

A sigh wrenched her. "For weeks I've been thinking you were with Joanne. It seemed the obvious conclusion." She moved away to look at him with angry accusation. "You must have known that that was what I was going to think. You deliberately let me suffer like that."

He grimaced, a wry apology in his blue eyes. "I'm sorry, darling. I was a bit resentful, I guess. All those rows we had when I was here last—I'd flown home with one thought in my mind, desperate to hold you in my arms again. Almost getting killed in Africa made me face the way I needed you. I'd have told you if you'd let me, but instead, from the minute you set eyes on me, you were spitting at me like a little cat and it made me mad."

"So you tried to make me jealous by flirting with Joanne," she said dryly.

Wicked amusement glinted in his eyes. "Tried? I succeeded, didn't I?"

"It wasn't funny," Nicola retorted, frowning at him.

"Don't glare," he said softly. "I told you she doesn't turn me on. The only person in the world Joanne cares about is herself. I'm not into ambitious ladies with an eye to the main chance. Not many men are."

"Joanne does all right," Nicola muttered, remembering watching the other woman turning her come-hither smiles on him and getting an amused response.

He looked sharply at her; his smile vanished.

"You believe me, don't you? Nicola, since the day I met you there's never been another woman."

"Never?" she probed, watching him closely. Ever since their marriage she had been troubled by doubts on that subject.

His eyes met hers frankly, directly. "I swear to you," he said. "I've never even looked at anyone else. I know I didn't write to you often—I'm not a letter-writer. But you were never out of my thoughts. I missed you all the time, especially lately. I'd have had you with me if it hadn't been so dangerous. You're so small and soft." He cupped her face in his hands, looking at her passionately. "I was scared stiff something might happen to you."

"Do you think I wasn't scared stiff? Do you think I didn't stay awake at night wondering if you were lying dead somewhere?" Nicola's voice shook.

He sighed wryly. "I know. I should have realized what it was doing to you but I was blind. I kept telling myself that you'd known what sort of life I led when we married so you must be able to cope with it. I couldn't believe you meant it when you said you were going to divorce me. I knew you still loved me. I thought you were just making idle threats. I thought that next time I came back we'd have a serious talk about it."

"You were behaving selfishly, you mean," she informed him with impatience.

"Yes," he said almost humbly. "I'm sorry, Nicky."

"So I should think." She looked at him through her lashes and he watched her, his strong face anxious.

"Don't go on being angry, darling," he coaxed. "Forgive me."

Her mouth curved in a teasing little smile. "I'll consider it. You are glad about the baby, aren't you? You haven't said a thing about that yet."

"I haven't had time to think about it," he said slowly. "I suppose I am. The baby makes the last link in the chain, doesn't it? I'm bound hand and foot. There's no escape for me anymore." He smiled at her, though, his eyes wry.

Nicola looked at his strong-boned, bronzed face with passionate intensity. "Do you still want to escape, Steve?" Wasn't that what it had all been about? He had married her because he fell in love with her but he had still wanted to escape. Their real struggle had begun only after their marriage. Steve had got married without intending to change his life at all. Was he, even now, really ready to accept that he was no longer a free man?

"That's what I had to decide," he told her. "That's what I went away to think about. And I had to face the fact that I could only be free if I left you—and I knew I would never be able to do that. I would kill anyone else who touched you. You belong to me." He looked at her, smiling. "And logic made me admit that, in that case, I belonged to you and I was no longer free anyway. I just hadn't come around to admitting it. It was all quite simple in the end."

"I wish I'd known this was going on inside your head," Nicola sighed. "The last weeks haven't been easy for me." She was understating with deliberate intention. She wasn't going to admit to him that she had almost gone out of her mind with pain.

"I'll make it up to you," he promised huskily, putting his lips against her bare shoulder, then his head came up and his mouth sought hers, kissing her fiercely, possessively, with a desire which made her tremble. "My love," he muttered. "When I came in here tonight and saw you in bed and Joe there—I thought I'd go crazy. I was so jealous I could hardly see straight."

"Poor Joe, you scared him silly."

"Serves him right," Steve said.

"He was being very kind to me," she protested, opening her eyes wide.

"He can be kind to someone else," Steve muttered. "He isn't offering any more kindness to my wife."

"You can't suspect poor Joe . . .?"

"Oh, can't I?" Steve looked at her dryly. "Poor Joe has been carrying a torch for you for months."

Nicola blushed and he gave her a probing stare. "Don't tell me you hadn't noticed? You're just the sort of girl Joe fancies—he must have thought it was his birthday, being here alone with you while you were in bed."

"That's very unfair," she said. "Joe behaved very well."

Steve grinned at her. "If you can be jealous, so can I. For one sinking moment I thought . . ." He broke off, his face hardening again. "It occurred to me that you might have started an affair with Joe out of revenge. You threatened to, remember? When I saw you together, that was the first thought in my head and I was ready to commit murder."

"I didn't mean it," Nicola admitted, linking her arms around his neck. "I love you too much."

"Not too much," Steve said thickly. "Never too much, my darling. I need every bit of love you've got." He kissed her throat, his lips heated. "And I need it now. If you weren't so ill, I'd do something about getting it, too, but it must wait."

"I'll be much better tomorrow," she promised, smiling.

"Tomorrow, then," he whispered, as he began to kiss her mouth. Only a few hours ago, Nicola thought, she had been in the depths of a grim and bitter misery but suddenly the world had turned on a new axis and her future was bright with promise. She had been so afraid that all she would have were those brief, burning memories. Instead she had a crowded procession of tomorrows stretching in front of her, each of them crammed to the brim with happiness.

*Silhouette Romance*

# 15-Day Free Trial Offer
# 6 Silhouette Romances

**6 Silhouette Romances, free for 15 days!** We'll send you 6 new Silhouette Romances to keep for 15 days, absolutely free! If you decide not to keep them, send them back to us. We'll pay the return postage. You pay nothing.

**Free Home Delivery.** But if you enjoy them as much as we think you will, keep them by paying us the retail price of just $1.50 each. We'll pay all shipping and handling charges. You'll then automatically become a member of the Silhouette Book Club, and will receive 6 more new Silhouette Romances every month and a bill for $9.00. That's the same price you'd pay in the store, but you get the convenience of home delivery.

**Read every book we publish.** The Silhouette Book Club is the way to make sure you'll be able to receive every new romance we publish.

This offer expires November 30, 1981

# Silhouette Romance

## ROMANCE THE WAY
## IT USED TO BE...
## AND COULD BE AGAIN

*Contemporary romances for today's women.*

*Each month, six very special love stories will be yours*

*from SILHOUETTE.*

*Look for them wherever books are sold*

*or order now from the coupon below.*

### $1.50 each

_Silhouette Romance_

___#49 DANCER IN THE SHADOWS Wisdom     ___#66 PROMISES FROM THE PAST Vitek
___#50 DUSKY ROSE Scott     ___#67 ISLAND CONQUEST Hastings
___#51 BRIDE OF THE SUN Hunter     ___#68 THE MARRIAGE BARGAIN Scott
___#52 MAN WITHOUT A HEART Hampson     ___#69 WEST OF THE MOON St. George
___#53 CHANCE TOMORROW Browning     ___#70 MADE FOR EACH OTHER Afton Bonds
___#54 LOUISIANA LADY Beckman     ___#71 A SECOND CHANCE ON LOVE Ripy
___#55 WINTER'S HEART Ladame     ___#72 ANGRY LOVER Beckman
___#56 RISING STAR Trent     ___#73 WREN OF PARADISE Browning
___#57 TO TRUST TOMORROW John     ___#74 WINTER DREAMS Trent
___#58 LONG WINTER'S NIGHT Stanford     #75 DIVIDE THE WIND Carroll
___#59 KISSED BY MOONLIGHT Vernon     ___#76 BURNING MEMORIES Hardy
___#60 GREEN PARADISE Hill     ___#77 SECRET MARRIAGE Cork
___#61 WHISPER MY NAME Michaels     ___#78 DOUBLE OR NOTHING Oliver
___#62 STAND-IN BRIDE Halston     ___#79 TO START AGAIN Halldorson
___#63 SNOWFLAKES IN THE SUN Brent     ___#80 WONDER AND WILD DESIRE Stephens
___#64 SHADOW OF APOLLO Hampson     ___#81 IRISH THOROUGHBRED Roberts
___#65 A TOUCH OF MAGIC Hunter

- - - - - - - - - - - - - - - - - - - - - - - - - - - -

**SILHOUETTE BOOKS,** Department SB/1
1230 Avenue of the Americas
New York, NY 10020

Please send me the books I have checked above. I am enclosing
$_____ (please add 50¢ to cover postage and handling. NYS and
NYC residents please add appropriate sales tax). Send check or
money order—no cash or C.O.D.'s please. Allow six weeks for delivery.

NAME_____

ADDRESS_____

CITY_____STATE/ZIP_____

## Simply the Best . . .
# Katherine Stone

# Put a Little Romance in Your Life With
# Fern Michaels

| | | |
|---|---|---|
| __Dear Emily | 0-8217-5676-1 | $6.99US/$8.50CAN |
| __Sara's Song | 0-8217-5856-X | $6.99US/$8.50CAN |
| __Wish List | 0-8217-5228-6 | $6.99US/$7.99CAN |
| __Vegas Rich | 0-8217-5594-3 | $6.99US/$8.50CAN |
| __Vegas Heat | 0-8217-5758-X | $6.99US/$8.50CAN |
| __Vegas Sunrise | 1-55817-5983-3 | $6.99US/$8.50CAN |
| __Whitefire | 0-8217-5638-9 | $6.99US/$8.50CAN |

Dear Readers,

October means turning leaves and crisp temperatures, but four irresistible new Bouquet romances are guaranteed to keep you warm!

We start off this month with beloved author Colleen Faulkner and the second in her Bachelors, Inc. miniseries as a small-town pediatrician falls for her newest patient's rugged dad in **Tempting Zack.** Next, Lynda Simmons offers **This Magic Moment,** a heartwarming tale of a couple who thought they'd parted for good—until they realize getting back together is just one kiss away.

In talented newcomer Elise Smith's offering, **Two of a Kind,** college sweethearts are reunited—in the college where they're both now working! This time around, a second chance at love is sure to make the grade. Finally, veteran author Jane Kidder explores what makes **Something So Right** when a couple who once did everything wrong discovers that putting the past aside is only the first step toward a future . . . together.

With four stories certain to capture your heart, you'll be happy to snuggle up with a cup of tea. And before you know it, it will be time to come back for another "Bouquet"!

Kate Duffy
Editorial Director

## USED TO BE LOVERS

"Regina."

Slowly, she looked up from the flower she'd been fingering. Will took a step forward. "Regina, I . . ." Will crossed the garden and stopped only a few feet from her, his back to the gallery. "We need to talk."

"We do? About what?"

"Us." He reached out and grasped her arms, pulling her to him. "I've come back. For you."

He bent his head and pressed his lips to hers.

There was no hesitation. The touch was electric. It was as if each had been waiting, untouched and unkissed, for eight long years. Waiting just for this moment. . . .

# TWO OF A KIND

*Elise Smith*

ZEBRA BOOKS
Kensington Publishing Corp.
http://www.zebrabooks.com

ZEBRA BOOKS are published by

Kensington Publishing Corp.
850 Third Avenue
New York, NY 10022

First Printing: October, 2000
10 9 8 7 6 5 4 3 2 1

Printed in the United States of America

*To Stephen*

# One

It was one of those early fall days that was almost ridiculously perfect. Regina Sutherland, at thirty the youngest member of the English department faculty of Idlewild College, stopped on the top step of Humanities Hall and turned to face the lovely vista. Just one more glance before the semester kicks in, she thought. One more moment of peace. With real appreciation she drank in the cool, crisp air and the pale, bright light of late morning.

No doubt the weather would shift back to summerlike heat and humidity for a day or two before autumn officially began later in the month. But for now, Regina would enjoy this preview of the most romantic season of the year in what seemed to her one of the most romantic parts of the country—the Hudson River Valley of New York State.

She'd always loved the vivid colors and spicy, earthy smells of autumn. A season of death, maybe, to some, but also a season that hinted broadly at rebirth. A season of vibrant color and dramatically shifting light and the comforting smells of fireplaces and damp, accepting earth. Regina knew she would never be able to live her life in a place where it was hot year-round. She would miss the spectacular change of seasons too desperately.

With a sigh of contentment, Regina turned her back on the inspiring view and pulled open the heavy wooden door. The English department—offices, faculty conference

room and student lounge—was located on the third floor of the old, stone building known as Humanities Hall. Though a small but serviceable elevator had been installed a few years before, Regina had never gotten into the habit of using it. She liked to climb the wide staircase to the first and second floors, then continue up the narrower extension to the third floor. The worn Oriental carpet that covered the somewhat rickety stairs, the shiny, well-polished oak banister—Regina felt like a heroine in a Victorian novel, ascending to her fate at the hands of the dark and brooding master of the house. She knew it was a silly fantasy but she enjoyed indulging it every time she placed her foot on the first stair in the stately entrance hall.

"Regina, hi!"

Regina smiled and walked over to join her friend Jane at a table laden with brochures and course descriptions.

"Jane, it's great to see you!" Regina hugged the tall, slim woman with genuine happiness. "How was the summer? And how's Mark?"

Jane laughed. "Both were—are—fantastic. My darling husband and I spent two weeks in Tuscany and did a whole lot of nothing. But eat and lie in the sun, of course!"

Regina could easily imagine Jane Cadwallader, professor in the Art History department, and her husband, Mark, owner of the only serious art gallery in Idlewild, traipsing across the hot and golden Italian landscape, probably hand in hand. Jane and Mark had been married for only a year and were obviously very much in love.

"I'd say I envy you," Regina said with a sly smile, "but I spent a month tramping across England, tracking down literary landmarks."

"That sounds like fun," Jane said, with a twinkle in her eye. "And that smile tells me you weren't exactly exploring the hills and valleys alone, were you?"

Regina laughed, her pale skin coloring slightly. "Well, there was one particularly attractive guy named Ian who,

um, offered to show me the sights. You know, tall, wavy blond hair, intense blue eyes. How could I refuse?"

"Oh, absolutely," Jane said with mock seriousness. "It was your duty to accept his offer. Keep American-British cultural relations healthy and all that."

"We did our countries proud," Regina affirmed. "But in the end it was the same as it always is. He gave me the it's-been-fun-but-just-one-of-those-things speech."

"Poor thing. Are you sad?" Jane asked, lightly touching Regina's arm.

Regina shook her head. "Honestly, no. It was fun while it lasted but well, you know, there's no place like home. And besides, Nigel and Lucy missed me terribly."

"Still have those scruffy beasts?" Jane teased. "They must be the luckiest formerly homeless kitties in the world, the way you spoil them."

Regina shrugged. "What can I say? It's the maternal instinct, I guess. You know, I *did* turn thirty this summer."

"Happy birthday!" Jane said. She stepped back and eyed Regina critically. "I must say, you're the youngest-looking thirty-year-old I've ever seen. How *do* you do it?"

"It's all in the genes," Regina said lightly. Though she was what was commonly thought of as a natural beauty—creamy white skin, lovely blue eyes, rich red hair and a womanly figure—she'd never paid much attention to her looks. And though everyone constantly told her how young she looked, Regina had never *felt* young, even when she was a child. An old soul, that was what she'd considered herself since she was mature enough to think about such things. When she was a child and adolescent, this sense had set her apart, made her feel different and often lonely. But at seventeen, when she started her freshman year at Idlewild College, things had changed. Suddenly, it was okay—more than okay, it was cool—to be who you were, and Regina had come to embrace those special things that set her apart from the majority of her peers.

Things like finding seventeenth-century madrigals more exciting than rock and roll.

Well, most of the time. A good dose of screaming guitar or classic country or moaning blues was a lot of fun in the right situation.

"Oh," Jane said, "speaking of attractive men, have you seen the new acting department head of English? Rumor has it he's seriously handsome and incredibly brilliant!"

Regina put her hand to her chest in mock horror. "Mrs. Cadwallader! You surprise me. And I thought you were a happily married woman! Anyway, you must be wrong about his being the acting department head. Dr. Nelson isn't going anywhere. She wouldn't give up her position for—well, for all the chocolate in Hershey, Pennsylvania! And you know what a chocolate fiend she is."

Jane frowned thoughtfully. "No, I'm sure I heard right. I was just talking to Mrs. Walker, you know, the art history department secretary. Believe me, she knows everything there is to know about everyone in this building. She said Dr. Creeden was hired just last week. He's got a one-semester contract. I thought that was kind of unusual, but I don't know any of the details, so. . . . Mrs. Walker even told me Dr. Nelson chose him herself."

Regina tightened her grip on the strap of the old, black leather bag she wore slung over her shoulder. "What— who did Dr. Nelson hire? What was his name?"

"Dr. Creeden. Will Creeden." Jane peered closely at her friend. "Hey, are you okay? You look, I don't know, kind of weird. Regina?"

For a long moment, Regina couldn't answer. What could she say? Was she okay? No, she most definitely was not okay.

Will Creeden. Here, in Idlewild. How long had it been? Seven . . . no, eight years now. Eight long and often lonely years. Eight years of considerate silence on the part of her friends—of Will and Regina's mutual friends. Silence

on the part of those acquaintances and townfolk who had the story wrong, sort of, and third or fourth hand, and who could never understand why Regina had outright refused Will's proposal of marriage. Or why Will had left town so abruptly. Why he had married someone else.

"Regina, you're scaring me." It was Jane, grabbing Regina's arm and shaking it. "What is it?"

Regina focused on her friend and took a deep breath. "I'm fine, Jane." She forced a weak laugh. "Really, I'm okay. It's just. . . ."

"Just what, Regina? You know you can tell me," Jane urged. She glanced briefly around the hall as if to make certain they would not be overheard.

Regina sighed again. "Okay, this is weird. Will Creeden and I were . . . we were involved. In love. For four years, through college."

Jane's face immediately took on a look of genuine concern. "Regina, you never told me there'd been someone important. I mean, you mentioned that one guy in New York, the lawyer, the guy you met during grad school. But his name was Eric, right? What . . . well, what happened?"

Regina laughed shortly. "Here's the condensed version. What happened is that Will asked me to marry him, right after we'd graduated, and I said no. Well, that's not strictly true. I said I needed some time, just until the end of the summer. I was in love with Will, but he was my first and only boyfriend. I wanted to say yes right away, but I was young and didn't want us to rush. My parents agreed with me. Anyway, Will got married to someone else that summer, while I was traveling in Europe with a girlfriend. Some girl he knew in high school or something. They, uh . . . they got pregnant. When I got back, ready to say yes, our friends Marty and Cindy were waiting for me at my parents' house with the news."

Regina shuddered, then forced a laugh. "Ugh, I can

still remember that awful day. Anyway, about a week later, Will took his wife and went off to the University of Chicago for graduate school and built an outstanding career. And that's the last I heard about him." Regina looked away from her friend's face. "Until now."

There was a moment of silence. Finally, Jane broke it by saying softly, "And here I am, just glibly telling you this man who meant so much to you is your new boss. Temporary boss, anyway. Oh, Regina, I'm so sorry."

Regina smiled. "There's no need to apologize," she said. "How could you have known? Anyway, well, I guess I'd better be ready for some major changes, huh? Dr. Nelson gone. . . ."

"Well, she isn't really gone," Jane said quickly. "I mean, Mrs. Walker said something about Dr. Nelson just needing some time to finish a book she's writing. And she still lives in town. I know how much she means to you—oh!" Jane pushed up the sleeve of her taupe silk blouse and looked at her watch. "I've got to run. Departmental meeting. You, too?"

"Yeah, in about a half hour," Regina answered. "Look, you go on. Don't be late on the first day of school!" she joked.

"Hang in there," Jane whispered earnestly before running off toward the elevator.

Regina watched the elevator's black painted door close behind her friend, then turned to the flyers and brochures spread out on the solid oak table against the wall. Anything to slow the rapid beating of her heart. Anything to prepare her for seeing Will again. One half hour. Better to spend it productively, she told herself sternly, than to rush off to the ladies' room for a good cry.

An acid green flyer announced: "Robert Browning and Elizabeth Barrett Browning: A Working Union." On appropriately red paper: "Satan in Seventeenth-Century Literature: Myself Am Hell." "The Romantic Poets: Life on

the Giddy Verge" on violet. Clean white for: "Heroes and Heroines in the Western Canon: Tradition and Innovation."

Regina flipped idly through the stacks of brightly colored flyers. Would a reluctant student really be attracted to a course on Alexander Pope because it was advertised on hot-pink paper? Regina smiled to herself. Not likely. Was the colored paper Will's idea?

Where was the flyer announcing her own course, the special one she'd developed three years ago, the one that made teaching two sections of Introduction to English Literature to uninterested freshmen bearable? Ah, there it was. Regina felt a surge of pride as she lifted the pale-blue sheet of paper. "Come Live with Me and Be My Love: The Evolution of English Love Poetry."

Developing the course had been a true labor of devotion. Regina still remembered how nervous she'd been pitching the idea to Dr. Nelson—and how thrilled she'd been when the older woman not only had praised Regina's work but had offered valuable suggestions for making the course even more exciting.

Love poetry. For one horrible moment Regina knew there was no way she would be able to teach the course this semester. How could she talk about musical language and deep emotion with Will here, in Idlewild, in this very building? How could she stand it? Knowing that the one man she'd ever really loved—her soul mate—had gone off with another woman, the moment her back was turned? Was Regina really to believe that by going to Europe for six weeks that summer, by holding off her answer to his proposal, she'd wounded him beyond repair? Hurt him so badly he'd turned for comfort to the first woman who'd thrown herself at him? Even if he had known Connie for most of his life.

How had she ever been able to stand it, all these years? The betrayal. The shame. The anger.

She'd been able to stand it because Will was in Chicago. Not down the hall. Not looking at her across a desk in conversation. Not sharing the student lounge at lunchtime. Not standing ten or twenty feet away with his arm around his wife at faculty cocktail parties. Not sitting next to her in meetings.

The departmental meeting. Regina shook herself from her reverie and slipped the flyer into her bag. Determinedly, she headed for the stairs.

When she reached the first landing, Regina stepped over to an old, not very clear gilt-edged mirror for a quick check on her appearance. Of course, she wanted to be presentable on the first day of the semester. But more than that, she wanted Will to . . . To what? To look at her and be pleased? To fall in love with her all over again?

To be filled with regret and longing?

Too late, she said harshly, silently. You're a married man, Will Creeden. You made your decision.

Her thick, dark, wavy red hair was newly cut and becomingly framed her face. The gray, double-breasted pantsuit flattered her very feminine figure and the deep-purple shell she wore under the jacket was a rich spot of color against the whiteness of her skin. Classic black loafers and small silver hoop earrings completed her simple, understated look.

Regina allowed herself a small smile of approval before moving on. She started up the next flight of stairs, her head down, enjoying the slight strain on her leg muscles, imagining these were not stairs that she climbed but foothills in the Lake District—

Regina reached out with one hand to steady herself against the banister and with the other grasped the arm of the person with whom she'd collided. "Oh! I'm so sorry!" she cried.

"No, it was my fault I was charging down the stairs and I didn't. . . ."

Regina let go of the man's arm as if she'd been burned. She could feel her face flood with warmth and knew she was blushing furiously. Her heart raced and her stomach fluttered and it was all she could do to stand there, clutching the banister. She wouldn't cry, she wouldn't laugh, she would do nothing until. . . .

Until?

"Hello, Regina," the man said softly.

"Hello, Will."

# Two

For the space of two breaths neither said anything more. And then both spoke at once.

"I'm sorry, really. . . ."

"I should watch where I'm going. . . ."

Will smiled. "Ladies first," he said, moving down to stand next to her on the wide step. "And please, don't apologize again."

"All right." Regina nervously touched her hair. "So . . . so I just heard about. . . . When—"

"My turn," Will interrupted. "I know my being here must be a surprise, Regina. I mean," he added hurriedly, "my being at Idlewild College. It came as a sort of surprise to me, too, even though Dr. Nelson and I had been talking about this move for most of the year."

"What!" Regina felt anger flare and knew her cheeks were red once again. "The year? But she never told me anything!"

"She wouldn't have," Will said matter-of-factly. "We kept our discussions private because, well, because there was no point in talking openly about something that might never have happened."

"But it did happen," Regina said quietly. "You're here and Dr. Nelson's gone. And she never told me about her plans." Regina gave a brief, harsh laugh. "I must say I'm a little hurt by her keeping such a secret. What I mean,"

she added quickly, "is that a new department head—even a temporary one—means a new department, doesn't it? As a professional, I want to know about changes that might affect my career."

"If it's any consolation," Will said, his voice even, "no one else in the English department knew about Dr. Nelson's decision to take this sabbatical. Frankly, Dr. Nelson herself didn't make the final decision until about two weeks ago. And since this is an unusual situation—I mean, the college's decision not to go through a standard hiring process—"

"Or to appoint one of *us* acting head," Regina interrupted.

Will coughed nervously. "Uh, right," he said. "Well, Dr. Nelson and I decided to wait for the start of the semester and tell the entire staff at one time." Will smiled ruefully. "Of course, the word's been leaking out since yesterday."

"Does everyone else in the department already know?" Regina asked.

Will nodded. "According to Mrs. Walker in art history they do."

Of course, Regina thought. So, neither Will nor Dr. Emily Nelson had given her any particular thought. They'd decided it would be fine to keep her, like all the other staff, in ignorance of such a major decision. Let her find out whenever. Wherever.

And why should they have considered me as special, Regina thought bitterly. I'm only Will's ex-girlfriend. The one who refused to marry him. And no matter how close I am to Dr. Nelson personally, I'm not a full professor. It was my decision to come back home after getting the master's, not go for another degree, but as a result, I'll probably never get tenure. What rights do I have with Will? None. And at Idlewild College? She decided she'd rather not think too closely about that question just yet.

"So, Regina, are you. . . . Where are you living now?"
Will asked, a little nervously.

"An apartment," she answered. "On Maple Street."

"Oh. That's a nice street. I mean, it was when. . . . At
least, I remember it being nice. How's Fido?" he added
quickly.

"Fido died three years ago, Will," Regina said. Amazing, she thought, how even now the thought of Fido could
make her so sad. The fifteen-pound male bruiser of a cat
had been her constant companion through college. When
she'd gone to New York City for graduate school, Fido
had moved in with Regina's parents. When she'd come
home after two years, there'd been no question that Fido's
home was again with Regina. Hugging his warm, furry
body and listening to his Harley Davidson-caliber purr
had helped her get through the long, miserable days after
Will's sudden departure.

"That's sad," Will said. "I—"

"Yeah, it's sad," Regina snapped.

Calm, she thought. Oh, please, stay calm.

She took a deep breath and attempted a bland smile.
"So, I guess it's all settled, Dr. Creeden," she said. "Welcome to Idlewild. Will your wife be. . . . Is she teaching
at Idlewild, too?"

Will looked intensely at Regina for a moment before
he answered. "Seems there's a lot about each other we
don't know anymore. I don't have a wife, Regina," he said
simply. "I thought you knew."

Regina took a small, half step toward him. He wasn't
married? For a moment, everything else fell away. All
concerns, like Dr. Nelson's unexpected sabbatical. All
surroundings. The beloved, grand staircase. The gilt-
framed oil paintings of horses and hunting dogs on the
walls. The background whir of a computer printer. Regina was aware only of Will's warm, brown eyes. His

strong, high-cheekboned face. His nearness. "I didn't . . . I'm sorry," she said.

"There you go again," Will said softly. "Always apologizing. Even for things that aren't your fault. Like my divorce."

"What happened?" she blurted. "I mean, was the divorce recent?" And then, a horrible thought struck Regina and she felt drenched with guilt for being absurdly pleased to learn that Will's marriage had ended. "Oh, Will, your child. . . ."

Will smiled briefly, tightly. "It's all right," he said.

"But divorce is always painful," Regina said softly. "I mean, I've heard it is. Will, you don't owe me the story. I shouldn't have asked."

Will stuck his hands in the front pockets of his suit pants, a habit Regina had tried to break him of for years. Obviously, no other woman had succeeded, she thought with a surge of nostalgia and affection.

"Well," he said, a bit more at ease again, "I don't know what I owe you or what you owe me. Yet," he added. "But let's just say I want to give you the story. It's a short one. My wife left me for another man. I don't blame her. It was my fault."

Regina shook her head. "I don't understand. How could her betrayal be your fault?"

Will took his right hand from his pocket and ran it through his hair. "Easy. I'd betrayed her first. From the start of our marriage, really." He looked carefully at Regina.

"How?" she said, slowly, though her heart had begun to race again. "How did you betray her?"

Will smiled sadly. "I was in love with another woman."

A thunder of footsteps startled Regina back to the moment. She stepped away from Will and closer to the railing as two work-study students, returned to Humanities Hall for another year, clumped past them.

"Hi, Dr. Creeden, Ms. Sutherland," the girl in dreadlocks said, and her preppy male companion added, "Hey."

"That reminds me," Will said quickly when the students were gone. "If I'm not going to be late for our departmental meeting, I've got to run. I'm on my way to the campus bookshop to pick up some materials I ordered."

Regina nodded. Will walked down a few steps then stopped and turned back. As if he knew Regina had been standing there, watching him.

He looked up at her, the noonday sun streaming in through the lower landing's large window, and smiled. Regina thought she'd never seen anything more beautiful than Will Creeden, tall and slim, his chestnut brown hair streaked with golden glints by the early autumn light.

"See you in a few minutes, Regina," he said.

"Yes," Regina replied. "A few minutes."

# Three

Regina ran up the remaining stairs, fueled by an energy she hadn't felt in what seemed like years. Will was back! And he wasn't still mad at her. On the contrary, Regina thought wildly, he'd seemed to be almost flirting with her!

When she reached the third floor she stopped for a moment to collect herself and then walked through the doorway of the English department faculty conference room.

"Regina! My dear!"

"Hey, it's our world traveler, home at long last!"

"A cup of extraordinarily fine coffee, Ms. Sutherland?"

Regina smiled. It was good to be back to the department, come what may in Dr. Nelson's absence. "Greetings, all!" she called and tossed her bag onto a chair on the far side of the well-used, burled maple conference table. The table dominated the room, leaving little space for anything but ten mismatched wooden chairs and a tiny coffee and microwave station. The cream-colored walls were decorated with art, mostly travel and theater posters contributed by the staff.

Regina eagerly accepted a cup of coffee from Aidan Ross, the one other instructor in the department without a Ph.D. His area of expertise was modern British and American writers, and he served as faculty adviser to the college's well-respected theater club. Lacking a separate theater department, Aidan collected interested—and tal-

ented—students from virtually all departments on campus. The students benefited not only from Aidan's exuberant love of theater but also from his ten years of experience on the New York City off-Broadway circuit. At several times throughout the academic year the theater club mounted productions, which varied from light opera to serious drama.

Nonstudents, Idlewild citizens of all ages and talent levels interested in theater, also benefited from Aidan Ross's expertise, as well as from his ability to make even the most inexperienced amateur feel important. The annual Idlewild Fall Fair, held on the college's campus, was one of the most popular town events of the year. For that event, the English department sponsored the production of a scene from a popular Shakespeare play. And for the past ten years, Aidan Ross had been directing the production, casting mostly townfolk and a few students in the roles of Beatrice and Bendict, Puck and Oberon. Almost single-handedly, Aidan Ross united Idlewild's two major communities in a mutually beneficial—and fun—effort.

At forty years of age, Aidan was still very attractive, though his love of good food and fine wine made him a bit more robust than his doctor liked him to be.

And then there was Dr. Maria Jackson. Regina gave a little wave to the fifty-year-old, ex-hippie professor of Victorian poetry. With such a small faculty, the staff taught classes in their specialties as well as in related areas. While Maria favored the Brownings, she taught a rollicking class on Charles Dickens and other major Victorian-era novelists. Dr. Jackson and her husband of thirty years, a surgeon at the teaching hospital located in a nearby town, lived in a rambling, white clapboard house on thirty acres of farmland, which, along with their children and grandchildren, they actually cultivated for crops. On

weekends they sold the produce at a stand along the main road leading into and out of town.

Finally, there was Dr. Miles Fetherston, a somewhat curmudgeonly gentleman of about sixty years of age, slightly hard of hearing but typically stubborn about this common indication of an aging body. With his shock of unruly, white hair, his tweed blazer, complete with worn suede elbow patches, and his gnarled, handmade pipe, Miles was the picture of old-fashioned intellectualism. Regina loved to listen as Miles read from *The Canterbury Tales* and other Old or Middle English texts, in close imitation of what scholars believed the language sounded like all those centuries ago. Dr. Fetherston had never married—as far as Regina or anyone else in the department knew—and seemed to relish his comfortable, solitary life as a bachelor.

Regina kissed Miles on his bristly cheek and took a seat at the table. "So," she said, "I guess everyone's heard the news?"

Aidan raised his eyebrows and turned back to measuring out another pot of coffee, made from his favorite gourmet roasted beans.

"Can't say I'm too surprised," Maria said, folding her arms across her ample chest. "Emily Nelson works harder than anybody I know. No disrespect to my colleagues. She deserves at least a semester off to finish that book she's been working on for the past four years."

Miles snorted. "Well and good, my dear," he said, "but where does that leave us? I've heard of this Creeden character, and I can't say that I like what I've heard. He's an *innovator*," Miles said, pronouncing the term with a sneer, as if an innovator were truly something disgusting to be.

Aidan turned around to face his colleagues. "Regina, what do you think?" he asked, his expression serious. "You're the youngest among us. The least likely to be set

in her ways. The most likely to accept what changes Creeden will institute. What do you think of all this?"

Regina looked from Aidan to Maria to Miles. Her colleagues. Her companions. Her friends, even. What did she really think about Will Creeden's being appointed acting head of the English department in Dr. Nelson's absence? A situation, Regina well knew, that could very likely turn into a permanent one. Especially if Dr. Nelson found herself enjoying her writing career more than she'd expected.

It was likely that she alone among this group of professional academics knew just how gifted Will really was. How intellectually strong and creatively spry.

"Well," she said slowly, "I have to admit I was shocked to learn Dr. Nelson had taken the sabbatical without telling any of us. Without discussing her decision. Or what would happen while she was gone." Regina glanced at Maria. "Honestly, I was more than shocked. I was . . . hurt, I guess. Though I know I have no right to be. What Dr. Nelson does with her life is her business," she added quickly.

"But there's no denying that in this case what she's doing with her life is going to affect us all," Maria pointed out. "Mind you, I'm happy for her." She chuckled. "I wouldn't mind some time away from the office myself, spend more time on the farm with my grandkids."

"But this could be just the beginning of major changes," Aidan pointed out, echoing Regina's own thoughts. "If Dr. Nelson decides to retire from the college. If Dr. Creeden stays on. We all need this job," he added quietly, then paused. "I'm sorry, I shouldn't presume. . . ."

"Oh, don't be so delicate," Miles huffed. "Some of us need this job for money, some of us for sanity and some of us for both. I do not hesitate to admit that I am one of the last."

"We still haven't heard from Regina," Maria said. "About Dr. Creeden."

Regina cleared her throat. Why did she feel on some level like a traitor to her colleagues? Did the fact of her past relationship with Will Creeden change the fact that he was now her boss, too? Could she really expect preferential treatment from him? No. Will wouldn't offer it and Regina wouldn't accept it if he did. Sure, his not telling her he was coming back to Idlewild to replace Dr. Nelson still bothered her but. . . .

"Well," she said finally, "I've read most of Dr. Creeden's published work and I find it solid. It shows both sound and creative thinking."

Miles guffawed and Regina frowned at him.

"Have *you* read Dr. Creeden's articles?" she asked pointedly. When Miles didn't answer, Regina went on. "I didn't think so. You should be ashamed of yourself, Miles, judging Dr. Creeden and his work based on . . . based on what, by the way?" she challenged.

Miles adjusted himself in his chair. "Based on gossip and hearsay, dear child, often the best and most reliable sources of information about the character of our fellow man. And woman, of course," he added, with a nod to Regina and Maria.

"So, you're condemning Dr. Creeden's character, not his work?" Maria asked.

"Well, as Ms. Sutherland so clearly pointed out," Miles conceded, "I have no academic basis on which to criticize the man's work. But my sources do tell me that our new department head is as overly fond of his own opinions as he is deaf to those of others. And there is some talk about his enjoying the company of several women of, shall we say, dubious character, both before and after his divorce . . ."

Aidan rolled his eyes. "Politics as usual. I wonder what Emily would say if she were here now."

"In my observational experience," Miles resumed, "a man's character is in direct relation to the quality of his work. A weak or vain character produces faulty or vainglorious work."

"That may be true. In which case, a good man produces good work," Regina pointed out. "And I've heard just the opposite of Dr. Creeden's character."

The trick now, Regina realized, was to defend Will without revealing exactly why she felt able to do so. Regina didn't want to let slip the fact of their former relationship until first talking to Will and agreeing on what to say or not say. And if there ever were to be a future relationship. . . . Well, the last thing Regina wanted to do was alienate her colleagues.

"What have you heard?" Aidan prompted.

"That he's reasonable and responsible and totally professional and—"

"Flattery will get you everywhere, Dr. Creeden!"

Regina swung her head to look at the door across from where she sat. Standing just inside the room was Will, his hair further tousled by wind, his tie tossed over his left shoulder as was his custom. Regina had always found something rakish about this habit. At that moment, she found it utterly annoying.

Standing next to Will was the person who'd laughed so seductively as she'd spoken of flattery. A gaminelike person, a girl-woman Regina thought, suddenly feeling too big, too much. The girl-woman's hair was pale blond, short and feathered around her small, narrow face. The eyes in that face—a deep, deep brown—looked huge. She's like a fawn, Regina thought. A gamine, girl-woman fawn. Except she looks too—too smart—to be easily startled or caught in anyone's headlights. She wore an artfully tattered, too-big pullover sweater in browns and tans and heather over slim-fitting brown suede pants. Regina couldn't see the girl's feet from where she sat but she was

sure the shoes or boots matched the rest of the casually stylish outfit.

Regina was aware that each of her colleagues was staring at the pair in the doorway. She saw Will's smile widen as he took the girl-woman's elbow and led her farther into the room.

"Welcome all," he said brightly. "Let's not waste too much time on introductions. We've got a lot of work to do this semester."

"Yes, I suppose you do," Miles murmured, glancing disdainfully at the gamine and then shooting his colleagues a look of triumph.

Will released the girl's arm and Regina noted with satisfaction that Miles's comment had made Will blush. Good, she thought uncharitably. She didn't know who this new person was but she did know—instinctively as a woman—that she did not like her.

"As I was saying," Will continued, now taking a step away from the newcomer, "I'm Dr. Will Creeden, the acting department head; Dr. Nelson's replacement. I mean, uh, in her absence. I'm acting head in her absence. Dr. Nelson, uh, Emily, can never be replaced, of course," he added hurriedly.

Regina darted a look at Maria, who lowered her head and bit her lip. If Maria started to laugh, Regina would be lost. Dr. Jackson had the most infectious laugh Regina had ever heard.

When not one of the group commented, Will went on. "And, well, I hope to help bring great changes to the Idlewild English department." He paused and looked at the carefully blank faces around the conference table. "Uh, not necessarily great," he added, "as in huge, though I suppose that could happen, but, you know, great as in important, like—"

The gaminelike person gently cleared her throat, and Will stopped talking. It was an oddly intimate interchange,

*Elise Smith*

Regina noted. As if the girl was used to rescuing Will in awkward social situations.

Regina clasped her hands together under the table and fought down a wave of nausea. Could *this* be the woman Will had referred to on the stairs? The woman with whom he'd been in love? Was *this* the woman who in effect had broken up Will's marriage?

"Yes, of course," Will went on, standing taller and shoving his hands in his pockets. He nodded to the girl and then to the group. "And this is Dr. Celia Keene. Her specialty is contemporary experimental theater and performance art. And she's the newest member of the Idlewild College English department faculty."

# Four

Regina ducked into her car, a six-year-old cream-colored Honda, just in time to avoid having to acknowledge or answer Will's call. If she got out of the parking lot quickly, she might be able to avoid him altogether. Which seemed, at the moment, to be a very good idea.

A quick glance told her that he was jogging down the steps of Humanities Hall now, heading, no doubt, in her direction. Regina snapped shut her seat belt, turned the key in the ignition and without glancing again to her left, pulled out of the space.

"Thank God," she breathed, careful to avoid a casual, accidental sight of Will as she drove slowly along the speed-bump-studded road that wound through and then out of the campus. He'd followed her out of the conference room after the meeting earlier, or, Regina thought, he had started to, but he'd been waylaid by Maria, too social and courteous a person to let the new acting head of the department just disappear after his introductory appearance.

Thank you, God, again, Regina thought as she steered the car onto Oak Leaf Road, bound for the home of Dr. Emily Nelson. She didn't think she'd have been able to talk to Will just then, not right after he'd presented Dr. Celia Keene. That in and of itself had been another shock. Regina had had no idea the department was in the hiring process.

No, she couldn't talk to Will just then. Not after he'd
spent the entire meeting sitting at Celia's side, acting, in
Regina's opinion, as if she were his—

"Darn," Regina said. And then she said it again, louder.
Almost unconsciously, her foot pressed down on the gas.

Why, why, why did Will Creeden have to show up in
her life now? Why *ever!* Everything had been going just
fine for her. Just fine. She enjoyed her job, enjoyed teaching, in spite of a very average salary, the stress of academic politics, and a sometimes huge workload. She had
friends. Good ones. She traveled for fun in the summers,
took research trips, too. She had a spacious, conveniently
located apartment and two adorable cats. Her parents were
loving and supportive and if sometimes a little too *there,*
well, that was better than being the daughter, the only
child, of a mother and father who didn't care about her.

The only thing missing from her life, she admitted, was
a man. Well, she dated now and then, but she meant a
man with whom she was in love. A man who was in love
with her and who wanted to get married and raise a family.
Just because she hadn't been serious with anyone since
the brief relationship with Eric, back in New York. . . .
Just because she hadn't been in love with anyone since
Will. . . . Well, it didn't mean her life was worthless or
bad.

Regina opened the driver's side window a crack and
took a breath of fresh air. Calm down, she told herself.
Just stay calm. Be reasonable. There was no use in asking
the universe to explain itself. No good in tangling with
unexplainable concepts like fate and destiny and the hand
of God.

Things happened and sometimes—a lot of times—you
just had to accept that they'd happened and go on. Deal
with the unexpected or unwanted reality. Handle it. Not
expect to understand it, necessarily. Or to make it go away
again.

If it was something you couldn't control—like Dr. Nelson's decision to take a semester sabbatical or the appearance of a new, full professor in the department or Will Creeden's surprising return to Idlewild—then you just had to. . . .

"I know, I know," Regina muttered, closing the window again, slightly chilled.

She was passing Bobone's Nursery now, on the right, outside of downtown Idlewild and along the road to Dr. Nelson's and the next closest town, Manderville.

The nursery. In spite of the awful combination of despair and anger that was threatening to overwhelm her, Regina smiled. Will had worked at Renato Bobone's place during college, preferring the tasks of digging, planting, watering—of cultivating and caretaking—to the more typical student's part-time jobs of waiting tables at one of the two diners in town or cashiering at King's Grocery.

Oh, Will, she thought, running her hand through her hair, pulling it away from her forehead. Those were such wonderful years. Each day full of new discoveries about the world and each other. Wonderful, yes, because wonders awaited at every turn. In those days, the eternal beauty of poetry had vied in Regina's heart with the ever-unfolding beauty of love. First love. True love. Real love.

Then why not lasting love?

For four years, Regina Sutherland and Will Creeden had lovingly constructed the image of a future. Of their future.

They were inseparable. The most compatible of couples. It was easy. They were so alike.

They shared dreams and passions, interests and goals. They both thought red raspberry preserves were the best and would do just about anything for a pint of cookies 'n' cream. Regina was a cat person and Will liked dogs better, but that was okay because they both loved animals, didn't they? They also preferred red wine to white and blues to

jazz. They liked to sleep with a dim light on in the corner of the room and hated getting up bright and early, no matter what time they'd gone to bed.

"Two of a kind," Regina's mother used to say, with an indulgent smile and a shake of her head.

They wanted a family. A boy and a girl, ideally, but they knew they'd be happy with whatever children God gave them. Regina was an only child, and so was Will. Neither had been particularly lonely growing up, but neither could deny having wanted on lots of occasions a brother or sister with whom to share TV cartoon shows and heavily iced cupcakes after dinner and whining complaints about teachers who gave *way* too much homework. So they would have two—or more—children, and together, the Creeden family would share cozy evenings before the fireplace, playing Monopoly or Scrabble or the latest video games. Would read favorite stories and books and sing favorite songs. Would have barbeques and picnics and go swimming in the lake on warm summer afternoons and sledding on Lady Hill on cold winter mornings. Spend Thanksgiving with Will's parents in Buffalo and Christmas with the Sutherlands in Idlewild.

It would be a simple life but a rich one. Regina and Will would work hard but never have a lot of money. They knew this, knew and accepted that as teachers and scholars they would never drive superexpensive cars or travel first-class or even be able to afford a second home. But they would have love. They would have enough. And enough was everything.

Sure, they'd been young—kids, really, making these plans, dreaming these dreams. But 'what did that matter? As far as Regina was concerned, their youth didn't make their goals any less valid. Their dedication any less real.

Besides, it wasn't as if Regina didn't know there would be hard times ahead. Sure, at twenty-one, fresh out of college, she had little real idea of what "hard times" might

mean. Realities like unemployment, major illness, a troubled child or the falling off of physical passion were dim notions Regina's mind registered only vaguely. And with the supreme confidence of youth, she had no doubt whatsoever that she and Will would handle any of those vaguely acknowledged problems with ease. After all, they shared a goal, a dream, a passion for a life and a lifestyle that suited them both right down to the ground.

They wanted, needed the romance of commitment.

But then came the shock.

Will had gone off and gotten married to another woman, just because Regina had asked for one last bit of time to herself—for herself. One last bit of space in which to be young and alone before accepting the burden and privilege of marriage.

All she'd needed was six weeks to travel across Europe with Katie—six weeks to walk through cities, her backpack bulging with a change of clothes, her camera and her journal; six weeks to ride from city to city on a Eurail Pass, crammed into nonreserved passenger compartments with other students or recent graduates from the United States, sharing bread and sausage and bottles of fizzy water, exchanging tips on the best hostels where you could take a shower and get a good night's sleep—just six weeks before saying the one word that would change her life forever. *Yes.*

She'd come home ready to say yes. Ready to settle down to the serious business of marriage and family and then graduate school. Ready to become Will's wife and to take him as her husband.

But it had been too late.

Will had broken their promise to each other, though to hear him tell it the one time they'd met before Will and his wife had left for Chicago, it was Regina who had broken their sacred pact. Not Will. Not Will at all.

What had he been afraid of? Had he really thought that

Regina would return from her European trip at the end of that summer and say no, she wouldn't marry him; it was over?

Had he been afraid of just the opposite—that Regina would say, "Yes, I'm ready, let's get married"? Had he really been afraid of marriage? But no, then why would he have married Connie?

Because she'd gotten pregnant. Because Will had gotten her pregnant.

Regina shook her head. It was impossible to figure out, impossible even now, eight years later, to understand why Will had done it. She'd never held him back, never failed to support him in every way she could. *Had* they been moving too fast? Well, yes, maybe. And Regina had been the one to slow them down.

It was too confusing, but even after all this time she couldn't let it go. That one time they'd met, Will wearing his wedding ring, twisting it nervously, he hadn't been clear about his reasons for sleeping with Connie, for marrying her. He hadn't been able to tell Regina anything that would help her to understand. He'd struggled for speech and then weakly blamed Regina. You weren't here, he'd said. I was lonely.

Why should Will be any clearer now about his motives, Regina wondered, than he was eight years ago. Lots of people, men and women alike, grew old without figuring out their motives, without questioning the direction of their lives or the quality of their loves.

What did she care, anyway? Regina turned right onto Dr. Nelson's long, tree-shaded driveway. Will Creeden was in the past. He had no part in her future.

She brought the car to a stop before the old but sturdy, white farmhouse. He was only her boss.

# Five

Dr. Emily Nelson had taught at Idlewild College for close to thirty years. Before that, she'd been a student at the college and before that, she'd been enrolled at what was then the only high school in town, Idlewild High. Indeed, Dr. Nelson had been born on a small farm on the outskirts of town to Martha and Joshua Nelson, whose own parents, as far as Regina knew, had been born, raised and died locally.

Emily Nelson was as much a part of Idlewild as were the hundred-year-old oaks that lined Main Street or the First Presbyterian Church on Elder or the Purity Diner, which still boasted a now old-fashioned working soda fountain and an egg-and-bacon breakfast for $2.50. In other words, in Regina's view, to think of Idlewild without Dr. Nelson was just not possible.

But she didn't have to think of Idlewild without her beloved friend and mentor, Regina reminded herself as she pulled into the grass-and-dirt driveway. She'd only have to get used to the college without her and hopefully, not for long.

Regina didn't bother to knock or ring the front doorbell. Anyone who knew Emily knew she preferred her guests to come right in through the kitchen in back. And anyone who knew Emily well also knew to pass right on through to the makeshift study that adjoined the kitchen. There

was no need for a dining room, Emily was fond of saying.
The kitchen was a good enough place for her to eat; her
friends should feel the same. So her mother's dining room
table was now a simple but massive desk, littered with
loose papers, folders, a 1962 Smith Corona typewriter and
a Power Macintosh G3. An electric pencil sharpener, taped
together because, though the frame was broken, the machine still functioned, sat in a cluster of half-empty coffee
cups. Several piles of books, haphazardly stacked, lined
the table's left edge. A printer sat on an old sideboard, the
drawers of which held supplies such as paper, pencils and
blank disks. On the wall hung an eclectic collection of
oils and watercolors and a few pieces of framed crewel
work done by some long-dead relative. A cracked earth-
enware pitcher of fresh wildflowers, perched on a strange
wooden stand, completed the scene that was Dr. Nelson's
at-home office.

Regina stood for a moment in the doorway of the room,
puzzled. Where was Emily? The kitchen door had been
unlocked, which it was unlikely to be if no one were home.
"Hello?" she called.

There was a muffled grunt from under the huge pine
table and then, slowly, a silvery head emerged, followed
by a wise and cheerful face with sparkling blue eyes.

"Uh, Emily?" Regina said, trying to control the smile
tugging at her lips. "What are you doing under the table?"

"My darned pencil rolled off, and I was just trying to
find it, my dear," the professor explained as she crawled
to her feet. "Couldn't find it, though. Must have been that
mouse. He's a tricky one, that mouse. Always taking my
things. Why, just this morning I lost my car keys and—"

"Are these the keys?" Regina held up a set of car keys
and jangled them. "They were right here on the desk,
Em." She grinned. "Really, what would a mouse want
with keys to an old broken-down Buick? Or with a
chewed-up pencil, for that matter?"

Emily inclined her head. "You never know, dear," she said, her voice serious. "You just never know. There are stranger things in heaven and earth. . . ."

"Like your taking an unannounced leave?"

There was a beat of silence, during which Regina wanted to poke herself for being so blunt. For sounding so mean and angry.

"Sit down, Regina." Dr. Nelson gestured to a slightly threadbare armchair shoved against a wall. She sat down heavily in her own swivel desk chair and sighed. "I was expecting you, you see. I suppose I do owe you an apology."

"And an explanation?" Regina prompted. "I'm sorry. It's just so sudden."

Emily grinned. "I'm not sure any adult owes another adult an explanation of her life and decisions. But I am sorry for not telling you before now. I'm sorry you had to find out like everybody else in the department."

Regina shifted in the lumpy, uncomfortable chair. "But . . . when did you start thinking about taking a leave? Will said something about almost a year but you didn't mention anything seven or eight weeks ago, when I left for England. Emily, are you okay?" Regina leaned forward, looked intently at her friend. "Are you ill? Is there something I should know?"

"Oh, there's lots of things I suspect you should know, my dear." When Regina rolled her eyes, Emily went on. "All right, my dear, I'll tell you what I can. But I'm not at liberty to speak for anyone but myself. You understand that, don't you?"

"You mean, you can't tell me about Will Creeden's part in this," Regina said flatly.

"Well, not everything, anyway. He and I—well, this arrangement works perfectly for the both of us. It was slightly unexpected for me, too, I must admit. When Will approached me—"

"It was his idea?" Regina interrupted.

"Patience, my dear." Emily shook her long hair away from her face, yanked her flannel shirt down on her chest and cleared her throat. "Will came to me as a longtime friend and colleague. I kept up with his work after he left Idlewild College, of course. We corresponded regularly, dashing off letters arguing certain propositions one or the other of us had made, the usual. Then, over the past two years, Will's letters became more personal. He talked more and more about his life outside of his work. His troubled marriage and then the divorce. And other troubles. I daresay I became a sort of mother figure to him," Emily observed. "As strange as that may sound."

"No," Regina said softly, shaking her head. "It doesn't sound strange at all."

"Well, be that as it may, eventually—by the end of last semester, really—Will began to talk about the need to take a leave of absence from the university. I don't think I'm breaking a confidence by telling you that much. But I can't tell you the exact circumstances surrounding his final decision."

"Like why he chose Idlewild," Regina said, not really asking a question so much as voicing an obvious, observable truth.

"Yes. Like why he chose Idlewild," Emily repeated slowly. "Anyway, I'd been thinking—dreaming, really—of taking some time off to finish this enormous book project I've been working on for what seems like an eternity. As it became clearer that I'd be doing Will a much-needed service by letting him come back to Idlewild for a time . . . well, we agreed to give it a try and we put the wheels into motion. It wasn't an easy decision for Will to make but it was a necessary one, his leaving Chicago and coming back here. I suspect the university people knew that because they made this odd arrangement easier than it might

have been." Emily smiled. "And that, my dear Regina, is the entire story."

"Not quite," Regina replied. "Though I'm guessing I'm not going to get much more out of you, am I?"

"No, you're not. But you might just get the whole truth from Will. In time."

Regina shook her head. "Oh, right. That doesn't sound likely. You remember . . . well, of course you remember, you were there, you taught each of us. We were together through college, and then I went away for the summer and Will married someone else. She was pregnant. End of story. At least, for me. I never knew you were in touch with Will all this time. Why didn't you ever tell me?" Regina asked, feeling strangely betrayed by her older friend.

"Maybe I should have, I don't know," Emily said. "But at the time I just couldn't see what good it would do—what purpose it would serve—to tell you Will and I were in touch. Would it have changed the way you felt about what had happened that summer?" Emily smiled a bit sadly. "You might even have hoped—unconsciously, of course—to use me as a way to keep alive a connection to Will that would have damaged you further. Held you back from living your own life. And my telling you I was still friends with Will might also have hurt our friendship, yours and mine. You were pretty angry, Regina. And you had a right to be. Lots of us were angry, even those of us who didn't have a right to be. Those friends of yours and Will—Marty and Cindy—they turned their backs on Will for a long, long time. Anyway, would you have been happy to know I could still be Will's friend, even after he'd hurt you so?"

Regina sighed. "No. Probably not. Oh, but, Emily, you didn't tell him about me, did you? I mean. . . ."

"I never broke a confidence, Regina," Emily said firmly. "I kept your life and our friendship apart from

Will. I honored your privacy. And now I'm honoring his. If the opinion of an interfering old woman counts for anything," Emily went on, more lightly, "I'd suggest you be open to the possibility of conversation with Dr. Creeden. Personal conversation."

"I loved him so much," Regina whispered as the tears gathered in her eyes.

"I know, my dear. I know. And he loved you, too."

"There's so much . . . there's so much I want to ask him," she whispered. "About the past. But also about now." Regina blinked away her tears. "Like how he can bear to be so far away from his family. Chicago's not the end of the world, but still. . . ." Regina gave a small laugh. "And if he's ever thought about me."

Emily Nelson stood and clapped her hands together. "I suspect Dr. Creeden has thought about you quite a bit. Now, no more musing and wondering in my presence or I'll slip and say something I shouldn't. Let's go into the kitchen and have ourselves a snack. That pesky mouse ate my lunch and now I'm simply starved!"

# Six

"Now, that is a beautiful Barbie!" Regina exclaimed. Not like the relatively simple doll of her own youth, which she'd dressed in clothes her mother had made from scraps of cotton and silk. This particular Barbie was called Very Velvet Barbie and wore a long, deep-red velvet gown.

"Her name is Mary," Annie announced, her dark-blue eyes serious and proud. "Her sister is Peggy. She has a ballet dress."

Regina looked over her shoulder to where Cindy stood at the kitchen sink, cleaning a head of lettuce.

"I didn't know three-year-olds played with Barbies," she said, half aware of Annie's low babble as she made her doll walk-hop across the kitchen dining table.

Cindy rolled her eyes. "This one does. If it's shiny, Annie likes it. Maybe later she'll show you her new bracelet. It's pink."

Annie seemed to be happily—and safely—occupied. Regina stood and joined her friend at the sink.

"Can I help?" she offered.

"Sure." Cindy nodded toward the sideboard. "Want to shell some peas?"

"Mommy!" It was Jake, the Barneses' five-year-old son, shouting from the playroom right off the kitchen.

"Want me to go?" Regina said, already heading toward the door.

Cindy chuckled. "Thanks. Sounds like he just wants to remind us he's still here. Jake's just like his dad. Always wants to be the center of attention."

Regina found Jake sitting on the floor of the indoor/outdoor room, surrounded by the evidence of two doting parents, four loving grandparents and Favoritest Aunt Regina. An erector set. Legos, the medieval castle and the parking garage. A computer and color printer on a low table. A large blackboard, covered with colored-chalk scribbles. Books—board and picture, paperback and hardcover. Boxes of crayons, paints and modeling clay. A bicycle. Another Barbie—that must be Peggy, Regina thought—and several baby dolls. A Raggedy Ann, easily three feet high.

It was overwhelming.

"What's up, Jake?" Regina said.

"Nothing. Want to play with me?"

Regina smiled fondly at the little boy. With his bright-blond hair and big blue eyes, pink cheeks and coltish arms and legs, he was a stunning child. His skin still glowed with the health of summer, evidence of a child who didn't spend a whole lot of time sitting in front of the television or playing video games. The Barneses were serious about their children being well-rounded, and that meant trips to the lake for swimming lessons and family canoe excursions, as well as the development of basic computer skills and early literacy, helped along by nightly reading-aloud sessions.

And as far as Regina could tell, neither Jake nor Annie felt the awful pressure to succeed that so many other young children today felt, what with tests required for admission to kindergarten and daily schedules booked so tight the children didn't have one moment to sit and play quietly. To think. To imagine.

"Sure," Regina said, plopping down next to Jake. "But I also promised your mom I'd help shell some peas. So

how about we play for a bit, and then you can help me in the kitchen."

Jake shrugged. "Okay," he said. "It's a trade."

Being with the Barnes family was one of Regina's favorite things by far. She'd been close to Marty and Cindy since college, back when she and Will used to double-date and simply hang around with them. Marty and Cindy's marriage had come as no great surprise to anyone who knew them. And the births of their two children were hugely welcomed events.

Still, as much fun as Regina had with the Barneses, at times being an intimate witness to their close family dynamic and strong marriage made her long for a loving husband and healthy children of her own. She wasn't jealous—no, that definitely was not what she felt. She was one hundred percent glad for her friends and would do anything to support their family. It was just that sometimes she worried she'd spend the rest of her life alone. Always the guest in someone else's home, always seated with the other single people at weddings even if they were total strangers, always the inexplicably unmarried friend in a world of husbands and wives.

Regina chastised herself whenever these glum thoughts took over. Reminded herself of her blessings and pondered the many ways her life could be so very much less happy. Thought of the divorced couples she knew or the ones who stayed together for a variety of reasons, even though they were miserable. She knew that marriage was not the solution to a problem. She knew it brought incredible joy and contentment but also knew it was an enormous challenge and hard, hard work.

And, as her mother, Joan, had said just the other day, "For God's sake, Regina, you're only thirty! You're still young. You have plenty of time to get married."

Regina smiled. It was nice of her mother to be so supportive and not to push her daughter into an unsuitable

marriage just for the sake of getting a few grandchildren or her daughter "taken care of." Regina had met a few of those mothers and found them unbearable—even if well-meaning.

Of course, Regina thought, handing Jake a Lego piece he couldn't reach, Bob Sutherland was a little less sanguine about his daughter's unmarried state. While he'd die before he'd actually come out and say something to Regina about finding a husband, telling her instead that most men were jerks (which he believed) who liked to marry the youngest eligible woman they could find and that maybe she should consider going out more with friends, to places nice, hardworking single people went (where were those places?), Regina knew he worried. He wanted to see his little girl happy and secure. And for Bob, happy and secure meant a marriage like his own, to his wife of thirty-two years.

Ugh. And now Will was back in Idlewild and somehow, looking down at Jake's bright hair and his face all intent on his primary-colored construction, Regina felt worse than she had in a long time.

Damn the man!

Everything had been going just fine until this morning, when Jane had told her the big news.

"Aunt Regina, you're not looking!"

Regina was yanked back to the moment by Jake's tugging on her sleeve. "What, oh, I'm sorry, honey. That's fantastic."

"Do you know what it is?" Jake asked, holding up the Lego thing he'd just created.

Regina frowned. "Well, let me see. It's not a car. I don't think."

Jake rolled his eyes. "No, it isn't a car. Where are the wheels?"

"Right. Not a car." Regina frowned again. "I—"

Dingdongding!

"I'll get it!" Jake cried, scrambling to his feet, racing toward the kitchen.

Regina followed.

"Don't let him invite any salesmen in, will you?" Cindy said as Regina hurried after Jake, well on his way to the front door. "Last week, by the time I got downstairs, he was pouring a glass of orange juice for a vacuum company rep."

"I won't!" Regina called. She reached the front door just as Jake swung it open.

"Jake, did you—"

"Hi, Regina."

In the doorway, the late afternoon sun golden behind him, stood Will Creeden.

"Who are you?" Jake demanded. "Why do you know my Aunt Regina?"

Regina rushed forward and put a nand on Jake's shoulder. "Jake, you know you're supposed to ask who someone is *before* you open the door. Not after."

Will grinned. "I used to do the same thing when I was his age," he said. Then, bending forward, he stuck out his hand. "Hi. My name is Will. I'm an old friend of your parents and your aunt."

Jake extended his hand in return and gave Will a manly shake. "Hi. I'm Jake. I guess you can come in."

Regina closed the door firmly after Will. "Uh, Cindy's in the kitchen," she said. "Marty's not home yet."

Suddenly, Will looked a bit awkward. "Oh. I, uh, I guess I should have called ahead. I, well, I kind of invited myself over," he admitted. "Just to say hi."

"Will!"

It was Cindy, standing at the threshold of the living room, drying her hands on a dish towel.

Will turned. "Hi, Cindy. I'm sorry. . . ."

"Stop apologizing and get over here!" Cindy met Will halfway and gave him a big hug. "Regina told me you

were back but with getting dinner ready and the kids and all, we haven't had time to talk about it."

Will smiled. "It's so good to see you, Cindy. And to meet Jake. And who is this lovely little girl?" he added, as Annie made her way out from behind her mother's legs.

"Annie," she said softly, holding Cindy's pantleg with two small fingers.

"This is Mommy's friend Will," Cindy explained. "He's going to stay for dinner with us." Cindy looked up at her guest. "That is, if you don't have other plans?"

Regina felt her heart race when Will quickly glanced back at her, almost as if asking her permission to stay. She managed a weak smile. Apparently, it was enough because Will turned back to Cindy and accepted her invitation.

"I'd love to stay. But only if you let me help with something."

"Cleanup," Regina blurted and then wished she hadn't.

But Will just laughed good-naturedly. "Cleanup it is. I'm a whiz with a sponge."

"Will? Want to see what I made with my Legos?" Jake asked now, tired, Regina guessed, of being ignored.

"I sure do, Jake," Will said. Then he smiled at Annie. "And I bet you have a Barbie I'd like to meet."

Regina's eyes widened and she saw Cindy's do the same.

How on earth had he known?

Annie nodded wildly, a grin spreading over her chubby pink cheeks as she did. "Her name is Mary."

"Well, then," Will said, "let's go!"

The children had been put to bed and the table cleared for coffee and dessert. True to his word, Will had managed to load the dishwasher, hand wash the pots and knives, and even wipe the countertops all before Cindy and Marty returned to the kitchen from the family's bedtime rituals.

"You are a whiz with a sponge," Regina said, laughing lightly as she measured coffee beans into the grinder. As the evening progressed, she'd felt more and more relaxed in Will's company. But that was probably due to the presence of their friends. Now, alone with Will in the Barnes's kitchen, Regina felt her stomach twinge nervously.

Who was Will Creeden, really? It had been so long. She'd changed, they'd all changed, hadn't they? Why had Will come back—and how long was he going to stay?

Regina ran the grinder to help drown out her whirling thoughts. She thought of her conversation with Emily that afternoon. After lunch, Emily had suggested, advised even, that Regina listen to Will. That she be patient and give him time and that she let things unfold at their own rate. What "things," Regina had pressed. Emily had shrugged. "Just things."

Well, no doubt about it, Regina thought, as she scooped the ground beans into the glass press, she'd get no closer to answers by obsessing. When you obsessed, you heard only yourself. You missed what the people around you were saying.

That reminded her of the conversation at the dinner table. It had been fun, on the whole, in spite of Marty's initial hesitancy to fully welcome Will back to the fold. But that was understandable. Marty was a very protective person. In his book, Will had hurt Regina and by doing so, hurt and offended the people who loved her. According to Marty, now it was Will's duty to prove himself worthy of their trust.

And Will seemed to understand and accept that. He'd shown no impatience or anger, had even answered a few of Marty's pointed questions with grace and humor.

Regina smiled now in spite of herself. She thought she'd die when Marty had asked Will, right out, what his intentions were. Will hadn't even batted an eye. "To rebuild a

good life," he'd said simply, and from what Regina could tell, honestly.

Will folded a dish towel over the lip of the sink and grinned. "Amazing what living alone will do for a guy," he said. "Suddenly, it's either clean the kitchen now or expect a visit from the Board of Health."

Regina laughed again. Will looked amazing. She'd be a fool to deny that all she wanted to do was run her hands through his wavy dark hair, lean her body against his. Beg him to kiss her. She hoped Marty and Cindy would return soon. She just could not afford to make a fool of herself, not after all these years and not with Dr. Celia Keene, her new colleague and Will's—friend?—on the scene.

"We're back," Marty announced from the living room, almost, Regina thought, as if he were warning the two in the kitchen to behave. Or, the man in the kitchen to watch his step.

"Perfect timing," Will answered, as the Barneses entered the kitchen.

Cindy looked around the kitchen and put her hands on her hips. "Not bad, Creeden, not bad. You've learned a thing or two since college, haven't you?"

Will laughed. "Oh, yeah. And I learned them the hard way."

"No pain, no gain?" Marty said, pulling a carton of ice cream from the refrigerator.

Will nodded. "Something like that."

The four friends gathered around the kitchen table. Cindy poured coffee and Marty dished out the cold vanilla fudge dessert. Once again, Regina felt her nervousness slip away. She'd just take it moment by moment. She'd listen to Will and—

"So, Will, um, now that the kids are in bed," Cindy began, "well . . . I guess I just wanted to say . . ." Cindy glanced appealingly at Regina and then at Marty. "I— we—just want to say how sorry we are. We heard about

the divorce. No details," she added hurriedly, touching Will's arm. "Just, you know, that you and Connie had gotten divorced. And, well, we're sorry."

Will bent his head for a moment, then looked at Cindy, his eyes bright with unshed tears. "Thanks, Cindy," he said, his voice rough. "That helps."

Regina's hand tightened on her spoon. Okay, that was tough, she thought, but Cindy is wonderful, so kind and direct. "Yes," she murmured now. "We . . . I'm sorry, too."

Marty took a long sip of his coffee. "What about Luke?" he asked quietly. "I guess he's with his mother. I mean, if you're back in Idlewild."

Will didn't answer immediately. Regina watched his face turn ashen and her heart went out to him. She wasn't a parent herself, but she thought she could imagine how sad it would be to have to live apart from your own child.

Will folded his napkin and sat back in the chair, still silent.

"That's okay, Will," Cindy said hurriedly, shooting Marty a look. "You don't have to talk about it. If it's too painful."

"How old is Luke now?" Marty went on, not unkindly. "About seven? Eight? We'd love to see a picture of him, if you've got one on you."

"Yes, Will," Regina said, forcing her voice to show only her sincere interest in the little boy, not the pain she felt thinking of that boy's mother. "Do you have a picture? I bet he's adorable," she added, with a small smile.

Suddenly, Will scraped his chair away from the table. Regina flinched at the sound—and the look on Will's face.

"Will!" Cindy said, reaching for him. "What's wrong?"

His voice was flat. "I'm sorry," he told them. "I . . . it's been a long day. Thank you for dinner. I think I'd better go now."

# Seven

Will steered the dark-blue Volkswagon hatchback along the dark roads leading back into the center of Idlewild. Every few moments he'd take one hand off the steering wheel and rub his temples. He had a whopper of a headache.

"I shouldn't have gotten so crazy," he muttered to the empty car. "I've got to learn to handle Luke's name coming up, people asking about him. I can't . . . this can't go on, Creeden!"

But it had been going on since Luke's death a year ago. And Will could detect no signs of the unbearable pain lessening, the brutally active sense of loss slipping away into numbness. Serene acceptance did not seem likely any time soon.

Foolishly, he now realized, he'd thought that by coming back to Idlewild, by coming home to Regina, the healing process would finally, finally begin. That back at the scene of his happiest youthful moments his heart, magically, would begin to mend and strengthen, a tough and necessary scar to grow over the raw and gaping wound Luke's death had inflicted.

Losing Regina—that had been bad. Losing his marriage—far more depressing than he had imagined. But losing his one and only child to a ravaging, unstoppable disease . . . well, that was the cruelest thing he knew.

But after his display at the Barneses' table earlier that night, Will was close to being convinced he'd made another colossal mistake. He wasn't ready to heal. He wasn't ready to talk about Luke. And, in such a condition, he certainly wasn't going to inflict himself on the one woman he'd always loved.

But would he have the strength to resist her?

Will turned on the radio low in an effort to distract himself from his own dark thoughts. It didn't work. He couldn't help but think he'd made one horrible mistake after another, beginning with cheating on Regina while she was in Europe. The effort it took not to descend into self-pity but to retain a sense of responsibility was exhausting. But he would not become a self-pitying wretch. He would pay for his mistakes, and if he couldn't turn back the hands of time and undo the foolish deeds, he'd make whatever reparations were possible in the here and now.

But how did a man live with the guilt? There was no way to forget, but was there really a way to atone, a way to make things right for the future? There had to be.

Will made a right turn onto Main Street and noted briefly that Idlewild's nightlife certainly had flourished into a lively scene. Idlewild was still a far cry from New York City but it was no longer the sleepy little town he'd known back in school. He counted three restaurants, two movie theaters and a pool and video-game place all teeming with people.

Almost home, Will thought, wearily. It was too late for Connie and him. More painfully, and not entirely his fault, it was too late for Luke. But was it too late for Will and Regina?

It couldn't be, he determined. He wouldn't let it be. If he was half the man he thought he was—one half the man he hoped he was—he wouldn't let it be too late for them.

He'd get back on track, starting now, and he'd win her love, this time forever.

Okay, Regina had her own mind, her own thoughts and feelings. He couldn't presume that it would be easy to change her opinion of him, if, after eight years apart, she was no longer disposed to love him.

However, he could—he would—presume that he had the right to try. He loved her. He always had. Didn't that give him some right to try to win her affection and esteem? And if he succeeded, if he did win her heart, wouldn't that atone for some of the selfish things he'd done in the past eight years?

Will thought of a commercial he'd seen on TV the night before. An ad for one of Elizabeth Taylor's perfumes, White Diamonds. "It's a woman's prerogative to change her mind," Burt Reynolds, the spokesman, said. Or some such similar words. "It's a man's prerogative to change it back." It was kind of an obnoxious ad, Will thought, and he hated Reynolds's raspberry-colored shirt. He, himself, wouldn't be caught dead in something so flamboyant. But there *was* something to what Burt said, though some slick marketing type had written the words for him.

Will pulled the car to a stop directly across the street from the building on Maple Street in which he'd rented a one-bedroom apartment. Before getting out he looked up at the windows he knew were Regina's. He knew because earlier that day, just after classes, when he'd signed the lease and moved in a few essentials—he'd been staying at Mrs. Ferencik's bed-and-breakfast for the past few days—the landlord had told him about his new neighbors, especially about the nice young teacher in the second-floor front apartment. But Regina's presence in the building had come as no surprise to Will. As soon as she'd told him where she lived, during that first meeting on the staircase, he'd set out to rent a place as close as possible. Luck or providence or fate had led him to a decent, available

apartment one flight up from Regina. At the time, Will had chosen to see such a fortuitous event as a sign that heaven was on his side.

Will turned off the car's engine and opened the door. Now all I have to do, he thought nervously, is tell her I'm her neighbor. Suddenly, as the chill night air touched Will's face and he shivered, his resolve wavered. Suddenly, he wasn't so sure he hadn't made yet another very bad mistake.

Will passed Regina's door without a glance. He knew she was probably still at Marty and Cindy's, maybe discussing his strange behavior, his abrupt departure. Well, his old friends had a right to dissect his unexpectedly bizarre conduct.

A turn of the slightly ill-fitting key in the lock and Will stepped inside his new—temporary?—home. Looked around at the stacks of unopened boxes, some filled with work-related material, others with personal memorabilia. Like Luke's first baby shoes and his kindergarten graduation diploma.

Luke's death certificate.

Will tossed the keys on the kitchen counter and fell onto the couch he'd recently purchased. Should he get up and get a beer? A cup of coffee? No, nothing. Will leaned his head against the couch's deep pillows and closed his eyes.

But sleep wouldn't come. Instead, he was bombarded with recriminations and memories and worries about the future. . . .

He couldn't fail to win Regina back.

Strange. It was so strange. Once upon a time, years ago, he never thought he'd be saying those words, setting that goal. To win Regina back. Why would he ever have

to win her back, when he'd never be stupid enough to let her go in the first place?

Damn it all, how *could* he have let her go? He'd been over it and over it. And still, he didn't fully understand why or how it had happened. At twenty-two years of age had he really been so weak, so young and insecure. . . .

Before Regina left for Europe after graduation—before she left him behind for six weeks—he couldn't remember ever feeling insecure. Why should he have? All through college, for four long years, he'd had Regina and all the dreams and wonders that went along with her. A loving family, too, since the day he was born. A first-rate academic record and a solid hold on his anticipated career path. Good friends, a part-time job he enjoyed, his health. Will Creeden was satisfied. He lacked for nothing.

But when Regina left, when she didn't leap to say yes to his proposal of marriage, it had blindsided him. It had almost destroyed him. No, it *had* destroyed him, had thoroughly shaken his sense of self, because the old, confident Will would never have done something so stupid and selfish and weak as to cheat on the woman he loved.

Because that's what it had been, in the end. Cheating. An ugly word. An ugly action.

True, at the time, he hadn't heard from Regina for weeks. And Connie, who'd had a crush on him since high school when they'd actually gone on a few dates, had spent those weeks showering him with affection and attention—helping to convince Will that if Regina really loved him she would have accepted his proposal of marriage, wouldn't have left for Europe, would send, at least, another postcard! No doubt about it, Connie had been husband hunting in a major way. But what had happened wasn't Connie's fault. Or Regina's. It was his own fault.

In his despair, he'd hurt everyone—Regina and her parents, his own disappointed folks and friends, Connie, his wife, and eventually, their son. Most of all, Will had hurt

himself. That was something he would never be able to admit to anyone, how badly he'd damaged his own heart and soul. He knew, beyond a shadow of a doubt, that he did *not* have a right to complain about his own pain.

But he'd grown over the years, changed, been hardened in the fire of experience. The pain hadn't killed him, only made him strong. Made him ready, willing and able to accept responsibility for all he'd done.

But not ready—not yet—to talk about Luke.

He walked straight to the box sealed in silver duct tape. With a box cutter, he sliced through the tape and pulled back the cardboard flaps of the box. Reached inside. . . .

The photo album was well-worn. Will had kept it by his side every day and every night in those months just after Luke's death. But in the past few weeks, since before leaving Chicago, he'd resisted looking through the album. Tried to train himself away from his obsession with the past. With Luke.

Tonight, after Marty's innocent, well-meaning but nevertheless devastating questions, Will needed a fix.

When Luke was born, Will's life had blossomed in a way he hadn't imagined possible. In those early years, still silently hurting and longing for Regina, he'd on occasion wished that Luke was her child. But he'd moved beyond that disloyal desire and come to realize that Luke was perfect as he was—and that he belonged to no one but God. Luke was outside of, above and beyond Will's former relationship with Regina and his current marriage to Connie. In Will's opinion, he and Connie had been chosen— for whatever unfathomable reason—to be Luke's guardians in life, his protectors and champions and even-

tually, his friends. Will's love for Luke was absolute and completely unselfish.

No matter how lonely Will became in his marriage, he had never grown lonely in parenthood. As a father, his life was filled with love and joy and pride. Luke's first steps and words, his curled fists in sleep, his wispy baby hair, his first crayon drawing and handmade Mother's Day card—everything about Luke was a miracle for Will.

It wasn't the ideal family, he knew. It didn't work the way a true family should have worked. Will would have liked to feel more deeply connected to the mother of his child, knew he should have. But he couldn't manufacture feelings for Connie. He treated her with the respect and kindness she deserved as a woman, mother, human being. When things got bad between them—when night after night, Connie stayed out late with her friends, when she forgot to meet Luke after kindergarten or to make his lunch for a school outing, even when she began to see other men behind Will's back—Will held on to his temper, never raised his voice or lashed out physically.

Maybe that was another mistake, he thought now, bitterly. Not hitting, he'd never resort to violence, but maybe he should have been tougher on Connie, demanded she respect if not him then their son—their family. Maybe even suggested—begged—her to go to therapy with him, to try to save the marriage. But the wilder Connie had become, the more Will had withdrawn—into himself, into his role as primary parent. Connie had not turned out to be a particularly devoted mother, so Will tried to pick up her slack in every way he could. Finally, by the time Connie filed for divorce, citing "irreconcilable differences," Luke had become Will's entire world.

Until Luke died.

The pain of losing Luke could equal no other, not even the pain of losing Regina. And yet, the pain of Luke's dying, especially at so young an age, had not killed Will.

After time—after a few weeks of inconsolable grief—the memory of Luke's life had rekindled in Will a small but steady desire to live and to love. To build again. In Luke's name, to build and to grow.

In his short, sweet and painful life, Luke had taught Will everything about living. He'd been a boy, even with Regina. Luke—his birth and then his death—had made Will a man. And a man he'd continue to be.

Or die trying.


Midnight. And still, sleep wouldn't come. Maybe now was the time for that beer, Will thought. No, better a small, neat whiskey.

Glass in hand, Will lowered the living room lights and returned to his place on the couch. And thought about coming to Idlewild.

When Will announced his decision to take an unprecedented, one semester leave of absence from the University of Chicago, his colleagues were stunned. They'd raised their eyebrows and speculated behind closed doors about the state of Will's mental health. A few had even gone so far as to make a play for his job. Closer friends were worried, asked if Will was feeling well, offered to listen if he needed to talk. No matter how you looked at it, leaving a prime position at a major university, even temporarily, for a job as temporary, acting head of a department at a small and not particularly prestigious college, was just not . . . well, normal.

Finally, friends, acquaintances and colleagues concluded it was the grief that had compelled Will to take the sabbatical, to take a break from his routine and from the city in which he'd spent virtually all of his married life. Who wouldn't want to get away? First, a messy and embarrassing divorce. Then the slow and painful death of an only and beloved child. No wonder Will Creeden was

making such an odd move. Those true friends just hoped
he wasn't permanently hurting his chances for career ad-
vancement, for tenure. Maybe if he continued to write and
publish while he was at Idlewild, maybe then everything
would work out okay.

Will listened to the voices of concern and tried his best
to ignore those voices that were more meanly critical. Ul-
timately, none of the voices made a difference. Will knew
his own mind, at least in this regard. At least in regard to
Regina. He had to go back, had to go back home to the
woman he'd never stopped loving. He had to try again.

Will stood, stretched. Finally, finally, he was ready for
sleep.

# Eight

Regina pulled into the driveway and turned off the engine. She sat for a moment before getting out, looking at the house in which she was raised. The house in which her parents had lived for all thirty-two years of their marriage.

She loved the house, no doubt about it. It was a classic Victorian, white clapboard with dark-green shutters and a widow's walk. The house had certain elements of whimsy, like the wraparound porch with gingerbread trim and the circular window over the entry.

Regina even thought she'd like to live in a house like it some day, with husband, children, pets. When she'd come home from New York City, after earning her Master's, her parents had expected her to move back in with them. Why not, they'd asked. There was plenty of space— her old bedroom, with the walls painted sunshine yellow, unchanged since the day she'd left—why should she spend money on an apartment in town? But it had been important to Regina to take her own place, make her own home in Idlewild, especially after having lived on her own for the previous two years. As much as she loved her mother and father—as much as she actually enjoyed their company— she was an adult, independent, and needed to live on her own. To make things easier on her disappointed parents, she'd agreed to see them once, even twice a week, for

dinner, brunch after church on Sundays, whatever. The deal had worked out just fine.

Regina closed the car door behind her and walked up the steps to the porch. A rocking chair, a bench, several potted plants and two small side tables, all painted pure white—the same pieces that her mother had bought years and years ago. Each was meticulously cleaned and repainted every spring.

She let herself in—the front door was usually unlocked when the Sutherlands were home—and called to her mother. "Hi, I'm here."

"In the kitchen, honey," Joan Sutherland called. "Come on in."

The kitchen was Joan's favorite room in the house. It was big enough to accommodate a wonderful, old, eight-foot-long oak table. Ten years or so before, Joan had had the back wall knocked out and replaced with floor-to-ceiling windows, which she had filled with hanging plants such as spider fern, swedish ivy and philodendron.

When Joan wasn't puttering around her prized kitchen, cooking or simply enjoying the view of the woods through both windows, she worked as a full-time wife and mother and a part-time real estate agent. She had the winning, open personality and the quick mind for figures that made a successful agent. People trusted her to be honest about the property in question, not to overwhelm them with a slick and hard sell and to answer, almost off-the-bat, questions about financing and the current real estate economy. Last, but not at all least, longtime residents of the town knew Joan and her husband from the Sutherlands' years of service on the PTA and from their involvement in their church. When such folk were ready to make a change in lifestyle, they bypassed bigger, newer agencies and called their old friend and trusted neighbor to take them through the process.

Another great benefit of Joan Sutherland's position of

trust in Idlewild was her ability to raise a significant amount of money each year for the Idlewild Fall Fair. In exchange for donations to support the fair and its benefactors, local businesses and small corporations received free advertising at the event in the form of banners and individual giveaway tables.

Bob Sutherland also volunteered his time and energy to the Idlewild Fall Fair. As an attorney with his own small firm that specialized in civil matters, Bob handled all business dealings for the event, such as the purchasing or renewing of liability insurance, selecting and making contracts with the vendors, and negotiating settlements of the occasional disputes that arose between vendors and the college. With Regina working for the college itself, the fair had become somewhat of a much-anticipated annual Sutherland family affair.

"Hey, Mom. What's up?" Regina placed her bag on a chair and gave her mother a kiss.

"You know, whenever you ask me what's up," Joan replied with a smile, "I feel I should have something fabulously exciting to tell you. As it is, I'm afraid all I've got is that the washing machine's on the fritz again."

"Ow. That is news. I think I'd die without my washing machine," Regina admitted with a shudder. "And I don't even have to clean up after Dad!"

Joan laughed. "How one man manages to make so much dirty laundry will forever be beyond me."

"Where is the old reprobate, anyway?"

"Oh, he's down in his workroom." Joan shrugged. "I called a repairman for the washing machine and your father's upset that I wouldn't let him handle it, so he's busy organizing his hammers and nails. Doing something manly, anyway."

"You locked up the chain saw, didn't you?" Regina asked worriedly. "Remember the last time he tried to use it and accidentally cut Grandma's cherry table in half?"

Joan raised an eyebrow. "I've never really been convinced that was an accident. But, yes, I hid the chain saw where your father will never find it. Behind the vacuum."

Regina and her mother burst out laughing. Bob Sutherland was just about the most perfect husband and the most perfect father a woman could want, but he did have his amusing foibles.

"Hey, what's all this racket?"

"Hi, Dad!" Regina quickly wiped the smile from her face and gave her father a hug.

"A man tries to get some work done, and he's interrupted by two cackling females." Bob grinned. "Okay, two beautiful, talented, intelligent cackling females."

"Good save, honey," Joan praised, patting her husband on the back. "Now how about you let Regina set the table and come help me peel these potatoes."

"We're having mashed potatoes?" Bob said, his voice rising in excitement. "I am one lucky man. Gorgeous women and mashies. Just remember I like them without any lumps."

Regina grinned slyly. "Your women or your potatoes?"

After her mother had cleared the table for dessert and coffee, Regina decided the time was right to tell her parents about Will Creeden being back in Idlewild. After all, he'd almost been their son-in-law. They had a right to know he was back—that he was now Regina's boss—and they had a right to know from Regina.

"Well," Bob said when Regina had given them the basics of a story that was still fairly sketchy to her. "Well, well, well."

Joan rolled her eyes. "Could you be a little more specific, Bob? Well what?"

Bob shrugged and took a sip of his milky coffee. "Well, I can't say I didn't expect this to happen one day."

"Expect what to happen, Dad?" Regina asked, genuinely confused.

"Are you doing this to torture us?" Joan said. "No, really. I want to know."

"Now, girls, all I mean is that for a long time now—after I got over wanting to tear his head from his shoulders—I've had a good feeling about Will Creeden. About his coming back to Idlewild. And to Regina."

"Oh, Dad! Come on!" Regina cried. "You can't really think Will's here because of me!"

"Really, Bob. Let's not go jumping to conclusions," Joan added, her pleasant face marred by a worried frown. "You, either, honey," she said to her daughter.

Regina huffed. "Don't worry. I won't."

"What about the baby?" Joan asked gently. "A boy, wasn't it?"

Regina took a sip of her own coffee and nodded. "Luke. He'd be about eight now. I'm guessing he's with the wife, in Chicago."

"You're not sure?"

"That's the weird thing, Mom." Regina paused. "Last night, Will showed up at Marty and Cindy's. We all had dinner together and then after the kids had gone to bed, Marty asked Will about Luke. It was . . . awkward, to say the least." Regina smiled sadly. "Will seemed to have been having a good time all night but the minute Luke's name was mentioned he looked like he'd been shot. I mean, I really thought he was going to break down in tears. It was horrible. Anyway, he never answered Marty's questions so. . . ." Regina shrugged. "I know nothing. And I'm certainly not going to pry, not after what I saw happen to Will last night."

Joan sighed. "It's a shame. Clearly, Will's still in pain over the divorce. He must miss that little boy so terribly." Joan shot a look at her husband then turned back to Re-

gina. "Another reason not to get your hopes up about Will. He's in no position to make you any promises."

"Believe me, Mom, I know and I'll be careful," Regina swore. "Frankly, I'm not even really sure how I feel about his being back in Idlewild. I'm . . . well, I'm both happy and upset, I guess." Regina laughed ruefully. "Okay, I'd be lying if I said my heart didn't race, just a bit, when I first saw him. But believe me, there's no way I want to go through the agony of another breakup with Will Creeden."

Bob looked solemnly at the Sutherland women. "You two have no faith," he said. "Sometimes a man just knows things. Or maybe he just has a strong feeling about something. That's all I'm saying. Give the guy a chance. I'm glad Will's back. He's doing the right thing. We'll just give him some time, let him move at his own pace. The man's been through a lot, and we've got to understand that."

"We?" Regina groaned. "Dad, please. Forget about him. Nothing's going to happen between me and Will. One little tingle means nothing. It was probably just shock at running into him—literally!—after eight years. The relationship is over. It's been over for a long, long time."

Bob Sutherland said nothing but gave his daughter a small, secret smile.

"I don't believe him," Regina said, turning to her mother.

"So, is he saying he's gone psychic?" Joan asked, her face still troubled.

"I think I'll give Mr. Creeden a call in a week or two," Bob Sutherland said musingly, ignoring his wife and daughter. "See if he wants to shoot some pool."

# Nine

Regina opened the door to her apartment and was greeted by the yowls of two hungry, slightly annoyed felines.

"Okay, okay," she said, gently pushing her way inside as they slithered between her legs, threatening to send her flying headlong onto the floor. "Mommy can't get your dinner if you don't let her inside," she added, reaching down to give both Nigel and Lucy a quick scratch.

Regina tossed her bag on the couch and with her furry friends attending her every move, walked to the kitchen. "What'll it be tonight, guys?" she said as she surveyed the contents of an overhead cabinet. "Pacific salmon or sliced lamb and rice in gravy? How about some of both?"

Loud and now frantic "meows!" confirmed Regina's choice. When the beasts were noisily well under way and their water bowls had been freshened, Regina grabbed a vapid but totally satisfying magazine she'd bought in a moment of weakness—*In-Style*—and flopped onto the couch. She'd flip through the glossy pages for a while, then head to bed. Talking to her parents earlier about Will's return to Idlewild had been unexpectedly emotionally draining. Maybe because the brief conversation had brought back a flood of memories about those days, then years, just after Will's marriage and move to Chicago. She'd hardly made it home in one piece tonight. At every

traffic light she'd slipped into a dreamlike state, flooded with images and names and events from six, even eight years before. At every light it took the angry, impatient honking of the driver behind her to bring her rudely back to the present.

But now that she was home . . . Regina drew her legs up under her and settled back into the cushions. Nigel and then a moment later Lucy jumped up to join her, busily licking their chops. And before she had made a conscious choice, Regina, magazine forgotten, had slipped off into a reverie.

What was there left to do after that? After Will? Go to New York City. Get the degree she'd planned on getting—with or without Will.

Besides, there seemed no way she couldn't go.

"Are you two trying to throw me out or something?" Regina demanded, sitting on the living room couch, her back straight and her hands flat on her thighs.

Her mother, perched next to her, frowned and patted her daughter's arm.

"Oh, honey, no," she said, her voice honest and momentarily reassuring. "Of course not. Your father and I just want what's best for you."

"What if staying here in Idlewild is best?" Regina countered, her own voice petulant. Like a child's.

"You only live once, Reggie." Mr. Sutherland sighed wisely and settled back further into his favorite deep armchair.

"Well, dear," Joan Sutherland went on, rolling her eyes slightly at her husband, "maybe staying here in Idlewild, getting your master's at the state university in Manderville, *is* best. But I'm just not sure you'll really know that to be true if you don't try life elsewhere, first."

Regina rubbed her temples. "And if I don't like it in

New York? If I hate the city? What if I can't handle the work?" Regina pressed. "What if I flunk out? There are so many incredible minds at Madison University. What if I waste the scholarship?"

"Now, dear . . ."

Mr. Sutherland leaned forward, elbows on his knees, and silenced his family with a raised hand. "Reggie, it's only money. We can make more, you can go to a different school."

There was a moment of silence. And then Regina looked at her mother. And then the two women burst out laughing.

"Bob, since when are you so full of clichés?" Joan chuckled, wiping her eyes.

Regina's father sat back, hurt. "Well, I . . . I just wanted to help . . ." he began.

Regina leapt from the couch and threw her arms around her father. "Oh, Dad, you did help!" she cried. "I'll go to New York. I'll get the degree. And I'll make you both so proud of me!"

"We're already so proud of you, Regina," her mother said softly. "No parents could be prouder."


There were plenty of things about New York City Regina Sutherland liked.

The sidewalks, for one. The hard, hollow sound of her heels on concrete, especially along Fifth Avenue at night, when most of the big, fancy stores were closed and hardly anyone walked from Fifty-ninth Street, where the Plaza Hotel sat in all its palatial magnificence, to Forty-second Street, where the streets always felt public, never private— never like Regina's own.

She liked the sexual energy of the hot summer nights in SoHo and the pleasing freshness of the spring mornings

in the West Village and the bright, white clarity of sunny winter afternoons in midtown Manhattan.

She liked the trees surviving—thriving, even—in tree wells along the curb. She liked the peal of church bells on Sunday mornings. She liked the lurid yellow of the taxis.

Maybe best, she liked the unexpected and powerful sense of community she found in her neighborhood—downtown, at the juncture of SoHo, Tribeca and the West Village.

Coming from a small town, she had small-town prejudices. Even though she'd tramped through Europe for a summer, she'd returned to Idlewild still a small-town girl, still wary of big cities as places of corruption and coldness.

Well, reading Grace Metallious's classic novel, *Peyton Place,* had helped the then seventeen-year-old Regina to abandon her naive view of small-town innocence. And coming to New York City at the age of twenty-one helped her to see and experience the warmth and buoyancy and friendliness of big-city life.

So another thing Regina liked was the fact that everyone who worked behind the counters of her local Korean grocery—open twenty-four hours a day!—and her laundromat, where her huge mound of sheets and towels and T-shirts and jeans were somehow, miraculously, folded into tiny, perfect little squares of clean cotton, and her post office and bagel shop and video store knew her name and her habits. And if Regina had a bad cold and didn't make it to the laundry on Saturday morning, as usual, Mattie, the owner for the past thirty years, would worry and keep her eye peeled for her young customer. And when Regina finally did come staggering in under a massive load of dirty dish towels and bedding and khakis, Monday morning, Mattie would immediately ask if Regina was all right. Tell her that she, Mattie, had been on the verge of coming up

to Regina's door—she lived in the building on the corner, right?—and checking in, seeing if Regina was okay, if she wanted anything, some chicken soup maybe.

And the other people in Regina's building on the corner. . . . She'd been enormously surprised when on the morning after she'd moved in, someone had knocked on her door. A bit fearfully, warily, Regina had asked who was there and peered through the fairly useless peephole.

"It's Mary. I'm your neighbor down the hall. I made some zucchini bread and thought you might like some."

Though the scene was distorted, Regina could make out a dark-haired woman and a big smile and a large square of tin foil being held up to the peephole.

From that day forward, Regina and Mary—and Sal from the third floor and Cary and John from next door—had been more than just passing acquaintances, nodding in the foyer, at the mailboxes, on the stairs. They'd been friends. They looked out for each other. Fed Mary's cats and watered Sal's plants when either was away. Attended Cary and John's seasonal parties. Picked up Regina's mail when she went home for a visit at Christmas and for a week in the spring and one in the summer. Called the police the minute someone spotted anyone—well, dangerous looking—hanging out on the street, or, God forbid, in the halls of the building.

It was good to feel needed and protected. Good to feel part of a small, casual but caring community. In that way, Regina's life in New York was much like her life in Idlewild.

In almost every other way, her life in the Big Apple was new and different. At times exciting, at other times, exhausting. Sometimes exhilarating and at odd moments, frightening.

For two years Regina went to classes and related lectures sponsored by the university's other graduate departments. For twenty-four months she read and studied,

discussed and argued. Stayed up late into the night, drinking bad coffee from a leaky paper cup, crouched over a tome in one of the high-walled carrels reserved for grad students on the library's fifth floor. Bid for time in the school's computer bank when her own laptop unexpectedly crashed. Wrote and rewrote, revised and revised again. Copied on to disks and printed out clean versions of papers. Handed them in, waited for them to be graded, evaluated. Smiled with hard-earned satisfaction when the papers came back with praises scrawled in red or blue ink across the cover sheet.

And when she wasn't engaged in the demanding, grueling and wonderful work of coming to understand the art of poetry, Regina took full advantage of the city. As full advantage as she could take on a student's stipend and the small salary she made from her job as a manuscript reader for Random House. But one of New York's best-kept secrets, Regina discovered, was the wealth of things to do for free. The variety of activities that could be enjoyed by just about anyone, at any but the absolute lowest of economic brackets.

So, Regina visited museums—the Metropolitan Museum of Art, the Museum of Modern Art, the Guggenheim, the Whitney, the Pierpont Morgan. Went to gallery openings at the small, sometimes dingy places where her friends or neighbors had mounted a show of paintings or prints. Attended off-off-Broadway theater, both experimental and traditional, both delightfully moving and embarrassingly bad.

Relaxed on the Great Lawn in Central Park on hot summer evenings and listened to the philharmonic, while sharing cold, sweet grapes and good crusty bread and rich cheeses with colleagues and friends. Sat high up by the ceiling, in the cheapest seats possible, at Lincoln Center's Avery Fisher Hall, listening to opera or marveling at a performance of the American Ballet Theatre.

Took long, long walks, from one end of Manhattan to the other; across the Brooklyn Bridge to the botanic gardens, the museum, and then to Prospect Park, to ride the paddleboats and carousel; along the white sands of Jones Beach on Long Island. Journeyed up to the Bronx—the Bronx!—to visit Wave Hill, a lovely garden on the Hudson River. Shopped in funky secondhand shops in the East Village and very occasionally, splurged with a purchase at Sak's or Barney's.

And the food! Regina marveled. Every kind imaginable, so easily had. Takeout. Order-in. Fast food. Gourmet. Italian, Ethiopian, Thai, Chinese, French, German, creative American. Pumpernickel bagels with fresh olive cream cheese at Essa Bagels in midtown and hot, twisty, salt-covered pretzels from street vendors. Coney Island hot dogs and thick, spicy slices of pepperoni pizza at the corner store on Bleecker Street and Sixth Avenue. Specialty markets that sold produce Regina's mother just couldn't get in Idlewild like Chinese cabbage and some she could get only rarely like broccoli rabe.

And then there were the people. When Regina stopped to think about her life in New York, which she did often, she realized it was the people who made it all so special.

In spite of what big-city snobs liked to believe about all small towns, Idlewild attracted its fair share of people who were . . . different. By which Regina meant not like . . . well, not like what small-town people were supposed to be like, she supposed. Narrow-minded and boring and stupid. True, Idlewild's population was comprised mostly of traditional, two-parent families, middle-class, of either German or English origin and Christian tradition. But there were several Jewish folk, too—enough to support a small but healthy synagogue community. And the college itself attracted a number of kids from across the country, kids whose families hailed originally from China, Africa, even the Dominican Republic.

But no getting around it, those kids were in the minority at Idlewild College. As were Chinese and African- and Dominican-American families in and around the town of Idlewild.

Not being incredibly ethnically diverse didn't make Idlewild a bad place. Regina believed this fervently. Neither did the fact that there was no large or openly gay community. As far as she knew, her hometown had no history of scandal, at least in matters of active discrimination. Idlewild was what it was. It was home. And she loved it.

But New York! For the first month in the city, Regina's head virtually spun with amazement at the sheer number of languages she heard spoken each and every day, on the sidewalk, in the subway, in the halls of the university. At the variety of skin tones and hair colors and clothing styles sported by tall and short, skinny and hefty, dark and light.

At the proud and unabashed men who held each other's hands while strolling through the Union Square Green Market. At the pairs of women who did the same, bringing home fresh muffins and fruit and flowers cut in the country.

Purple hair and body piercings on the twenty-somethings. Drag queens at the Halloween Parade. Women of all ages hurrying along the sidewalks, dressed in regulation corporate blue or black suits, smart, sleek briefcases slung over their shoulders. Old natives of the city, once immigrants, still speaking their mother tongue—never English—trailing shopping wagons alongside privileged kids skateboarding their way to school, baggy pants billowing in the hot breeze blasting from the subway grates. Impeccably groomed Wall Street mavens, on line for the automatic-bank-teller machine, chatting with arty young mothers in leggings and skimpy T-shirts, their smiling babies adorable in funny hats. Society ladies and extreme-sport bike messengers, racing across the avenues. Women in the modest veils

of their religious traditions and women in the shortest shorts imaginable, side by side on the street corner, half lingering, half listening to a grungy man playing percussion on empty, overturned plastic tubs.

And the most amazing thing—the most truly amazing thing—was that no one stared or hissed or laughed at each other. It wasn't that people didn't care about each other. No, Regina had seen firsthand how friendly these New Yorkers were. It was just that no one cared to criticize. Live and let live. Be who you need to be. Be who you are. That was why so many lost souls came to New York City, Regina realized. She'd grown up hearing the myth of magical New York. Hearing stories of so-and-so, who'd always been, well, different, picking up after high school and without a backward glance, clutching a one-way ticket, gotten on an exhaust-bellowing old bus bound for New York.

It was a place of dreams. Not perfect. Not at all! New York was too dirty and expensive. It moved too fast and was too competitive, too full of pretentious, posturing types who by their very presence in the same restaurant could make the less hip cringe, feel improperly dressed and hopelessly overweight and force them to forgo the piece of black forest cake they'd really wanted to order.

Maybe worst of all, the city routinely wore down its hardworking, decent-living inhabitants with the grim and depressing reality of too many homeless, too many angry youths. Too many guns and too much poverty.

Still, bizarrely, there was no denying that it was a place of promise. Of hope. Where whoever you were was just who you were supposed to be. And that was just fine with everyone else.

New York—the mecca for the different. The ultimate destination for the ambitious. Haven for the lonely. Bright lights, twenty-four/seven. Streets paved with gold. If you could make it there, you could make it anywhere.

Living in New York, Regina almost forgot Will.
Almost.


"Regina! Cool! You made it."

Rick grabbed Regina to him and planted a big, wet kiss
on her lips.

There goes my lipstick, Regina thought distastefully, as
she smiled faintly and pulled back from her boyfriend.
The kiss had tasted too much like whiskey for her pleasure.

It had been only two months and already Rick Hayes,
lead guitarist and vocalist for a hot local rock band named
Mood, thought he owned her. Well, to be fair, Regina admitted, he wasn't being possessive, exactly. It was more
like he just assumed she'd be there, whenever, wherever
he wanted her to be.

He was sweet. In a way. But oblivious. Like when he'd
called her the other night at 2:30 A.M. The ringing phone
had torn brutally through her dream, sending her tearing
out of bed for the phone, panicked, angry, disoriented.

It had been Rick. He'd just finished a gig and it was
great and someone said a record producer or scout or
something had been in the club and wasn't that great!

It was great, Regina had agreed. But did he know it
was the middle of the night? And had he remembered that
Regina had a final at 8:00 A.M.? The very next—no, *this*—
morning?

No, Rick really didn't know what time it was. And he
hadn't remembered, and he was sorry, really, and he promised to make it up to her that night. Hang with her, or
something. Get some sushi.

Regina looked around the smoky, dark little club and
spotted an empty table near the back. By the door. When
Rick was dragged off by a band mate, Regina made her
way to it.

Sighing, she sat on the rickety wooden chair and planted her untouched bottle of light beer on the sticky tabletop. Two months ago she'd met Rick at a party thrown by another student in her department, a loud and crowded party in a tiny studio apartment in Little Italy. Rick seemed to have been drawn to her immediately—and she to him. Maybe that was because since coming to New York six months earlier, Regina hadn't been out on a date with anyone. Between enormous amounts of schoolwork and adjusting to a totally new way of life—learning to negotiate the subway was a major task in and of itself!—and setting up a simple but functioning apartment and getting to know her neighbors. . . . Well, Regina told herself repeatedly, there just wasn't time to meet a man, let alone to date him.

There just hadn't been time, though once or twice she'd been introduced to someone by a colleague, at a university function. And once, in the eleventh-floor hallway at Random House, where she'd gone to pick up her weekly reading, she'd spotted a man who, for some reason, made her turn, look. But he'd been getting on an elevator, the door sliding closed rapidly behind him. Now she couldn't even remember what color hair he'd had or how tall he'd been.

So, what had made Rick different? Why had Regina agreed to go out with him? Partly because it had been a long, long time since she'd been held. And kissed. Partly because she couldn't deny her body's strong response to his dark eyes and wide, vibrant smile. And, Regina admitted later, partly because she was a little ashamed, a little embarrassed in front of her new friends. Why wasn't she seeing anyone, Mary had asked, over and over, worrying about Regina's happiness like a mother hen. And then at the party, Regina's colleague Gail had encouraged her—well, almost dared her, actually—to go over to Rick. To flirt and smile and talk.

"What do you have to lose?" Gail had asked. "Oh!"

Her hand had flown to her mouth. "I'm sorry. You do date men, don't you?"

No question. It was time to take a step. Get back into the world of men and women and relationships.

And once she'd made the decision to flirt and smile and talk, she'd discovered that Rick was really nice. Smart, though maybe not school-educated. Sweet, though maybe a bit self-centered. But wasn't that the way with all artists, Regina told herself philosophically. If you wanted to date an artist, you had to accept certain facts, like groupies waiting outside the house and absentmindedness inside the house and creative self-absorption just about everywhere.

When Regina was ready to leave the party, Rick offered to walk her home. She found the gesture charming—and alarming. He'd walk her home—and then what? Would he expect to be invited inside? Upstairs? Would he. . . .

But she'd swallowed her nerves and reminded herself that Will Creeden was at this very moment probably in bed, in his wife's arms. And that even though the only man she'd been with since she was seventeen was Will Creeden, she was not a child. She was a woman. A smart, responsible woman, fully equipped with the ability to say no. Firmly, if necessary.

She hadn't had to say no. Rick had walked her to the front door of her building. He hadn't held her hand along the way, though at one point he'd taken her elbow and gently tugged her back from the curb as a car sped by. Now he smiled and asked if she'd like to meet the next day some time, for coffee maybe or pastry somewhere, maybe at Cafe Grande Artiste on Greenwhich Avenue or Tea and Sympathy.

Regina had smiled back, surprised, impressed, pleased. Rick took her number, promised to call—and then lightly, quickly, kissed her on the cheek.

Two months ago.

Regina sighed again and crossed her legs under the small table. Rick was okay, really, she thought. He wasn't the problem. He was sweet and talented and truly in awe of her work in literature, even though he didn't quite understand that her work actually was *work*.

And he was cute. No doubt about that. Regina leaned a bit to the right to catch a glimpse of Rick through the ever-growing crowd of hip students and artists and locals. It wasn't hard. Rick stood out. He was tall, but not too tall. Perfect for hugging. Thin but not too thin. In other words, sexy without being wimpy. Let's face it, she thought, the man has a butt to die for. "To die for"—one of the phrases she'd picked up since living in New York.

The man's hands were perfect—strong, well-sculpted, skilled at coaxing incredible music from his guitar and from Regina. His eyes were a decadently rich brown. His hair, the same deep color as his eyes, waved back from his forehead and cheeks, cut just right, not too full, not too short. Thick enough for Regina to grab when he trailed kisses down her stomach and then. . . .

No, the problem definitely wasn't Rick, Regina thought, taking a small swallow of the beer. The problem was her.

The problem was always her.

Put another way, she thought, as Mood began to tune up, the problem was that no one ever was Will.

A little over six months after she'd met—and broken up with—Rick Hayes, Regina met another man. Well, she had met lots of men in the interim—at school, at friends' apartments—but no one interesting or appealing enough to make her take notice—and make her take action.

Eric Harrison was as different from Rick Hayes as day is from night. Where Rick was dark, Eric was blond and blue-eyed. Where Rick was charmingly irresponsible, Eric

was devoutly responsible. Where Rick was a struggling musician, barely able to make rent the first of each month, Eric was a lawyer, three years out of Princeton, specializing in corporate real estate, making a big name for himself at one of the top firms in the city, and the proud new owner of a duplex condo in a high-rise on Seventy-fifth Street and First Avenue.

Eric's family had money and they'd made it the old-fashioned way. His grandfather had founded and run a printing company for almost forty years before selling it for a very tidy sum.

Eric's father, Stephen, was also a lawyer, partner in a large and respectable firm that counted several giants of the financial world and even a few of the more sophisticated, monied celebrities as its clients. To Mr. Harrison Sr. work came first, family and all other duties and pleasures second and third. He wasn't a bad parent, just a fairly absent one.

That was okay, because Mrs. Harrison was the on-duty, on-call parent, a stay-at-home mother who could easily have afforded to hire a nanny but who never saw the need. She liked the work of parenting. She liked being the kind of mother who greeted her children when they came home from school, liked preparing their afternoon snacks and listening to their lessons after dinner. What she liked less was waiting for her husband, who loved her, she knew, to come home, exhausted, with barely enough energy to kiss his wife on the forehead and mumble a question about the children before collapsing into bed. But Samantha Harrison was as committed to her job as Stephen Harrison was to his, and together they made a strong and united team.

Regina had been slightly intimidated by the Harrisons the first few times she and Eric joined them for dinner, either at a quiet, classy restaurant or at the family's Upper East Side apartment. Both Stephen and Samantha had

earned graduate degrees at prestigious universities, regularly attended charity events at various museums, and hobnobbed with the rich and powerful of Manhattan and the Hamptons. Their younger son, Eric, was a successful attorney and their older son, Frederick, a successful broker with a beautiful wife, a toddler, a baby on the way, a tastefully decorated house in Sag Harbor and a highly desired loft in Tribeca.

But Eric's parents were what Regina's father would call "real people," not interested in putting friends or colleagues at a social disadvantage, not wanting a guest to feel uncomfortable or ill-at-ease. They were unfailingly congenial, interested in Regina's work at the university, in her parents, in her feelings for their son. Regina soon learned to enjoy time spent with the Harrisons and came to look upon them as friends. And when Eric began to talk, occasionally and lightly, about marriage, Regina felt a surge of happiness at the prospect of having Stephen and Samantha as her in-laws.

Briefly, she wondered how Eric would like her parents as in-laws and decided that Eric would be the luckiest son-in-law alive.

For a time, everything seemed just fine. Maybe more than fine. Perfect. Eric treated Regina with respect and kindness. She responded with warmth and appreciation. He brought her coral roses every Monday. She went to his firm's softball games and cheered him on whenever he came to bat. They fell into a routine of seeing Eric's parents every Sunday for brunch, and sometimes during the week for dinner. They spent two fun-filled weekends at Fred and Sally's house in Sag Harbor.

Sometimes, with all the socializing, Regina had to cancel getting together with one of her friends or stay up until two in the morning to get her work properly done. But being with Eric, being a part of his world, was worth the

small sacrifices she had to make: losing touch with a few good friends, falling slightly behind in her studies.

Trouble came when Regina's faculty adviser told her she'd been chosen to attend an important conference. A conference at which she would read a paper she'd submitted to the MLA for publication. A paper that had been chosen to appear in the next issue of the journal.

She had a month to prepare. To extend her research, be ready to answer difficult questions the learned audience might pose, argue her case eloquently, and convince her listeners of her considered views.

It was an enormous privilege to be chosen to read. And to be published! She was only in the master's program, not even a full Ph.D. candidate yet.

Regina was going places.

Eric wasn't sure he wanted to go with her. Or maybe it was that he didn't want her to go at all. That was more like it, Regina thought.

Preparing for the conference required extra hours in the library, at her computer. It meant she had to cancel at least half of each week's social commitments.

"Just for this month," Regina explained. Again. "I can't go to Atlanta unprepared. My reputation is on the line here."

The argument had escalated slowly, over two weeks or more. Regina made concessions where she could. After all, she loved Eric. Not with an overwhelming passion or energy, but she cared for him, cared about him. Their love-making was basic and comfortable and required very little of Regina, herself—body or soul. Though sometimes she wished she felt more intensely about Eric—or that he felt more erotically about her—it didn't really matter. Not in the scheme of things.

Anyway, she liked the Harrisons and missed their company, too. But surely they understood? There was a limit to how much time she could spend away from her work

and keep her professional commitments. At least Eric should understand. His own father spent an extraordinary number of hours at the office. . . .

"But my mom's waiting for him when he gets home. I work long hours and when I get home, you're still at work. When I have free time, which isn't often, you're not available."

Regina considered before she spoke. Even bit her tongue so she wouldn't blurt something she'd regret. "Eric," she said slowly, keeping control, "are you saying that it's not all right for me to have a career—one that sometimes requires intense concentration and odd hours—because I'm a woman?"

Eric didn't speak immediately.

"There's a very important client dinner next Thursday," he said finally. "All the attorneys are bringing their spouses or fiancées. Or girlfriends. It's really important to me that you be there, Regina."

Regina felt her stomach go cold. This couldn't be happening. It couldn't be ending this way.

"Eric," she whispered. "I'm leaving for the conference next Thursday morning. You know that. I can't make the dinner. I'm sorry."

Eric sat forward on the secondhand upholstered chair Regina had bought at a flea market the summer before. He looked down at his expensive, highly buffed, leather wing tips. "Is that what you'll say when we're married?" he asked. "I'm sorry, I can't, I have a prior commitment?"

"Eric, what do you want from me?" Regina demanded, kneeling on the scarred wood floor before him.

"A woman who's always there," he said simply. "Who will sacrifice her own life for me. And our children. Like my mother did for my father and me and Frederick."

Regina shook her head. "That's unreasonable. I mean, I want to be like your mother, of course. She's kind and generous. But I also want to be like me. I need to be who

I am. I'm a scholar. And I'm going to be a teacher. You knew that about me," Regina said quietly. "You knew that."

Eric raised his head. Looked at Regina with an expression of puzzlement. And pain.

"I knew. But I didn't know that it's not what I want. What you are. Someone with a career. . . ."

"A passion," Regina corrected. "A need."

"Whatever. . . ."

"Not 'whatever'!" Regina cried, rising to her feet. "It's not about money with me. Or expense accounts or power. It's about words. About stories and poems. It's about art. It's about opening young minds to the beauty of the written word. Why can't a woman be a good wife and mother and care passionately about those things? It doesn't make sense, Eric. It just doesn't make sense."

Eric stood. "Maybe you're right, Regina. Maybe I'm hopelessly old-fashioned or just being dumb about all this. But I can't come second. I'm sorry."

He showed up one night, about two weeks after the conference. Regina was surprised. She hadn't expected ever to see or hear from Eric again. She'd spent time getting used to that idea and now. . . .

It was late. She'd been watching a movie she'd rented earlier that afternoon. An old Katherine Hepburn movie she'd been only half focused on. Mary had brought her dinner, just in case, she'd said, Regina didn't feel up to cooking. A healthy portion of pasta—Mary's own homemade noodles—with a traditional sauce of black olives, red peppers and anchovies. For dessert, a thick slice of cherry pie, also homemade. It was important, Mary said, for Regina to eat, to keep up her strength. So far, Regina hadn't touched the food.

She let him in, wishing she were wearing something

neater, more appealing than ratty old jeans and one of her father's forgotten T-shirts.

"Hi," he said, shyly.

"Hi."

"How was the conference?" he asked then, his face coloring slightly. "I thought about you."

Regina gave a small smile. "Thanks. It was good. Tough but good. The paper was well received."

"Oh, Regina." Eric rushed to her, grabbed her up and held her tightly against him. She could feel him harden, hear his breathing becoming heavier. "I'm so sorry. I don't know what made me leave you. I've thought about it. Really thought about it, for weeks. I think I can change. No, I *have* changed."

"Eric?" Regina pulled away from him, stepped back out of his arms. Folded her own arms across her middle. "Who did you take to that dinner? The one I couldn't go to?" she asked calmly.

Eric shoved his hand through his hair. "Wha—? Well, I—"

"You didn't go alone, Eric," Regina said sadly. "I know that."

He stood as if completely confused. Regina thought she should help him.

"You made me feel like some sort of freak, Eric," she said simply. "I don't like you for that." Briefly— unwittingly—she thought of Will. He'd believed in her, supported her. Saw nothing unusual or odd in her passionate desire for both family and work.

"But," she went on, "you deserve to get what you want. Or need. Everybody does. I'm sure you found a nice substitute for me that night. Someone better for you than me. Someone who wants only you and nothing else."

Eric hung his head. He looks like a naughty boy, Regina thought, a ten-year-old who's been caught snatching candy from the five-and-dime.

"What can I say?" he mumbled.

"Nothing. There's nothing to say. Good luck, Eric."

When he'd gone, Regina rewound the Hepburn movie and started it again. Poured herself a glass of wine, heated Mary's wonderful pasta and prepared a loaf of garlic bread.

It was going to be okay.


New York. It was a miracle and a challenge and finally, a very good, cherished memory. Because at the end of Regina's last semester, when she'd been awarded a master's degree in literature, when she'd been accepted into the Ph.D. programs at several prestigious universities, she knew it was time to go home.

"But, Regina," John pleaded. "C'mon. I'm supposed to believe you're going to be happy in that sleepy little town after spending the past two years in New York! This is the city that never sleeps. Idlewild probably rolls up the sidewalks at nine P.M."

"Eight, actually," Regina quipped. But John was right. She was taking a risk moving home. And as she got older—she was twenty-three now—Regina felt less and less that she had the energy or the desire to go into a life decision armed with the convenient out of knowing she could simply reverse her steps, backtrack, pretend she'd never gotten off the right path in the first place.

She was only twenty-three, but Regina Sutherland felt it was time to settle down.

# Ten

It was only five-thirty in the afternoon and Will had been at it for only two hours, but already he wanted to throw himself on the couch he'd bought just last week, open a beer and turn on the TV. Unpacking was hell, and he'd thought packing was bad. Why couldn't he just dump everything out of the boxes and let it lay where it fell? Eventually he'd find everything he needed. Eventually everything would sort itself out, make it to the proper drawer or shelf or closet. Right?

Wrong. Will stretched, decided to have a beer anyway and vowed he'd keep working until. . . . Well, for a while, at least. Until maybe he heard Regina come home. If that didn't happen any time soon, until a good football game came on or a good, mindless adventure movie maybe. He was tired and a bit overwhelmed by the fact that he was here, back in Idlewild, after all these years. A bit nervous about the semester to come. And as always, haunted by thoughts of the child he'd left behind.

Yeah, a night of macho shoot-'em-up action sounded highly relaxing. He'd just be sure not to mention his proclivity for cheese spread, extra-salt pretzels, Chuck Norris and Arnold Schwarzenegger to his more sophisticated—let's be real—his more uptight colleagues.

Will took a swig from the bottle and looked around at the chaos that was his new home. It was a great apartment,

he thought. Top floor, which didn't bother him a bit. Walking several flights of stairs a day couldn't hurt his aerobic capacity any. The view from the living room in front wasn't anything to write home about, just the other side of Maple Street—more three- and four-story brick apartment buildings and a few Victorian-style homes, all now converted to multifamily dwellings. But from the back, from his bedroom, Will could see the not-so-distant hills ringing the town, hills now beginning to blaze orange, yellow and red. The kitchen and dining area were small, but Will figured he wouldn't be throwing very many dinner parties, so what did it matter? His only point of contention was with the bathroom, which, for some unfathomable reason, had never been modernized. The faucets and other fixtures had to be thirty, forty years old, at least, and if the kitchen sink was any indication, Will suspected the water pressure in the shower was not always what it should be. Not a selling point for a guy who needed to feel the hot water pounding on his neck and back each morning before he could face the world.

Still, the apartment had one overwhelmingly positive feature, for which he would gladly forgo good water pressure. The apartment was one floor upstairs from Regina Sutherland's apartment.

Will picked up the box cutter and sliced open another carton. He tossed aside the top layer of crumpled newspaper and looked inside. Memorabilia, he realized. Stuff he'd saved from high school and college days. A box he hadn't opened since his marriage and move to Chicago. Yearbooks, a pennant from a homecoming game, a few ticket stubs and some photos shoved in a yellowing envelope.

Maybe this box was better left intact, Will thought, hesitating to dig any further. Maybe now was just not the right time to delve into the past, so soon after having met and

spoken with Regina. So soon after almost breaking down in front of her at the mention of his son's name.

Maybe he should let the box sit for a while, a few weeks or so, until he was more settled in Idlewild, more sure of where he stood with Regina. Until he could stand the memories, if memories were all he would ever have.

Will began to fold the cardboard flaps over the top of the open box. Then he spotted it, one fragile bit of his past, peeking through a wrapping of tissue paper. He couldn't resist. Gently, so as not to further damage the already imperfect piece, he lifted the tissue paper package from the box. Brought it over to the kitchen and laid it reverently on the counter. Took a deep breath and slowly began to pull away the sheets of crumpled tissue.

And there it was. A delicate ring of dried flowers, more fragile now than it had been when the blooms were fresh and the vines green. Now it was a pale, brittle thing but still beautiful. It had lost its color and scent, true, but the circlet was still brimming with the essence of Regina. Still a token of the love he had born her. The love he bore her still.

Will turned the crown over in his hands, remembering the care he'd taken to weave it from grapevines and fresh flowers. It had been a labor of love, Will cursing himself with every misstep, his clumsy fingers awkward with the soft, live blossoms. But he'd wanted no help, asked for none, and finally, at the end of a very long evening, it was finished. Maybe not a thing of beauty in and of itself, but surely, resting on Regina's glorious mane of hair, a vision to hold close forever.

He placed the crown back in the center of the tissue paper and sighed. He'd given it to Regina the next morning—the day of the Idlewild Fall Fair, the day Regina played Ophelia in the mad scene from *Hamlet.* She'd cried when he'd given it to her, knowing more than anyone how difficult it must have been for Will, not the most creative

fellow with anything not intellectual, to craft this gift. It was the best gift she'd ever received, she'd said through blue eyes crystal with tears. She'd treasure it always and forever.

The following June, just before Regina had departed for Europe, Will had found the circlet on the top of her dresser in her bedroom. He'd picked it up, amazed he'd fashioned such a thing, sure it would have fallen completely apart by now. "Will?" Startled, he'd turned to find Regina looking at him, her packing momentarily forgotten. "It's still the best gift I've ever received," she said, her voice low. "It always will be." He'd shrugged in return, briefly wondering again, for the millionth time, how she could be leaving him for six weeks, why she hadn't been able to agree to their marriage immediately. When he'd said nothing, Regina had continued. "Why don't you keep that for me while I'm gone, okay? Just until I get back. I'll think of my crown and know it's in safe keeping." She'd paused and come to him, drawn him close. "And when I return, you can give it to me again. And I can say thank-you again," she'd added, kissing his cheek, then moving to his lips.

Whoa, not the place to go. There'd been just too much loss all around, Will thought, folding the tissue paper over the crown. Too much letting go. Remembering those last days with Regina was more than he could tolerate just yet. Better to push the memories away when they rose to make his heart ache. Take things slowly.

As if to confirm his self-protective instincts, his doorbell rang, further bringing him back to the present. Back to reality. "Who could that be?" he mumbled, crossing to the door. And then, in a flash, "Regina! Who else do I really know here anymore?" Will hurried his final steps, momentarily sorry he'd made such a mess with the empty boxes, tossed them haphazardly over the room, not broken them down, neatly stacked and tied them with twine. Fi-

nally, he reached for the doorknob, pulled open the door. . . .

"Celia. Oh. It's you."

"Well," she said dryly, an eyebrow cocked, "that's not exactly the reception I was hoping for." She took a step forward, gently brushing past Will and into the apartment. "But it'll do. For now."

Will shook his head and closed the door, trying to re-orient himself, remember his manners. "I'm sorry, Celia," he said, an awkward half laugh escaping his lips, making him feel like a dopey teenager. "It's just . . . I was un-packing. . . ."

Celia perched on the arm of the futon and smiled slowly. "It sounds to me like you were sitting around ex-pecting someone else to suddenly appear at your door."

Will attempted a look that said no way and nervously stuck his hands in the front pockets of his jeans. Okay, Celia wasn't the visitor he'd have preferred, but still, she was a guest and a colleague, and he'd better get his act together, and fast. Stop acting like an immature idiot. Be-sides, he'd have to be a stone—and he wasn't—not to see just how attractive his guest looked just then: long, shapely legs crossed, black tights, short skirt and knee-high, calf-hugging, high-heeled boots. She was the stuff of most men's fantasies. And though Will had no intention of get-ting involved with Celia Keene—none—what was the harm in enjoying the innocent companionship of a sexy woman? Especially one his intellectual equal.

He laughed again, casually, more believably now. "What brings you to my hovel?" he asked, moving toward the kitchen. "Want a beer? I've got some wine, too. Or water. . . ."

"A glass of wine would be nice," she interrupted. "If you're sure I'm not bothering you."

Will uncorked the bottle of Chardonnay with a *pop!* and carefully poured out a glass. Good thing he'd found

the box with his kitchen supplies this morning, he thought, making his way across the mess to Celia. "It's not too cold, so it should be perfect," he said.

Celia reached out for the glass, her small, slim fingers brushing his, ever so briefly closing over his hand for a moment. "Thanks." She grinned. "Just the way I like it."

"In a glass?" Will joked, stepping back to the kitchen for his own already opened beer. Humor. The way to go was humor. It kept people away and it allowed people in, depending on how you used it. Okay, Celia was very sexy—which was nice, very nice—but she was one of those women who made Will just a little too nervous, made him feel like he was in a locked room with a very pretty but very dangerous wild animal, like he was in way over his head, playing a game of which he didn't know all the rules. Not that he couldn't handle himself, he thought, grabbing the bottle and taking a big swallow, as if to prove his assertion. He was just a little out of practice was all. He thought of how uncomfortable Celia had made him at his first staff meeting, causing him to fumble his words, lose his train of thought, almost forget to introduce her.

The thought of the meeting pulled him up short. And for God's sake, Will, he told himself, as he turned back to the room, Celia Keene is a colleague. Technically, he was her boss; she, the most junior level member of his staff. Their professional positions alone would protect him, if for some reason things got out of hand. Will Creeden took his professional and related ethical responsibilities seriously.

Celia took a sip of her wine, raising her eyes above the glass and looking at him. "So, any plans for this evening?" she asked when she'd lowered the glass.

"No. Well, more unpacking, if you can call housework plans in the way I think you mean it," Will said, his back against the counter.

Celia smiled and shook her head. "I don't think so. Why don't you come out with me? See what this sleepy little town has to offer in the way of nightlife." Celia took another sip of wine and crossed her legs in the opposite direction, giving Will another view of physical perfection. "I was planning to do it on my own, but then I thought, since we're both new here, really, why not have a partner? After all," she added, a slow grin forming on her lovely lips, "everything's more fun with a partner."

Suddenly, the temperature in the apartment seemed to soar and Will felt a strange trickle of sweat on the back of his neck. Okay, he could handle her, he thought, but he'd far prefer to do it in public. Not in the confines of this place. Face it, he was way more out of practice fending off wild females than he'd realized. Several years of marriage and then long months of caring for a dying son had kept him out of the social scene, rendered his confidence shaky.

"Sure," he blurted, looking away from her pinning gaze. "But I don't want to stay out for long. You know, first day of classes tomorrow and all. A man needs his beauty sleep," he added feebly. So much for humor.

Celia rose and finished off the wine. "Fine. We'll go to Idlewild's one and only art-film house, that little place on Plum Street. What is it called? The Boulevard. We'll see the new Jaramusch movie and have a cappuccino. And I promise to have you home safe and sound by bedtime. Okay?"

Will gulped. "Okay."


"That movie really was amazing," Will said, setting his empty espresso cup in its saucer. "Thanks for dragging me out tonight. Once the semester gets started," he added, carefully choosing his words, "who knows when I'll have time to just hang with a colleague."

Celia leaned forward across the small marble table and grinned. "All work and no play," she breathed. "You know what that brings, don't you?"

Will raised an eyebrow. "A raise and promotion? Tenure?"

Celia sat back and inclined her head. "Touché, Dr. Creeden. I'll be sure to keep my play hours to an absolute minimum. Or, at least, I'll be sure to keep them secret."

Will laughed. "Good. Remember, I might not look particularly frightening, but I am the big bad boss. I don't want my very first duty on the job to be reporting you to the disciplinary board for slacking off and ignoring your duties to the department."

They sat at one of the ten or so tables at the far end of the theater lobby. Some time after Will had left Idlewild, the owner of the one and only theater that showcased foreign or so-called arty films had decided to cash in on the seemingly universal coffee craze. Mr. Philip Leitch opened a small café where theatergoers could enjoy a variety of overpriced coffees, pastries, fruit juices and small sandwiches. The Boulevard's loyal clientele had immediately patronized the café, some would say with a vengeance. After three years, Mr. Leitch was still doing a brisk business. All except one of the tables were occupied.

"I won't forget, sir," Celia replied, pouting. "From this moment on I'll unquestioningly obey your every command and grant your every wish, meet your every need and anticipate your every desire. . . ."

Will held up his hand and smirked. "Let's just start with your showing up for your classes, okay?"

Celia's eyes widened and for a moment, Will thought she was going to cry. She looked just like a small child rebuffed by her favorite uncle—and Will felt himself tighten, harden. Crap. Was he going to fall for this sensitive-woman-in-distress thing? Besides, even if his answer had been curt, he was just trying to

keep things on a friendly, almost impersonal level. She was the one who turned his every remark into something suggestive or leading.

Damn, but she looked so vulnerable. Why did he have to be so uptight, such a hardnose? They'd been having a good enough time before he'd acted like a jerk.

"Celia," he began, reaching across the table for her hand. "I'm—"

"Will. Hey."

Will withdrew his hand from Celia's as if it had been burnt. "Marty. Cindy. Hey." Silently, he cursed the fact that his voice sounded artificially bright, falsely casual. Guilty almost. He stood. "Have a seat, won't you? I'll pull another chair over from—"

"That's okay, Will," Marty said shortly. "We're on our way. I've still got to drive the baby-sitter home."

"We just wanted to stop and say hi," Cindy added with a smile. She looked expectantly at Will and for one horrible moment he didn't know what the heck she was waiting for.

"Oh, yes," he blurted, still standing. "This is Dr. Celia Keene. She's just joined the English department. We . . . we were just at the movie." Will gestured wildly at the lobby. Then he dropped his arm and smiled weakly.

"Very nice to meet you, Dr. Keene." Cindy—ever gracious Cindy—reached to shake Celia's hand and Will breathed for what seemed like the first time since the Barneses had arrived.

"Celia, please." Celia shook Cindy's hand in return and favored the husband and wife with a cool but perfectly polite smile. "And you are?"

Will sensed Marty bristling again and broke in. "Ha ha. Where are my manners," he said stupidly. "Celia, meet Marty and Cindy Barnes. We went to Idlewild College together."

"Regina Sutherland, too," Marty added, nodding a re-

luctant greeting in Celia's direction. "She's still a good friend of ours."

Will felt his anger begin to rise. And I'm not your friend, is that it, he thought. What the hell was happening here? What right did Marty have to be so rude to Celia? To act like Will was committing a crime by sitting in a public place having a cup of coffee with someone. A woman. A woman not Regina.

But Celia was equal to the occasion. She smiled vaguely, shook her head once, and then, as if suddenly remembering a small and unimportant detail, said, "Oh, yes, of course. Ms. Sutherland. She seems very nice."

Poor Cindy, Will thought, as he watched her smile falter just the slightest bit. "Well," she said, "Marty and I really have to be going. It was nice meeting you, Dr. . . . Celia. Good seeing you, too, Will. Marty?"

Cindy took her husband's arm. "Yeah, see you around," he said as his wife hurried him off to the lobby exit.

With a huge sigh, Will dropped into his seat. He was stricken by his old friend's condemnatory attitude, grateful for Cindy's social grace. Worse, he was embarrassed. Mortified to learn that he'd not been forgiven for what he'd done to Regina. That if Cindy trusted him now, after all the time that had gone by, Marty still did not. Even after the four of them, Will, Regina, Marty and Cindy had spent an amicable evening together at the Barneses' home. Marty had immediately thought the worst of Will. Probably thought he'd abandoned his child. Assumed he was out on a date with another woman.

But wait. First of all, there could be no "other" woman because at this very moment, there was no primary woman. At least not officially. Will might want Regina but he didn't have her yet. So he was free to spend time with whomever he pleased. Especially a colleague. Was it his fault this particular colleague was a beautiful woman? Was he breaking some kind of law about catching

a movie and a cup of expensive coffee after six o'clock in the evening with a female colleague, when both, as far as he knew, were single? And when he, at least, had absolutely no intention of getting physically involved?

What was Marty's problem, anyway? He'd acted like he was Regina's overprotective father—

"Uh, Will? Your friends might have gone, but I'm still here."

Will snapped his head around to look at Celia. "Oh. Yeah. Look, I'm sorry about Marty," he said. "I . . ."

Celia shrugged. "I'm used to it. To that kind of reaction, I mean, suspicious and all, when someone sees me with another woman's man. What confuses me, though, Will," she went on, tilting her head and studying him, "is that I was under the impression you weren't involved. Have you been holding out on me? Keeping a deep, dark secret?"

Oh, boy. That question hit too close to home. But he was not about to discuss his feelings for Regina Sutherland—or his goal to win her back—with this woman he hardly knew. He hadn't been out of the game so long as to realize how stupid a mistake that would be.

"No," he lied, his voice firm. "No, there's no secret. And I'm sorry for Marty's rudeness." Will sighed and ran a hand through his hair. "And look, Celia, I'm sorry for being such a jerk before. It's just . . . I'm a little tired and strung out. I'm under a lot of pressure."

For a second time, Will reached for Celia's hand. This time, he held on. "What a night you've had." He shook his head. "You must think I'm a real jerk. You shouldn't have to deal with my bad moods." Will withdrew his hand and sat back. "Let's call it a night, okay? I'll drive you home."

Celia folded her arms on the table and looked carefully at him. Again, Will felt himself tighten as he waited for her to speak. And waited. She held his gaze and when he thought he couldn't take it any longer, she spoke.

"You're a very special man, Will Creeden," she said, her voice low. "Are you sure I can't persuade you to prolong the evening?"

For one damning second Will wanted to say yes, to stay with her, to follow where the night might take them. It had been a long time since he'd been with a woman. Too long. Since before his divorce from Connie. But then, as he knew it must, the better part of him took control and he shook his head. "Thanks, Celia. For the compliment and the offer." He stood and put on a goofy smile. "But I turn into a pumpkin at precisely 11:34 every night."

And then his anger at Marty's suspicions flared. He wasn't going to let anyone make his decisions for him, ever again. He'd make a friend of Celia if he wanted. To hell with his so-called old buddy. "How about I take a rain check, okay?"

She smiled. "It's a deal."

# Eleven

At exactly six o'clock, eastern standard time, the alarm clock on the night table beside the bed sounded loudly, at which point a horrible grumbling was heard from beneath the blue-and-purple paisley comforter, hanging half off the right side of the mattress.

That frightening and almost masculine noise was Regina Sutherland coming reluctantly to life. Long gone were the days when she would bound energetically from the peace of sleep and the coziness of bed to greet the new day. About fifteen years gone. Now, at thirty years of age, and for some reason she just could not—or did not want—to understand, morning came just too early for her taste. Even when she'd gone to bed at a reasonable hour, as she had the night before. Just one more hour of sleep. . . .

"Oh, ugh, blah . . ." Regina flailed until her hand turned off the offending alarm clock, knocking it off the night table in the process. Good thing her bedroom was carpeted. She'd have lost an awful lot of small electronic time-telling devices otherwise.

The first day of classes. Not a day to be late to work. Definitely a day to consume a full two cups of the strong black coffee she preferred. Regina sat on the edge of the bed for a moment before standing, getting her bearings, blinking away sleep. She shivered, feeling now the chilly

morning air that crept in through the partially open window. Fresh air, Regina thought mechanically. A good thing, good for your health . . . that's what her father always said.

Regina reached for her robe—also on the floor—and pulled it on. Then she stood, finally, belted the purple terry-cloth garment around her waist and slipped into the matching purple slippers. Both had been a gift from her parents the Christmas before last. She spared a glance at the two furry beasts at the foot of her bed, still deep in sleep, and grunted.

Out of the bedroom. Into the bathroom, where Regina managed to avoid looking in the mirror. It was a good thing she wasn't seriously involved with a man, she often thought. How could anyone stand to look at her in the morning, hair a wild bush on top of her head, face slightly swollen, skin paler than usual and eyes red. Ugh! Of course, she supposed that if the man loved her—was in love with her—he wouldn't mind. Or if he did mind, wasn't totally thrilled with her morning appearance and grumpiness, he'd have the kindness not to say anything about it. The kindness to hide his true feelings. Regina smiled as she shuffled to the kitchen.

Beans ground, coffee-press cleaned and waiting, water boiling, Regina was beginning to feel somewhat alive. Halfway through her first cup of the French roast, she began to feel the excitement that always came with the first official day of the fall semester. It was an excitement she'd felt first on her own inaugural day of kindergarten, and every first day since. New school shoes, stiff and shiny. New pencils, #2, tall and yellow, sharpened and packed carefully in her pencil case. Notebooks with clean, not-yet-grimy pages. Folders in red and green, and blue binders that pinched the fingers. Pink erasers in the shape of hearts and stars. Bic brand pens, blue ink.

True, the first day of a new semester was now a lot

more complex than it had been when she was a kid. Being an adult and a teacher saw to that. But it was also more exciting in its own way. It was the first day of a new season of challenge and hard but rewarding work. It was a day for anticipating pleasures, like having a particularly gifted student sign up for one of her classes. A day for hoping that she would be granted the opportunity to coach a poor or average student into making great strides, finding his or her own strengths. True, she didn't relish the sometimes boring interdepartmental meetings, or the—thankfully—few times she'd been involved in the disciplining of a student who'd committed plagiarism, wittingly or unwittingly, or who'd cheated on a test. And she didn't know any faculty member who actually enjoyed holding regular office hours. Most times, kids avoided stopping by to chat with a teacher like they'd avoid the plague or being seen with their parents at a movie on Saturday night. It seemed they only came when there was a problem—a forgotten deadline, trouble at home that was causing trouble in the classroom, a dog that'd eaten a paper. Only once in a rare while did a student come by during a teacher's office hours to talk about the work in an interested, enthusiastic way.

Still, Regina thought, as she took a corn muffin out of the toaster oven where it had been warming, she loved her job and looked forward to each new semester.

"Well, there you are, sleepyheads!" Nigel and Lucy had finally made their appearance, lured, no doubt, by the smell of the corn muffin, the smell of butter. Regina suspected she lived with the only two cats in existence who didn't wake their human companion at an ungodly hour, demanding to be fed, sticking a sharp nail into a lip, standing on a windpipe, sitting on a face.

The cats meowed and rubbed against Regina's legs, twining in and out, threatening to send her flying as she prepared their breakfast. A small bit of Tender Vittles,

mixed with another small bit of wet food. Fresh water, though she knew Nigel would rather eat mice than drink water. A tiny bit of butter on a finger for each to lick. Lucy liked cream cheese better, but this morning, she wasn't complaining.

After breakfast, a once-over of the kitchen, a rapid straightening of the bedroom. Then shower, makeup, hair. Choosing her clothes and a few pieces of jewelry to complement the outfit. Her papers had been in order, packed in her black leather bag, since the night before.

Regina was just fastening an earring when the doorbell rang. "Who could that be?" she mumbled, padding across the living room in her stocking feet, smoothing the skirt of her gray, lightweight wool suit as she walked. "Who is it?" she called, simultaneously grasping the doorknob and opening the door.

"Oh!" Regina stood frozen, mouth open, hand still clutching the doorknob.

"Uh, can I come in?" he asked. "It's kind of cold out here."

"What? Oh, yeah, sure. Come in." Regina stepped back, certain now she was blushing, and let Will pass.

Will Creeden was wearing a towel. And nothing else. Unless you could count soap as clothing and Regina was pretty sure you couldn't.

"I bet you're wondering what I'm doing here like this," he said. Sheepishly. Holding the edge of the towel at his waist. Hair soaped and sculpted into a wild mane. Water droplets gleaming through the dark hair of his chest. And his stomach.

Yes, that was the word, Regina thought. Sheepish. He looked sheepish and adorable and irresistible, too. Sexy. Mischievous. Suddenly, she could think of lots of words to describe the way Will looked at that moment.

Regina smiled and folded her arms. Tilted her head and looked at Will appraisingly. "No, not at all. I'm used to

half-naked men—half-naked *wet* men, I should say—
showing up on my doorstep. There's a new one pretty
much every day. Although . . ." Regina tilted her head the
other way and frowned, as if assessing a piece of ripe fruit
in the market. "Although," she went on, amazed at her
own boldness but unable to resist, "I must say that you're
a particularly fine specimen of half-naked wet man."

Will cleared his throat. "Um, yes, well, thanks. I
guess."

Regina laughed. "Don't mention it. Please. Ever again.
So, why are you here? In my building? Like that," she
added, gesturing at the towel draped low around his middle, then dropping her hand rapidly.

Will smiled hopefully. "Surprise!" he said. "I'm your
new upstairs neighbor."

"My . . . what?"

Will repressed a shiver. "Your new neighbor. I've been
moving in in bits and pieces for the past few days. I'm
surprised we didn't run into each other before now."

Regina shook her head. "I've been, I've been busy, not
home a lot." Then, she laughed. "Uh, when were you planning on telling me about this neighbor thing? Or . . ." She
smirked. "Is this special appearance part of some bizarre
welcome-wagon plan in reverse?"

Will laughed. "Actually, I wish I'd been so clever. But
really, my water suddenly stopped. I mean, the pressure's
not great up there on the top floor, but it never just went
off in the middle of my shower. Could I . . . I was wondering if I could. . . ."

"Use my shower?" Regina supplied.

"Yeah, that's it. Uh, do you mind?"

Will's face looked so hopeful. Unsure. Like he really
thought she might refuse him the use of her shower, send
him off to work—his own big first day—a sticky mess.

"Of course," she said, finally shutting the apartment
door. What would nosy Mrs. Brown from next door say

if she saw Will Creeden, the new tenant and a bigwig at the college, dripping and gorgeous in Regina Sutherland's living room! "And I think you'd better get under some hot water fast if you don't want to catch your death of cold," she added, the thought of interfering busybodies killing—almost—the more intimate, exciting and extremely unprofessional thoughts she'd been entertaining about the acting head of the English department. Better to act like a concerned friend than a woman who suddenly wanted nothing more than to tear away the towel around Will's waist and accept whatever sweet consequences were to come.

"Thanks, Gina." Will smiled and Regina felt another surge of desire course through her body. Gina. He hadn't called her that since he'd come back to Idlewild. It had been his nickname for her, back when everybody else had shortened her name to Reggie. Back when she and Will had been lovers. Back when they'd been everything to each other.

Now, he'd moved into her building. Shown up at her door in a towel. Called her Gina. These had to be signs of something, didn't they? Something good?

He hesitated, as if waiting for something. "Oh." Regina forced herself to speak normally, casually. "The bathroom. Right through there. Sorry."

Will grinned again and turned to head for the bathroom.

"Will?" It was a risk, but, oh, God, she had to take it.

He stopped and turned back to face her. Waited, his eyes dark and warm. A lock of damp hair, curled over his forehead.

"I . . . I didn't think you'd remember that," she said, her voice not as steady and nonchalant as she'd hoped it would be. "Calling me Gina."

A silence filled the room then. No, Regina thought later, more of a stillness, something palpable and weighted and at the same time, something ungraspable, indefinable.

Suddenly, the room had become an undeniably erotic space within which she was willing to stay with Will forever.

And then he spoke. "I remember everything," he said, quietly, intensely. "I remember it all."

*"Reaorwwww!"*

"Ow!"

"Nigel! Bad boy!"

Regina dove after the big gray cat who'd taken a nasty swipe at the strange male animal in his domain. The cat who'd broken the emotionally charged moment between this interloper and his mother. She scooped him up, barely preventing him from taking another swipe at Will, who'd backed up against the wall, petrified.

Regina couldn't help herself. The sight of Will, fearless, intrepid Will, Will, her hero, cowed by a cranky furball, was just too much for her. She burst out laughing. "Oh," she gasped. "I'm sorry, Will. But it's . . . you just look so funny."

Will grinned warily and sidled toward the bathroom. "That's okay. Just keep that beast away from me."

Nigel hissed and Will scurried into the bathroom, slamming the door behind him. "Regina?" he called, weakly.

"Yes, Will?"

"It's good to be back."

# Twelve

What a morning! Regina had gotten to the campus in plenty of time to take care of any last-minute emergencies, like a literature class that had been scheduled for the same time and place as a chemistry lecture. Once that mini crisis had been handled by administration, Regina had rushed off to the old classroom to post a notice of the change. Then dashed off to the new classroom to check out the space and greet the students. By the time all twenty kids had realized they were in the wrong place and made it to the right place, ten minutes of the class time had been wasted.

Then one of the students informed her that the bookstore had not received a shipment of the collection of poetry Regina had ordered, though someone from the bookstore had confirmed the shipment's receipt three days earlier. The second mini crisis solved—the bookstore was, indeed, in stock with the book—Regina introduced her new students to the scope of the course, its content and requirements.

That had gone fine until a show of hands revealed that a full two-thirds of the class had never heard the terms *synecdoche* or *trope*. Okay, so the kids were a little less advanced in their study of poetry than Regina had hoped, but that was fine. As long as they wanted to learn, were

interested in the material, she'd work around the fact that the basics were missing.

And then there'd been one of the intro courses, a whopping twenty-five kids, most of them completely uninterested, just there to fulfill one of their core requirements.

Oh, well, Regina thought with a sigh as she climbed the stairs of Humanities Hall. The morning could have been a lot worse. Then she smiled as she remembered how the morning had begun—with a wet and soapy Will appearing at her door, wearing only a towel.

Regina glanced at her watch. Good. If she'd read the department teaching schedule properly, Will should be upstairs now, enjoying his lunch break, comparing notes with Maria or Aidan. Regina hurried her steps. No doubt about it, she was looking forward to seeing Will Creeden again.

Voices, lots of them, from the student lounge. Regina hefted her leather bag more comfortably on her shoulder and strode into the room.

There, squeezed onto an old and very small love seat, sat Will Creeden and Celia Keene. Perched on an arm of the love seat and gathered on the rug at their feet were students, listening raptly to Will and gazing adoringly at Celia.

Regina stopped as if struck. There was something so— so domestic, intimate even, about the scene. Celia and Will, hip to hip, shoulder to shoulder on the love seat, the students surrounding them like their. . . .

Will was talking about a movie or at least that was what Regina surmised, not having been there for the start of the conversation. And the kids were hanging on his every word.

Regina stood, not moving, for what seemed like hours. And then Celia looked slowly away from Will's face and toward Regina, as if she'd known all along that Regina

was there, in the doorway, paralyzed. A slow and lazy smile spread across her face. A smile of victory, Regina thought. She looks like a smug little cat.

"Regina." It was Will. He'd finally just seen her. "Hi, come on in," he went on.

One by one the students turned to stare at Regina. Waiting for her to accept Professor Creeden's invitation to join their impromptu salon.

"Yes, Regina," Celia added, running a slim, manicured hand down the thigh of her tailored suede pants. "Why don't you join us. You have seen the new Jaramusch film at the Boulevard, haven't you? We're discussing it now." Celia's smile grew. "I'm sure we'd love to hear your considered views on the piece."

This isn't happening, Regina thought. This is too awful. No, she hadn't seen the stupid movie, how could she, it had only opened yesterday. That meant . . . that meant. . . .

She felt like a stranger, the newcomer, the outsider. But it's my department, Regina thought, all in the space of a second or two, and these are my students, why, I've taught just about every single one of these kids.

"Regina?" Will said, prompting her to speak. To stay. Or to go.

Regina started, looked from left to right rapidly. "Oh, yeah, thanks, but I've got an appointment. I'm meeting someone at the . . . at the cafeteria," she said, painfully aware that her voice was too high and that she was babbling.

She turned to go, aware that the students were turning away from her, disinterestedly, wanting to get back to the business of listening to Will. And Celia.

"Before you run off," Celia called.

Regina turned back. What else could she do?

"Before you go," Celia repeated, "you should know that Will and I highly recommend the film."

# Thirteen

"Regina, would you get me that order list, the one on my desk blotter, please?"

"Sure, Jane." Regina hurried into the office behind the gallery's main viewing space. Helping Jane and Mark set up for their next opening was the least she could do for friends. Besides, it was fun to be in the gallery, to watch people wander in, look at the art on display, react to it in an astonishing variety of ways. Depending of course on the particular medium being shown, whether it was painting, sculpture, prints, drawing, and the particular style in which the work had been created—representational, abstract and any combination of the two—people seemed either to love or hate the pieces. And most every show elicited both extremes, some people praising and pulling out wallets to make a purchase, others, frowning, shaking their heads in disgust or frustration, hurrying out the door without a backward glance.

Art was whatever you wanted it to be, Regina thought for the millionth time, as she snatched the piece of paper from her friend's desk and hurried out front with it. The caterers were there and Jane was double-checking that they'd delivered exactly what she'd ordered for the evening's event.

While Jane finished confirming the delivery with the caterers, Regina looked around at the paintings that had

been hung just that morning. They were by an artist named Jason Berrios, mostly still lifes—cups and saucers, vases of flowers, an overturned glass or two—in a representational style that reminded Regina of Cézanne. The paintings were strong, skillfully executed, simply framed. In her opinion, beautiful.

Let's see how they go over tonight, Regina thought dryly. Usually, those people who were invited to the gallery's openings—as well as those few drop-ins, mostly younger people, Idlewild students and the like—were sophisticated or at least well-behaved enough to praise whatever work was being shown, even if in truth they loathed it. Those who didn't have the nerve or the stomach to praise what they didn't like, at least opted for tactful silence. The public's real assessment would make itself clear in the final number of sales the gallery made over the course of the show.

"Perfect." Jane appeared at Regina's elbow, smiling. "Everything's in order, right down to the mini quiches. Mark always says you can't have a gallery opening without mini quiches."

Regina laughed. "That's just because he likes to eat them."

"Scarf them is more like it," Jane admitted. "Especially the ones with ham. Now, we should get out of the way and let these people set up. Let's go out back and get a breath of fresh air."

The two women passed through a sliding glass door at the back of the gallery's main room and into the small, enclosed garden that served perfectly to accommodate overflow at the more popular opening parties. Mark had designed the space to be predominantly lush and green, like a romantic forest glen in a fairy tale. The few flowers that bloomed were mostly white, including white azalea bushes in the early spring, roses and tulips and white lilac later in the year. A stone gargoyle was attached to one

wall, from where he spit water into a small stone pond. A pergola spanned the width of the garden at back. The walls of the garden themselves were covered with crawling vines. At night, small white lights twinkled from the corners of the garden and an assortment of hurricane lanterns added a warm glow. Even now, in late September, the space was magical.

"Whew!" Jane plopped down in one of the elaborate wrought-iron chairs. "Now all we do is cross our fingers and hope it all goes off well."

Regina joined her friend in another of the chairs. "It'll be a smash. Your openings always are." Regina grinned slyly. "Even if the art is ugly."

Jane stuck out her tongue and then laughed. "You're right. Remember that awful woman last year, the sculptor with the frizzy black hair and humongous attitude?"

Regina shuddered. "Ugh. And those horrible—what were they, exactly, those things she made?"

"Those were 'spheres of influence', my dear," Jane answered, tilting her head up and sniffing. "Important statements about society."

"More like lumps of cow . . ."

"Now, Regina!" Jane scolded, glancing over her shoulder to the inside of the gallery. "We wouldn't want any potential clients to hear us talk badly about our artists, would we?"

"Definitely not," Regina agreed, mock solemn. Then she lowered her voice. "But why *did* you and Mark give that woman a show?"

Jane sighed. "Don't get me wrong, I love Idlewild, love living here. It's Mark's home and I've been happy to make it my own. But honestly, sometimes it's just impossible to find new talent. *Any* talent, actually, who's halfway decent. The pool is just too small. In a place like New York, there's another potential star getting off a Trailways bus every

other minute. Here, well, sometimes we take what we can get."

"This painter Jason Berrios," Regina said, "he seems very good."

Jane smiled brightly, her mood uplifted. "Yes, doesn't he? I'm really pleased Mark found him. Seems he's been working alone quietly in a barn his father converted into a studio for him. He'd never even shown anyone his work until Mark ferreted out rumors of a solitary young painter."

"And how, exactly, did he do that?" Regina asked, quirking an eyebrow.

"My husband is a natural sleuth, a born detective, a sniffer-outer of artistic talent," Jane replied loftily. "In other words, he got friendly with the mailman, a particularly chatty fellow, who, knowing Mark owned a gallery, thought he'd be interested in the fact that young Jason had been receiving packages of paint and other supplies from a well-known art-supply house. The rest is history."

Regina shook her head. "Ow. Remind me never to get on Mark's bad side."

"And to have your Victoria's Secret purchases delivered in plain brown wrapping." Jane shifted forward in her seat. "Enough about Mark and the nosy postman. I want to know what's going on with you."

"You mean with me and Will, don't you?" Regina corrected.

Jane shrugged. "Okay, you got me. So?"

"Well . . ." Regina considered for a moment, drawing her gray wool blazer closer around her. "Well, nothing's going on, really. I mean, Will's been making some changes to the department, improvements, really, from what I can tell. Nothing too major yet. Some scheduling and minor paperwork procedure changes, things like that."

"What do your colleagues think of him?" Jane pressed.

"Miles is still pretty cold to Will, kind of huffy and

standoffish. Celia Keene," Regina said, with an uncomfortable laugh, "the new person, thinks Will walks on water. Aidan is Aidan, a total gentleman. If he's worried about what Will's going to do to the department—and I think he is—he's not letting it show. Maria's always ready to give anyone the benefit of the doubt. She's too warm to shut anyone out without serious proof he's a jerk." Regina hesitated.

"And you?" Jane prompted. "What do you think?"

"Honestly," Regina said, after another moment's silence, "I don't know what I think. Exactly. Or what I feel, either. I mean, Will's been courteous to me, a good boss and a pleasant neighbor, but . . . but nothing more. After that first time when we ran into each other on the staircase—after that night, really, because we met later at the Barnes's—we haven't had anything that remotely resembles a personal conversation." Except for the morning Will had come by asking to use her shower, but Regina didn't feel like revealing that bit of information just now.

"And you'd like a personal conversation?"

Regina smiled ruefully. "I'd be a lying fool if I said I didn't. I—okay, part of me wants to sit down alone with Will and clear the air. Yell at him for what he did to me. Punish him, somehow, for all the hurt, all the ruined memories and shattered dreams. Another part of me wants to listen to him, assuming he's got something to say, something that would help me understand and put the whole messy past to rest. So that I could forgive him. So that I could get on with my life."

"So why don't you ask him to meet?" Jane asked. "It seems a reasonable thing to do, I think. He's not avoiding you, is he? He probably just expects you to make the first move.

"Why should I make the first move! Why doesn't he take the initiative?" Regina blurted angrily. "If he wants

to talk with me, he should ask, shouldn't he? He should choose a time and place and. . . ."

"What else is going on here, Regina?" Jane asked shrewdly. "Why are you so afraid to approach him, ask for what's owed to you? Do you really think he's going to say no? I mean, refuse to get together and talk?"

Regina hung her head and sighed. "Oh, Jane," she said softly, "I don't know. Will meant everything to me once. The world. He was like—like an organ, a vital organ I couldn't live without. Imagining life without Will was like imagining living without a heart or stomach or kidney." Regina laughed and looked up at her friend. "Doesn't sound very romantic, does it? But it was," she said firmly. "He was a part of my body and soul and mind. When he left, I didn't know how to breath. Didn't believe I'd survive."

"But you did," Jane said softly. "You did more than survive. You lived, you built a life."

Regina shifted in her chair and sighed. "Oh, yeah, I got a degree and have a career, friends. I appreciate my life, really. I'm very lucky, blessed, even. But in a way . . . in a way I've never gotten over Will. Never came fully back to life. Never loved again. I'm a poor imitation of who I was, Jane," Regina said, with a sad smile. She pointed to her heart. "In here, where it matters."

"And that's why you won't ask him to see you? I don't think I really understand."

"That—and the fact that I think he's seeing Celia Keene," Regina said quickly.

"What!" Jane shook her head. "Are you serious? No, that can't be true. I would have heard it from Mrs. Walker."

"Miles thinks it's true," Regina said. "And Will and Celia did go to the movies together."

"And? You and I go to the movies together. You and Mark went to the movies together when I was at that con-

ference last year. That awful adolescent comedy I refused to see. Are you and Mark involved?"

Regina looked shocked. "Of course not!"

"Well? People go to the movies together, Regina. Think about it. Will and Celia are both new in Idlewild. Why shouldn't they spend some time together, get to know the town?"

"I guess. . . ."

"Do you have any concrete evidence they're involved?" Jane went on.

"No, but—"

"Regina Sutherland, I'm ashamed of you! Jumping to conclusions."

"I know, I know, but . . . but what if he is seeing Celia?" Regina said, her eyes suddenly clouded with fear. "I don't know if I could bear to hear him tell me that. Oh, even if he isn't seeing Celia or any other woman, what if. . . ."

"What if . . ." Jane prompted gently.

"What if he tells me he never loved me? I mean, never loved me in the way he said he did, the way I thought he loved me. The way I loved him. What if I learn that the past was all a lie? Or what if he did love me then, but doesn't feel anything now." Regina stopped talking and put her head in her hands.

"Oh, Regina." Jane rose and knelt at her friend's side. "You want him back, don't you? You're still in love with him. You want to put the past to rest so you can build a future with Will. Is that it?"

Regina nodded, too choked with tears to speak.

"And that's why you're so afraid. Confronting Will seems like too big a gamble, too huge and risky a chance, is that right?"

Again, Regina nodded as Jane put her arms around her shoulders.

"Well, let's see," Jane continued softly. "What happens

if you don't talk to him? Nothing. Nothing but endless, lonely years of not knowing. No closure. No truth, just frightening guesses and probably, someday, anger at your own cowardice. Regret."

Regina tried to pull away from Jane but her friend held on.

"Shush. Now sit there and listen to the happily married woman who's trying to give you some good advice. What happens if you do talk to him? Well, there are lots of possibilities. Too many to count, really. But one of those possibilities is that you find out Will still loves you. That he's back in Idlewild for more than a career move. Although why he'd come *here* to advance his career is beyond me," Jane added with a chuckle. "Anyway, it seems to me there's only one thing for you to do, Regina. So that whatever happens, whatever Will tells you, whatever he feels, you can at least live with yourself. You know what that is, don't you?" she whispered. "You know what you have to do?"

Regina nodded. Sighed. Lifted her head into the growing deep blue dusk and took a deep, steadying breath. "Yes," she said. "I'll talk to him tonight."

# Fourteen

"It's a marvelous party, Regina!" Dr. Emily Nelson snagged another fresh jumbo shrimp from the large bowl of crushed ice on the main banquet table. "Marvelous shrimp and that pâté is simply decadent!"

Regina laughed. "Admit it. You don't really care about the art. And forget about the people. You're just here for the free food!"

Emily harrumphed. Quickly glanced round. Leaned conspiratorially closer to Regina. "Of course, my dear. But don't tell Jane. I don't want to offend her."

Emily was right. It was a good party. From what Regina could tell, people really liked Jason Berrios's work and were happy to meet and chat with the young, unassuming artist. The mood was bright, the laughter genuine, the food and wine superb. Jane and Mark stood to make a profit with this show and Jason might just have found himself a mentor, someone who would safely guide him through the often nasty, dog-eat-dog world of the big galleries.

"By the way, Regina." Regina shook herself from her reverie and turned back, smiling, to her older friend. "You look smashing tonight. Radiant, even!"

"And I think you've had too much wine!" Regina retorted, eyebrows comically raised.

Emily shrugged and took another sip. *"In vino veritas,* my dear. That color becomes you."

Heavy cream. That was the best way to describe the color of the lacy, silk-backed sheath Regina wore. The dress was slim fitting and cut to cocktail length, showing Regina's trim ankles to advantage. Long, tight sleeves gave the dress a decidedly romantic air while a round, low-cut neckline, worn with some serious support underneath, made virtually every man in the room look twice. Strappy satin sandals, their taupe color perfectly matching the satin taupe of her evening bag, completed the ensemble. The look was thoroughly sophisticated and completely sexy at the same time.

"And if I may say so," Emily went on, "wearing your hair up that way, off your neck, slightly piled on your head . . ." She sighed. "Why, I hardly knew you were the same no-nonsense Regina from the English department!"

"That was the point," Regina murmured, her eyes again scanning the crowd for a glimpse of Will. As far as she could tell, he'd yet to arrive. Come to think of it, was she even sure he had planned on coming? "I needed a little firepower."

"Yes, sometimes men do need to be hit roundly upon the head."

Regina stifled a laugh. "You are incorrigible!" she hissed. "Now get away from the shrimp. Give someone else a chance. Mingle. It'll do you good."

Emily sighed again, dramatically. "If I must."

Regina watched her friend and mentor wander off, probably in search of more food and a quiet corner from which to watch the event unmolested by unwanted chit-chat.

Regina took a fortifying sip of her own wine. He'd be here. Or he wouldn't. Either way, there was nothing she could do about it. Might as well enjoy myself, she thought. See how Jason is holding up under the glare of the lime-light.

"Regina!" It was Jane, suddenly at her side. "Thanks so much for all your help! Isn't it great?"

Regina looked at her friend and smiled. "It is; the opening's a wonderful success. And you look so lovely!" Regina winked. "I'm surprised Mark hasn't whisked you off to the garden for a stolen kiss."

Jane winked in return. "Ah, but he has!"

The tall, slender art-history professor wore a basic little black dress with empire cut bodice and A-line skirt. A strand of pearls, a pair of single pearl earrings and her wedding set—a simple platinum band worn below a diamond studded platinum band—were her only adornments. With her medium-heeled black peau-de-soie pumps and pale blond hair sleeked into a French twist, Jane was, as always, the personification of elegance.

"Have you seen Will?" Regina asked now, commanding her voice to be cool and nonchalant, even though her heart was beating a fast tattoo.

Jane frowned. "No, I haven't. And just about everybody else who responded in the positive has arrived." Jane brightened and patted Regina's arm comfortingly. "Now, Regina, don't get all worried and miss the fun. He'll be here."

Regina laughed lightly. "And if he doesn't come, that's fine, too. I worked too hard this week not to enjoy some downtime with Idlewild's gliteratti!"

As if her words had summoned him, suddenly, Will Creeden stood in the entranceway. Tall, dressed in a dark three-button suit, his thick hair waved off his forehead as if it had been styled. . . .

Will? Wearing mousse? Gel?

"Professor Creeden! Glad you could join us this evening!"

Regina stood perfectly still as Mark Cadwallader made his way through the crowd to greet his guest.

Or, more precisely, Regina noted, her hand tightening on her wineglass, his guests.

Because with Will, holding his arm as possessively as any wife or girlfriend would, was Celia Keene.

# Fifteen

"So, Regina, Will tells me you studied at Madison University." Celia smiled blandly. "Life in New York City must have been quite a challenge for a small-town girl."

Stay calm, Regina told herself. Take the high road. "Actually," she said, her voice bright, "it was a lot of fun. I love the city."

"So, you've seen the new Jackson Pollack show at MOMA, then?" Celia asked.

"Uh, no, I haven't." What was there to do but tell the truth?

Celia arched a perfectly shaped brow. "Well, surely you caught the Cindy Sherman retrospective last summer? At Rochambeau Galleries?"

Regina could feel herself flushing and for what seemed like the tenth time that evening, mentally cursed her pale complexion. "No," she said. "I—" Regina attempted a nonchalant laugh. "The truth is, I haven't been to New York since the summer after graduation. I've just been so busy, I guess, what with the college and, you know, my family." Stop babbling, Regina scolded silently. Don't make excuses for your life.

"Regina prefers to take her holidays abroad," Emily Nelson interjected. "In fact," she went on, turning to face Regina, "didn't you just return from a month in England?"

Regina breathed a silent thank-you to her old friend. Why did this Celia person get her so rattled!

"Yes, as a matter of fact, I did. Just came back from England. Have you ever been?" she asked Celia.

The little blonde shrugged. "Many times. I have to say, though, I far prefer France. The food is much superior, the shopping is fantastic and the men. . . ." Celia smirked and lightly touched her hand to her chest. "Well, the men put the Brits to shame. If you know what I mean."

"Oh, my dear." Emily's voice was sly. "I'm sure we all know exactly what you mean."

"Will, hi." Regina smiled as Will joined the three women. The conversation had to take a more pleasant turn now. Didn't it?

Will handed Celia one of the glasses of Merlot he'd fetched from the bar. "Fantastic show, Regina," he said with enthusiasm. "Mark really found himself a winner with this Berrios kid. Don't you think so, Celia?"

Will looked down at his lithe companion. Celia gave a slight, noncommittal shrug and took a sip of her wine.

For a brief, fleeting moment, Will looked embarrassed. "Of course, this isn't New York or L.A. or. . . ."

"Thank God, is what I say." Emily drained her glass and placed it on the empty tray of a passing waiter. "Well, kids, I'm off. It's way past my bedtime and my cabdriver is probably about to leave me stranded."

"Good night, Emily," Regina said, leaning down to kiss her friend's cheek. "And thanks," she whispered.

"Don't let her get to you," Emily whispered back.

Dr. Nelson took her leave of the group and wended her way to the door. When she'd gone, there was an uncomfortable silence that Regina, in a sudden panic, just did not know how to break.

Celia did it for her. "You mentioned your family, Regina," she said smoothly. "Do you have children?"

Regina saw Will's eyes dart to her face. She avoided returning his glance. "Oh, no," she said lightly.

"Then you're married?" Celia pursued, her tone all innocence. "Funny, I hadn't heard anything about that."

Nervously, Regina put a hand to her hair. "No, no I'm not married," she said. "I . . . what I meant was. . . ."

"Regina has a very close-knit family," Will said quickly, turning to Celia. "I'm an only child, too, so I know how that can be."

Celia laughed. "I've got a foolproof solution for the parents-breathing-down-your-neck syndrome," she said. "Move away from home."

"It's not . . ." Regina blurted.

At the same time, Will said: "I didn't mean . . ."

Regina smiled awkwardly at Will. "Sorry. Look, will you excuse me?" she said to Celia. "I've really got to check with the caterers, see if everything's okay, that they're not running out of anything. Good-bye."

Ignoring Will's look of mingled embarrassment and panic, ignoring Celia's look of smug success, Regina turned and with as much dignity as she could muster, walked to the back office.

She'd never felt more miserable.

# Sixteen

Regina checked the watch on the wrist of the bartender. Ten o'clock.

Will hadn't left Celia's side since they'd arrived together almost an hour earlier. Why would he, Regina thought bitterly. In that strapless silver minidress, Celia looked like a sprite or a fairy from a recent film production of *Midsummer Night's Dream*. Everyone, even the women, was captivated by her shimmering appearance.

Ten oh five. Regina sighed. Another agonizing hour of this dreadful party to endure. Then there would be the good-byes and then, finally, she could go home. Alone.

She just hoped she didn't run into Will and Celia in the stairwell of her building. In spite of herself, Regina smiled. Now wouldn't that just make the evening complete!

But darn the woman! Why did Celia Keene, someone who probably didn't even weigh one hundred pounds soaking wet, intimidate her so? When Regina was in her presence she couldn't seem to help but feel awkward, like a country bumpkin. Immature, like a girl who had never cut the strings of her mama's apron—and that was certainly not the reality. Unsophisticated. Unsuccessful.

Lonely.

That was the worst part. Celia Keene made Regina Sutherland feel her loneliness like she'd never done be-

fore. Or, maybe, like she hadn't done since those first months after Will's marriage to Connie.

And loneliness was a horrible thing. She had friends and family and a fairly decent choice of local men to date, but the truth was that Regina was lonely. None of those people touched her soul the way. . . .

The way Will Creeden had. The way Regina had hoped he might still.

Regina sighed and decided she'd better move out of this one spot by the bar or someone would think she had a drinking problem or a crush on the bartender. Nodding at guests as she went, Regina made her way toward the back of the gallery. Toward the garden.

Well, there was no way—no way!—she was going to approach Mr. Creeden after tonight. In spite of Jane's opinion, it was clear—very, very clear—that Will and Celia were a couple. At least, on their way to becoming a couple. And Regina wanted no part of that misery. She'd just keep her mouth shut and smile prettily. Maybe think about applying for a job somewhere else next academic year.

A high, flirty laugh. Instinctively, Regina looked in its direction. And saw Celia, surrounded by several smiling men, including Will. Celia holding court.

Celia Keene could have her choice of any man in Idlewild, and she'd chosen Will Creeden.

So be it.

Anger flooded Regina. Anger and shame. How could she have been so stupid! To harbor feelings for Will all these years. To think that maybe he still loved her, too. She was pathetic!

Regina walked more quickly through the well-dressed crowd of party-goers and into the garden. An older man and a woman in yellow sat side by side against the west wall, talking earnestly. Other than that, the garden was empty of guests.

Perfect. Regina Sutherland might be lonely. But right then, all she wanted was to be alone.

Celia's laugh was captivating. Almost everything about her was captivating. Will could not deny it. But since Regina had walked off to speak with the caterers, his eyes had followed his first love.

He'd wanted to go to her. Had tried a few times to move off. But each time, Celia had found a reason for him to stay—a story he had to hear, a bit of Irish cheese he just had to taste, something in her eye that needed tending to, maybe an eyelash. She'd only had to touch his arm, lightly, seductively, and he'd complied, stayed by her side. After all, he'd reasoned, she was new in town—even more new than he was—and probably didn't know anyone else at the party. Many people, anyway.

But now there was no reason he couldn't go off to find Regina. Spend some time with her. Celia had somehow managed to gather around her what looked to Will like every eligible bachelor in Idlewild—and some not so eligible men, too. There were a few wives who were going to be pretty furious when they found their errant husbands drooling over the sparkling Ms. Keene.

Fine. Will had no doubt that Celia could handle herself with just about anyone. Especially irate women. He didn't quite get it, but something about Celia seemed to make other women dislike her. First Cindy. Then Emily and Regina. He wondered how Jane would take to Celia.

There she was. Will watched as Regina began to walk toward the back of the gallery, away from the bar, where she'd been standing for the past ten minutes.

Perfect. He'd join her in a moment.

A peal of lovely laughter from Celia.

Will's head automatically turned toward the sound. When he looked back up, only a second or two later, he

saw that Regina had stopped. That she'd also turned toward the sound of Celia's voice. That she'd probably just seen Will turn his attention to the delicate blonde.

Damn! Will recognized that look on Regina's face. Well, part of it. The anger was clear. There was something else there, too, but he couldn't quite make it out.

And now she was heading, more purposefully, toward the back door. Toward the garden.

"Excuse me," he murmured. Celia didn't even seem to hear him, so intent was she on the story one of the other men was telling. Something about the guy's visit to Cannes. Or a corporate takeover. Something.

Will threaded his way through the revelers. He hoped they would have some privacy in the garden. He had a feeling they'd need it.

She stood at the far end of the walled garden. A vision, to Will's eyes, in creamy lace. Graceful and lush at the same time.

"Regina."

Slowly, she looked up from the flower she'd been fingering. Will noticed the man and woman who had been seated along the west wall rise, make their way back to the party.

Will took a step forward. "Regina, I—"

"Won't Celia miss you?" she said. It was not a question. It sounded to Will an awful lot like an accusation. And a complication of which he hadn't quite been aware. Regina Sutherland was jealous.

"I doubt it," he answered, keeping his voice calm. Neutral.

"But she is your date, isn't she?"

Will took another step into the garden. Realized the air was cool and fresh after the closeness of the crowded gallery.

"We came together, yes," Will admitted. "But only because her car is in the shop. I offered her a ride."

"What a gentlemanly thing to do."

Will sighed. He was getting nowhere fast.

"Look, Regina . . . do you want to sit?" Will gestured toward the same two chairs Regina and Jane had occupied that afternoon.

"No, thanks. I'm fine standing," she said, her voice cold.

"Okay. Okay." Will crossed the garden and stopped only a few feet from Regina, his back to the gallery. "We need to talk."

Regina made a look of false surprise. "We do? About what?"

Will laughed. "Don't play dumb with me, Regina. I know better than anyone how smart you are. We need to talk about Celia. About what you think is going on between Celia and me."

"Okay." Regina took a step away from Will and folded her arms across her waist. Her voice was unsteady. "Okay, what I think is that you two are a couple. It's pretty obvious. And that's fine with me."

Will met and held Regina's eyes. "No," he said firmly. "No, Celia and I are not a couple. And no. It wouldn't be okay with you if we were."

Regina let her arms fall to her sides. "Aren't you presumptuous, Dr. Creeden! After all these years, to think you know what I feel."

"Yes, I am presumptuous. About some things. About you."

It was now or never. He hadn't wanted to come to her in anger or misunderstanding. Hadn't wanted to approach her under less-than-perfect circumstances.

But what were the perfect circumstances to ask Regina—to what? Take him back? Give them another chance? He'd never had a well-thought-out game plan.

At least now, at this very moment, he knew Regina still cared for him. If she didn't, she wouldn't be fighting him

this way. Protecting herself from more hurt. From him. From the presence of another woman.

He stepped forward. Saw her flinch slightly but not back away.

Will reached out and saw his hands grasp her arms, saw them pull her to him.

"Hello, Regina. I've come back."

He bent his head, pressed his lips to hers.

No hesitation. The touch was electric. It was as if each had been waiting, untouched and unkissed, for eight long years. Waiting just for this moment of reawakening.

Will felt his body spring to life. Felt the blood course through his arms, legs. Felt himself harden with a longing and passion he hadn't known since. . . .

Since Regina.

Her lips were soft and inviting and warm. He wanted to stay there all night, pressed to her. Holding her.

But there would be time.

Slowly, gently, he withdrew. Searched her face for any sign of belated anger. Saw only peace and joy and eyes hazy with desire.

"Why haven't you. . . . Why have you been avoiding me?" Regina whispered.

Will shook his head. "Not avoiding. Just going slow. I wanted to know that you didn't hate me. I needed to know there might be some chance before . . . before I took a risk and kissed you."

Regina smiled. "It's okay. As long as you finally got around to kissing me." She paused, traced the slight dark circles under his eyes with one slim finger. "The Will Creeden I knew was a major workaholic. Sleep always came second when there was work to be done. Something tells me you've been burning the midnight oil, learning this new job."

Will nodded. "There's that, too. It's been hard, coming back, Regina. To you, to Idlewild. In so many ways. I . . .

maybe I should have gotten more things in my life settled, have waited even longer to come to you."

"Sh!" Regina placed her finger on Will's lips. "No regrets."

Will kissed her delicate fingertip. Looked deeply into her eyes. "No regrets. But we need to go slow, Regina. I need to go slow. I want to be careful. I don't want to lose you again. Can you accept that?"

"Yes," Regina whispered. "I can."

# The Publishers of Zebra Bouquet

are making this special offer to lovers of contemporary romances to introduce this exciting new line of novels. Zebras Bouquet Romances have been praised by critics and authors alike as being of the highest quality and best written romantic fiction available today.

# Each Full-Length Novel

has been written by authors you know and love as well as by up-and-coming writers that you'll only find with Zebra Bouquet. We'll bring you the newest novels by world famous authors like Vanessa Grant, Judy Gill, Ann Josephson and award winning Suzanne Barrett and Leigh Greenwood—to name just a few. Zebra Bouquet's editors have selected only the very best and highest quality romances for up-and-coming publications under the Bouquet banner.

# You'll be Treated

to tales of star-crossed lovers in glamourous settings that are sure to captivate you. These stories will keep you enthralled to the very happy end.

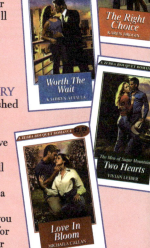

## 4 Free Novels
As a way to introduce you to these terrific romances, the publishers of Bouquet are offering Zebra Romance readers Four Free Bouquet novels. They are yours for the asking with no obligation to buy a single book. Read them at your leisure. We are sure that after you've read these introductory books you'll want more! (If you do not wish to receive any further Bouquet novels, simply write "cancel" on the invoice and return to us within 10 days.)

## Save 35% with Home Delivery
Each month you'll receive four just-published Bouquet romances. We'll ship them to you as soon as they are printed (you may even get them before the bookstores). You'll have 10 days to preview these exciting novels for Free. If you decide to keep them, you'll be billed the special preferred home subscription price of just $3.20 per book; a total of just $12.80 — that's a savings of over 35% off the cover. If for any reason you are not satisfied simply return the novels for full credit, no questions asked. You'll never have to purchase a minimum number of books and you may cancel your subscription at any time.

# GET STARTED TODAY –
# NO RISK AND NO OBLIGATION

To get your introductory gift of 4 Free Bouquet Romances fill out and mail the enclosed Free Book Certificate today. We'll ship your free books as soon as we receive this information. Remember that you are under no obligation. This is a risk-free offer from the publishers of Zebra Bouquet Romances.

Call us TOLL FREE at 1-888-345-BOOK
Visit our website at www.kensingtonbooks.com

# FREE BOOK CERTIFICATE

**YES!** I would like to take you up on your offer. Please send me 4 Free Bouquet Romance Novels as my introductory gift. I understand that unless I tell you otherwise, I will then receive the 4 newest Bouquet novels to preview each month FREE for 10 days. If I decide to keep them I'll pay the preferred home subscriber's price of just $3.20 each (a total of only $12.80) plus $1.50 for shipping and handling. That's a savings of over 35% off the cover price. I understand that I may return any shipment for full credit–no questions asked–and I may cancel this subscription at any time with no obligation. Regardless of what I decide to do, the 4 Free Introductory Novels are mine to keep as Bouquet's gift.

BN100A

Name _____

Address _____

City _____ State _____ Zip _____

Telephone ( ) _____

Signature _____

(If under 18, parent or guardian must sign.)

Orders subject to acceptance by Zebra Home Subscription Service. Terms and Prices subject to change.
Offer valid only in the U.S.

If this response card is missing,
call us at 1-888-345-BOOK.

Be sure to visit our website at
www.kensingtonbooks.com

**BOUQUET ROMANCES**
Zebra Home Subscription Service, Inc.
P.O. Box 5214
Clifton NJ 07015-5214

# THE PUBLISHERS OF ZEBRA BOUQUET

are making this special offer to lovers of contemporary romances to introduce this exciting new line of novels. Zebras Bouquet Romances have been praised by critics and authors alike as being of the highest quality and best written romantic fiction available today.

# EACH FULL-LENGTH NOVEL

has been written by authors you know and love as well as by up-and-coming writers that you'll only find with Zebra Bouquet. We'll bring you the newest novels by world famous authors like Vanessa Grant, Judy Gill, Ann Josephson and award winning Suzanne Barrett and Leigh Greenwood—to name just a few. Zebra Bouquet's editors have selected only the very best and highest quality romances for up-and-coming publications under the Bouquet banner.

# YOU'LL BE TREATED

to tales of star-crossed lovers in glamourous settings that are sure to captivate you. These stories will keep you enthralled to the very happy end.

## 4 FREE NOVELS
As a way to introduce you to these terrific romances, the publishers of Bouquet are offering Zebra Romance readers Four Free Bouquet novels. They are yours for the asking with no obligation to buy a single book. Read them at your leisure. We are sure that after you've read these introductory books you'll want more! (If you do not wish to receive any further Bouquet novels, simply write "cancel" on the invoice and return to us within 10 days.)

## SAVE 35% WITH HOME DELIVERY
Each month you'll receive four just-published Bouquet romances. We'll ship them to you as soon as they are printed (you may even get them before the bookstores). You'll have 10 days to preview these exciting novels for Free. If you decide to keep them, you'll be billed the special preferred home subscription price of just $3.20 per book; a total of just $12.80 — that's a savings of over 35% off the cover. If for any reason you are not satisfied simply return the novels for full credit, no questions asked. You'll never have to purchase a minimum number of books and you may cancel your subscription at any time.

# GET STARTED TODAY –
# NO RISK AND NO OBLIGATION

To get your introductory gift of 4 Free Bouquet Romances fill out and mail the enclosed Free Book Certificate today. We'll ship your free books as soon as we receive this information. Remember that you are under no obligation. This is a risk-free offer from the publishers of Zebra Bouquet Romances.

**Call us TOLL FREE at 1-888-345-BOOK**
**Visit our website at www.kensingtonbooks.com**

## FREE BOOK CERTIFICATE

BN100A

**YES!** I would like to take you up on your offer. Please send me 4 Free Bouquet Romance Novels as my introductory gift. I understand that unless I tell you otherwise, I will then receive the 4 newest Bouquet novels to preview each month FREE for 10 days. If I decide to keep them I'll pay the preferred home subscriber's price of just $3.20 each (a total of only $12.80) plus $1.50 for shipping and handling. That's a savings of over 35% off the cover price. I understand that I may return any shipment for full credit-no questions asked-and I may cancel this subscription at any time with no obligation. Regardless of what I decide to do, the 4 Free Introductory Novels are mine to keep as Bouquet's gift.

Name _____

Address _____

City _____ State _____ Zip _____

Telephone ( ) _____

Signature _____

(If under 18, parent or guardian must sign.)

Orders subject to acceptance by Zebra Home Subscription Service. Terms and Prices subject to change.

Offer valid only in the U.S.

**If this response card is missing, call us at 1-888-345-BOOK.**

**Be sure to visit our website at www.kensingtonbooks.com**

**BOUQUET ROMANCES**
Zebra Home Subscription Service, Inc.
P.O. Box 5214
Clifton NJ 07015-5214

# Seventeen

"I am going to burst out laughing at any minute," Regina whispered. She sat staring dead ahead, not daring to look at Will. The minute they caught each other's eyes, it would all be over.

They'd be thrown out of Doodles and Drafts' monthly poetry reading for misbehavior. Conduct not becoming scholars of literature. Let alone fine, upstanding, adult citizens attending a social function in the town's revered independent bookstore.

Her mother would never let her hear the end of it. Her father would say he wished he'd been there to throw rotten tomatoes and laugh along with them.

"This is so amazingly bad." Will spoke softly and without moving his lips. "I don't know how much more of this I can take without, I don't know, guffawing or something."

It was Wednesday night, four days after the gallery opening. Regina hadn't spent any time alone with Will since those moments in the garden, when he'd kissed her. When she'd welcomed him home.

He was taking it slow, as promised. Regina had seen him around the department but hadn't socialized with Will—hadn't actually gone anywhere with him—until this evening.

"Just remember," she whispered. "This was your idea."

"Great. Our first date and I blow it."

Regina hugged the word to herself. A date! And a first date usually implied a second date, didn't it? Extraordinary that at thirty years of age the idea of going on a good old-fashioned date with a man could be so appealing, so exciting. Will had asked her out for the evening, made the plans to attend the poetry reading and then to dinner at Chang's Chinese Banquet afterward. He'd even picked her up at her apartment, a whole flight of stairs away, and when they reached his car, opened the door for her before going around to open the driver's side door.

It was like old times, Regina thought.

*"Rain! Pain! Ran! Pan! Rin! Pin!"* the featured amateur poet intoned, gesturing wildly with his left hand.

"Rin?"

"What, in God's name, does that mean?" Will hissed.

"Sh!" Someone in the row behind them leaned forward to scold. "This is art!"

It was the last straw. Just too much. As hard as she tried, Regina simply could not stifle the giggle erupting in her throat.

"Hee-hee hee-hee . . ."

Eyes wide, mortified but still smiling, Regina clapped a hand over her mouth.

Too late. Will guffawed.

The poet on the makeshift stage glared at Regina and Will. The people in the row of folding chairs in front of them turned and frowned.

Regina lowered her eyes. Folded her hands in her lap. She couldn't meet the eyes of her accusers. She could feel her face flame.

"Sorry," Will whispered to the staring faces. "Sorry. Won't happen again."

"I am so going to die," Regina whispered, when the program had resumed.

"Please don't," Will whispered back. "Not for at least another fifty years, okay?"

Regina leaned across the small, wall-mounted sink and looked at her face in the mirror. God, her neck still showed traces of red. She'd been laughing so hard and trying so hard not to do it aloud.

She knew from experience that makeup would not help cover the blotches. Only time would lessen their obviousness. But another coat of lipstick couldn't hurt.

Regina hefted her shoulder bag to the sink and began to search for her makeup bag. She knew she really shouldn't carry so much stuff all the time. The morning meteorologist on the local network affiliate had predicted no rain for the next three days, and here she was carrying an umbrella!

Ah, there it was, the makeup bag. Regina unzipped the small, plastic-lined case and rummaged further for the pinkish brown tone she wore most days. She found the tube, uncapped it, and looked up again at the mirror.

"Oh!" she cried. Not ten feet behind her, staring into the mirror at her, was Celia Keene. And she did not look happy.

Celia continued to stare as Regina turned from the mirror image of her rival to face her in the flesh. "Celia. What are you. . . . I mean, I didn't see you at the reading."

Celia's face melted from cold to witchy. Not a very big change, Regina noticed.

"You know you're deluding yourself, Ms. Sutherland," she said, the ghost of a sly smile appearing on her lips.

Regina laughed, a bit nervously. "What do you mean?"

Celia walked farther into the ladies' room, until she came to stand at the sink next to the one Regina stood before.

Regina noted for the first time that Celia didn't quite

come up to her own shoulders. But a power emanated from her frail body, big enough to cower women twice her size.

"I think you know what I'm talking about," Celia said. "But I'll spell it out for you, since for some reason you're insisting on playing dumb."

Regina waited, the open lipstick tube still clutched in her hand, half disbelieving this crazy scene was taking place. Was Celia going to start a fight? Regina thought wildly. Here, in the women's bathroom of Doodles and Drafts? Regina had never been in a physical fight and was in no mood to break that streak now! Although she did have the size advantage over her opponent, she wouldn't have been surprised to learn that Celia was experienced in the not-so-fine art of catfighting.

"You're deluding yourself if you think something's going to happen with Will," Celia said now. "He's just having some fun, wasting some time."

Before Regina could stop herself she blurted her protest. "That's not true!" she cried. "Anyway, what business is it of yours, what Will and I do?"

Celia chuckled. "Oh, it's my business all right. Because when Dr. Creeden gets tired of slumming with the girl-next-door, he's going to come to me. A woman much more to his liking. You know"—Celia rudely looked Regina over from head to toe—"a woman of style. And a woman of intellect."

Regina stood quivering. She couldn't tell what she felt more—anger or shame. Okay, so she wasn't tiny and perfect and always dressed like she'd just stepped out of *Vogue*. How did Celia afford her extensive wardrobe on a teacher's salary, Regina wondered briefly. And she didn't have a Ph.D., like Celia. But . . . but she was a good person, and smart and attractive in her own unique way.

Why am I even arguing this? Regina thought, totally angry now. This woman is insane! And she's totally out

of line. I should pity her, that's what I should do. She must be in love with Will but he's in love with me! And he would never leave me. Would he?

"Nothing to say, is there?" Celia grinned, turned toward the door, then looked back. "That's okay. You know what they say about the truth hurting and all. You'll get over it. Again."

Regina watched, numb, as the door swung shut behind her colleague. Slowly, she turned back to the mirror. The harsh florescent lights highlighted the fact that her face was now blotched and red with embarrassment and barely controlled rage. She looked horrible. She felt horrible.

*Get a grip, Regina.* She breathed deeply. *Get a grip.* She brought the lipstick to her face and carefully applied it. Washed her hands and dried them under the electric dryer on the wall.

And then she was ready to rejoin Will. Go to dinner with her date. Her friend. Her. . . .

# Eighteen

A bottle of wine or a housewarming present? Why not both, Regina thought, so she purchased a bottle of a good red wine she remembered Will liking and then a bread-board from Williams-Sonoma. Not very romantic, she thought, but practical. The Will she'd known had had a bad habit of using sharp knives on his mother's counter-tops.

Anyway, she thought, as she tied a bow around the board and another around the bottle, maybe an unromantic gift was the best thing. Sure, she and Will had kissed that night in the garden of the gallery, and sure, since then they'd been spending lots of time together, but Will hadn't made another attempt to kiss her. She'd held back, too, more out of respect for his wishes to go slow than for any lack of desire on her part.

If it were up to me, she thought with a smile, I'd have jumped his bones that first night, in full view of the party guests.

Regina glanced at the clock on the kitchen wall. Seven P.M. Time to leave. After one more check in the mirror. Regina hurried into her bedroom and closed the door in order to look at herself in the full-length mirror she'd hung on its back.

Was the outfit okay? The occasion—dinner with an old friend, former lover and possible romantic partner—called

for nothing too outrageous and nothing too bland. They weren't dining out on the town but neither were they going to a ball game. Jeans were out. So was anything slinky or overtly sexy. Still, she did want Will to know she was a woman so a matte silk blouse in a lovely shade of light gray, top two buttons open, worn with a pair of fitted black wool pants seemed just the thing. Stack-heeled black shoes and a small black bag for lipstick and powder completed the look.

Regina hurried out of the bedroom and gathered wine, bag and bread board. Oh, she thought, of course, keys! A moment later she was climbing the stairs to Will's apartment, heart racing in anticipation.

And fear. Definitely fear. What was she doing, trying to recapture the past? To do so was futile. Didn't all the poets and philosophers say so? Didn't her own mother advise against such a thing? But I'm not trying to recapture or recreate the past, Regina argued silently. I'm just . . . I'm just hoping to start again with Will. Just hoping to put the past to rest and move on to building a future.

Regina reached the top step and smiled. Something smelled heavenly! Living alone after his divorce really had changed Will, she thought. Why, he'd become a regular domestic god!

She stood a moment outside his front door. Took a deep, calming breath. Tried to put all expectations for the evening out of her mind and tell herself she would simply enjoy each moment as it unfolded.

Yeah, right, she thought, as a grin spread across her face, unbidden. Quickly she gathered herself again and with only a slightly trembling finger, rang the doorbell. A second later she could hear the tread of masculine feet approaching the door and then Will's voice calling, "Regina?"

The door was flung open before Regina could respond. The grin returned to her face. Will looked fabulous.

Maybe he wasn't every woman's version of the ultimate male but he was hers, all right. In a simple white cotton button-down shirt, sleeves rolled partway up his forearms and a pair of black jeans, his thick, wavy hair swept off his forehead, Will Creeden was. . . .

"Hey."

"Hey, yourself," she said. Then she held up her gifts. "I brought you something."

"So I see. Come on in." Will stepped back as Regina entered the apartment. "So, what do you think?" he asked as he closed the door.

"I think wow." Regina turned to face Will. "You've done wonders with this place!"

Will smiled proudly and Regina imagined the little boy he once had been, showing his mother the room he'd just cleared of toys. "Thanks. I've been working on it every night for about an hour before going to bed. You know, something about being thirtysomething really changes you. Suddenly, living out of boxes just doesn't cut it."

Regina surveyed the living room, kitchen and dining area. Will didn't have lots of furniture and even fewer odds and ends, but what he did have was clean and well coordinated.

"After my divorce," Will explained, as Regina moved toward the kitchen, "I had to invest in a set of pots and pans and dishes and glasses. So those are pretty new. The couch and stuff, too. In fact," he added thoughtfully, "now that I think about it, very little is left—"

Regina looked at Will. "Yes?" she asked, puzzled at Will's having broken off so abruptly in midsentence.

Will avoided Regina's eyes and walked past her, into the kitchen. "What? Oh, nothing," he said, picking up a wooden spoon. "I just realized," he added, his voice bright, "I'd better stir this sauce. Can't have lumpy sauce!"

Regina watched Will as he bent over the pot and stirred.

Well, she thought, that was odd. When he'd opened the door, Will had seemed perfectly relaxed. Now, after the mention of the divorce, he seemed nervous. Though why shouldn't he be nervous, she realized. We've both been hurt. I'm scared. Excited but scared. Why wouldn't Will be, too?

"So, what are we having for dinner?" she asked now, coming closer to peer at the makings Will had spread out on the kitchen table and counter.

Will looked over his shoulder at Regina and his momentary tension seemed to be gone. "I hope you like lamb," he said.

Regina closed her eyes and put a hand to her heart. "You didn't." She opened her eyes now and laughed. "My favorite! With that amazing mint-and-apple sauce your mother used to make! I knew I recognized that smell, even in the hallway. It's been ages since I've had it."

"Since you last had dinner at my family's house," Will said softly, turning away from the stove to face her. "A night or two before you left for England, right after graduation."

"Oh, Will."

Will came forward and placed his hands on either side of Regina's face. "I've made you suffer, Regina," he said. "I can't tell you how sorry I am for that."

"You don't have to, Will," Regina responded, her eyes filling with tears, her heart opening to him.

"Yes, I do," he answered. "But more, I have to make it up to you somehow. I have to prove myself again. I have to earn your love. If you'll let me."

Regina smiled. "You've always had my love, Will," she whispered.

Will answered by pressing his lips to hers, gently. "And you've always had mine," he said. "But you've never had my homemade green-bean casserole, so dinner comes first!"

Regina laughed and kissed Will on the tip of his nose. "Oh, all right," she said. "If you insist."

Will went back to preparing the meal, and Regina took the liberty of opening the wine she'd brought. After she'd poured them each a glass and kissed Will on the ear for good measure, she decided to take a closer look at the apartment.

"Just don't give it the white-glove test," Will joked. "I'm not that good a housekeeper."

While ever more savory aromas wafted from the kitchen and the rich red wine warmed her, Regina strolled leisurely through the living room. On one level of a high bookshelf sat a row of framed photographs. A black-and-white photo in an old silver-gilt frame showed two of Will's ancestors, his great-grandparents, Regina remembered. There was a photograph of Will and his parents, taken when Will was about five, when the family had gone on a summer vacation to the Grand Canyon. There was no picture of Connie, Will's ex-wife. But Regina hadn't expected there to be.

Something was wrong, Regina realized suddenly. At least very odd. Quickly, she glanced around the living room and dining area. No. She could see no pictures of Will's son, Luke. Unless there were some in the bedroom, a more private place. Of course, she thought, Luke was a terribly sensitive subject with Will. He hadn't once mentioned his son since that horrible night at the Barnes's when Marty's innocent questions had led to Will's abrupt departure.

And frankly, Regina hadn't had the nerve to ask about Luke, either. The way she figured it, Will would talk about his child when he was ready. He'd tell her about Luke's life with Connie, his mother, in Chicago. Tell her how sorely he missed his son and how he longed to be with him. Tell her how he wanted so badly to take Luke to

school each morning and tuck him into bed each night. To play catch with him and be part of his daily existence.

Until then, until Will was ready to share Luke with her, Regina vowed she'd keep silent. Wouldn't ask questions about the divorce or what came after.

"Hungry?" Will called.

Regina smiled. "Have you ever known me to answer no to that question?" She walked toward the dining table, simply though perfectly set with linen placemats and brass candlesticks.

"No, I haven't, Ms. Sutherland," Will replied. "So have a seat and get ready to be wowed."

Dinner was fabulous. The lamb was done to perfection, the green-bean casserole yummy and the salad fresh and tasty. Regina had teased Will about his obsession with ranch dressing—he'd placed a big bottle of it smack in the center of the table—and he'd responded by bringing out a bottle of red wine vinegar and one of oil for her.

"Why don't you relax while I make some coffee," Will suggested after they'd cleared the table together.

"Sounds fine to me," Regina agreed. "After I visit the little girl's room."

Regina grabbed her small black bag and left the living room. The bathroom was just past what had to be Will's bedroom, the one other room in the apartment Regina had not explored. As she passed, she resisted the urge even to look inside. The door being open made such an urge even more tempting. I'll see the bedroom when Will's ready for me to see it, she told herself firmly.

But by the time she'd finished fixing her makeup, Regina's self-control had fled. Just a quick peek, she vowed. I'll only be a moment.

A bedside lamp shone warm and dim, making the entire room seem welcoming. Regina stepped inside. A large

bed, covered with a dark-blue comforter. An old dresser, on top of which were piled a few well-worn books. A trunk, a night table. That was about it. It was simple without being sparse. Cozy and masculine.

Regina was about to turn and sneak out when something over the dresser, something on the wall, caught her eye. She stopped. Caught her breath. Took another step into the room. Then another.

Yes. Over the dresser, carefully mounted on the wall, was the circlet of flowers Will had made for her all those years ago, for her part as Ophelia in the Idlewild Fall Fair play. A little worse for the wear of time, but still, in Regina's eyes, the most beautiful thing she'd ever seen.

Oh, Will, she thought. How much time we've lost. She thought her heart would break all over again, looking at that simple, enormously meaningful gift. She came closer and with one finger, gently touched the circlet.

"Regina."

She turned. In the doorway stood Will.

"I can't forget," he said.

She nodded, felt she didn't have the power to speak.

Without another word, they walked toward each other. When they met, their arms reached for, then held each other close. Then Will's lips found hers and with an urgency that lifted Regina off her feet, he kissed her.

Hungrily, greedily, Will kissed Regina's lips. She could feel them swelling with desire. Every part of her body was flushed with need. A need for Will to be inside her. Now.

With a groan, she pushed his mouth from hers.

"Come on," she breathed, leading him to the bed.

"No rush, Reggie. We've got all night."

"And I don't want to waste a minute of it. Undress me."

Will smiled and came forward.

"Gladly."

Regina could see his fingers tremble as he began to unbutton her blouse. Then it fell from her shoulders, revealing her generous white breasts in a lacy black bra. Will put his arm around her, bent her back. He pushed aside the soft material, exposing first one, then the other breast. He caressed each slowly with his other hand and teased each nipple into hardness until Regina cried out.

"Please, please. . . ."

His hand lowered to the button, then zipper of her pants. He expertly worked them open. Then, on his knees, he slowly, slowly pulled them past her hips, over her thighs.

Regina thought she would collapse with anticipation. She grasped him for support, clutched his thick, wavy hair. . . . Then the panties slipped away . . . slowly . . . slowly. Tantalizingly, Will kissed her stomach, then lower, lower, until. . . .

"Oh, God!" she cried.

And he took her to heaven.

The last time Regina and Will had made love—but she hadn't known it was the last time! Or that it was going to be the last time with him for more than eight years. And now . . . to be facing the only man she'd ever loved, naked, vulnerable, after so long apart, so long without his touch, it was magical. It was a miracle.

She couldn't control herself. Didn't even try. She wanted to climb him like a vine, slide herself up his strong thighs, against his hardness, along his muscled chest. Stop only when he pulled her onto him. . . .

"Where are you going?" he whispered, huskily, hands clasping her buttocks.

"Where you take me," she answered, placing her hands on either side of his face.

* * *

She was poised on top of him. Ready and eager. Moist and open and throbbing with need. Her hands were on his chest, now glistening with sweat.

"Say it," he urged.

"Will. Please. Make love to me. Now."

And with a thrust that made her gasp, he entered her. She rode him wildly, pressing against his hand that had found her again, wanting it never to stop, this man with her, inside her. Part of her.

She cried out. He'd done it again for her, given her this ecstasy.

"Let me be on top of you," he whispered.

He rolled her onto her back, still keeping inside. He looked down at her face transformed by passion and began another, slower rhythm. Smooth and now faster until he reached his own climax.

When it was over, they lay still, hearts beating madly against each other's chests.

Regina closed her eyes and said a silent prayer of thanks. Will had matured as a lover, had learned to spend more time seeing to her pleasure, teasing her, tantalizing her before bringing her to a delicious, mind-shattering climax. Will Creeden had always been a generous lover but . . . now!

Regina squirmed against his thigh and a tiny thrill ran up her stomach. She breathed in the scent of his skin like it was a life-giving elixir. Both clean and musky, the freshness, the richness of an ocean breeze along the shore.

She kissed his neck. Savored his particular taste, his salty sweat. The dim, bracing remains of shaving lotion or cologne. This was where she was meant to be. Stretched on his body, her face next to his, cheek to cheek. This was home.

# Nineteen

It was all too familiar. Depressing and sad and heart-breaking and every other negative he could think of. But he couldn't stay away, had to be there, had to believe that somehow, by offering his time and what little emotional energy he could muster, he would be making amends. Maybe, too, he would be helping himself.

Or maybe that was too much to hope for.

Will steered the car into the visitors' parking lot around back of Idlewild Memorial Hospital. It was a local hospital, the first stop for a lot of people being sent on to larger medical-care facilities with departments and staff that specialized in a particular rare disease or life-threatening condition.

But like pretty much every hospital Will had known, it had a children's ward. He'd been in a children's ward himself as a kid, when he'd broken his arm falling out of a tree in his parents' backyard. Looking back, from the perspective of a parent who'd lost a child, he realized that what had seemed like a horrible experience at the time, wasn't so bad at all. At least he'd come out of it alive.

Also like every hospital Will had known, Idlewild Memorial welcomed volunteers. This would be Will's first day on board. He'd asked to be assigned to the children's ward.

Will turned off the engine and took a deep breath. The

morning was to be taken up with a series of training sessions. Then there'd be an informal lunch with the other new volunteers and the staff who ran the volunteer program. Will grimaced. He hoped the cafeteria at Idlewild served better food than the last hospital Luke had been in. Will had long outgrown his taste for sandwiches from a machine. Although before he'd gotten to the point where he could no longer eat, Luke had had a bizarre fondness for the cardboardlike ham and cheese on white.

After lunch would come the difficult—and maybe wonderful—part of the day. Will would be introduced to the patients. Will's job? To read to the children, play games with them, hold their hands if they were scared. Nothing more and nothing less.

Still, the whole thing seemed an enormous challenge, one Will wasn't entirely sure he was prepared to take on. But it was a challenge he'd committed to and he was determined, from this day forth, to be a man of his word.

Will got out of the car and began to walk around to the building's front entrance. It was a beautiful morning, the air fresh and crisp, the sun bright. In spite of his nervousness about what lay ahead, Will couldn't help but smile as he remembered last night with Regina.

It had been an amazing thing, making love to Regina after eight long years apart. Like coming home but also like starting over, both comforting and thrilling. In the end, they'd finally fallen asleep, side by side. Like it should be, Will thought. Two of a kind.

Almost. People in a real, honest relationship didn't lie or withhold important information from each other. He knew that. He knew Regina was as honest a person as he could ever hope to love.

But early that morning, Regina had gone to her apartment to feed the cats, the look on her face a bit wistful. And before she left, Will had said nothing about his plans for the day. Part of him desperately wanted to ask Regina

to spend it with him—making love again and again, putting together an enormous brunch of eggs and sausage and muffins, taking a late afternoon walk.

But he'd said nothing, held back from asking her to be with him, refrained from telling her about his volunteer work at the hospital.

Why? Part of him was angry he hadn't just told Regina about the hospital, maybe asked her to drive over with him or to meet him afterwards.

Okay, he wanted to pace things, not rush, take things easy and slow. Sure. But the real difficulty came when Will realized he just couldn't mention his volunteer work because that would lead to questions and questions would lead to Luke and. . . .

He was back in Idlewild. He was in love with Regina Sutherland. But he still wasn't ready to share Luke with anybody. He regretted that, but it was true.

Will opened the door to the hospital lobby and stepped inside.

The middle-aged nurse smiled kindly at Will. "Are you ready to meet our little Joy?" she said, coming to a stop just outside Room 202 in the children's ward. "She was admitted just yesterday so she's still a bit shy. Her parents are so scared, I'm afraid they aren't being much help in reassuring their daughter. Right now they're in conference with Joy's physicians and you'll have about an hour before they come back."

Will answered with a nod and nervous smile of his own. "Yes, sure," he said, "I'm ready." He was aware his throat was dry and his voice somewhat scratchy. For a split second he worried he had the beginnings of a cold and if that was the case, there was no way he could meet and spend time with a sick child, one whose immune system was broken down or seriously overtaxed.

But then, in the next second, he realized his symptoms indicated nerves, fear, not bodily illness. He was okay. At least, he was pretty sure he'd be okay.

"Have you worked with cancer patients before, Mr. Creeden?" Nurse Clarke asked now.

What to say to that! No, technically, he hadn't worked with cancer patients. But yeah, he'd certainly had his share of caring for one. Again, to admit the truth would mean listening to questions he just wasn't ready or willing to answer.

"Uh, no, no," he said quickly. "I, uh, just thought, you know, I'm new in Idlewild, well, I just moved back after almost ten years away and. . . ."

Nurse Clarke smiled. "I see. You thought volunteering at the hospital would be a good way to get involved in the community, meet some people, right?"

Will smiled gratefully. "That's it, exactly," he confirmed.

"Good then. Shall we go inside?" Nurse Clarke moved ahead of Will and entered the small room. Will followed.

On the right side of the room, a freshly made bed stood empty. On the left, another bed, this one with slightly rumpled sheets. And under those sheets, propped up against two fluffed pillows, sat a pale-skinned, wide-eyed, round-faced little girl with a head of wild red curls. Will's first, awful thought was that little Joy would lose those gorgeous curls before long. His second, more hopeful thought was that if all went well, God willing, before too long they'd grow back, maybe thicker than ever.

And his third, strange and disconcerting thought was that this child could be Regina's child, with her distinctive skin, hair and eye color.

"Good afternoon, Joy." Nurse Clarke fussed briefly with the thin blue blanket at the foot of the girl's bed, then efficiently checked the two intravenous drips leading from a standing machine to the little girl's arm. "I've brought

along a friend to see you. His name is Will and he'll be happy to read to you today, if you like, until your mommy and daddy come back."

The little girl's wide blue eyes were solemn as she looked from the nurse to the strange man in the doorway.

Will smiled. "Hi, Joy," he said, softly, fighting against memories of a similar bed, similar machines, the too familiar and competing odors of stale air and strong disinfectant. "My name is Will."

When the child continued to stare, Will's parental training quickly kicked in. "You know," he said, taking a step farther into the room, closer to the bed, "if you don't want me to read to you today, that's okay. I'm going to be coming to see you a lot so we can read some other time." Slowly, Will sat in a big vinyl chair a few feet from the bed. Joy had followed him with those solemn eyes. "You know, I think someone told me this TV has Nickelodeon. Do you like to watch some of those shows?"

Joy nodded.

"Me, too. I like *Teletubbies* myself."

A tiny sparkle came into the child's eyes. "That's for babies," she said softly.

Will grinned. "I know. But I really like Tinky Winky."

"I like Franklin," Joy said. She reached under the covers and pulled out a stuffed turtle. "Here."

"Well, look at him!" Will pet the toy Franklin on its head. "Is he your good friend?"

Joy nodded vigorously.

From the far side of the bed, Nurse Clarke caught Will's eyes and smiled. "I'll be back soon, you two," she said. "Have fun, now."

# **Twenty**

"Lucy! That cheese is not for kitties!" Regina swatted lightly at her dairy-loving ten-pounder and laughed. It wasn't that she minded giving Lucy a small piece of cheese. It was just that she was pretty sure guests wouldn't be thrilled at finding cat hair in their meals. "On the floor, now. And Mommy will put something in your dish."

The calico jumped off the kitchen counter and landed at Regina's feet with a thud. Regina sliced a piece of the Parmesan and put it in Lucy's favorite green dish. Amazing how fussy cats could be, she thought, and not for the first time, as Lucy dug in. Regina knew that even if Lucy were dying for a snack, she wouldn't eat it if it were in a different dish or bowl. Worse than a man, Regina thought. In some ways, anyway.

A man. Regina grinned as she worked, chopping tomatoes, putting garlic cloves through a press, grating cheese. It had been too long since she'd had a man in her bed—or since she'd been in his. But now . . . now she had not just any man but Will. Will Creeden, her one and only love. He was back and he was hers.

Last night had been fantastic. Regina shivered remembering how Will's lips and hands had reawakened sensations, feelings, desires and needs she'd thought had gone for good. Today, life looked a whole lot more interesting than it had yesterday, and Regina had a feeling life was

going to continue to seem a whole lot more interesting before she and Will were through.

But we'll never be through, she thought happily, scraping tomato chunks into a small bowl. Because last night she and Will had stood on the threshold of a new world and welcomed it with open hearts and hands. Today was only the very beginning of the rest of her life—and of their life together.

Regina laughed aloud. She sounded like a cereal commercial or something! But it *would* be wonderful. And she would forget all the pain Will's previous marriage had caused her. She'd all but forgotten it already, Regina thought with surprise. From now on, she would keep in mind Will's own painful experiences; she would learn true compassion and put aside judgment and not be so selfish. From now on she would focus only on the bright and shining future she and Will would share. Who knew? Maybe they would be better for each other now, having gone through a marriage, various relationships, several years in New York City and Chicago, respectively. Maybe now they could come together with a maturity they never would have gained if not for those years apart. Maybe now that their souls had been tempered in the fires of experience, they would know better how to love and care for one another.

Like this afternoon, Regina thought. All she'd really wanted to do was spend time preparing Will's favorite pasta sauce, a basic, garlicky red he could consume by the gallon, if he allowed himself that luxury. But first she'd had to run some errands and do some light housecleaning and start preparing a talk for an interdisciplinary lecture series starting in early December. Finally, after those once pleasant but suddenly boring tasks, she was free to do something special for Will.

I'm in love, she realized, grinning again though there was no one there to witness her joy. And she'd spend an-

other night with the man she adored, first over dinner and then pursuing a far more interesting and intimate activity.

Of course, she'd yet to talk to Will today, so she hadn't been able to actually invite him over. But she'd left a message on his answering machine and wherever he was, she was sure to hear him when he came home. The walls in their apartment building weren't exactly soundproof—both a good and a bad thing, depending on what or who you were listening for. This morning, not long after Regina had gotten back to her own apartment, she'd heard Will's footsteps in the hall and then the front door slam shut.

Truth be told, she'd hoped Will would suggest they spend the day together, or at least a part of it. But he hadn't and that was okay. She and Will were adults, with full and responsible lives. They couldn't be expected to drop everything else to spend all their time together after just one evening of romance. Even if they did share a past.

For one brief moment, a horrible doubt forced its way into Regina's mind. What if last night hadn't meant anything special to Will, like it had to her? What if he'd made love to her out of pity or sorrow or guilt? Thrown her a bone after all these years. . . . What if he couldn't wait to get away this morning, away from Regina and everything she reminded him of?

Regina put her hands to her head. Stop it, she commanded herself. Just stop it. What are you doing to yourself? You know Will's not like that.

Wasn't he? Wasn't he just the type to love and then leave, a cruel part of her mind argued. The type to make promises of fidelity and then to trample those very promises into the ground? He'd done it to her once, left her, betrayed her. What was to prevent him from doing it again? People didn't change, did they? Men didn't change.

"Oh, God," she whispered. "Please help me. Please

help me believe in Will, trust him." Maybe if she knew more about Will's state of mind when he'd married Connie, maybe that would make it easier to trust now, to believe he wouldn't abandon her a second time.

No. No excuses. True love wasn't about perfect circumstances and demanding full, explicit confessions of troubles in a long-ago past. It was something bigger and yes, better than petty fears and insecurities, jealousies and angers. Regina knew that if she was to love Will in the way he deserved to be loved—in the way a good woman should love a good man—she would have to believe his words and his actions starting now, from this very moment forth. She would have to believe that this Will, the adult Will, would not make the same mistake twice. Would not hurt her.

Yes, she would trust him. She was afraid she had no choice. Regina took a deep breath and put the ingredients for the sauce aside. She glanced at the clock. Four-thirty. Still early. She'd force herself to concentrate on some work, wait to hear from Will, confirming a time for dinner, then finish preparing the meal.

Plenty of time, she thought, trying to regain some of the contentment she'd felt only an hour earlier. The most precious gift of all. Finally, there was plenty of time.


With a sigh, Regina saved her document and stretched. At least she'd fully outlined the talk she was to give. She'd let it sit for a few days, then go back to it with a fresh perspective. It was amazing how a little time away from a situation or project brought new insights and a more honed critical sense.

Regina looked at her watch and was startled. Eight o'clock already. Time had flown. And no word from Will. She hadn't heard him come home—not that she'd been consciously listening, she told herself—which meant that

he was still out. That meant he probably hadn't gotten her message, unless he'd called in to his answering machine and why would he have done that?

For any number of reasons, Regina realized, annoyed with herself. Why was she starting this silly guessing game again? She shut down her computer, stood and walked to the kitchen. Well, there was no point in not finishing the pasta sauce, was there? Will might still call or come by. And besides, the sauce would keep if he didn't show up. And you might want to eat something, Regina reminded herself dryly.

But first, some music, a little Frank Sinatra to sing along to. She chose a CD of Frank's years at Capitol records, pumped the volume just enough to feel slightly guilty about the neighbors, freshened her lipstick during a quick stop to the bathroom (shades of her grandmother, she thought with a grin—the woman had preached the power of lipstick to help a woman feel put together no matter what her troubles) and headed back to the kitchen.

Shooing away wailing felines, Regina sang along with the Chairman of the Board, sipped a glass of wine and set to work on the sauce. For almost an hour she was kept busy by Frank's sexy crooning, the demands of creating a fresh salad and dressing and the other elements of a good meal.

Frank sang mournfully, asking about this thing called love. I wish I knew, Regina thought, suddenly torn from the simple tasks before her and faced with the reality that it was now nine o'clock and she'd still had not heard from Will. She looked at the sauce simmering slowly on the stovetop and she felt her heart sink within her. What had she been thinking? How did she even know that Will would still like her red sauce? She hadn't made it for him in more than eight years. Why had she presumed to know who he was anymore, what he liked and disliked? Why had she assumed anything at all about Will Creeden? For

all she knew he had spent the day with Celia Keene, was planning to spend the night, too. After all, he and Regina hadn't said anything specific about an exclusive relationship, had they?

Stop it, stop it, stop it! Regina told herself angrily. Will had denied any romantic involvement with Celia. Didn't she believe him? What was she, an adolescent? Obsessing this way over some guy. Not just some guy, she corrected. The most important guy. But how would you feel if he knew what you were doing to yourself tonight, she countered. Would you want him to know how little you think of yourself?

Regina was disgusted. For the past eight years, she'd been on her own. She'd made strides in her career and dated men who were educated and handsome and kind. One night with Will and she was becoming someone she'd never been, someone she never thought she'd become. Someone weak and silly. Love uplifted and made you feel good about yourself, strong, not unsure and scared. At least, mutual, reciprocated love made you strong. She'd just have to calm down and take this revived relationship with Will one day at a time. She'd have to stop thinking about disaster and betrayal before she and Will even had a chance to explore this new relationship. She'd have to have courage.

And I will have courage, Regina vowed. She poured herself another glass of wine and raised the heat under the pot of sauce. Some pasta, salad, more Frank and some Mississippi Delta blues. She'd have a fine time tonight with the company of an attractive, smart, funny woman named Regina Sutherland. Maybe she'd even check out the pay-per-view channel, see if there was anything good being offered, like a comedy, maybe one with Bill Murray.

Footsteps. Even from the bedroom, where she was propped up in bed watching a late-night movie, she heard

them, coming up the hall stairs, pausing then, for almost
a full minute, just outside her door.

Will. Regina hit the volume button on the remote and
listened harder in the silence. Would he knock? Why was
he standing there—waiting, thinking? And then, the footsteps again, moving away and back toward the hall stairs,
slowly and—sadly? Then, moving up the stairs, one by
one. Another moment of silence, and then a door closing.

Regina frowned. What was that about, she thought, sliding down farther against the pillows. She looked at her
watch. Almost midnight. But she wouldn't start worrying,
wondering. She was over that now. Tomorrow, she'd simply ask Will where he'd been. Say—calmly, maybe
brightly—how sorry she was they hadn't been able to
hook up, get together for dinner. With a smile, offer to
give him a plastic container of sauce—ask first if he still
liked garlicky red, promise him she'd made too much for
one, remind him he could freeze it for some other time.

Oh, Will, Regina thought, staring blindly at the television screen. Are we going to be okay? Can we put the
past to rest and create our own future?

# Twenty-one

It was amazing how one minute, you could be so scared, so convinced the happiness you'd just found was ephemeral. And then, in the next minute, a secret smile from your lover could revolutionize your world, make you beam with joy, make you feel strong and cherished and absolutely able to conquer the world.

If conquering the world was your thing. And it's not mine, Regina thought, glancing meaningfully back at Will across the hall as they passed, a stream of hurrying students between them. It's enough that I have Will in my life.

Regina rounded a corner and casually looked over her shoulder as she did. Will had been stopped by an eager young freshman Regina recognized from one of her introductory classes. Clare something-or-other. Clare Sheridan. And the way she was gazing up at Will adoringly made Regina smile. She couldn't be jealous of a virtual child. Besides, it was wonderful how Will inspired kids of all ages, how they really seemed to listen to whatever it was he was saying.

And this paragon of manhood was hers! All hers. Regina kept on toward the English department, laughing to herself. Paragon of manhood! What was she saying! Since Saturday night her mind had turned to a steaming, bubbling stew of rekindled romance and reawakened desire. If truth be told, Regina felt downright goopy with love.

Sure, Sunday night, when Will had come home so late and Regina had sat brooding over Sinatra, cold, hard fear had just about overcome her softer, warmer feelings for Will. But then, Monday morning, Will had come by her apartment early, eager to apologize for his having missed her dinner invitation, asking if maybe they could reschedule for that very evening. True, he hadn't offered any specific explanation for where he'd been all day and into the night. He'd simply said he'd been busy, running countless errands pertaining to his new home and job. And after a moment's hesitation, Regina had decided she didn't need to ask for specifics. Didn't need to know details. Asking might imply she was wary and suspicious of Will and love wasn't about distrust. For the first time in a long time, she was being called on to be courageous and she would meet that challenge. Although she wouldn't have minded accompanying him on those errands. . . .

So, Monday night they'd reheated Regina's famous sauce and then fallen on the couch in a mad, almost desperate embrace, clutching each other's bodies, tearing away clothing. In the end, she'd lain on top of him, their stomachs glued together with sweat, the earthy smell of sex tantalizing enough to lead them on again.

Tuesday night, Regina had joined her mother at a meeting of her Women's History Club. The effort it took not to spill the truth about her and Will was mind-boggling, but Regina wasn't yet ready to share Will with anyone, not even Joan Sutherland. She'd gotten home around ten o'clock, to find a note from Will slipped under her door. He'd gone to see Dr. Nelson and would meet Regina in the morning to ride together to the college.

But next morning, dressed and ready to go, Regina had knocked on Will's door only to find him just rolled out of bed and looking a little worse for the wear.

"Emily keep you up late?" Regina had teased, raising an eyebrow at Will's mess of hair and unshaved face.

A look of puzzlement flitted over Will's face. "Wha—" he began, then said, "Oh, right, well, yeah, I was up pretty late."

Regina had rushed off to the campus. She'd seen Will only briefly during the day and always in the presence of the other department members. He'd winked at her behind Miles's back once but that was the extent of their personal communication.

At least until Wednesday night. Maybe it was her imagination, but sex with Will was getting better and better almost by the minute. Regina struggled to stop the grin she knew was sliding across her face. With the gentlest of touches, Will could bring her to a height of sensation from which she felt she would never recover. Each time after, she lay trembling slightly, incapable of speech, clutching his arm, vaguely aware of his smiling down at her, of his hand on her breast.

Regina shook her head and opened the door to the department's conference room. Okay, down girl, she told herself sternly. This is not the time or the place. Thursday afternoon, lunch break, Miles snuffling at one end of the table, Celia. . . .

Well, that'll put a damper on anyone's erotic dreams, Regina thought. Lunch with Celia Keene.

Regina closed the door behind her and put her bag on the table. "Hello, Miles," she said. "Celia."

Miles grumped a greeting and went back to his roast beef sandwich.

Celia, however, did not respond. Regina took a seat, wondering at this most recent display of hostility or disdain—or whatever it was—Celia Keene felt for Regina Sutherland today. This childishness was getting boring.

"So, Regina." Celia suddenly looked up from the book she'd been perusing and smiled brightly. "You've been looking like the cat who ate the canary this week."

Startled, caught off guard by Celia's close-to-home comment, Regina laughed nervously. "I do?"

Celia closed her book with a small slam. "Yes, you do."

Okaaaayyyy. She would not give this woman anything. Regina shrugged. "I can't imagine why."

"Miles, don't you agree?" Celia pressed, her voice rising. "Doesn't our Regina look, well, a little smug lately?"

Miles scowled at having his lunch interrupted. "I am not in the habit of regarding my colleagues quite so closely as you seem to be, Miss Keene," he replied.

"That's *Dr.* Keene," Celia snapped.

In response, Miles took a lusty bite of his sandwich.

Good old Miles, Regina thought, opening up her own sandwich on the table before her. She noted her colleague's bottle of designer water and wondered briefly if Celia Keene ever ate.

For a few moments, there was relative silence, only the sounds of chewing and angry page-turning to be heard.

Finally, Regina, ever eager for harmony, spoke. "So, Celia, are you all settled in at home?"

Celia gave a half smile. "Of course. Unfortunately, I'm not fond of home entertaining so you'll have to take my word for it."

Regina resisted rolling her eyes. She hadn't been asking for an invitation, for God's sake! Just making polite conversation.

"Actually," Celia went on, toying with the pages of her book, "I'm considering looking for a permanent place, buying instead of renting. Because I'll be here—in Idlewild, I mean—for some time, it seems silly not to make the investment."

"Really? So, you're planning to stay in our sleepy little hamlet?" It was Miles, suddenly interested in the conversation. "I'd have thought you'd hurry back to the metropolis as soon as possible. I must say," he added archly, "you

don't seem to quite—how shall I put it?—fit in here in Idlewild."

Celia laughed and looked pointedly at Regina. "Well, there are certain compelling reasons for my staying on in town and at the college. One must go where the opportunities are to be found, you know.

Miles sat back in his chair and glared. "And what, pray tell, are those compelling reasons, Miss Keene?"

Before answering, Celia stood and gathered her book and bottle of water. Then she gave both Miles and Regina a look of undisguised pity.

"You'll find out soon enough," she said. "And once again, Dr. Fetherston, it's Dr. Keene, not miss. If you are having trouble remembering such a minor yet important matter of respect, I'm afraid I'll have to ask Dr. Creeden to speak with you."

Regina sat stone-still, lunch half eaten, as Celia made her way around the table and to the door. She didn't turn around when she heard her new colleague shut the door behind her.

"I don't trust that woman as far as I could throw her," Miles snarled.

Regina shook herself and laughed uncomfortably. "Well, you're lucky this isn't the World Wrestling Federation. Although . . ."

"Miss Keene suffers from an inordinate sense of her own importance. My dear, I would take great care in her presence," Miles advised.

"And I'd watch my back," Regina added. "I don't think she's above a sucker punch."

"She's after someone's job, no doubt."

And after someone's man, Regina thought grimly.

# Twenty-two

"Wasn't that a wonderful sermon?" Joan Sutherland asked her husband and daughter as they emerged from the comforting dimness of the church to the pearly gray and blue sky of a cool autumn morning.

The Sutherland family often met on Sunday mornings to attend church services and then to treat themselves to a big brunch at the Leaping Lords. In Regina's opinion, it was their most fun family tradition. Especially the Eggs Florentine.

"Reverend Morris is such a brilliant speaker," Regina agreed.

"The man makes sense, is what I like about him," her father added.

Regina laughed. "That, too."

"Well, Regina, I hope you don't have your heart too set on the pumpkin muffins at Lords."

Regina glanced over her shoulder at her mother.

"Why?" she asked. "Do you want to try someplace else?"

Joan smiled slightly. "No. But I think someone else does." She raised her eyebrows and nodded ahead. "Something you haven't told us, dear daughter?"

Regina, frowning, turned back to see Will Creeden standing at the end of the small church grounds, a slightly

awkward smile on his face, a huge picnic basket over one arm.

He looked so hopeful and adorable and. . . . "Will!" she called, gesturing for him to join them at the foot of the stairs.

"Let's see how the young man conducts himself in front of his future in-laws," Bob whispered.

"Dad!" Regina hissed.

"Bob!" Joan threatened.

"Sir, it's good to see you again." Will joined them and put out his hand to shake Mr. Sutherland's. The men greeted each other with the shake and a nod and then a smile.

"Mrs. Sutherland." Will turned to Regina's mother. "It's good to see you, too. Regina's told me you're doing well."

Though less exuberant than her husband, Joan greeted Will kindly. "Yes, thanks, Will. Bob and I are just fine. And how are things going at the college?"

Will rolled his eyes slightly and laughed. "Well, let's just say it's a challenge. An enjoyable one," he added hurriedly, "but running a department, even as acting head, is probably the hardest job I've ever had in my professional life."

Regina grinned. "But Will's doing just great. He's no Emily Nelson," she teased, "but then, he's much better-looking."

Bob laughed heartily and Will looked like he was going to slip away through a crack in the pavement.

Joan raised a questioning eyebrow at her daughter, who shrugged.

"Uh, well," Will began, clearing his throat, avoiding Regina's amused eyes. "Uh, I was hoping I could spirit away your daughter for a picnic," he said, looking from Bob and Joan. "It's such a nice day and before long we'll all be slogging through snow and ice. I know the three of

you probably have plans," he went on in a rush, "so if it's not a good time, that's fine, we can do it some other day."

Bob seemed to draw himself up. "Well," he said, almost in a drawl, "it's okay by her mother and me if it's okay by Regina. She's the one you should be asking, Will."

Will finally looked back at Regina. "What do you say?" he asked, his voice low and to Regina, thrilling. Holding promises of a very special day. "Would you like to go on a picnic with me?"

Regina frowned and tilted her head. "Do you have deviled eggs in that basket?" she said.

Will's face fell. "Oh, no, but, you know, we could stop at the store."

Regina laughed roundly. "Of course I'd like to go on a picnic with you, Will," she said, taking his arm and looking up into his face. "Deviled eggs or no deviled eggs."


"This is fantastic, Will!"

Regina twirled in a complete 360 degrees to see the view spread out around them. They stood on a sort of promenade or lookout point, surrounded by hills covered in flaming-orange, fiery-red and blinding-yellow leaves. Various grasses of green, brown and silver sprouted at their feet. The sky was a true autumn blue, almost too pretty to be real.

"Indian summer at its best," Will said, coming up from behind Regina, encircling her waist with his arms "Maybe the last day before it gets too cold to eat outside, who knows?"

Regina leaned into Will, her blood beginning to rush.

"So, is that the only reason you wanted to take advantage of the warm weather?" she asked huskily. "So we can eat alfresco?"

Will laughed low and let his hands spread down against her abdomen. "Actually, I was hoping. . . ."

Regina twisted in his arms to face him. Hungrily, they kissed.

"I think I'd like to take my jacket off, sir," she breathed.

"Have I convinced you, then?"

"Wasn't difficult, was it?"

The picnic sat forgotten. A hamper of food and wine would wait, a ready-made celebration for later.

He led her to a grouping of sprawling oaks and laid out a soft blanket. Then, in the bright autumn light, skin caressed by the warm autumn breeze, he began to undress her, slowly, tenderly. Until her own moans of desire, her own urging, made him hurry, lift her breasts from her bra so that the undergarment framed and lifted them to his waiting mouth.

"Will . . ." she breathed, pressing closer, closer. "Please . . ."

Quickly, he eased her down to the ground, continued to suck on her breast while letting a hand trail tantalizingly down, down. . . .

She arched against his fingers, wet and ready and almost crying in need. He lifted his head, took her mouth in his and with a light, knowing movement, brought her to climax.

"Will," she cried, "I want you inside me, please!"

Gracefully, he lifted himself above her, slid down, then in.

"Gina," he murmured, one hand cradling the back of her neck. "Oh, yes . . ."

Half dressed, they ate their picnic.

Will grinned. "What are you smiling about? You look incredibly adorable right now."

Regina laughed out loud. "I'm smiling about life, silly.

How fantastic is this? A beautiful day, good food. Amazing sex with you." As she spoke she could feel herself grow warm again with the desire for this man. It hadn't been a half hour since their lovemaking but already she was hungry for him.

And he knew it. She could see it in his eyes. Somehow they grew darker, more intense.

He stood and held out his hand for her.

Regina took it and pulled herself to her feet. Slowly, irrevocably, holding her shoulders, he walked her backward to the oak tree under which they had been sitting. She gasped when her back met the bark and pulled him to her. She wanted to be crushed by this man, consumed.

"Kiss me!" she commanded.

He did. With urgency, as if this were the last kiss they would ever share.

She felt him go hard. Thought she could feel the heat through his jeans, through her skirt. Moaning, she slid a hand against him. Fumbled for his zipper. "I want you to take me here," she said huskily. "Against this tree."

He said nothing but roughly pulled her skirt up to her waist.

"Are you sure?" he whispered.

"Yes."

And then he lifted her up and onto him.

She cried out, clutched him, pressed herself onto him, held him tight.

"Harder!" she gasped.

They came together, under the autumn skies.

# Twenty-three

Six-thirty. Damn. If he didn't hurry he'd miss seeing Joy tonight. In a few short visits Joy had come to mean so much to him, her every smile a gift from God, her every little whim his absolute command. No doubt about it, Joy's presence in his life was helping him heal. He only hoped his presence in her life was having some sort of positive effect.

Will edged the speedometer up to sixty-five. He'd take his chances with a particular member of the local sheriff's office, a guy whose sole purpose in life seemed to be to catch drivers going even five miles over the county road limit.

It had been an amazing day, maybe the best in years, certainly since he'd come back to Idlewild. He'd met Regina outside the church she and her parents attended, the same one they'd attended since Regina was a small child. He'd braved meeting the Sutherlands for the first time since he'd left town more than eight years ago. And then he'd spent a gorgeous autumn afternoon making love to the queen of his heart.

Will grinned as he remembered the glow of Regina's hair in the golden afternoon light. The curve of her shoulders as she reached up for him. The whiteness of her skin against his own, darker coloring. How she'd opened for him, grasped him to her, called his name softly at first,

embarrassed by the prospect of being discovered. And then, as he'd brought her to climax, how she'd called his name more loudly, with need and desire.

Six-thirty-five. He'd better get his mind off Regina and on the task at hand, Will thought, squirming slightly in his seat. He had a present for Joy, and he'd promised to read her a story before she went to sleep. He wondered if she liked the classic fairy tales, like Cinderella and Snow White, Sleeping Beauty and Rapunzel. The pre-Disney versions. Well, he'd just have to find out. Good thing he'd brought Luke's *Big Book of British Fairy Tales* with him tonight.

Six-forty-five and counting. Will wondered now if he'd disappointed Regina by not finishing the evening with her. After their picnic and outdoor lovemaking, he'd driven her home, walked her to her door and with a promising kiss, said good night. Told her he'd see her in the morning.

He recalled now the look of puzzlement on her face, the passing sadness. Had there been also a note of fear or distrust? No, he'd been imagining that. And Regina had recovered quickly, thanked him brightly and with another thank-you kiss for a fabulous afternoon, wished him a good night and closed her door.

He'd told her he wanted to go slow, hadn't he? Yes, but that was before they'd first slept together, that night after dinner at his apartment. Regina had a right to expect more from him now, Will knew. After all, she was giving so much more of herself to him now that they were making love, more than just her body, certainly.

Soon, he promised himself, silently. Soon he'd be ready to tell Regina all, talk to her about Luke. Ask if she could still love a man who'd failed his own family so badly. Promise to start fresh with her, build their own family, if she would have him.

And he'd like to get to that point of strength before

Regina asked him another question about his son. And she would, she had the right to.

He hoped he had the courage to look her in the eye and come clean with dignity. He hoped she wouldn't blame him for Luke's death, the way he'd blamed himself. The way Connie had blamed him, after the funeral. He couldn't believe she'd actually come. But she had, and right there, within feet of Luke's grave, she'd attacked him. Detached herself from all responsibility as wife and mother and attributed Luke's death to Will's own falseness in their marriage. Blamed him for using her eight years earlier, catching her at a moment of weakness. Said that none of this would have happened if Will hadn't taken advantage of her that night, when they were both drunk.

Maybe she'd been crazed with grief, more likely, bitter with disappointment. But Connie's words had penetrated Will's own sorrow and inordinate sense of responsibility and stuck, way down deep.

Seven o'clock. Will pulled the car into the hospital's parking lot and with a sigh, turned off the ignition.

He hoped he wasn't too late.


"What do you mean, she's not here? I can see that!" Will gestured down the hall, toward Joy's empty room. "Where did she go? When?"

The night nurse at the nurses' station spoke in a voice and manner trained for calming irate and emotional visitors. "First, may I ask who you are? What is your relationship to the patient?"

Will sighed and ran a hand through his hair. "I'm a volunteer here," he said. "I was scheduled to be here tonight to read to Joy before bedtime. Look, if you can't tell me where she is, can anyone else? Her toys are gone, her—"

The woman held up a hand and continued to read down a list on the desk in front of her. "Yes, you're Mr. Will Creeden?"

"Yes, that's right," Will said impatiently.

"Here, this is for you." The woman held out a small, sealed envelope. "It was left for you by Nurse Clarke when she went off duty several hours ago."

The buzzing in Will's head that had started the moment he'd seen the envelope grew, and suddenly threatened to overwhelm him. His face felt hot, his skin prickled all over with pinpoints of heat, his vision swam. He was going to faint.

"Mr. Creeden?" The voice came through a thick fog, the loud buzz of approaching unconsciousness. "Are you all right, Mr. Creeden?"

All right . . . no. Yes. Yes. "Yes," he blurted, using every ounce of his strength and nerve to come back from the brink, to see and hear clearly, to stand firmly. "I'm . . . I'm fine. Thanks."

The nurse's face was dark with doubt but she nodded. "Why don't you have a seat over there?" She gestured toward a group of three plastic chairs and a small table strewn with out-of-date magazines.

"Yes, okay, I . . ." Slowly, one foot put carefully in front of the other, Will made his way to the chairs, ashamed, scared, clinging to control. Joy had not been scheduled for release any time soon. What had happened?

Will eased into the chair farthest from the nurses' desk, dropped the book of fairy tales onto a small table and stared at the envelope in his hand. He'd wrinkled it, almost folded it in half, in the sweep of despair. He took a deep breath and inserted a finger under the flap. Slid out a single sheet of folded white paper, torn from a memo pad. And read the note from Nurse Clarke.

* * *

"Sir! Mr. Creeden!"

Will didn't stop, didn't answer to his name being called by the night nurse. He just kept running, out of that place, away, far away from that place of death and despair.

"Mr. Creeden, are you all right!"

*Whoosh!*

Will threw open the door to the stairwell and charged down to the second, the first floor.

*Woosh!*

Through another door and then the lobby and then finally. . . .

Out into the night. Will bent over and tried to catch his breath. Took deep lungfuls of cool, fresh air. Then stood straight and threw his head back and looked into the sky as if it contained the answer. As if the few bright stars twinkling overhead could tell him.

Tell him why another child had to die.


An hour later. It had taken Will almost an hour to make it home. He drove slowly, like a much, much older man. Dragged his legs up the stairs. Didn't stop when he passed Regina's door. Didn't even think about stopping.

He closed the door to his apartment behind him and immediately looked for the blinking red light of the answering machine.

One blink. One message. That would be the message from Nurse Clarke. The note said she'd tried to call him, to speak with him personally, but finally, regretfully, had just left a message on his machine. And written a note for him, to be left with the night nurse.

It had been unexpected. Cardiac arrest. Irreversible. Tragic. Her parents had been with her, thank God, Nurse Clarke wrote. She hadn't died alone.

But she'd died.

Nurse Clarke hoped this one bad experience wouldn't

prevent Will from continuing with his volunteer work. He
had a natural way with children. He could do so much for
a sick or dying child.

This one bad experience. . . .

The phone rang at nine-oh-five. Will let it ring. He was
in no mood or condition to speak to anyone. He didn't
even know how he felt. Sad. Depressed. Frightened. Angry. Hopeless?

Yeah, maybe hopeless came closest.

"Will, hi, it's Celia. I was hoping to find you home."

In spite of himself, Will tuned in to the voice speaking
softly into his living room.

"My bad luck. I know it's kind of late on a school
night—" Here, Celia stopped to laugh lightly. "But I was
wondering if you'd like to come over to my place. I guess
I'm just being selfish. I've been working all day on those
ideas for the fair I mentioned to you the other day."

Will searched his mind. Yes, she'd said she had some
ideas for improving the fair, bringing the production of
the Shakespeare scene, the centerpiece of the entire event,
into the twenty-first century. He hadn't paid much attention to her the other day, he'd been too busy rereading a
student's paper before class. He did now recall that later
that day he'd had a fleeting thought that the production of
the play, and the fair as a whole, a tradition more than
twenty years old, shouldn't be tampered with. But . . .

He'd missed the rest of Celia's message. Will got up to
play it back and then thought, Why not? He sure as hell
wasn't being productive sitting around here, staring at the
chip in the ceiling paint. Briefly, he thought of calling
Regina, instead. Of telling her everything, about Luke and
Joy and his own heartache.

But the thought of all the emotion, all the grief and

despair and. . . . He was tired. Too, too tired. Tired and hopeless.

And what did it matter now, anyway?

He grabbed his bag off the couch and rummaged for his date planner/phone book. Scanned the *K* page. Dialed Celia's number.

Fifteen minutes later, he was ringing her doorbell.

# Twenty-four

"Why do certain people insist on holding a weekly departmental meeting first thing Monday morning?" Miles Fetherston was grumpy. He was a congenitally grumpy person. This everyone knew and accepted. But on Mondays, particularly Monday mornings, he was more than grumpy. He was a pill. A curmudgeon. Even, some would say—

"Miles, you old fart." It was Maria Jackson. She spoke with a twinkle in her eye. "When are you going to stop complaining about what you don't have the power to change."

Miles harrumphed. "Never, I assure you."

"Miles's moods are one of the inevitables in this world," Regina added, winking at Maria. "Like death and taxes."

Aidan Ross joined the others at the small conference table. "Now, now," he said pleasantly, ever the peacemaker, "Miles just hasn't had his coffee yet. Here, my personality-challenged colleague, try this." Aidan handed a steaming mug of his special brew to Professor Fetherston, who took it with only a small grumble.

"So," Regina said now, opening the steno pad in which she kept notes on everything from which bills needed paying to which poems needed rereading, "it's about time we started finalizing some of the details of the English department's role in the fair. Particularly, of course, the

Shakespeare selection. I mean, I'm assuming we're doing everything pretty much the same as last year? A comedy, maybe *As You Like It?*"

Maria nodded. "Why fix it if it ain't broke. Aidan? You're in charge. Tell us what needs doing and we'll do it."

"I agree that our participation in last year's fair was quite successful," he said. "Thanks to everyone's help. I do have a few small ideas for improving—"

"Good morning, all."

Will Creeden strode into the room with his usual briskness. Regina felt herself blush and battled to control an uncontrollable reaction to the sight of her lover. Even being in the same room with this man made her hot and turned her mind to porridge. Images of yesterday's lovemaking in the fresh, open air surged through her mind and body, making sitting still and professional almost an impossibility.

And then, like Will's shadow, into the room slipped Celia Keene. Regina's blush cooled. Celia was too close behind Will for them not to have approached the door together. Why had she hesitated a moment, come in behind him? And why am I obsessing over something I'm completely making up, Regina wondered, annoyed now.

"Humph." Miles.

"Good morning, Will. Celia." Aidan, ever gracious.

Maria waved a hand, too busy chewing a muffin to speak.

Before Regina could muster an intelligible greeting, Will turned around to Celia, now seated closest to the door. "Ceel, would you close the door, please? We've got a lot to do this morning and I don't want unnecessary interruptions."

*Ceel?* Regina bristled.

And what kind of business could possibly require a

closed door? The English department and its staff were certainly not known for their outré habits and behavior.

Could someone. . . . Will didn't have the power to fire anyone did he? She'd heard mutterings from her colleagues in other departments, rumors that the college might just be interested in replacing its nondoctoral staff with full Ph.D.'s. Regina shook her head. Stop it, she ordered herself. Just listen to what he has to say. Besides, Will wouldn't fire or reprimand anyone in public, in front of his or her colleagues, would he?

Will took a seat and drew a manila folder from his bag. "I hope everyone had a good weekend," he said, glancing quickly at the staff, careful not to let his eyes linger on Regina. "Because the next few weeks are going to be pretty busy for us all, with midterms and getting the annual fair in place."

"Yes, we were just talking about that before you came in," Maria said, wiping her fingers on a napkin. "Last year's fair was such a success—"

"I'm sure it was," Will interrupted. "And it was also very much like the one the year before it. And the one the year before that."

Miles narrowed his eyes. "Your point, sir?"

Regina couldn't help the horrible feeling growing in her stomach. Or her heart. Somewhere inside, maybe all over. Her heart began to thump, and she felt slightly nauseous. Something was not right.

Will shifted in his chair and met Miles's gaze directly. "My point," he said calmly, "is that it's time for a change. At least as far as the English department's part in the event. Time to shake things up a bit, time to let some new talent have their turn at running things."

Regina darted a look at Aidan. His face was dispassionate, expressionless though polite.

Then she looked at Celia and knew that Will's "new talent" was looking right back at her.

Aidan cleared his throat. "How will this affect the organization of the scene's staff, Will?" he asked.

Will put up a hand as if to ward off objections. "There'll be a place for everyone, I'm sure. At least a job to take on, either before or during the fair. Scripts have to be printed, flyers circulated, the department's booth has to be manned, and whatever money we take in counted and—"

"Is Aidan in charge or isn't he?" Miles demanded.

"Miles!" Maria protested.

Regina couldn't speak if she wanted to. The lump of anxiety had settled in her throat.

Will glanced at Celia and then back to the group. "I've decided to let Dr. Keene direct and stage the Shakespeare scene at this year's fair. She has some wonderfully innovative ideas—"

"What!" Miles thundered. "That scene is the centerpiece of the fair. Aidan's been handling the casting and directing for the past ten years!"

"Will . . ." Regina stopped. Celia looked at her inquiringly.

"Yes, Regina?" she said, with a small smile. "Were you going to say something?"

Again, Regina felt the blood rush to her face. But this time, the reason had nothing to do with lust. "Yes," she said, working to keep her voice steady, "I was. Will, isn't this a little sudden? I mean, well, I think we'd all have liked to have been consulted on such a major decision."

Maria nodded. "In the past," she began, calmly, nonaccusatorially, "Dr. Nelson encouraged us to make decisions about the fair as a committee or team. I have to say it worked to the fair's advantage."

Will sat back in his chair. "Dr. Nelson isn't heading this department this year," he reminded. "I'm sure her methods were productive but that's no reason not to make changes that will benefit—"

"Who?" Miles sneered. "Benefit who, Dr. Creeden?

Certainly not the Idlewild community. Our little town likes its fair and its Shakespeare the good, old-fashioned way."

"Dr. Fetherston, I assure you Dr. Keene will mount a production worthy of this college. She has a strong reputation for challenging artistic boundaries with—"

Regina couldn't help it. She laughed, not happily. "Challenging artistic boundaries? Will, I appreciate what you're saying, but you know as well as I do that this is not a venue for experimentation! This is a traditional small-town fall fair. A cherished annual event. It's about dunking for apples and homemade-pie contests and a chance for the community to mingle with the college folk. It's about raising money for projects that benefit everyone, like a new wing on the public library."

"It's always been about bringing the college and the community together," Aidan said quietly. "Not about dividing them."

"Just what are you all objecting to, specifically?" Will shot back. "My asserting authority or my appointing Dr. Keene in charge? Do you object to her because she's the new person on the staff and none of you is generous enough to give her a shot at the job? Or do you all resist the notion of a challenge to your own narrow conceptions of art?"

There was silence. The air was thick with anger. Regina thought she would explode. How could Will have said such mean-spirited things to his staff? To her! It was . . . it was impossible. A bad dream.

"Perhaps," Maria said quietly, after a few moments, "perhaps we should hear from Dr. Keene. Perhaps her ideas are less, ah, disruptive to the spirit of the fair than we're assuming." Calmly, with dignity, she turned her head to Will. "None of us in this room are opposed to change in and of itself, Dr. Creeden. I think such an accusation is unworthy of you—and certainly of us."

Will nodded. "Maybe my judgment was unfair. But it

was based on the fact that certain members of this staff refuse even to listen to a new idea before they reject it. That's not acceptable in a scholar."

Will Creeden was being downright belligerent, Regina realized. Like he wanted to create dissention, start a nasty fight. But for what reason? To what end? What had happened between, well, yesterday afternoon and this morning to have produced such a gross change in his personality?

Another horrid silence. Regina thought she would cry and be sick at the same time. That and guilty of murder.

"Well," Celia said brightly. The only person in the room untouched by the controversy her very presence had caused. "If anyone's interested, the first change is that we'll be using professional actors and not amateurs from the town and the school." She smiled falsely. "In case your milkman asks to audition for the lead. And, Aidan"—Celia reached across the table and patted his arm—"I'm sure there'll be a place for you. You can help me . . . well, we'll come up with something."

Aidan allowed a tiny, frozen smile to reach his lips. "You're too kind, Dr. Keene. I'm willing to do whatever I can for the good of the fair."

Will cleared his throat. "Right, then. Let's move on. Next order of business."

Regina heard nothing after that.

# Twenty-five

Regina looked up from the paper she was grading. Was that a knock on the door? There it was again, less tentative, a little louder and more definite.

"Coming," she muttered. She knew who it was, who it had to be. And she was in no mood to talk to Will now. But if she didn't answer the door and get the confrontation over with, things would only get worse. Anger would grow and fester and a problem that might have been solved in a half hour would take months to get over.

Regina pulled open the door. And waited.

Will stood there, looking a bit sheepish, a bit confused. "Can I come in?" he said finally.

Still silent, Regina stood back and let Will pass into the apartment.

"Am I getting the silent treatment?" he asked with a small laugh. As if he knew the answer but were still afraid to hear it.

Regina sighed. "No, Will. What can I do for you?" she said, sitting back down at the table with her work.

Will hesitated, then sat at the table with her. "Can we talk?"

"What about?" she said, her voice tight.

"Come on, Regina, don't play this game with me," Will replied. "You're upset about something and I want to know what. Was it something I did?"

Regina's eyes widened. "Do you mean to tell me you really don't know why I'm angry?" she said. "After what went on at the meeting today?"

"Well," Will began, looking down at his hands, folded on the table, "I know some people don't like the idea of Celia's taking over as director of the play."

Regina laughed sharply. "Some people? How about the entire department, Will." She stood and began to pace. "I mean, I can't believe you interfered this way. For ten years the play's been under Aidan's control and it's always come off just great. There was no need to basically fire him. But to replace him like you did," she said, stopping to glare at Will, "in front of everyone, and to give Celia, of all people, his job, that was just unconscienable."

The gloves were off. Regina hated to fight. She hadn't planned on fighting, had sworn she would stay calm and be reasonable. But right then, face-to-face with Will, she really felt she had to stick up for herself and the others in the department. Didn't she? In a way, she was their spokesperson. Wasn't she?

Especially after he'd basically insulted everyone's intelligence!

Will made an expression of disbelief. "Okay, wait a minute," he said, sitting back in his chair. "Let's just back up here for a minute, Regina. I don't consider my decision to allow Celia a shot at directing the play 'interference.' Unless I'm mistaken, I was appointed the acting departmental head and as such, I have the authority to make such a decision."

"But does having the authority give you the right?" Regina shot back.

Will was silent for a moment. His face hardened. "Yes, in this case, I believe it does."

"Well, I don't agree." Regina folded her arms across her chest and leaned against the back of the couch. "The

least you could have done, Will, the very least, was tell me beforehand that you were going to replace Aidan."

"Why? So you could warn him? Turn the department against me?" Will said nastily.

For a moment Regina was too stunned to reply. "No," she said finally. "Because we're seeing each other. Because we have a relationship. People in relationships talk about things."

"This is business," Will said stubbornly. "I don't have to consult with anyone else in making decisions as head of the department."

"Not even me?"

Will sighed. "Regina, if I show you any preferential treatment, the department would figure out that we're involved and I just don't think that's a good idea right now. It could undermine us both professionally," he finished defensively.

Regina laughed. "Oh, I don't think it's my career you're worried about, Will."

"Look, I just think we should keep our relationship a secret, that's all."

"Forever?"

"For now."

"From Celia, too?" Regina spat. "How convenient."

"Regina, come on."

"No, Will, that's okay," Regina said slowly. "I guess maybe we don't have the kind of relationship I thought we did. You know, close. Honest. I just had no idea at all that you were thinking of replacing Aidan with Celia. But Celia, on the other hand, must have known something. It occurs to me now that you and Celia must have had lots of conversations about her 'ideas.' It occurs to me that she must have been working you for this job since the beginning of the semester, Will."

"What are you implying?" Will demanded.

"Oh, I'm not implying anything. I'm saying it outright.

I think you lied to me when you told me there was nothing going on between you and Ms. Keene. That night at the gallery opening. I think you've just been having fun with me. You know, give the old girlfriend a thrill. Poor thing never left her home town. Never got married. Never—"

"Regina, stop it," Will shot back. "You're being paranoid."

"Paranoid? Me? Okay, Will, answer this. Where did you go last night? That Sunday, too, the day after we first had dinner at your place. It's like you sneak out and then sneak back in and never once have you mentioned where you're going. I've tried not to ask, to give you the benefit of the doubt. I've tried to tell myself you have a right to your privacy, that you'll share your life with me when you're ready." Regina paused. "But now . . . where do you go, Will? Who have you been seeing?"

Nothing. He gave her nothing, just stared stonily at the table.

After a moment, Regina laughed. "What's the big secret, Will? You think I'm being paranoid? I just think I'm being smart. Finally. All those years ago, Will, you slept with another woman the minute my back was turned. I don't know why I ever trusted you this time around! How stupid could I be!"

She hadn't known, hadn't realized until this moment that she was still so hurt and angry and scared. She'd been a fool to start up with Will again before examining her heart and mind. Before exorcising the demons of despair. Her mother was right, everyone was right. You couldn't go home again.

Will rose from his seat. "Regina, please. . . ."

Regina stepped back. The tears began to flow. "No, Will. No more talk. I don't know who you are anymore. I don't want to talk to a man who would hurt a guy like Aidan Ross, like you did this morning. I don't want to talk to a guy who thinks he can just march back into his

old town and change a beloved tradition on a whim because of a woman like Celia Keene. I don't want to talk to a person who could betray me twice in one lifetime," she added quietly.

Will rushed from around the table. "Regina, don't do this. Don't destroy us. Please don't push me away! I—"

"Leave, Will," she said. "Just go."

Regina clenched both fists at her side and willed herself not to collapse. Willed herself not to rush to the man she'd loved so strongly for so long. So foolishly for so long. She could barely see him through the tears streaming from her eyes and that was the way she wanted it.

She did not want to see him walk out her door for the last time. Bad enough that a few seconds later she heard the door shut with a bang.


Regina spent what was undoubtedly the most horrible night of her life lying awake, staring at the ceiling, thinking grim thoughts. Bad enough to be fooled once, she thought over and over. Worse to be fooled twice.

This time it was my fault, she told herself. This time, I should have known better.

But by morning, Regina had convinced herself that for better or worse—and someday, after a period of worse, it would be better—she was over Will. Truly over him. Maybe she'd been humiliated along the way, but she convinced herself she'd reached the goal she should have set in the first place. Independence from Will Creeden.

After two cups of strong coffee, a small glass of grapefruit juice and a toasted bagel slathered in butter, Regina felt ready to meet the day, if not to greet it with open arms. A final squeeze to Nigel and Lucy and Regina was out the door.

Only to run—almost physically—into Will Creeden.

"Regina, I was just coming to see if you wanted a ride to work," Will blurted. "Maybe we could talk on the way."

Regina calmly locked the door behind her. "No, thank you, Will," she said, her voice as steady as could be expected after the horrible scene of the night before. "I'll be taking my own car."

"Regina . . ."

She turned away from the door and began to walk toward the stairs. Will stepped into her path.

"Please, Regina," he whispered, shooting a glance around for nosey neighbors. "Let me explain. We can't go on like this. You have to talk to me; we have to work this out. For God's sake, we work together! We live in the same building."

Regina stood as still as her trembling body would allow. She clutched the strap of her bag tighter. But she just couldn't look Will in the eye. If I look at him, she thought wildly, it will start all over again and I can't afford the pain. I can't afford to waste more of my life pursuing a foolish dream.

"I'm sorry, Will," she said, her voice quivering. "You should have thought of that before you came back to Idlewild."

# Twenty-six

"How can you eat ice cream when it's only forty-five degrees outside?" Regina asked, tucking into her own cup of steaming corn chowder.

Cindy shrugged. "It's got to be to least seventy-two degrees in here," she said, taking a big spoonful of vanilla soft-serve.

"Mommy, can I have some, too?"

Regina raised her eyebrows at her friend and waited.

"Not until you've finished your juice, Annie," Cindy told her three-year-old. "Then you can finish Mommy's ice cream."

"She'd better hurry," Regina said, laughing.

The two women and little girl sat at a small table in the food court of the McKinley Mall. It was the biggest indoor mall within fifty miles of Idlewild and as such, attracted a steady stream of shoppers, pre- and postholiday. Sometimes, Regina and Cindy made a morning or afternoon excursion to the mall just to get away for some girl talk. They didn't necessarily go to buy anything. Just looking at elaborate party dresses and computer upgrades, new bedroom sets and state-of-the-art kitchen appliances was plenty of fun. Of course, a visit to the food court was an essential component of each trip.

Today, though, the visit had been Cindy's idea. She'd promised Annie a new nightgown. Maybe more important,

her best friend was in sore need of some cheering up. So
far, their visit seemed to be doing the trick. Regina was
actually laughing, though whether she was simply pretending to be lighthearted to make Cindy feel she'd ac-
complished her goal was anyone's guess.

"So . . ." Cindy began, "how're you doing, Regina?"
Automatically, she wiped her daughter's juice-covered
chin, then looked carefully at her friend.

Regina put down her plastic spoon and frowned. "Honestly, I don't really know. I mean, it's only been a few
days since Will and I broke up. And it has not been fun
having to deal with seeing him every single day on campus. I think I should be feeling a lot worse than I do but . . .
I kind of think I'm in shock. Does that sound silly?" she
asked, looking earnestly across the table.

"Not at all!" Cindy assured, patting Regina's hand.
"And it might not be the worst thing right now, to feel a
bit numb. Look, the pain will come, it always does. But
maybe by the time the shock wears off, you'll be better
able to deal with the pain. Right?"

Regina smiled. "Right. I think." For a moment she
toyed with the spoon. "Maybe there's something else going on," she said finally, quietly. "Maybe I'm . . . maybe
I'm finally really over Will Creeden."

Cindy didn't get a chance to answer.

"Mommy!"

"Oh, Annie!" Cindy cried, grabbing for a wad of paper
napkins. "Now, how did you manage to do that?" The
little girl had dumped a half cup of ice cream on her shirt.
Combined with the juice already dribbled there, she was
now a sticky mess.

Annie giggled. "It's cold."

"C'mon, kiddo." Cindy stood and took Annie's hand.
"We'll be right back," she promised. "After I hose her
down."

Regina watched mother and daughter hurry off to the

ladies' room. She sighed. It had been so nice of Cindy to ask her along today. Certainly, she didn't need Regina's help in picking out a new flannel nightgown for a three-year-old. Regina appreciated her friend's caring efforts. Even if Cindy never herself had experienced the kind of heartache Regina had suffered—and was still living through—she always made it a point to be as compassionate and sympathetic as possible.

Regina popped open the top of a can of Diet Pepsi and took a sip. Maybe things are working out for the best, she thought. Maybe Will Creeden was really not meant to be a part of her future. . . .

"Fancy meeting you here."

Regina almost choked on her drink. She put the can down and with a crumpled napkin, blotted her chin.

Standing before her was Celia Keene. The very last person Regina ever expected to find at the mall on a Saturday afternoon.

"Celia," she managed to say.

Celia raised her eyebrows at the napkin strewn table, then pointed one slim finger at a fuzzy yellow Pokémon toy. "I gather you're not here alone?"

What the heck did this woman want, Regina thought frantically. Celia hardly ever spoke to her at school and certainly never in a chatty, friendly way. In fact, since the disastrous meeting at which Will had announced Celia's replacing Aidan as director of the fair's play, the two women had avoided each other like the plague.

Celia didn't know, did she? That there was another, more awful reason Regina was avoiding her?

What was Celia up to?

Regina smiled falsely. "No, I'm here with my friend and her daughter. They'll be back in a minute."

Celia smiled back, just as falsely. "Don't worry. I won't stick around where I'm not wanted."

"I don't know what you mean," Regina replied quickly,

suddenly feeling big and awkward in her bulky Irish knit sweater and loose-fitting jeans. Celia's slim, black leather, hip-length jacket must have cost a small fortune.

"What I mean," Celia said, smirking, "is that I'm sure your friend wouldn't appreciate having a cup of coffee with the woman who—" She paused, tilted her head. "Who's been sleeping with your former boyfriend since the summer. Though I'm sure he's denied it, to spare your feelings."

Regina felt her face flood with color. "What are you doing here?" she demanded, fists clenching in her lap.

Celia shrugged. "Why, observing the locals in their quaint little habitat, what else? After all, now that I live in Idlewild, it's my duty to learn about the locals. Though I daresay I'll never come to understand them."

Regina shook her head angrily. "Like you care about Idlewild's citizens! That's a laugh. If you gave one hoot about them at all you wouldn't be excluding them from the fair the way you are. You—"

"Regina, you misunderstand me." Celia carefully, calmly adjusted the strap of her sleek leather purse before continuing. "I never said I cared about you Idlewild folk. It's just that as a stranger in a strange land, it's incumbent upon me to learn the habits of the natives. As it were."

Regina was speechless. How was she supposed to answer this person? How was she supposed to speak civilly to such a nasty woman? And what had she meant by that remark about Will?

As if reading her mind, Celia spoke. "I'm assuming that woman in the coveralls and turtleneck carrying the rather hefty—and somewhat dirty—child is your friend," she said. "The woman looks vaguely familiar. . . ." Celia shook her head, as if dismissing the possibility she could personally know someone like Cindy Barnes. "Well, they seem to have made a detour at a candy shop. As if either needs more weight. . . . Nevertheless, I'll be on my way.

Just one more thing." Suddenly, Celia's face seemed to narrow and darken. "I let Will make love to you. I knew he needed to work it out of his system. Something about guilt. But he's over that now. He's through with you. He's done his penance and he's come back to me. Where he belongs. Face it, Regina, you never were woman enough to keep Will Creeden satisfied."

Regina sat rigidly, unmoving, almost not breathing. Had Will told Celia everything about Regina's relationship with him? He couldn't have. Why was this happening? Why!

Celia turned to leave, then paused. Winked. "I hope you had a little fun with my man."

Celia Keene walked off, leaving Regina alone. Alone and tortured. The humming in her ears had grown louder, until now it threatened to explode from her head. She felt like she would die right there, right then. Like she would just combust, like all the humiliation, pain and anger raging inside her would simply cause her to self-destruct, in front of everyone, sitting right there in the food court of the McKinley Mall.

"Regina?" It was Cindy, back from the ladies' room, Annie clutching a bag of jelly beans for her brother. "Was that the new teacher in your department? The one——"

Regina looked up at her friend, eyes brimming with tears.

"Celia said she and Will have been together all along," she whispered.

Cindy sighed angrily. "That . . ." She glanced at her daughter, then back to Regina. "You know what I mean. You don't believe her, do you? Come on, Regina, she's lying, playing with you."

"Why?" Regina demanded. "What did I ever do to her?"

"Nothing. But with people like that, mean people, people who get off on causing others pain, it's not about you.

It's all about them. About their own unhappiness and lack of self-respect. Don't you see?" Cindy pleaded. "You can't let her get to you. Feel sorry for her instead. She's pitiful and weak and pathetic. She only has power over you if you give it to her."

Regina wiped her eyes and smiled wobbly. "I think I already have."

# Twenty-seven

This is probably the closest thing to a traditional town meeting Celia Keene's ever attended, Regina thought, as she entered the general meeting room of Idlewild's town hall. With her were Joan and Bob Sutherland, involved, as usual, to the best of their abilities in the annual Fall Fair.

As her parents walked off to greet friends, Regina scanned the growing crowd. Pretty much everybody was here, if by everybody you meant any Idlewild resident with any sort of part to play in the designing, organizing and building of the fair.

Up in front, already seated and enjoying a conversation with one of the town's librarians, was Dr. Emily Nelson. Standing to Emily's left were Jane and Mark Cadwallader, also surveying the room. Regina caught Jane's eye and gave a wave.

Aidan Ross and Miles Fetherston were seated together quietly—unobtrusively—toward the back of the room. Neither was speaking.

Marty and Cindy had planned to attend, but both children had come down with a twenty-four-hour stomach virus and both parents were on full call. Regina would fill them in later.

Maria Jackson, her husband and their son and daughter-

in-law had just come through the door behind Regina and greeted her as they passed.

And scattered throughout the room, faculty from other departments in the college; local business owners, from shopkeepers to bankers; full-time mothers with children in Idlewild's grammar and high schools; even clergy from the various congregations around town. On the whole, Regina noted, Idlewild seemed to be well represented tonight.

Only one person seemed to be missing.

"Hello, Regina."

Regina whirled. He was standing just behind and to her left.

"H-hello," she said.

They stood there awkwardly for a moment and then Will cleared his throat.

"I'd better . . ." He gestured toward the front of the room and, head lowered, walked past.

Regina put her hand to her throat, felt her pulse beating harshly. Quickly, she walked over to join Aidan and Miles. No way was she interested in sitting within easy view of Will Creeden.

"Regina," Aidan greeted, with a genuine smile. "Come to sit with us?"

Regina nodded and sat to Aidan's left. "Hello, you two. No bad behavior tonight, right, Miles?" she added with a weak grin. "Remember, we represent the college."

Miles pulled down on his vest and sat up straighter in his chair. "My dear, I will be, as always, a model of decorum."

I just hope Dad will be, Regina thought suddenly. No sooner had she told her parents about she and Will getting back together than she'd had to break the news of their separation. Bob Sutherland was generally a mild-tempered man, but when someone made his wife or daughter unhappy. . . . Look out, Will, Regina thought.

And then she caught sight of Celia Keene walking down the middle aisle to join Will and other fair directors up front.

Although, if Mom feels like letting off a little steam, Regina thought, smirking, I'd be happy to arrange a meeting between Mrs. Sutherland and Dr. Keene.

"Penny for your thoughts?" Aidan said, though his eyes told he knew exactly what Regina was thinking.

"Did you know?" Regina asked suddenly. "About me and Will?"

Aidan smiled kindly. "Yes. We all did. And I'm so sorry . . . about everything."

Miles frowned. "Always said that Creeden was a bad seed . . ."

"Miles," Aidan scolded.

Regina sighed. "And I'll be good, too," she promised. "Besides, even I have to admit that she looks fabulous tonight."

"A trifle overdressed for the occasion," Miles said dryly, "but it's her moment of triumph, my dear, don't you see. The moment when she addresses the local yokels and lifts them from wallowing in their own filth and ignorance."

Aidan coughed discreetly. "Yes, I daresay you're right, Miles, but Regina's right, too. Celia does look lovely."

Like a sylph, Regina thought. But a sylph with guts and style and power. Celia wore a slim, pearly grey sheath, cut to the knee, with black Audrey Hepburn heels (must be from New York, Regina noted; there was no store in Idlewild that carried such shoes these days). She carried a matching black handbag and her only adornment seemed to be a pair of mobe pearl earrings. Her hair was styled smoothly and swept behind her ears, emphasizing the smallness—the perfectness—of her face and skull.

Once again, Regina felt monstrous in her presence. Monstrous and somewhat provincial.

The whine of feedback interrupted any more gloomy thoughts. Everyone who was still standing took seats and Idlewild's mayor, Barbara Carrington, opened the meeting.

It was mayhem.

Well, Regina thought, not the entire meeting. Thankfully, most of the fair's organization was remaining unchanged. The disastrous part was, to her, the most important part. The part that dealt with a scene from a popular Shakespeare play, annually directed by the college's English department. Specifically, for the past ten years, by Aidan Ross. Performed by students and Idlewild residents of all ages and abilities. Costumes handmade—and annually repaired and altered—by local women who donated their time, effort and materials. Props and the stage made by local weekend handymen and a professional carpenter or two. Refreshments at the department's booth made and served by the town's librarians—Michael Roberts, Julia Kennedy and Miss Agnes Tresch.

In other words, a truly homemade production.

Until now. Until Will Creeden took over as acting head of the department and appointed Celia Keene as director.

"Costumes will be provided by the Backhand Theater Company, located in Manhattan," Celia told the group. "They will be on loan so they must be treated with great care. Therefore, only professional seamstresses will act as dressers. Actors from the RagTag Troupe, also located in Manhattan, will perform all of the roles, in exchange for a small fee. Only professional, licensed carpenters will be selected for the construction of a brand-new stage and scene set. Applications for these positions can be picked up at the Idlewild College English department. Several people will then be chosen for interviews. Refreshments will be catered by Minna's Table, located . . ."

"Let me guess," Miles mumbled. "In Manhattan?"

People protested. They questioned calmly at first but when Celia wouldn't budge and nothing Will said made sense to them, they questioned more loudly and more angrily.

"This fair is about two things, always has been," Mr. Joyce, owner of a small jewelry store and a former King Lear, stated. "Good will and profit. Now I don't see any good will in this new situation and what with paying for food and professional actors, I certainly don't see any profit!"

Will, a little pale, assured Mr. Joyce that Celia Keene would come in on or under budget. He did not address Mr. Joyce's other concern.

"What's wrong with the costumes we've already got?" Mrs. Plumber argued. "Why, some of those pieces were made brand-new just last year! Plus, there's some of us ladies that look forward to working together on the costumes."

In Regina's opinion, Celia's answering argument about the need for superior quality craftsmanship fell on largely deaf ears.

"Who the heck are we doing this production for anyway?" Bob Sutherland asked. "Idlewild or some Broadway producer? This is supposed to be about having fun, not impressing some out-of-towner."

"And why isn't that nice young man Aidan Ross in charge?" demanded an elderly woman Regina knew only barely. Mrs. King, she thought, from a small assisted-living residence downtown.

"I'm guessing this means Dr. Keene doesn't want any student actors, either," Aidan said tightly. "How will I explain. . . ."

Regina sighed as the battle raged on. In all honesty, she did understand some of Celia's desire to make a mark and spruce things up. She was sure others in Idlewild would

also welcome some fresh ideas. But the new director's proposed changes were too sweeping, too radical. And, especially from the podium, Celia Keene projected no warmth toward or real interest in her audience. Why should anyone accept what she was suggesting?

Will fielded another question, trying hard to seem upbeat and one hundred percent behind the new scheme. But did he really believe Celia's ideas were best for Idlewild, Regina wondered. In his heart of hearts?

And even if he did believe in the scheme, would he have the nerve to say no to Celia, at least to some of her ideas, in order to appease the local population?

Doubtful. Though you'd be wise to do it, Will, Regina told him silently. Particularly if you plan on sticking around town.

Aidan leaned close to Regina's ear. "I think I've had enough," he whispered. "Miles and I are going to have a late dinner at McEvoy's. Celebrate the new regime," he added dryly. "Come with us, Regina."

She hesitated.

Aidan went on. "Come with us. There's nothing you can do here now."

# Twenty-eight

"It didn't go very well, did it?"

Will knew the answer to his own question. He just wanted the miserable failure to be confirmed.

"My dear," Emily Nelson said, settling in a comfortable wingback chair, "that is the understatement of the century."

Will watched his friend and sometime mentor take a slow and careful sip of the cup of hot tea she had prepared for herself. He'd asked for something stronger and now sat toying with a glass of whiskey.

For a long moment, Will said nothing more. Flashes of the disastrous and seriously eye-opening meeting earlier that evening attacked his head. The townfolk's almost universal disapproval of Celia's proposed renovations. The Cadwalladers' silent condemnation. That puzzled him, actually. Jane and Mark were among the most forward-thinking residents of Idlewild. For sure, he thought, they would support Celia's efforts. His efforts.

Will took a sip of the amber liquid. Fought an onslaught of self-pity. Nothing's gone right since I came back to Idlewild, he thought. Nothing I do produces anything but failure.

First Joy. Then Regina. Now the town and for all he knew, most of his colleagues at the college. Certainly his department staff were no fans.

"You know," he said suddenly, "you never really did tell me why Celia Keene was hired." Will laughed. "Not that anyone knew the circumstances surrounding my being hired. No one does, but you."

Emily Nelson sighed and placed her half-empty teacup on a small side table.

"There were a few reasons. The first, I reject as invalid, but even department heads have to answer to the larger administration."

"What do you mean?" Will asked.

"What I mean is that two of the English department's staff do not hold doctorates. Aidan Ross and Regina Sutherland. My understanding is that some muckety-muck on the college's marketing team—can you imagine!—decided we should be weeding out those members of the teaching staff without a Ph.D. after their name. The plan, I believe," Emily finished dryly, "is to replace Aidan or Regina with Dr. Keene, some time over the next year."

"Nice," Will muttered. "So, why Celia? If the college wants to attract more money by boasting a 'better' staff, why not go for someone with more years of experience, someone with a reputation."

Emily laughed. "That, my dear, would be you. It's no accident the administration agreed so readily to our little substitution plan." Emily shrugged. "They hope I decide to retire, at which point you will be offered the position as head of the department. And, of course, tenure."

Will took another sip of the whiskey. "Well, I should have seen that one coming," he said. "You know, don't you, that stealing your job has never been—and never will be—one of my motives for coming back to Idlewild?"

"Of course, don't be silly."

"So, you haven't answered my question about Celia."

"Time was short, the pressure was on . . . and her resume landed on my desk at just the right moment. True, there are thousands of unemployed Ph.D.'s out there, des-

perate for jobs. But not everyone wants to come to Idle-wild." Emily raised her eyebrows. "And not everyone pro-claimed to be such a devoted follower of Dr. Creeden. She knows your work as well as I do, Will. Say what we might about her, er, personality challenges, she is bright."

Will grunted. "I know. I read her thesis, sat in on her classes. She's got a brain, and an original one, at that. The students seem to like her. But—"

"But she's brash and self-centered and insensitive. Maybe even downright cruel."

Will grinned. "You forgot manipulative."

"And quite attractive." Emily sniffed. "If you like that sort of thing."

"What, blond, slim, fashionable?"

Emily stood and walked to one of the room's many bookshelves. She pushed aside a dusty volume and re-trieved the bottle of whiskey to refresh Will's glass.

"Speaking of women," she began, pouring a drink for herself, as well, "have you told Regina the truth? Well," she added, sitting again, "of course you haven't. If you had, you wouldn't be sitting here alone with me, bemoan-ing your fate."

"What truth?" Will said bitterly. "About Luke? That the child she thinks is alive and well in Chicago is really dead? That's one ugly truth. Here's another. That my at-tempt to exorcise my demons by working with other sick kids ended spectacularly with Joy's death."

Emily's voice was grim. "Yes, Will. Those ugly truths. And the truth about why you couldn't tell anyone but me about your work at the hospital. I just don't know what you're so afraid of."

Will looked seriously at his friend. "I don't know, either, Emily, I really don't. Not any more." He sighed. "But it's too late to fix things with Regina. I've hurt her so often, in so many ways. God, she must think I'm her

own personal nightmare, a Dr. Jekyll and Mr. Hyde put on this earth to torment her."

"Now, Will—"

"Emily," he interrupted, "I swear I didn't plan or expect it and I'm certainly not proud of it, but I let my grief about Joy slam me. Hit me like a baseball bat to the head. Suddenly, it was Luke's death all over again. Emily, I let the shocking pain of that night turn me away from the one person who could have really helped me. I let it take me right to Celia, a person who just wants to tear things down. Destruction to go along with the death."

"Regina thinks you and Celia are an item, no doubt."

"Oh, yeah. I swear, Emily, I've never touched Celia, never even wanted to. Okay, she's attractive, but it's kind of like how a bad accident is attractive. It draws your interest and disgusts you at the same time."

"Strong words."

"I mean them. I always knew Celia was dangerous. Right from the start. And I knew her interest in me was, uh, more than just academic. But still, I let her get to me. I let her make me want to tear things down, too. Destroy my relationship with Regina. Alienate my staff. Anger the town. Hey, if you're the one destroying, it's harder to be destroyed, right? If nobody likes you in the first place, you can never be hurt. Foolproof plan. You might be lonely but you won't feel pain."

"You could remove Celia as director, reinstate Aidan," Emily suggested quietly.

Will shook his head. "I wish I could. But my gut tells me that would cause even more trouble. I made a professional decision—okay, a bad one—and I have to stick by it. I need to show some commitment to something."

"Will, you need to see a grief counselor." Emily raised a hand as if to ward off Will's protest. "Now, I'm not a huge fan of therapists or headshrinkers, but even I know

there are some times in life when we all need a little help getting past our troubles."

"I did see someone, right after Luke died," Will admitted.

"Why did you stop?"

Will was silent for a moment. "I stopped, I think, because I was beginning to . . . not to forget, but to let go." He raised his eyes to Emily's. "And I just wasn't ready to let go."

"So your grief has become your companion, your link to Luke. It's destroying you. And it's hurting others. Will, that's wrong."

"I know, Emily. I know."

# Twenty-nine

It was a Thursday night, and it seemed to Regina that half of Idlewild was out at some restaurant or browsing at some late-night bookshop or just strolling the streets of town. The weather might have had something to do with it, she thought. A golden autumn afternoon had given way to a crisp, fresh autumn evening, with a sky full of stars and the lovely aroma of crackling fireplaces. Briefly, Regina thought of the autumn days in New York, of the smell of roasting chestnuts sold by street vendors, of the way the city seemed to be at its most beautiful and exciting. If and when I ever go back to New York, she vowed, entering her favorite restaurant in Idlewild, I'll go back in the fall.

No sooner had the door to Bellissima closed behind her than Regina caught sight of Jane and Mark, seated at their usual table. She checked her watch—no, she wasn't late. The Cadwalladers were always early!

Regina gave her coat to Donna, the restaurant owner's adult daughter who worked the coat check and as hostess. When her coat was hung, she followed Donna through the small and intimately lit dining room. Bellissima had only ten tables and was devoted to serving the best in Northern Italian cuisine, with special care taken to fresh ingredients and healthy portions. The wine list was superb and the waitstaff very friendly. All in all, dining at Bel-

lissima with good friends was one of Regina's favorite ways to spend an evening.

Though, to be honest, since the night she and Will had broken up—"parted ways," as her father would say—Regina hadn't felt much like socializing. Still, she knew that talking to friends about work and events in their lives—in other words, putting aside her own troubles for the moment and focusing on the joys and sorrows of another—was a far healthier way to spend the night than alone in bed with a pint of Ben & Jerry's, sitcoms and a big dose of self-pity.

Even a burger at McEvoy's with Aidan and Miles had been fun, even if Miles had sent his hamburger back twice.

"Thanks, Donna," Regina said, sitting in the comfortable chair Donna held out for her.

"Good to see you all tonight," the hostess responded warmly. "I'll have some fresh bruschetta brought over immediately."

Mark put a hand to his heart. "Ah, Donna! If Jane ever leaves me, I'm coming right to your door."

Jane laughed and swatted Mark on the arm. "Trust me, Donna," she said dryly, "you wouldn't want him."

When Donna had gone and the waiter, a young cousin, had brought over the fresh bruschetta, along with a bottle of imported olive oil and a small plate of black and green olives, Jane turned to Regina.

"You left the meeting early the other night, Regina," she said, pouring her friend a glass of the house red wine Mark had ordered. "We looked for you afterward. How are you doing?"

Regina took a sip, swallowed and smiled. "Much better than a moment ago," she said. "Really, though, I'm fine. Well, not exactly fine but good enough not to spoil our time together."

Mark leaned across the table and patted Regina's hand. "Depressing each other is what friends are for." Mark

paused. "Well, that's not exactly what I meant. I meant, uh, if you can't depress friends, who can you depress!" Mark smiled.

Jane raised her eyebrows at Regina. "Well said, darling."

"Thanks, you guys, but really, I'm okay." Regina picked up her menu and sighed. "I don't know why I even bother to look at this thing," she said. "Every time I come here I order one of three dishes. How did I become so boring?"

"It's not about being boring," Jane said earnestly. "It's about knowing what you like. Setting priorities and limits. Holding out for the best."

Regina stared at her friend. "Somehow I don't think you're talking about food anymore."

"Subtle, isn't she?" Mark commented.

The three friends went on to enjoy a plate of appetizers that included a piece of olive and onion tart, roasted red peppers and a salad of orange slices, toasted walnuts, crumbled gorgonzola cheese and a variety of greens. For entreés, each of which came with a small order of pasta, Jane chose a veal marsala, Mark ordered the osso buco. And Regina, throwing caution to the wind just this once, opted for a main course portion of black pasta with clams.

"This is just fantastic," she said happily. "I'm adding this to my list of favorites."

The waiter arrived with a second bottle of wine and Jane laughed. "Going to be one of those nights, is it? Okay, what are we celebrating?" she asked.

Mark shrugged. "Us? Friendship? The future?" He winked at Regina. "Romance?"

Regina blushed. "I think I'm going to take some time off from romance," she said. "Besides, I think I've already dated every eligible bachelor in Idlewild."

"What about Bruce McNeil?" Mark asked, pouring a glass of wine for each of them.

"What!" Jane whispered. "The man is a convicted criminal, Mark!"

Mark frowned. "Oh. I forgot. Tax fraud. Okay, what about Jim Griffith? He's a hell of a nice guy—"

"And about seventy years old." Regina held up her hand. "That's okay, Mark. I'm perfectly capable of reviewing the list myself. But not tonight. Tonight, I just want to enjoy myself."

"Good for you," Jane said, shooting Mark a scolding look. "How about we order the cheese plate for dessert?"

"As long as I can also have a chocolate gelato," Mark said. "Please?"

Jane grinned. "I've got you just where I want you, don't I? Yes, you may have a gelato, too." While Mark ordered, Jane turned to Regina. "Oh, Regina, I meant to ask if you could read a draft of a paper I'm writing. I'm having a bit of trouble with the middle section and I could really use some help."

"Sure, Jane. I'd be happy to—" Regina broke off, simply unable to continue her sentence. Her eyes locked on the sight of Will and Celia standing just inside the door of the restaurant, their coats still on, their faces flushed with cold.

"Oh." It was Jane. Clearly she'd just seen Dr. Creeden and Dr. Keene, too.

"A little late to be starting dinner, isn't it?" Mark commented coldly.

"Not necessarily," Jane said quickly. "Maybe they were both working late and ran into each other at the campus library and just decided to, you know, catch a bite to eat."

"At Idlewild's most intimate restaurant?" Mark replied. "The guy's on a date."

"It's okay," Regina said, a bit too loudly, looking pleadingly from Mark to Jane. "Please, just let's forget they're here. And there's no need to condemn Will or to make excuses for him. Okay? I'm not involved with him. He's

not my concern. What he does or does not do with Celia Keene after-hours just doesn't matter to me."

When neither Jane nor Mark responded, only looked worriedly at their friend, Regina relented. "Okay, look, I still care. Maybe more than I realized. But there's nothing I can do about their being here, is there? So, please, please, let's try to enjoy the rest of the evening."

Just then the waiter returned with the desserts and coffee. Regina sat back to allow him more room to work. Almost inadvertently, she glanced again toward the door. And saw Will staring at her. On his face, a look of what? Hope? Embarrassment? Regina couldn't even guess, she felt so flustered.

She didn't meet his eye. Just watched as Donna led Will and Celia toward a table for two. Watched as Celia scooted her chair closer to Will's. Saw Will shoot another inscrutable look her way and Celia smile at her like a feline in firm possession of the bowl of cream.

Regina did not return Celia's smile. Why should I, she thought bitterly. It certainly wasn't a friendly greeting smile! Instead, she slowly turned back to look at the Cadwalladers. Her real friends.

"So, Jane, as I was saying," she went on, "I'd be happy to look at your paper. Why don't I stop by your office in the morning and pick up a copy?"

"I could e-mail you the draft, if it's easier," Jane offered.

Regina nodded. "Great. That way I can make any comments or suggestions right on the file and e-mail it back to you as soon as I'm finished."

"Peter!" Mark gestured toward a man who was approaching from the table farthest in the back of the restaurant. "What brings you to Idlewild?"

Mark stood and shook the man's extended hand.

"Mark, great to see you!" the man replied. Regina could not help but notice his sparkling blue eyes and genu-

ine smile. Not to mention his beautiful, well-cut suit, broad shoulders and trim hips. "I just came in to town to take a client to dinner. He left about five minutes ago, but I thought I'd sneak another cup of coffee before the drive home."

Mark grinned and turned to his wife and Regina. "Peter Thompson, I'd like you to meet my wife, Jane, and our friend Regina Sutherland. Regina teaches at the college, in the English department."

"Peter, nice to finally meet you," Jane said graciously. "Regina, Peter's with the bank who helped make the gallery possible."

"Cititon Bank, in Appleton," Peter added, for Regina's benefit. "Just two towns away."

"Join us for a while?" Mark suggested, returning to his seat.

Peter smiled at Regina. "Thanks, I will." He sat next to Regina—in full view of Will and Celia across the room.

Regina gathered her nerve. Told herself now was a perfect time to begin to get on with her life. Turned to Peter and smiled her best and most inviting smile. "So, Peter," she said, "do you come to Idlewild often?"

"Well, not too often lately," he said, his smile becoming a little shy, "but I could happily be persuaded to visit more frequently."

The Cadwalladers beamed. Regina said, "I'm glad to hear that."

And across the room, Will Creeden frowned.

# Thirty

"Almost there," Regina said with an exaggerated huff-and-puff. "Just one more flight and we'll be home."

"And then we can have our snack, right, Regina?" Jake questioned, his eyes bright with anticipation. "I want cupcakes!"

Regina tugged a little on Annie's hand to encourage the child to make the next step some time in the next century. "Well, I was thinking more along the lines of apples and peanut butter," she said calmly. "I think cupcakes are better after dinner, don't you?"

Jake hauled himself up the next few stairs by tugging at the banister. "Well," he considered. "I guess. Is it the chunky kind?"

Regina grinned. "Of course! It's my favorite, too."

"Okay, then, come on!" Jake, suddenly full of energy, bounded up the final few steps and stood on the landing, hands on his hips, looking down at his aunt and sister. "You'd better hurry," he said bossily. "My tummy is making a big noise."

Taking the hint, Regina scooped up Annie and hurried to join Jake. At the door to her apartment she set the child down next to her brother and rummaged in her bag for the keys.

"Mommy does that, too," Annie noted, pointing to Regina's bag. "She has lots of things in there."

Regina laughed. "Someday you'll have lots of things in your bag, too, Annie."

"Daddy doesn't have a bag," Jake said. "He puts everything in his pockets."

Regina inserted the key into the lock and opened the door. "That's why your mom bought him cargo pants," she said.

"I want cargo pants!" Annie exclaimed, running for the couch and tossing herself into its fluffy pillows.

"You don't even know what they are," Jake said.

"Yes, I do!"

"Then what are they?"

Regina set her bag on the kitchen table and turned back to her charges. Unfortunately, Annie's eyes were widening by the second and now . . . uh-oh. Tears.

"Jake," she said, hurrying forward, "why don't you take off your jacket and get the peanut butter from the fridge, okay? I'll be right there to help."

Regina stepped aside as the little boy raced for the kitchen. Then she walked over to the couch and sat next to Annie. Gently, she unbuttoned the girl's sweater and took off her knitted hat. "Hey, don't cry," she said, giving the child a kiss on the top of her head. "Who cares about silly old cargo pants anyway? Come on, let's get our snack and then how about we take a nap before Daddy comes to pick you up?"

Annie nodded and took the hand Regina offered. Together they walked to the kitchen to find Jake unloading every condiment he could find from the refrigerator.

Regina picked up a jar of hot brown mustard. "Hey, this doesn't look like peanut butter to me," she said, laughingly.

Jake looked very serious. "Well," he explained, "I'm tired of jelly on peanut butter. Once Mom gave us honey instead and it was really good. So I thought I'd try some other stuff, too."

Regina picked up the jar of mustard, as well as one of horseradish, and returned them to the refrigerator. "You know, Jake, it's great to try new foods," she said, inwardly wincing at the thought of Jake with a mouthful of horseradish, "but I'm pretty sure these spicy things aren't meant for peanut butter. I think we should stick to honey. And how about some maple syrup?"

"I want an apple!" Annie announced.

Jake shrugged. "Okay."

"Good boy. Sure, Annie," Regina said, hoisting the chunky little girl into a kitchen chair and sliding the chair close to the table. "Let me clean and slice one for you."

As Regina worked to prepare the children's snacks—as she poured glasses of milk and sliced apples and helped spread peanut butter on half slices of whole wheat bread—she realized, suddenly, how tired she was. It was a physical exhaustion, too, not a feeling she was used to. Mental exhaustion, sure. Especially after writing a paper or struggling through a colleague's convoluted so-called intellectual discourse. Emotional exhaustion, no stranger. Hadn't every woman over the age of fifteen experienced her share of heartache and trauma?

Though Regina was an active person, she was no athlete. So the exhaustion that came after a day on the slopes or a serious workout on the courts was almost foreign to her.

Regina smiled as she watched Jake work a mouthful of peanut butter and Annie pretend-feed a small, rubbery baby doll she'd brought with her today. Taking care of children, even for one afternoon, was hard, hard work. You had to be mentally alert, emotionally sympathetic, even empathetic, and physically strong. If I ever have children of my own, she thought now, I'm going to have to join a gym, no doubt about it. Though her friends with children, namely Cindy, assured her that as a mother, you

found the strength and stamina, from some deep reserve of love and interest. Regina hoped that was true.

"I have to use the bathroom," Jake announced, pulling Regina fully into the moment.

"Do you want me to come along?" she asked neutrally. Regina was very conscious of Jake's desire to be grown up, as well as his need to be a thoroughly taken-care-of child. She'd leave the decision to him.

Jake looked thoughtful for a moment. "No," he said then. "I'm okay."

"Sure. You know where it is, right?"

Jake rolled his eyes. "Aunt Regina! I've been here, like, a bazillion times!"

Regina suppressed a smile. "Of course," she said seriously. "I forgot."

Jake dashed off from the kitchen. Annie, chattering under her breath to her doll, seemed oblivious that her brother had gone. Sensing from Jake's drained glass and empty plate that snack time was over, Regina began to clear the table, all the while keeping one eye on her younger charge. She's almost ready for a nap, Regina noted, watching the blue eyes flicker closed and open again, closed and open.

It had been a wonderful day. Perfect fall weather, even with the pearly gray sky and chill air. The three of them had gone to the playground in the park and slid down the slide, swung on the swings and teetered this way and that on the seesaw. Though she was decidedly too big for the rides—she didn't even want to think about how she looked bumping down the slide and onto a pile of sand—Regina had had a great time.

"Jake's not here."

Startled, Regina looked at Annie. "Oh, I know, honey," she said. "He went to the bathroom."

And then it dawned on her. It had been—Regina

checked her watch—more than five full minutes since he'd left the kitchen.

"Sit right there, Annie," Regina said quickly. "I'll be right back."

Regina dashed into the hallway, toward the closed bathroom door.

"Jake?" she called, trying to hide the rising panic in her voice. Anything could happen to a child in a bathroom! For God's sake, he could drown. "Are you okay?"

A half moment of silence. And then a voice, small, almost scared and just a little bit proud. "Aunt Regina?"

"Yes, Jake?"

"I can't open the door."

Regina put a hand to her racing heart and sagged against the doorjamb. Thank goodness! He'd only locked himself in. "You're not hurt, are you?" she asked.

"No."

"Okay, Jake." Regina leaned closer to the door. "Don't worry, I'll get you out."

It was all her fault. She'd been meaning to get that old lock fixed or removed for ages now. She never should have neglected that chore for so long.

But now was no time for self-recrimination. Now was the time for action.

And what am I supposed to do? Regina thought wildly. I could call a locksmith but the expense and by the time someone gets here . . . Marty will be here any minute! Some baby-sitter I am.

With one last assurance to Jake, Regina hurried back to the kitchen. Annie still sat contentedly in her seat. What should she do!

And then it came to her. Simple and easy, a solution she should have thought of first thing.

Will. She'd call Will. He was just upstairs, wasn't he? If he's even home, she argued silently. If he even wants to talk to you again.

And then Regina shook her head. No, she thought. I don't need him. I can handle this myself. Purposefully, she strode over to the small drawer in which she kept a few basic tools and supplies. She pulled open the drawer. And stared. What . . . how. . . .

"Aunt Regina!" It was Jake, his voice now more than slightly scared.

"I'm coming, Jake!" she cried. Regina Sutherland might not need Will Creeden, she thought grimly, reaching for the kitchen wall phone. But Jake Barnes does.

"We'll have you out in a second, buddy." Will knelt before the locked bathroom door and inserted a screwdriver into the keyhole. At least, it looked like some sort of screwdriver. Regina shook her head. She had to get her act together and learn something more about home improvement than how to make a hot plate out of wine corks.

Regina glanced back toward the couch, where Annie slept peacefully. How nice to be a child, Regina thought, briefly. At least, a well loved child. Too bad we grow up and forget just how good we had it as children!

"Bingo!"

Regina turned back to see the bathroom door fly open and Jake erupt into Will's waiting arms.

"Uncle Will!"

Over Will's shoulder Regina could see Jake's flushed face. No sign of tears, though. He'd been as brave as he could. And now, with this rescue, he'd found himself another hero—and honorary uncle.

"Jake, I'm so sorry," Regina said, kneeling next to Will and the boy. "I promise I'll get that lock fixed right away, okay?"

"No problem, Aunt Regina," Jake blustered, pulling away from the adults. "It was fun. And I wasn't even afraid."

Regina smiled. "I know you weren't. But if it's all the same, I'm going to get the lock fixed anyway."

Jake shrugged and raced for the living room.

Regina was left alone with Will.

She stood. Battled with a sudden rush of embarrassment. "I'm . . . thanks for coming down," she said awkwardly. "I'm sorry I had to call you like that."

Will stood, too. Wiped his hands on his jeans. "Regina," he said, with a slight shake of his head, "you can always call on me. Don't ever think that just because—" He stopped, also embarrassed. "Look, just don't think I'm not there for you. Okay?"

Regina nodded. Then nervously touched her hair, the collar of her shirt. "Um, can I get you something to drink?"

Will looked down before answering. "I really should be go—"

"Uncle Will! Come look at my Pokémon cards!"

It was Jake, tugging on Will's arm, leading him toward the living room.

Will shot a glance at the boy, then at Regina.

"Go ahead," she said. "Marty will be here soon anyway to pick them up."

Will's expression showed his gratitude, and he followed Jake to the living room.

Regina detoured to the kitchen, struggling to still the mad beating of her heart. What was she feeling! Desire? No, no, no, she told herself. Just . . . nervousness. Anxiety, something. It was awkward being in the same room with someone you'd just broken up with, everybody knew that. Someone you'd seen on a date with another woman. And to have called him for help in an emergency. . . . She was embarrassed, yes, ashamed she'd been unable to take care of the situation herself.

Be honest, Regina, she told herself now. You're embarrassed that the sight of Will crouching in the hallway, jeans

molded to his strong legs, thick, wavy hair curled on his neck had made you feel so full of need. So desperately in love with him. Had made you want to touch him so badly—

Buzzz!

The doorbell! Marty, thank God. Regina hurried to the door to let him in. When the children left, there would be no reason for Will to stay.

"Marty, hi!"

Marty smiled. "Well, that was an enthusiastic greeting," he said. "You'd think we hadn't seen—"

Marty stopped speaking.

"What?" Regina said, turning to look at whatever it was that had caught Marty's attention.

It was a scene of domestic contentment. Will, sitting cross legged on the floor, peering intently at each card Jake showed him. Annie, awake now, on the couch and bouncing her doll on Will's head. Jake, thrilled to have a new audience.

"Oh . . . you see . . ."

Will looked up. "Hey, Marty," he said casually, meeting Marty's gaze.

Marty nodded. "Will."

"Daddy!" Jake jumped up and bounded over to his father. "Uncle Will rescued me!"

"What?" Marty turned to Regina.

"No big deal," Will said, getting up from the floor, too. "I'd promised Regina I'd replace the old lock on the bathroom. Before I got around to doing it, Jake locked himself in. My fault. I'm just glad I was home when it happened."

"But no harm done," Regina said swiftly. Will had lied for her. He didn't need to have done that! Marty wouldn't have been mad, and even if he had been. . . .

"Uh, thanks, I guess," Marty said with a small laugh.

Will cleared his throat. "Well, I've got to be going

now," he said. "Jake, see you around, okay? Bye-bye, Annie."

"Will—" Regina began.

"Bye, Regina," he said, slipping past the group and out the door.

When he had gone, Marty turned to Regina. "What just happened here today?" he asked.

"Oh, Marty, I'm sorry, I really did mean to have that lock fixed."

Marty shook his head. "No, no. Forget the lock, like you said, no harm done. I mean"—he looked at Jake gathering his cards in his binder and Annie doing her best to help her brother, then back to Regina—"what happened between you and Will?"

"Nothing, Marty," Regina said, willing him to believe her own lie. "Absolutely nothing."

# Thirty-one

"Miles, what's going on with the Chapman kid, the one in your—"

"I know for which class my own student is registered, thank you, Dr. Creeden."

Here we go again, Regina thought, tuning out the tense voices around the small conference table. These days, practically everything Will said was met with suspicion or downright rudeness. Well, Miles was really the only member of the department to speak rudely to his boss, but there certainly was no love lost among the other members.

Including me? Regina wondered. In public, at school, she spoke to Will with distance but with respect, too. There was no warmth in her voice, no invitation to conversation in her choice of words. But she'd been raised to keep her temper in check—at least in a work environment.

But when they were alone . . . Regina glanced at Will, pretending instead to be studying a poster on the wall behind him. No doubt about it, he'd changed since the start of the semester, less than two months before. His face was sterner now, not at all hopeful. He appeared more driven than energetic, but not driven in a pep-rally, team-spirit sort of way. More like a man with his nose to the grindstone. More like a man just wanting to make it

through to the end of the day so he could scratch it off on his calendar. One down, only. . . .

Only how many more to go? What would Will do at the end of the semester? Go back to Chicago? Had he come into her life so suddenly, so dramatically, to leave it again so shortly, so abruptly? Maybe this time for good?

Regina's eyes flicked to Celia Keene, sitting, as always, at Will's right. What really was the point of Will's being here, in Idlewild? She couldn't say in regards to his career. That had always been a mystery. Regarding his personal life . . . well, if he had come back for Regina, he'd failed. Or I failed, she thought now. No matter, it was no one's fault. They were two people who'd rushed in where angels feared to tread. They'd neglected first to understand the past, to put it to rest. They'd been foolish to try to start over. Hadn't they?

It was all so confusing!

Take Will's secret life. He had one, she knew, but in spite of Celia's declaration to the contrary, Regina just couldn't fully believe Will and Celia were a couple. Lovers. Certainly during work hours, there was nothing to give them away, no covert glances or smiles.

Then again, Regina reminded herself, Will had wanted to keep her own relationship with him a secret from the rest of the staff. Why not Celia's relationship with him? And she had seen them at dinner together.

Regina suppressed a sigh. This line of thought was getting her nowhere. But coming right out and asking Will what he did after hours, where he disappeared to nights or afternoons, if he was really dating Celia, hadn't gotten her anywhere.

Trying to find out about Will through friends had also, so far, proved a dead end. A week or two ago, the day she'd baby-sat for Jake and Annie Barnes, after Will had left the apartment, after he'd rescued Jake from the locked bathroom, Regina had asked Marty, casually, if he'd heard

anything about Will's habits. Marty, befuddled by the concept of gossip, had looked at her like she was crazy and said no. The one or two times she'd approached Emily Nelson about Will, she'd been met with kindness but an absolutely firm reply: "I will not break a confidence."

For God's sake, Regina thought now, frustrated, what could be so important? And so in need of being kept a secret?

So many unknowns . . . and the bottom line? Regina looked at Will and felt a strong, familiar surge of fondness and sympathy, an urge to care for and help and . . . an urge to make love to him.

*I'm still in love with the man. There, I've said it, not out loud but to myself.*

Regina shot a look around the table to see if her wayward and private thoughts could been detected on her face. Good. No one was looking at her. Will was saying something about—something, his voice dull. Maria was sitting tall, pretending professional interest. Aidan was sketching on a small pad held on his lap, his down-turned face also a mask of professional thoughtfulness. Miles was moving around in his seat, occasionally harrumphing. Only Celia looked perfectly calm and collected and . . . triumphant.

Because she's gotten her man, Regina thought. But why Will? She'd never have picked out Will as Celia's type. Was it simply a game of conquest for Celia? Did she not care at all about Will, the person, only Will the most powerful man she knew—for the time being—in this small town and college? If that were the case, Celia wouldn't stay with Will for long. She'd move on to richer, more politically powerful men.

So much to sort through! And now there was Peter Thompson, Mark's friend. He'd called her the night before, and they'd spoken for almost an hour. Regina couldn't deny she'd enjoyed the conversation. Peter was smart and funny and interested in lots of the same things

she found enjoyable. Plus, he came with the Cadwalladers' recommendation, which was no small thing.

Problem was he'd asked her out for this coming weekend. There really was no good reason for Regina to say no, so she hadn't. They were going to have dinner together Saturday night and then. . . . Well, come what may. Was it wrong to date one man while in love with another? Maybe. But if the man she loved was not in love with her, what were her options?

Still, Peter Thompson was a good man and Regina didn't want to mislead him. She'd have dinner with him Saturday, ask herself honestly how she felt being with him and take it from there. If there were no sparks, she'd come clean. At least, tell him she wasn't ready to get involved with someone right then.

"Regina, are you with us?" It was Will's voice, impatient but polite.

Regina startled to attention, felt her face flush. Saw Celia smirk.

"In case you missed it," Will went on, "Celia's informed us that everything's in order with the actors, etc., for the fair. Now, what do you think of my proposal?"

Regina hesitated. "I'm . . . I'm sorry, Will," she said earnestly. "I was . . . would you repeat it? Your proposal, I mean."

Celia laughed. "Late night, Regina? Or just coming down with the flu. You look a little . . . unwell."

"There's no need for Dr. Creeden to repeat his proposal!" Miles Fetherston huffed. "I think it's absurd!"

Saved by the grumpy gus, Regina thought gratefully. But she'd better start paying attention, nonetheless.

A heated, impassioned argument was breaking out all around her. Over a suggested minor change to the department's midterm schedule! This is ridiculous, Regina thought. All this anger for nothing! Will doesn't deserve this disrespect. We don't deserve this chaos.

She listened with half an ear and watched the unhappy
faces of her once harmonious colleagues. She noted the
tightness around Will's mouth and wished more than ever
that Will Creeden had never come home.

# Thirty-two

Regina sat up straight in the uncomfortable library chair and stretched, hands over head, until she felt her spine loosen. Then she stretched her neck, first to the left and then to the right, until she heard the satisfactory *crack!* that released some of the kinks and tension in her body.

She'd been sitting in that same hard wooden chair, bent over a table that was too low for convenience for the past three hours. Since the end of her last class, in fact. She lowered her arms and glanced at her watch—a sturdy Swiss Army model—and her eyes widened in surprise.

Nine-thirty! And she hadn't even eaten dinner. Suddenly, Regina's stomach rumbled. Amazing how lost in her work she could become, so that until she stopped for the night, things like hunger and thirst and the passing of time went unnoticed.

Regina began to stack her papers neatly, close the books she'd been using and pile them in the center of the table. She'd go home, feed Nigel and Lucy, pop something in the microwave, put off grading the papers from the Introduction to English Literature class until tomorrow. Well, maybe she'd take a few of them into

bed with her, give them a quick glance before falling off to sleep.

Shouldering her bag, Regina stood and made her way to the lobby, covering a large yawn with the palm of her hand.

When she reached the main entrance/exit of the building, she saw that it was raining. It must have started while she'd been doing her research. Regina peered through the wet glass of the doors and sighed. No umbrella. And she'd walked to the campus this morning, so no car. Well, not much to do about it but carry on!

She pulled open the door and stepped outside. Rain or no, it was a gorgeous fall night. In fact, Regina thought, standing on the top stone step and glancing at the view before her, the rain made the night that much more beautiful.

Everything seemed to sparkle in the soft light from the old-fashioned street lamps that stood sentinel at the end of the library walkway. Hardy green leaves, still on their boughs, shone almost eerily in the glow. Other leaves, already yellow, red and orange, stood out in the lighted night like fancy candies or baubles. The painted black banister of the stone staircase glittered with raindrops and the air was fresh and cool.

Regina took a deep, cleansing breath. She was suddenly aware that she felt calm. Inexplicably calm. For the first time since the semester had begun, Regina felt almost peaceful. Peaceful and confident and—well, contented. She was glad she'd walked to work that morning. Glad she had no umbrella and that her light wool jacket had no hood. She'd walk home slowly, enjoying the feel of the rain on her face, the scent of wood fires in the air. . . .

"Regina?"

She gasped and whirled around, hand to her heart.

"Oh, my God," she breathed. "You scared me. I didn't hear you at all."

"I'm sorry," Will said, zipping his jacket against the weather. "I didn't mean— Look, I didn't know you were at the library tonight, Regina, but I'm glad I ran into you. I'm sorry about the meeting today. Sorry everything is such a mess."

"Will? Stop apologizing." She smiled. "You're beginning to sound like me."

Will laughed. "God forbid! But really, I didn't mean for things to get so tense, so out of control. I just . . ." Will shrugged. "I just shouldn't be dumping my management problems on one of my staff. I'm sor—"

"If you say, 'I'm sorry' one more time, Dr. Creeden," Regina cut in, "I will not be held responsible for my actions. I mean it, Will. I've had a hard day and it's late and I'm hungry and I just want to enjoy the sound of the rain for a minute before walking home." She smiled. "Okay?"

"Okay," he said. "If I can join you?"

Regina nodded and Will moved to stand next to her. Together, they stood in silence, listening to the crisp patter of rain and the strange rustling of the night breeze through wet leaves and across slick branches.

"Remember, Regina?" Will said softly. Wistfully, she thought. "Remember how we used to go for late-night walks in the rain and snow? Up to Lady Hill and down to the lake. Sometimes just around the campus."

Regina turned slightly away from him, to look out at the night, to prevent him from seeing the tears that had gathered in her eyes.

"I remember," she said. That's all I seem to do, she added to herself. Remember.

She was tired of remembering. It got you nowhere fast. It was painful and unproductive. It was a waste of time and worse, it was boring.

She turned back to Will, her tears now fiercely blinked away.

"The past is the past, Will." She hurried on when he opened his mouth to speak, to protest. "I know that's a cliché, but it's true. It was silly of us to try to recapture it. Revive it, whatever it was we were trying to do. It was silly and maybe even wrong." Regina imagined herself standing taller. Straighter. "We have to move on now. Just move on, get past all the anger and regret. Okay? Be colleagues. Friendly acquaintances."

He was silent for a moment, a moment in which Regina could see the hurt in his eyes.

"Not even friends?" he said finally, with a small smile.

"Probably not," she said gently. "Not for a while, anyway."

"You know," Will said, his voice low, "my intentions in coming back to Idlewild were good."

"You know what they say about the road to hell, don't you, Will?" Then she shook her head. "I'm sorry. That wasn't really fair. I—"

"Please, Regina. Don't start. Don't apologize to me again," he pleaded. "Don't ever apologize. We'll be whatever you'll let us be. I'll accept that. Colleagues, friendly acquaintances. I won't like it," he added honestly. "But I'll accept it."

Can *I,* she thought suddenly. Desperately. Can I?

All she said was, "Thank you, Will."

Will released a deep, almost relieved breath, as if, Regina thought, he was clearing away their old dynamic and starting a brand-new type of relationship, for the both of them. His eyes twinkled and he smiled mischievously. "I walked to work this morning, too," he said. "What do you say? Want to make a run for it?"

She couldn't help herself. She was grateful he hadn't fought her. Even if she was still in love. Even if part of

her wanted so badly for him to fight *for* her. Not let her go.

She smiled back and nodded.

"Then, come on!" Will grabbed Regina's hand and she laughed as he pulled her down the smooth stone steps and into the night.

## Thirty-three

# Thirty-three

It was only one week before the annual Idlewild Fall Fair and Regina had never been so little involved. At least, so little involved in the workings of what she still thought of as Aidan's popular amateur production. And as far as she could tell, none of her colleagues had anything at all to do with what they all begrudgingly admitted had become Celia's secret project.

Questions and offers of help were met with a smug blankness or downright refusal. Whatever Celia was doing to put together the Shakespeare scene—down to the choice of play and scene!—was being kept severely under wraps.

"Don't you think . . ." Aidan began, hesitant. "Well, don't you worry a bit, given that we know nothing of the proceedings? What if Celia really does need help with—"

"Then she damn well better ask!" Miles roared. "Every one of us has made ourselves available to the illustrious Miss Keene, and she's cavalierly rejected each of us in turn. If she won't allow us to help, the play's on her head."

"Still," Maria mused, "I'd hate to see anything go wrong. For the sake of the community, of course."

Regina shrugged. "I agree. But what can we do? Will's not demanding that Celia include us. I don't think we have a choice but to let her do her job."

Each day, the conversation was the same. Celia had

taken to eating—or not eating—lunch elsewhere, not in the faculty conference room along with her colleagues. She'd implied she was just too busy to waste time when there was just so much to be done.

Collectively, the English department washed their hands of the affair. Well, Regina thought, maybe not Will. For all they knew, Will was in thick with Celia's planning. Sure, in meetings he asked Celia for an update as if he, too, were really in need of the information. Not that she really answered. But who knew what Mr. Secrecy was really about, Regina thought bitterly. And sadly. Behind the scenes, Celia could be feeding him all sorts of information. Or lies.

To take her mind off the approaching event—and off Will Creeden—there was Mark's friend Peter Thompson. Regina had been out with him once, to dinner. She'd had a nice time, there was no denying that, no point in denying it. But maybe, if the memories of Will hadn't been so fresh and clear in her mind, she'd have had more than simply a nice time. It was hard to sit across from a man who was undeniably attractive by most every woman's standards, undeniably intelligent and funny, and not feel somewhat interested in pursuing some sort of relationship. But . . .

Okay, the truth was that being with Peter, talking to him on the phone, did not take her mind off Will. Maybe it was just too soon. Or maybe she never would get over Will Creeden, her first and only love.

Still, at her mother's suggestion, Regina had made another date with Peter. Her father, waxing poetic as always, had reminded her that nothing ventured, nothing gained. She wasn't exactly not looking forward to the date, but neither was she embracing the idea. This time, they'd go to a movie, then somewhere for dessert and coffee. She'd see. At the very least, she'd show her parents she wasn't about to collapse. Not in public, anyway.

She'd do her job. Go on the date. She'd be fine. And maybe someday, much more than that.


"Hold me."

She moved into his arms to leave him no choice, though she knew he could not—would not—deny her that simple request.

She sighed, tremblingly, as his arms encircled her, as her body pressed into his—so wonderfully familiar and yet, oddly new and thrilling. The hard, flat stomach. The strong, tight neck. The taut, unrelenting thighs. Had he always been so solid, so. . . .

"Regina." His voice was a whisper that made her shiver and press even more closely against him. His hands ran lightly down her back, then up to her neck. With one hand he grasped her hair and pulled her head away from his chest to look deeply into her eyes.

Regina felt herself open to him. She met his gaze but with eyes glazed with desire. She was his, and a small cry of need escaped her lips.

Whatever he wanted, as long as it was her, as long as—

"Will!"

Regina sat up in bed, heart racing, hands trembling. She reached to her side and found no one.

Sighing, she sank back onto the pillow. So much for moving on, she thought, knowing she'd never get back to sleep after that dream.

Earlier that evening, Peter Thompson had dropped her off at her apartment door. Regina knew he'd wanted to be asked in, for coffee and more, but she just couldn't bring herself to offer the invitation. Not even for just coffee. She'd said good-bye, avoided making any promises for another date and slipped inside the apartment. She felt a bit like a rat. Peter was a good man, and he deserved her being straight with him.

Now, after the too vivid dream of Will . . . Regina vowed she'd call Peter first thing in the morning. Well, not then, it would be Saturday, and besides, she had to run off to work at the fair. At least, to be part of it in some small way.

With a sigh, Regina closed her eyes and asked God for one small favor. That she return to her dream of Will.

# Thirty-four

"Celia. What are you doing here?"

Regina pulled her robe tighter around her and kept the door only half open to her unexpected visitor.

It was six o'clock in the morning. At ten o'clock, the fairgrounds, erected on the college commons, were scheduled to open to the public. Regina had set her clock for seven, but a frantic knocking on her door at 5:56 had wrenched her from bed.

"Can I come in?" Celia said. "Please."

Regina shook her head and stepped back into the apartment. "Uh, yeah, sure. But shouldn't you . . . ?"

"Oh, Regina, you've got to help me!"

Stunned, Regina closed the door behind her without turning away from her colleague. She'd never seen Celia like this. For the first time since Regina had known her, Celia looked scared.

Scared and a wreck. Her face was without makeup and her hair looked unwashed. Okay, Regina looked no better, but she'd just flown out of bed and was in her own apartment!

"What's going on?" Regina said, moving toward the couch. "Why don't you sit?" she suggested.

Celia did more than that. With a cry of anguish, she threw herself into a chair and buried her head in her hands.

Now Regina was worried. She didn't like Celia Keene,

but she didn't wish her harm, either. Had someone hurt her. . . .

"Everything's ruined," Celia moaned. "You have to help me, cover for me, anything!"

"Wait, is this about the fair?" Regina demanded.

Celia lifted her head. "Yes," she said, voice trembling. "Will you help me?"

Regina listened. It was worse than she could have imagined.

"Why didn't you say something sooner?" Regina demanded.

Celia hesitated. "I thought . . . I thought it would all work out."

Regina ran a hand through her hair. "Yeah, well, you thought wrong."

"So," Celia sobbed, "will you do it? Say I'm too sick to be there?"

"Instead of telling the truth, which would be that you're too cowardly to take responsibility for your mistakes and try to correct them?" Regina laughed dryly. "Yes, I'll do it. But not for you," she added quickly, as a small gleam came into Celia's eyes. "I'll do it for Will. I'll do it for Idlewild."

"Oh, thank you, Regina!" Celia gushed. She patted her hair and sat up straight. "None of it's really my fault, you know. How should I have known—"

"Save it," Regina snapped. "We're not friends, Celia. I don't like you. In fact, I can barely tolerate you. The last thing I want to hear from you at six-o'clock in the morning is self-justification. Bad enough I had to endure the drama queen performance."

Suddenly, Celia's tear-stained face hardened. "Fine," she said, standing. "I have a terrible headache. I'll be going home now."

Cindy was right, Regina thought. Celia Keene is pathetic.

When Celia reached the door, Regina spoke again.

"Remember, Dr. Keene. I'm not doing this for you. And don't dare to ask me for anything. Ever. Again."


A half hour later, after a quick shower, phone calls to Aidan, Miles and Maria, and a message left on Will's and Emily's answering machines, Regina sat behind the wheel of her Honda.

I don't know whether I'm more angry at Celia or at myself, she thought, pulling the car away from the curb. How had she let such a person get to her? Celia Keene had proven herself not only arrogant and rude but immature and irresponsible, too. The woman might have a doctorate, Regina thought, but she didn't have an ounce of organizational skill. She was nothing more than a spoiled child.

And I'm not much better, Regina thought grimly, driving down an almost deserted Main Street. Insecurity had bred mistrust and both had blinded her to two important realities. One, Celia's childishness. And two, Will Creeden's pain.

Will hadn't told her everything about his life. But what he had told her—that he was not involved with Celia Keene—Regina now knew for sure was the truth.

Maybe I have some growing up to do myself, Regina realized as the campus came into view.


"Kids, we have a situation."

"A situation? How about a disaster? A nuclear meltdown!"

Regina put her hand to her head. "Whatever. The point is, the actors didn't show. They're claiming we—Celia—reneged on two deal-breaking points in their contract."

Miles opened his mouth again.

"Don't ask," Regina said quickly, "I don't know. I do know that up until eleven o'clock last night we had performers and now we don't."

"What do we do?" Maria said. "We'll just have to cancel—"

"No." It was Aidan. "I'll round up as many of the experienced local people as possible. Find some scripts. At least paperback copies of one of the plays. We'll read through, something. It's not unheard of to use scripts onstage."

Miles frowned. "What if they won't do it? Have you forgotten that our popularity with the masses is at a disastrously low ebb at the moment."

Aidan shook his head. "It's not us they're angry with. It's Celia." He looked at Regina almost apologetically. "And Will. They'll listen to me."

Regina nodded. "Aidan's right. Let's do it. Next problem?"

Aidan hurried off and Regina checked her notes.

"Right. No costumes."

"What!" Miles thundered. "There was a dress rehearsal just yesterday."

Regina shook her head. "No, there wasn't. Celia lied."

"P-H-D," Maria muttered. "Piled higher and deeper."

"Celia took on more than she could handle," Regina confirmed. "In the first place, her arrogance, or maybe ignorance, prevented her from delegating tasks. And in the second place, from asking for help when everything began to fall apart."

Miles sneered. "I would place money on the probability that up until her appointment as director, Ms. Keene never had been in charge of anything more complicated than choosing her own clothes each morning."

Regina continued. "I don't doubt it. She told us she'd hired local seamstresses but the truth is that no one would work for her. So, a few days ago, she made a deal to rent

some costumes from an agency run by a friend of the manager of the acting troupe."

"Reneged on a deal point?"

"No. Bounced check."

"Well," Maria said, "we do have the costumes from last year. They'd need to be dug out, and I'm not sure they'll fit whoever Aidan rounds up."

"See what you can do, Maria," Regina ordered. "Even if each person has a hat or tunic, some piece of a costume, it'll work."

When she'd gone off, Miles turned back to Regina.

"Let me guess. The caterer . . ."

"I can't figure out what happened there," Regina admitted. "Celia's story was amazingly convoluted. My best guess is that she forgot to place an order."

Miles drew himself to his full height. "My dear, I am at your service. I shall at once apply to the generous ladies of Idlewild for contributions of cakes, cookies and those little apple tarts I like so well."

Regina laughed. "I knew I could count on you, Miles!"


*Crash!*

"Oh, my God, was anyone hurt?"

"Stand back, I'm a doctor."

*Disaster comes in threes.* It was all Regina could think of as she watched people race to the pile of wood that had, until just a moment ago, been a very makeshift performance platform.

"Who the heck did she get to make that?" Regina muttered.

"All clear, no one hurt," the man who'd said he was a doctor shouted. Oh, right, Maria's husband. Thank God for small favors, like Dr. Doug Jackson's being on hand for free medical care.

"No professional carpenter, that's for sure," Aidan com-

mented. "Talking out loud to oneself is a sure sign of distress. How are you holding up?" he asked.

Regina laughed. "I'm fine, Aidan. When you live with cats, you get into the habit of talking to yourself out loud. Even when they're not around to give you an excuse for doing it."

"Well, it seems my troupe will be performing at ground level," he said now, focused again on the matter at hand. "Unless . . ."

Regina watched as Aidan wandered off, no doubt to solve this latest problem. The fourth disaster, Regina thought now. Actors, costumes, food and stage.

What a morning. Regina sighed. And she still had to face Will, explain why Celia was no longer running the show. Deal with his anger and embarrassment. Resist the urge to say, "I told you so!"

But that wouldn't be a problem. Since the night they'd run home from the library in the rain, things between Will and Regina had been better. At least, they'd been a bit more comfortable with each other and Regina was thankful for small favors. Like his coming to her in her dreams.

"Regina!" It was Maria, hurrying toward her. "The key I have for the costume room snapped off in the lock! I managed to pry it out but . . . I know there's another key somewhere in Will's office. At least, Emily used to keep an extra there."

Regina nodded. "I'm on it. Look, before I go, have you seen Will this morning?"

"No, and that's odd, isn't it?"

"Maybe. But maybe he's just assuming that everything's under control so he doesn't need to show up 'til later."

"Regina? Thanks to you, everything *is* under control."

# Thirty-five

Regina hurried through the door of Will's small private office. Not much about the room had changed since Will had taken over for Dr. Nelson. The room was still jammed with books and paper files; a slightly dirty-looking Mac; other standard issue office equipment, including a phone, stapler, and tape dispenser; and a spindly floor lamp that had stood in its corner for at least twenty years. Regina wasn't even sure it still—or had ever—worked.

Unlike Regina, who liked to personalize her professional space, neither Will nor Emily seemed to care about family photos and trinkets in the workplace.

No time to think about why. Regina scanned Will's desk and figured it'd be best to start with the drawers.

But two minutes later, each drawer searched, she'd found no duplicate key to the costume room. A KitKat wrapper, several dried-out rubber bands and a nail clipper but no key.

Regina sighed. On to the desktop. She'd have to search thoroughly while maintaining—or restoring when she was done—some order to the seemingly messy, paper-strewn surface.

File folders, receipts from the campus bookstore, students' tests and papers. . . .

What was this? A few folded pieces of paper with her name scrawled across the back of the outermost sheet in

Will's distinctive handwriting. Regina glanced up at the door. The hallway was silent. She'd seen no one else in the building.

Still, the letter had been on Will's personal desk, possibly buried under a pile of papers for a reason. It was not hers to open and read, even if it was addressed to her. Sort of.

Who would know if she unfolded the carefully creased pages and read? Regina rolled her eyes. I would know, of course, she admitted, and I'd hate myself for it. But could she live with the awful curiosity that would follow if she didn't read it? Maybe it wasn't a letter to her from Will at all. Maybe it was something more official, something concerning her professional life. Did the possible contents of the note justify the action of reading it?

Regina groaned. Who was she kidding? She would read it, fast, and get back to the business of the fair. She would deal with the guilt later.

Regina turned her back to the door and quickly unfolded the plain white sheets of paper. Oh, God, it was a letter to her, from Will. Dated just a few days before. Regina swallowed hard and read.

Gina,

I love you. A subtle way to open a letter, isn't it? But those three words are the world to me.

Regina, Luke is dead. He died a little over a year ago. It was cancer.

There's more you need to know. In the divorce, I was awarded custody of my son. Of course I wanted him, but if Connie, his mother, had wanted custody, I would not have protested. She did not. She did not want any part of our child.

Luke and I moved in to our own apartment. A few months later, he was diagnosed with cancer. His mother did not participate in his care. Luke died

thinking his mother did not love him and, Regina, I lied to him and told him that his mother loved him very much. But how could she have loved him, and abandoned him?

Then again, I couldn't blame Connie as much as I might have. My relationship with her was dishonest from the very beginning. I wasn't in love with her. And for a long time, I didn't even love her, not really. Not in the way a wife and the mother of one's child should be loved.

Should be treasured.

That night I spent with Connie, during the summer you were in Europe . . . I was so hurt, feeling so lost and abandoned. I'm not blaming you for anything, Regina! And I'm not making excuses. Only telling you, finally, what really happened and how.

You'd been gone for about three weeks. After the first week, I hadn't heard from you. I told myself you were just having a good time, too busy or broke to make a long-distance call every day. But your silence hurt all the same. I didn't know where you were, how you were. For the first time in four years, I knew absolutely nothing about you. I was lost without you.

I guess the hurt slowly turned into anger. I'd asked you to marry me. You'd said maybe. And then you'd gone away. And after the first week, I heard nothing.

Suddenly, I found myself not trusting you. Convinced you were seeing other men. Convinced you'd come back to Idlewild and refuse my offer. Do you remember that I'd put off final plans for starting grad school that fall? Your answer to my proposal was all-important. Everything else revolved around that answer.

But there was silence. My future hung in the balance. It was during that time that I ran into Connie

again. At the mall of all places. She was working in Spencer's. I'd gone in to kill time before a movie. We started to talk and then made a tentative date to meet later that evening, when she got off work. To catch up on old times. Connie was so friendly, seemed so caring, so happy to spend time with me.

You know in high school we'd gone on a few dates, nothing major, just the movies and a burger. Back then, Connie had been more interested in me than I was in her. For a high school kid who just wanted to have some fun—who was years away from even thinking about settling down and getting married—the attention was too much. But now, the attention seemed just right. I resisted taking our friendship to a romantic level, even though Connie made it clear she was interested in our dating. I was loyal to you, I kept hoping you'd call, I wanted you to come back and say "Yes, Will, yes, I'll marry you!" But you didn't call and instead of loving you all the same, as I should have, I convinced myself that Connie, who was right by my side, loved me more than you did.

And then, one night we went to a party together. I can't blame what happened on Connie or the beer or sentimentality or the fact that two of the couples there were boasting about their recent engagements. I made a choice. I drove Connie home that night. At the time she was sharing an apartment with a girlfriend. The friend was out of town. Connie invited me up. She'd set the scene perfectly. The lights were low. Candles were lit. The music was romantic. The wine was plentiful. I made a choice.

It seemed like only weeks later that Connie discovered she was pregnant. I was shocked. Sorry. Full of regret. I'd already decided to break it off with Connie. But I'd been raised to take responsibility for

my actions. I waited one more day for you to call, to write. And then I asked Connie to marry me. From that day forward, I vowed to be a good husband and father.

The rest is history.

I should have told you all this when I first came back to Idlewild. I couldn't. I couldn't tell anyone but Emily Nelson, and she knew parts of the story before I was able to speak. She knew from our mutual acquaintances in Chicago. She approached me and pushed until I let her in. She urged me to let you in, too, and I was trying but I was too ashamed of my failures as husband and father—and friend. I was too eaten away by grief. I came to Idlewild with the intention of being a man about it all and well. . . .

Gina, how I wish you could have known Luke! You would have been his true friend. He was—he is—a beautiful spirit. I would like to show you pictures of him and share with you stories of his short life. But I know it's too late for that now.

I was fooling myself when I came to Idlewild when I did. But all I could think of was you and how much I needed and wanted you. I did not realize that until I'd really come to terms with Luke's death—until I was able to share him and the pain of his loss with anyone other than Emily and the grief counselor I saw for a short time last fall—I was in no condition to make a romantic commitment. How could I really have loved and cherished you when I couldn't love myself? When I was tortured by memories of Luke?

You asked where I went those days and nights. I know it seemed like I disappeared. I know you came to think I was involved with another woman.

The truth is that I was volunteering at Idlewild Memorial Hospital. Last fall, the grief counselor had

suggested that working with other very sick or dying children might in some way help me face the reality of death. Maybe demystify death for me, I don't know.

I should have told you where I was going and why. I wanted to. But at the last moment I knew that I couldn't. You'd ask questions, you might want to be a part of the work and I was shocked to realize I still couldn't share my pain. To share it is to release it and, as Emily has so wisely pointed out to me, my grief has become my tie to Luke. With grief in place, there's no room for anyone else but me and Luke. And I wanted—needed—it that way.

The funny thing is, after I met with the little girl to whom I was assigned, I began to feel some of the grief lift. Just a bit, but it was something, some relief. For the first time in a long time, I began to believe in the possibility of happiness. You and I were together, after all.

Her name was Joy. And she suffered irreversible cardiac arrest on the Sunday we met for the picnic. When I got to the hospital that evening, I found an empty room and a note from the nurse.

I won't ask if you've ever felt despair. I know you have. That night, I was ravaged by it. All hope died. I knew I would never recover. Every person I loved, I hurt.

I'm not proud of how I felt that night. Along with the black despair there was a large dose of self-pity. And a growing desire to destroy, to lash out at the universe, to say, Fine, you don't want me to be happy. Fine, I'll concentrate on unhappiness.

Gina, I hated myself enough at that moment to allow Celia Keene a further power over me. She called and I met her. I let her convince me to give

her the job as director of the fair's play. Why not? What did anything matter anymore?

And I swear that until that next night when you accused me of being in a relationship with Celia, I was blind to what was really happening. To what I had been letting happen all along. That night my eyes began to uncloud. Just a little, but it was a start.

You could say I was punishing myself by wanting you but at the same time making sure you'd denounce me for the horrible person I was. The person who'd failed you and his wife and his own child—and now a little girl named Joy. You could say a lot of things but the bottom line was that I was sick. I thought I could handle Luke's death on my own but I couldn't.

Regina, I know you have no reason to believe me! But if you can, believe just a little that I never meant to hurt you or bring you or your family any pain.

I have no right to ask for your forgiveness or understanding. I have no right to ask for yet another chance. I know I've lost you. But—and this sounds odd—I'm becoming a better man for your having denounced me. A better man for having lost you in the dreadful way I did.

Regina, there are so many things I want to say. . . .

Tears blinded her. She could read no more. She held the pages to her breast. "Oh, Will," she sobbed. His son, his only child, gone. . . .

"Regina?"

She whirled, clutching the letter guiltily. It was Emily Nelson.

"My Lord, Regina, what is wrong?" the older woman exclaimed, bustling into the room. "You were gone so long Maria began to worry. Regina, what is it?" she added,

putting her arm around the younger woman's trembling shoulders.

"I know," Regina whispered through her tears. "About Luke."

"Did Will tell you?" Emily asked quickly.

Regina shook her head and held out the letter. It took Dr. Nelson all of three seconds to assess the situation.

"Didn't your mother ever tell you not to snoop?" she said gently, helping Regina into Will's desk chair. "Well," she sighed, "it's probably for the best. From what I could tell, Mr. Creeden wasn't doing a very good job rebuilding his personal life on his own. So," she added, kneeling by Regina's side, "what are you going to do? And you'd better make up your mind quickly, my dear, because I simply cannot stay down on these old rickety knees for long!"

Regina smiled and wiped her eyes with a tissue she'd snagged from a dusty box on Will's desk. For a moment she didn't answer but that was just because she thought she'd burst out crying again. And then, through her snuffles, she said, "I'm going to make that silly man marry me."

# Thirty-six

"By the way, my dear," Emily said, glancing slyly at Regina as they hurried across campus to the commons, "I received quite an interesting resignation letter this morning from a certain Dr. Keene."

Regina laughed. "Doesn't surprise me. What did she say? Did she say anything about the fair? Apologize?"

"Nothing. No apology. She's just walking away."

"Leaving us to clean up her mess."

Emily shrugged. "So be it. Do you want to hear the rest?"

"Of course!"

"Well, it seems Celia's father, an 'internationally important businessman,' whatever that means, has requested his daughter be his traveling companion. He's off to Paris for a year, and then, as Ms. Keene put it, 'who knows?' "

"So much for moving away from home," Regina said dryly. "Do you know she implied I was tied to my parents' apron strings?"

"I do now. Anyway, Miss Keene goes on to say that of course she'd be a fool to turn down such an opportunity to further study the masterpieces of European culture and the—"

"Blah-blah-blah."

"Exactly, my dear."

Suddenly, Emily stopped in her tracks and pulled on Regina's arm.

"Enough about Celia Keene. There's someone over by the Math department's famous caramel-apple booth I think you might want to talk to."

Regina followed the direction of Emily's pointing finger and saw Will, his back to them, helping Harry Wakefield of the Math department secure a hand-painted sign to the booth.

Suddenly, her heart began to race and with a shock, Regina realized she was embarrassed to approach Will. Or too shy. She felt something awkward. Almost like how she felt the first time he'd approached her their freshman year, in the cafeteria.

"Macaroni and cheese," Regina blurted.

Emily frowned. "Pardon me, my dear?"

"Macaroni and cheese. That's what I was eating for lunch the day Will came up to me in the cafeteria. I'd seen him around but we'd never spoken." Regina laughed and put a hand to her chest. "I couldn't believe he was interested in me. He was so—"

"Before you get any mushier," Emily suggested dryly, "why don't you go and say something."

Regina nodded and was vaguely aware of Emily's walking off. Heart racing, stomach fluttering, Regina began to walk toward Will across the leaf-strewn commons.

The closer she got to the booth and the man she'd always loved, the more she was convinced she had no idea what to say. She hadn't had any time to prepare anything, to find the perfect note of forgiveness and apology and. . . .

"Will?"

He turned. Opened his mouth as if to speak. . . .

"Will, I know," she said.

He closed his mouth and a million emotions seemed to

flicker across his face, through his eyes. One of those emotions, Regina thought, was pain. Another, relief.

"How?" he said softly.

"That doesn't matter right now," she answered, taking a step closer to him, willing herself not to cry, not just yet.

"Are you angry?" he asked.

Regina shook her head and managed a small "No." Took a deep breath. "No," she repeated, more firmly, "I'm not. I'm sorry. For everything and about everything."

"I'll make it up to you."

Regina smiled through eyes now clouding with tears. "Oh, I know you will. Starting tonight."

The surprise on Will's face was enormous, and Regina burst out laughing.

"Do you mean. . . ."

"That I still love you? That I want and need you? The answer to those two questions would be yes."

With a motion so fluid Regina barely knew what was happening, Will pulled her to him and kissed her. He wouldn't let her go but held her to him in a fierce and protective and thankful hug.

"Will," Regina whispered, her arms tight around his neck. "There's one condition."

She felt his tension as he spoke. His fear. "Okay."

"Good. You have to marry me. Soon."

Will pulled away enough to stare excitedly at her. "Do you mean. . . ."

Regina laughed. "Oh, no, silly! I'm not pregnant! But I hope to be before long."

The look of happiness on Will's face sent a huge thrill through every inch of Regina's body.

"Regina," he said, "do you realize what this means? I . . . the thought of you having our baby, the idea of us marrying, starting a family—" Will laughed. "It's fantastic!" He hugged her to him again. "Gina," he said, quietly

now, "since losing Luke nothing has seemed right. But right now, with you in my arms and my wanting, really wanting a family again. . . . You've given me back my life."

"So," Regina drawled, nuzzling Will's neck, "that means yes, you'll marry me?"

Will laughed again. Regina thought it was the most beautiful sound she'd ever heard.

"Oh, yeah. It means yes!"


"Knowing you know about Luke . . . well, it feels so good," Will said, as they strolled across the commons. "I . . . I think I know now why I couldn't talk about him. Couldn't share him with anyone, even you. Couldn't let go."

"It's a process, Will. Letting go. Sometimes it never fully happens. And in this case," she said, "it shouldn't. It won't. You'll always be Luke's father, and he'll always be your son. No matter what else happens, that truth will never change, will always be the same. Now you've just got to stop being afraid."

Will smiled. "It's already happened, Gina. Thanks to you."

Regina tossed her head. "No problem, Dr. Creeden," she quipped. "It's my field of expertise. It's what I do. As of now, anyway. You know, unconditional love. It's what a wife's all about."

"Whoa, you're really getting into your new role," Will said, raising an eyebrow. "I'm impressed. And lucky. But enjoy the fiancée part first, okay? I've heard that can be fun."

"Don't worry, I will," she said, kissing his hand, the one held in hers. "I've got a lovely little ring all picked out."

"No more lies. No more secrets," Will whispered, drawing her close again.

Regina looked up into the eyes she adored. "Oh, what a tangled web we weave, when first we practice to deceive."

"Something like that." Will kissed her quickly. "Come on. Let's go finish the miracle you started."

# Thirty-seven

The applause was deafening. At least, it sounded that way to Regina. Personally, she'd never clapped so hard in her life.

In only a few short hours, Aidan Ross had managed to pull together and stage a performance worthy of his most practiced work. Judging that it was too last minute a situation to bother with an entire scene from one particular play, he'd hurriedly contacted both the college's and the town's librarians. With their help, he'd rounded up a handful of paperback Shakespeares and conducted a quick search for those lighthearted scenes that most often ended the writer's classic comedies.

And what happened at the end of such scenes was this: People got married. Or they got ready to get married. Society was restored. All was well that ended well.

Maria had gathered up enough partial costumes so that each actor, including Mr. Joyce of King Lear renown and the students in the theater club who'd rushed to the rescue, wore some article of Elizabethan garb.

And Miles, God bless his heart—or stomach?—had issued a battle cry heard round the town. From each corner of Idlewild came women bearing plates of warm cookies and gooey cakes and fresh apple tarts. Those last were made specially for Miles by the recently widowed Mrs. White. A woman, Regina noted now, of some beauty and

a decided interest in the bachelor Fetherston! Stranger things had happened and Regina, smiling up at Will, could vouch for that.

"Thank you, ladies and gentlemen," Aidan announced over the slowly dying applause. "Thank you for your generous support of our humble entertainment."

With a twinkle in his eye, Aidan looked directly at Regina. "Most of all," he went on, "we have the lovely and talented Miss Regina Sutherland to thank for taking a potential disaster and turning it into a rousing success!"

Regina laughed and covered her face with her hands.

"He's right, you know," Will said, squeezing her to his body in a one-armed hug. "Without your energy and leadership, we'd never have been able to pull this off."

Will stepped slightly away from her and spoke clearly over the din. "Aidan, I'd like to say something, if that's all right."

Aidan bowed graciously, and Will made his way to the very makeshift but stable stage some of the senior members of the theater club had hastily erected that morning.

"What is he doing?" Regina murmured, suddenly feeling very, very shy.

Will cleared his throat and looked at the gathered group of Idlewild citizens and college people. "I want to thank you all," he began, "for putting aside any resentment you might have harbored toward me or Dr. Keene for my unpopular and unwise decisions regarding Idlewild's fair and coming instead to its rescue." A friendly noise from the crowd encouraged him to continue. "I learned a few lessons today," he went on, his voice, to Regina, the littlest bit wobbly, "and I also want to thank you all for teaching me those lessons. I won't forget them, I promise."

"Here, here!" It was a voice from the back of the crowd.

Regina whirled to see Emily Nelson and her own parents walking toward her.

Emily spoke again. "There's more to celebrate here to-

day," she said, gesturing dramatically to the crowd, "than just the return of our beloved Aidan Ross to the stage. In fact," she continued slyly, "I believe Will and Regina have an announcement they would like to make to us all."

"Emily!" Regina hissed, not displeased.

"My dear," she replied, "I am done with keeping secrets. From now on, in fact, I refuse to keep any secrets for anyone so you mustn't tell me anything you don't want the entire town of Idlewild to know."

"What is it, Regina?" Bob Sutherland asked, the smile budding on his face revealing he was already in on the big news.

Regina turned back to find that Will was rapidly making his way toward her. She held out her hand for his and smiled.

"We've been discovered," she said, laughing.

"Good. I want the world to know." Will looked to Regina's parents. "Joan, Bob. Regina and I are going to be married." He grinned. "As soon as possible!"

A resounding cheer went up from the people around them. The Sutherlands hugged their daughter and soon-to-be son-in-law. Emily Nelson pounded Will on the back and kissed Regina's forehead. Out of nowhere appeared the Jacksons, Maria and Doug, as well as Miles Fetherston, accompanied by a very comfortable-looking Mrs. June White, all offering the couple happy congratulations. Regina took Will's hand and smiled brightly up at him.

"It's going to be great," she whispered.

"It already is."

# COMING IN NOVEMBER FROM
# ZEBRA BOUQUET ROMANCES

### #69 WHEN YOU WISH by Lori Handeland
__(0-8217-6748-8, $3.99) Desperate to get funding to supply sick children with security blankets, Grace Lighthorse is forced to work with Dr. Daniel Chadwick—a loner who doesn't believe in alternative medicine. Daniel has no intention of giving up his grant to Grace, who believes in a lot of foolish things—including the potent magic of a moonlight kiss.

### #70 HER BEST MAN by Lisa Plumley
__(0-8217-6718-6, $3.99) In order to keep her best friend from marrying a hussy, Macy Vandevier-March arranged to have the groom kidnapped, then flown on her jet until he came to his senses. But Macy just discovered that the man she's uncovered at 27,000 feet is handsome, dark and blissfully unaware of his predicament. He's also the wrong guy . . .

### #71 MOUNTAIN DREAMS by Cheryl Holt
__(0-8217-6747-X $3.99) When Allison Masters is exiled to Jackson Hole, Wyoming to manage a modest inn, she feels totally out of place and almost lets herself be seduced by country singer Beau Beaudine. But when Beau is booked for six months at her inn's bar, they both begin to believe that the intoxicating desire they shared could be the start of something real . . .

### #72 A NIGHT TO REMEMBER by Adrienne Basso
__(0-8217-6720-8, $3.99) When sophisticated Joshua Barton asks Eleanor Graham to be his date for the weekend at his father's estate, sweet kisses melt into a night of glorious passion. But it's going to take a lot of gentle persuasion from Joshua to convince Eleanor to believe in fairy tale endings . . .

---

Call toll free **1-888-345-BOOK** to order by phone or use this coupon to order by mail. *ALL BOOKS AVAILABLE 11/1/2000.*

Name_____

Address_____

City_____ State _____ Zip _____

Please send me the books I have checked above.

I am enclosing                                           $_____

Plus postage and handling*                               $_____

Sales tax (in NY and TN)                                 $_____

Total amount enclosed                                    $_____

*Add $2.50 for the first book and $.50 for each additional book.

Send check or money order (no cash or CODs) to:

**Kensington Publishing Corp. Dept. C.O., 850 Third Avenue, New York, NY 10022**

Prices and numbers subject to change without notice. Valid only in the U.S. All orders subject to availability.

Visit our website at **www.kensingtonbooks.com.**